THE UNIT

THE UNIT

R.A. RICHTER

Redwood Publishing, LLC
info@redwooddigitalpublishing.com

Author's Note

Disclaimer and Warning: This is a work of fiction. Any reflection of real events is pure coincidence. In addition, this novel includes graphic and violent scenes, profanity and other material that may not be appropriate for certain readers. Read at your own peril.

Library of Congress Control Number: 2018946416

ISBN Paperback: 978-1-947341-27-2
ISBN eBook: 978-1-947341-28-9

Printed in the United States of America

Cover Design: Redwood Publishing, LLC
Interior Design: Ghislain Viau

SECTION I

CHAPTER 1

Los Angeles, CA

The early morning sun drifts through the light blue curtains and rests softly on the kitchen table. Young Sean slides his small hands slowly over the yellow linoleum surface. It feels cool, smooth, comforting. The warmth of the sun feels good. A fragile smile plays across his face as he tilts his head back, closes his eyes, and takes a deep breath. *It's okay here. I'm safe here in this dream.*

Lowering his head, he lets his eyes rest on his mother, standing against the wall just a few steps from the worn screen door that leads out into the backyard. His little brother, Jack, resting his head against Mom's waist, is smiling as she gently strokes his head. Dad is sitting across from Sean, a far-off expression on his face, a cigarette hanging at the corner of his mouth. He is wearing a green army uniform. A moment stuck in time, lived over and over. So many times, his dreams take him back there, to that moment, that home.

The muffled sound of a cell phone yanked Sean away from that vivid memory of that innocent, happy day in Selinsgrove, Pennsylvania. After last night, after too much to drink and smoke, and then a couple of Ambien, the warm memories tried to hold him back. Now the sound of a phone brought him back.

His eyes opened and he lay disoriented, staring into the unfamiliar room.

"What the hell," he said, as he stumbled to get out of bed and search for the phone. The hotel room came into focus, still dark in the early morning hours of downtown Los Angeles. He threw his clothes off the large desk from where he had flung them the night before, groping for the phone.

"Jesus, who the hell is calling me so fucking early?" he said, as he picked up the hotel phone. "Oh shit, must be my wife. Is the goddamn sump pump backed up again? Hello? Hello?"

There was no answer, but a phone was still ringing.

"It's your cell phone," said a gentle voice from under the sheets.

He turned toward the voice hidden in the bed. He had forgotten the young Asian woman was there. Another typical night out with the boys.

"Oh Christ, right, it's my cell. Where the fuck is it?" He moved toward the faint sound, knowing the voicemail would pick up any second. He sat down on the edge of the bed and leaned forward to pick up his pants from the floor. Just then Sean felt the touch of her hand, reaching up, massaging his neck and shoulders. He closed his eyes. He turned his head toward the girl; he remembered now, this wasn't the first time, and wouldn't be the last.

The ringing stopped. *She'll wonder where the hell I am at five o'clock in the morning. I'll call her back, tell her I was fast asleep, took a couple of Tylenol PM, and slept like a baby,* he thought.

He hesitated, gingerly pulling the covers back. Not wanting to stare at just another bad choice. He was making them more often. *A*

4

good life, after all I've been through. The guilt had never left; sometimes it faded and days would go by, and then there it was. The memories, the injustice, the moments, still hidden after all these many years. He nodded his head slowly and gently, as if agreeing with himself, but there was no peace to the memories that consumed his thoughts. The therapy had helped, but the guilt had been building up each day. The tide coming in, waves crashing relentlessly. It wasn't his fault; he had been only eight. But even back then he had found himself looking for a path to forgiveness. So many missed opportunities to see his brother, all that was left.

Sean reached for his pants, a habit, his routine. Searching for his wallet, while a nameless woman lay quietly under the covers. He cautiously pulled it out of his crumpled-up pants. He stared at the ID in the dim light. A badge: Philadelphia District Attorney's Office, Sean McGinnis, Assistant District Attorney. He was on assignment, working with the local office, investigating a series of homicides that had been plaguing the Philadelphia suburbs for years, with a connection to Southern California. Finally, a solid lead, leading to an arrest and then a cop's celebration at a topless bar just outside of LAX Airport in Los Angeles, California. A twenty-dollar lap dance and then another bad choice. Sean pulled the covers up over her shoulder and sat staring at the blackout curtains that was allowing only that sliver of light that seemed to cast his ID into the silhouette of the man he should be.

He pulled out the cell phone, walking over to the window. Just one missed call.

"You have one new message from 987-1234 at 8:09 a.m.," came the automated voice. He didn't recognize the number. *Thank God, it's not my old lady. Who the hell is calling me at five in the morning?*

The voice on the message began, "Big brother." Sean pushed the cell phone hard against his ear. Could it really be his little brother, Jack? He hadn't seen or talked to him in more than twenty years.

"Sean, how you doing? It's me, Jack. You do remember your brother." The sarcasm was thick in his brother's voice, with an uncomfortable hesitation. "Yeah, whatever…" The guilt came flooding in after so many of years of therapy he learned how to live with the pain and the fear and to block out the memories, but not the guilt.

The phone went dead. "Fuck!" He hadn't noticed the low battery message; of course, he hadn't charged it last night. Sean scrambled out of bed. The charger was still in his overnight bag. After plugging it in, his hands trembling slightly, he went back to the bed, staring at the ceiling.

He had made so many excuses to himself over the years. Why had he never reached out to Jack? It must have been so tough on the little guy. The thought of seeing or talking to him now was starting to bring it all back. The depression and fear were always just under the surface. He was so tired of being scared and sad.

To his friends, Sean seemed like the happiest guy in town. He was a good husband and a good father to his two young kids; he had a great sense of humor, always the life of the party, with a big smile and a big hello. From the outside, Sean McGinnis appeared to have it all.

The fact was that he had lived these past thirty years an angry and bitter man on the inside. He had made a list of all those he hated and blamed: his father, the Army, but on the top of the list — the men who had raped and murdered his mother decades before.

Now even after years of therapy, what he could never get out of his mind was never learning the truth. When it happened, he was eight. During his entire childhood, he believed what the cops and his grandparents had told him. A drug addict killed his mother looking for money, and then when they told him his dad was killed by a sniper in Vietnam, he believed that too. *Why shouldn't I believe what I was told? I was eight fucking years old.* But as he grew older he would often ask his grandparents for more details: Was the guy who hurt their mother ever caught? Was there a trial, a court case? What about his father, was his body never found? So many fucking questions and doubts and never any answers.

Wasn't his fault that he and Jack didn't keep in touch. He forced himself to believe that the two of them had just drifted apart after being split up. He had never wanted to get split up, but what could he do? He was eight, Jack was six.

Sean sat on the chair next to the bed, staring at the charging phone in the dim early morning light; he could hear the girl breathing, soft and steady.

"You Korean girls can sleep through a monsoon," Sean said under his breath.

"I'm not Korean, I'm Vietnamese."

Sean turned toward the girl, "Sorry. Your English is perfect, were you born here?"

"No, I was born in Saigon during the American War. My father was an American soldier."

"You mean the Vietnam War?" Sean asked cautiously.

The young woman pushed herself up, sitting cross-legged.

"For us it was the American War. Try not to forget, you came into our country, your army killed over a million of our people. I know, I know, you were there to save us from the northern hordes. Good job…"

She looked older than he had thought the night before, when the lights were dim and he had too much to drink. "Let's get some room service. I'm starving."

Sean turned and sat on the edge of the bed. "Take a shower if you like. I'll order breakfast."

"That would be nice, thanks," she said and walked toward the bathroom. She turned and added, "My name is Ling."

Sean nodded with a smile of approval. She had passed the test. He tested everyone, at least since he was eight.

"I'm afraid that I have forgotten my manners. My name is Sean McGinnis."

Sean threw on his T-shirt, turned back to the desk, and picked up the phone to call room service.

"They said they're busy. It could take a half an hour."

"Fine with me. Why don't you come in the shower?" she said in a seductive voice.

Sean smiled, he needed this distraction. The call from his brother couldn't be good. It was probably about money.

Sean stepped into the bathroom, the hot shower fogging up the room. Ling was facing him through the glass shower door; she opened it slowly, invitingly.

Sean breathed in deeply, slowly pulled off his shirt and his shorts, and stepped into the shower. She was tall, coming up almost to his chin. Her wet, jet-black hair clung to her shoulders. "You're beautiful," he said.

Ling gently stroked his face and said in a soft voice, "I know," then smiled as she gently brushed her lips against his wet body. He could feel his heart beat faster with anticipation. She stopped and turned slowly, her back up against his chest. She reached for his hands and moved them around her waist, toward her flat belly. His hands moved downward until he could feel the mound just below her pelvis; she gasped softly while he kissed her neck.

The knock on the door startled him; for a moment he had been lost in the sensation of pleasure.

"Room service."

"Hold on," he shouted, "just getting out of the shower..."

Sean grabbed the robe that hung on the inside of the bathroom door. "Hold on, I'm coming," he said again. As he opened the door, he was greeted with a smile from the young man. "Good Morning sir, would you like me to set up your breakfast? "Sure," said Sean. The young waiter set up breakfast and turned, "Have a good day sir." He handed Sean the bill and walk out of the room. "All clear," said Ling with a hint of humor in her voice. Sean turned to see the young girl stroll towards him, with her robe hanging open so that he could sneak a glimpse of all of her. "We almost seem like an old married couple," said Ling with a smile. They both ate their breakfast, saying very little, lost in their own thoughts.

"How's your breakfast?" asked Sean, and continued without waiting for an answer. "I've got to listen to a message. I think my phone should be charged by now."

"Would you like me to go?" she asked.

"Please stay a bit, it's nice having you here. This will only take a minute."

Sean held the phone hard against his ear while the message from his brother continued from where it left off.

"I've got something to tell you, but not on the phone. Can you come home? It's about Dad and Mom. It's not what we were told, Sean. Dad and Mom were purposely murdered, this wasn't

9

some random act. Look, I don't want to get into it now; this isn't the time or the place. Just call me. I'm staying in Selinsgrove, at the Smiths. Call me, Sean. Please, Sean. I found the letters." The message ended.

Sean walked back to the bed, sitting on the edge. He felt his heart beating faster as he started hyperventilating. He had learned how to control this stress reaction: breathe slowly and focus on an object close by. It helped, he began to feel calmer even while the pain and fear that he had learned to suppress flowed into his body, like warm cocoa going down his throat on a cold winter morning.

Standing up from the edge of the bed, he walked over to the window. He drew back the curtains and peered down to Rodeo Drive below. It was still early in L.A., and the street was empty except for one person jogging past the chic stores.

In a flash he was back, all the way back, to a cold winter morning, sitting with his father and grandfather on the banks of the Susquehanna. His mother said they were crazy; she didn't understand fishing in the dead of winter. No one else got it, but Sean didn't care. This was his space, his own little world with his two best friends.

"Are you okay?" asked Ling, with a trace of concern in her voice. "You seem far away."

Sean looked at her. He smiled and said, "I'm back."

"I think it is time for me to go." Ling handed Sean a small note. "Call me if you like." She leaned in close and kissed one check and then the other. "You're a nice person, Sean McGinnis."

He watched her walk out the door. He closed the curtains and slipped under the covers trying to drift back to sleep. His first meeting was not until eleven.

The letters, he remembered the letters; Jack had found the letters.

He was used to his mind drifting in and out of bizarre places while trying not to listen to the dripping faucet or the thoughts in his head. He had worked through this with his therapist: in the moments before falling asleep, he would play a round of golf in his head, and by the time he got to the ninth hole, he was usually fast asleep. Sean loved the game and was able to feel the club in his hand and see himself looking down the fairway. He could picture the guys watching his setup and then the swing, slow and sweet, and then the flight of the ball moving through the clear blue sky until the ball finally, after what seemed like forever, would land softly in the middle of a manicured fairway.

Sean was passionate about life. Maybe it was because of what had happened to his parents. A zest and hunger for everything the world had to offer. He pushed himself, his kids, and his wife. "Don't leave anything on the table" was his mantra.

He was really good at everything in his head: golf, sex, and revenge. The revenge part had always been just a fantasy, but a fantasy that had taken on a life of its own. Maybe now there would be answers to questions that had haunted him most of his life.

The curtains kept the room in almost total darkness. He felt safe under the covers. He turned to look at the clock radio on the table next to the bed, it was 7:15 a.m. He stared up at the ceiling and thought about that moment. The moment when everything turned sour and bitter, when everything he cared about came crashing down at his feet, and there was nothing he could do except watch it happen. How often he imagined standing in the corner of the room, helpless, unable to do anything. He was not there, it was Jack who had witnessed it all. Sean could only imagine and perhaps that was worse. He was not Jack, poor Jack, so silent. All the years of therapy seemed to fall apart, and now he found himself back, staring at that quiet and terrified kid, sitting on the porch outside his grandfather's house as all those people came by, patting him on the head like he was a fucking lost puppy and saying to him that everything was going to be all right when his father got home. When his father got home from Vietnam everything would be all right… But in the end it wasn't all right, it would never be all right. But now, maybe Jack had found out something that would end the memories and the anger that Sean had lived with for much too long. He was tired of feeling this way. He was tired of hurting.

The world saw a happy-go-lucky family guy with a good job and a good wife and two great kids and friends and everything looking great, with a smile on his face and a joke on his lips, but behind the smile and past the jokes, deep inside, he saw the young boy who, on the day of his mother's funeral, sat by a river, looking from side to side, looking for his father and his mother and seeing nothing, nothing but the river moving through the Pennsylvania countryside as it had done for so many millions of years, and finally he fell asleep.

Sleep had taken him home again, but as he woke and rubbed the sleep from his eyes, he was back in Los Angeles. It was just before 9 a.m. when he reached for his cell phone and dialed.

"Hello." There was a moment of uncomfortable silence. "Is that you, Sean?" asked the voice on the phone.

"Yeah, it's me. How you doing? Thought you died and gone to heaven."

"Right," answered Jack. "Is that supposed to be funny?"

"No, Jack, guess not, just trying to…," Sean stopped. "How you been, Jack? I know it's been a long time, but I think about you all the time, even though I try not to."

"Sean," said Jack, "cut the shit, will you? Look, Sean, if we've got nothing else, let's at least have a little honesty between us."

Sean broke in and said, "I've got a phone too, Jack, it goes both ways. But let's not get into this right now. We will talk about how fucked up I am later. You said that Mom and Dad were deliberately killed. Do you mind telling me what the fuck you're talking about?"

"Not over the phone. You come home and I'll tell you exactly what happened to our parents. You won't fucking believe what I found out. And you definitely won't believe what I found in the basement. Remember the letters that Dad sent to Mom that disappeared all of a sudden? Well, they just reappeared in the Smiths' cellar. Sean, do you want to find out what really happened or you want to spend the rest of your life believing the bullshit?"

"No, no, I definitely want to find out what happened, but where did you find those letters? I thought they were lost."

"I'll tell you everything when you get here. When can you come out?"

"I don't know, I've got a life."

"You don't have shit," said Jack. "Your whole fucking life is based on a big fucking lie, and if you want to find out the truth then you'll make the goddamn time to come out here. Look, Sean," continued Jack in an agitated tone, "I don't know about you, but my whole life got thrown into the fucking toilet. I don't want to get into this now, are you coming out or not?"

"Okay," said Sean. "I'm in L.A. for another two days and then I'm coming home. I'll call you on Wednesday."

"Sean, don't call me. When are you coming out?"

"Fine. I'll be there on Saturday, this coming Saturday afternoon. Where should I meet you?"

"Meet me at the Dunkin' Donuts in Selinsgrove. It will be good seeing you," said Jack sarcastically. "It's been too long."

"Yeah," said Sean, "it'll be good seeing you too."

CHAPTER 2

Selinsgrove, PA

Jack hung up the phone on the kitchen wall and went to sit down at the table; he thought about how many times he had sat there waiting for his stepfather to give him permission to leave. He looked around the room, the dirty windows, and the dull and peeling wallpaper. Nothing had changed in all these years. The old clock on the wall said 12:10. He was hungry but didn't feel like eating. He hadn't felt like eating much for a long time. So instead Jack reached for a can of beer, a sly smile at the corners of his mouth as he lifted the can and took a sip.

Well, Sean, he thought, *you are finally going have a chance to be here for your little brother. Time to step up, big brother, cover my ass, fight for me, like brothers do. All these years, where the hell were you? How is it possible you left and never looked back? Well, now I've got your attention, now you will show up because I have something you want. I have the answers, at least I know what questions to ask, and one way or another you are going to help me find out who is responsible for fucking up my life. This time you're not going to walk away from your*

14

little brother while the bad guys beat the shit out of him every goddamn day. He swallowed another sip of beer and let his left hand slid along the table's edge. He slowly reached up toward his mouth, a jagged tooth protruding from his gums. The painful memory had come and gone over the years, feeling those hands grabbing his hair and then bringing his head crashing down onto the side of this table, a sharp excruciating pain driving through his young face. He had tried to put the memory out of his mind. But even with the therapy, the doctors, it was always there, just a smile away, always visible for the world to see.

Jack sat back and put his right foot up on the chair next to him. He was tired of being angry, tired of hating, tired of being sad all the time…

Jack opened another beer. *Well, at least I've graduated from being a junkie to being a drunk. People respect you more if you're a drunk.* He laughed hard and coughed loud, wiping the beads of sweat that had formed on his forehead. He stood up and walked to the bathroom, feeling a slight burning as he urinated. *Must be the cold,* he thought. He brushed back his long blond hair that had fallen into his dark brown eyes.

The six months in prison had done him a world of good. Nothing to do every day but stay straight and work out. He didn't have to do too much time for possession of a controlled substance. The thirty pounds Jack lost over the last six months made him look trim, but in the mirror, his skin seemed a bit yellow and his eyes seemed too set back in his head.

Back at the table, Jack pulled the worn cardboard box filled with letters close to him. The half-empty can of beer sat next to the ashtray with the cigarette butts still smoldering. He had been reading the letters since late the night before. No sleep and a six-pack of beer were making him drowsy. He put his head down on the kitchen table; he drifted off into dreams of the past.

Selinsgrove, PA 1970

There was an early morning mist and a slight chill in the air. The small town of Selinsgrove was at peace. A black Ford pulled up to the small house on the quiet street and two men got out slowly and looked around. The trees were still full of leaves and the grass was a warm green. They both turned toward the sound of a woman, dressed in a housecoat, dragging a garbage can down her driveway toward the curb. They watched as she picked up the paper, left the garbage can at the curb, and turned back toward the house, never looking up from the morning paper.

"What do think?" the shorter guy said, tilting his head toward the woman.

"Let's not complicate this; she didn't see anything. Let's just do what we have to do and get the hell out of this bullshit town."

"It looks like a nice town," the first guy said. "Wish I grew up in a town like this."

"Yeah, sure, you know they don't allow any white trash Italians in this part of the world. Didn't you see the sign that said no Italian gangsters?"

"Get the fuck out of here," said Tony Ramo. "Come on, stop fucking around. We got work to do." They walked up to the house and Tony rang the doorbell. John Murphy towered over Tony, 6'4" with a worn face for his age and short black hair. Tony was short, but built like a tank; large hands and even larger shoulders. John took off his sunglasses and placed them carefully in the inside pocket of his uniform and replaced them with wire-rim glasses that he laid neatly on the edge of his small nose. He reached over Tony and rang the bell again. There was no answer. He knocked hard.

Then a voice on the other side of the door said, "Keep your shirt on, I'm coming." A young woman answered the door. She was pretty, with a nice smile.

"Morning, miss, my name is Sergeant Gray," said Tony Ramo, "and this is Sergeant MacLean," pointing at John Murphy. "We're with the Department of Defense. Are you Kate McGinnis?"

Kate took in a deep breath, fear suddenly tightening across her face. "Is Jerry okay? What's the matter?" she whispered.

John smiled and said, "Look, Mrs. McGinnis, everything is fine. Can we come in? We need to talk to you."

"Of course, come in. Sorry the place is a mess. Would you men like a cup of coffee?"

"No, thank you, ma'am. We won't be taking too much of your time. How are your sons, are they off at school?"

"What is going on? Why do you want to know about my boys, what are you here to tell me?" A look of suspicion played across her face and her welcoming smile turned hostile. She stood straighter, taller, posturing to a more protective stance. It hadn't always been this way. Once a shy and tentative young girl, she had become cautious ever since Jerry's abandonment of her family for reasons that still made no sense to her.

"Nothing to be upset about. We know your husband. He wanted us to stop by and say hello to you all."

"What did you say your names were? I don't think Jerry ever mentioned you." Kate moved aside as the two men entered the house.

The taller of the two men glanced up at the staircase leading to the bedrooms, then around to the living room on the left. "Bowling for Dollars" was playing on the small TV. He smiled to himself. Memories of sitting with his mom and dad watching that together on cold winter nights in St. Louis.

A sinister smiled played across the big man's lips. John began, choosing his words carefully, "Your husband is in a bit of trouble. Seems that he had been sending information to you that could compromise the security of our forces over there in Vietnam and we need to take a look at the letters that he's been sending you. So, if you'll be kind enough to let us take a look at anything you have received, I'm sure we can clear this little issue up right here and now."

The look on Kate's face betrayed her thoughts; confusion and doubt. "I don't know what you're talking about; we get letters almost every day, nothing special."

"Let's take a look at them, if you don't mind," said John Murphy.

"I do mind and unless you guys tell me what's going on here, you both can just get the hell out of my house."

John moved closer to Kate, the expression on his face suddenly changed. Tony had seen this before, the moment before it all went terribly wrong. He hoped that he was mistaken this time. "I'm going ask you real nice, Kate: Where are the letters, every goddamn written word your husband sent to you?" The look in John's eyes frightened Kate, but she stood her ground. Kate was not one to back down from a fight. In that moment, she knew that she was out of her league; she was frightened, but mustered up the strength to say again, "Get the hell out of my house, right now."

John Murphy smiled and said to Tony, "What do you think, Sergeant? You think maybe we should just forget the whole thing?"

Without hesitation, John turned and crashed the back of his hand into Kate's face. The strength of the slam hurled Kate to the living room floor. She opened her mouth to scream but before the sound could reach her lips, John grabbed her by the hair with one hand and pulled her close to his face. "I'll ask you one more time, where's the fucking letters?"

"In the closet," she cried, "in the closet right there, please don't hurt me." Tony walked to the closet and there on the top shelf was a box filled with files and letters. This had to be what they were looking for.

Up the stairs, at the edge of the landing, just barely out of sight, six-year-old Jack crouched close to the wall. He had a bad cough and Kate had decided not to send him to nursery school that day. The young boy sat quietly, still in his pajamas, too frightened to move or say a word.

John had his knee on Kate's stomach and he smiled and said, "Sorry for getting a little rough with you, Mrs. McGinnis, but please understand, the information here could cost the lives of a lot of good soldiers."

Kate looked up at John and said, "You got what you want. Now get the hell out of here and you can bet your ass that the Army is going to hear about this."

John turned his attention to Tony, who was going through the letters and said calmly, "You got everything?"

Tony looked up and said, "Yeah, looks like he dated everything. There's a ton of shit here, right up to last month. Let's get the hell out of here."

John still held onto Kate by her hair and shook his head slowly as he said, "Wish I could, but I'm afraid that we've gone too far, I got to take this pretty little thing out of the equation. We need him, and this is the only way to secure his loyalty, take away his reason to come home."

He reached down and pulled her to her feet. Kate lashed out but was no match for John's strength.

"Let me go, you son of a bitch, who the fuck do you guys think you are? What the hell is this all about?"

Tony knew what was coming; he'd seen this before. This was crossing the line, hurting Jerry's wife was unnecessary. Putting the fear of God in her was enough. Tony Ramo was no choirboy, he was a street thug, but compared to John Murphy, he was an amateur. John Murphy was a sadistic psychopath with no conscience.

John turned back to Kate and ripped her shirt open. She screamed. Tony dropped the box of letters and grabbed John by the arm to stop him.

John turned and sneered at Tony, "We need that son of a bitch, so shut the fuck up and get out of my way."

John threw Kate down on the couch. Before she could scream again, John put his hand over her mouth. Kate tried to push his hand away, but John Murphy was too strong and only the moans could be faintly heard.

"We need to make this look like a robbery gone bad. Crackhead breaks in to rob the place and unfortunately finds the lady of the house at home, and in a drug-crazed state, rapes and kills her." John continued, "It's orders, Ramo, I swear to God, it's orders."

"Orders!" yelled Tony, "Orders from whom?"

"The founders. We need him, the war is coming to an end. We need Jerry to manage the investments and the disbursements. I've got to make it impossible for him to ever come back home. Now, get those fucking boxes out to the car. This won't take long."

Kate had control of only one thing, her eyes. She glared at the monster above her. Terrified at first, and then a calmness came across her fragile face. She pushed the monster away, as happier thoughts drifted into her mind. As John Murphy pushed into her, he said, "Well, honey, the last thing you're going to know is me and, oh, by the way, I'll be sure to send your love to your husband." His cruel smile reappeared as he put his hands around her neck slowly and applied pressure ever so slightly and then more and more. Kate's eyes rolled back in her head as she gasped for breath. Just before she died, she looked up to see her young son watching it all.

Tony stood for a moment outside the door. He waited for silence, and then slowly turned the knob. He stared at Kate's body, then John, and said, "You didn't need to do that."

John fastened his pants. "You know what, let's get the fuck out of here while the getting is good."

Young Jack crouched and pushed himself even closer to the wall he had been hiding behind. He sat there for a long time after they left. Finally, he stood up and walked downstairs toward his dead mother. He sat next to her and covered up her body with the blanket that had kept him warm during the cold nights since his father had left. He reached out to hold her hand and could feel the warmth of her skin. He sat there with his mother and cried silently until the knock on the front door.

CHAPTER 3

Selinsgrove, PA 1970

Everyone looked up. Kids can feel it when the principal walks into their class, and Sean McGinnis was no exception. He figured somebody was in real trouble. He was shocked when the principal, after whispering something to his teacher, walked up to Sean's row and stopped at his desk. "Sean, come with me, son," he said.

"What did I do?" said Sean, trying to sound brave and feeling scared at the same time.

"Nothing," said Mr. Albertson in a soft, almost sad voice. "Just come with me, son, and bring your books." All the kids were staring at him.

Sean picked up his stuff and started walking down the hall when he felt an arm around his shoulder. Sean looked at the principal with a curious look. He walked to the office silently, his head down, trying to figure out what he had done to get himself in so much trouble. Two police officers and a woman were waiting for them in the office. The lady walked over to him and took him by the hand and told him to sit down. She said that she worked for the city and was there to help him and his brother.

She sat next to Sean on the couch and told him to be brave, and that everything would be okay in the end. Then she told him that his mom had been killed, and since his dad was in Vietnam, he and Jack would have to immediately move in with either his mom's parents or his dad's. Just then Sean's grandfather Burt McGinnis walked in past the two cops. He walked right up to Sean and hugged him hard.

"What the hell are you guys doing? You shouldn't be talking to him, unless I was here, you should have waited." He let go of Sean and kneeled down next to him.

"Don't worry, son, we'll be okay."

There was nothing vague or confusing about what that lady had said. "Your mom is dead." In the blink of an eye, everything that was warm turned cold, and everything that made him feel safe suddenly felt terrifying. And in that moment, Sean's whole life turned around, nothing would ever be the same.

Sean's grandfather looked at the two cops and said, "You had no right coming here, you should have waited for me. What are you doing here anyway? The kid doesn't know anything, go do your job, find the bastard who killed Kate."

One of the cops, Joe Buck, had known Burt for more than twenty years. They were fishing buddies and old friends. "Okay, Burt, but we need to ask Sean some questions."

"Not now," said Sean's grandfather. "I'll bring him down to the station in the morning. I've got things I need to do."

Joe looked down, he knew that time was important in the investigation. He leaned in close to Burt. "Shit, Burt, anything the kid could tell us would be real helpful."

Burt McGinnis reached out, took Sean's hand and said, "Don't worry, Sean, me and Grandma will take care of you and Jack. Everything is going to be okay."

Sean looked at his grandfather and couldn't figure out whether he was angry or scared, maybe both.

Sean stumbled along the familiar hallway as they left the school, but it was like he was watching his grandfather and himself from a faraway place. It wasn't really him walking down the hallway.

"Come on, son," said Burt, "Let's get out of here. We need to get your brother."

Sean followed, his grandfather's warm hand holding his.

Sean loved his grandpa's car; it was a big red Cadillac. Just driving down Main Street in that car made him feel special. He would sit up real tall and straight, proud, but not today. Today he slumped against the window. His breath was fogging up the glass, making the world seem clouded over. He was going to be okay; Grandpa would take care of everything. "Me and Jack are okay," he whispered to himself over and over. "Dad will come home soon, me and Jack are okay."

"Where's Jack, is he okay?" Sean asked.

"Yeah, Sean, he's okay." Burt reached across the seat and lay his heavy hand on Sean's shoulder. He kept talking, quiet, like he was talking to himself. "They think that maybe he was there the whole time and they think that maybe he saw the whole thing, but he's just sitting there not saying a word. Grandma is with him. They think that maybe he is in shock, and we have to just wait until he can tell us who did this."

Sean didn't say a word, just stared out the window. Burt stopped talking and looked over at his grandson, nodded at the silence and the back of the young boy's head. "Don't worry, Sean. Let's give your father a call. We need him to get home to us as soon as he can." Sean glanced over at Burt and then turned back to the window.

The light turned red, and Burt stopped the car. Burt put his hand out and reached for Sean's hand; the boy slid over and put his head on his grandfather's shoulder. He thought that he should be crying, but not yet. Maybe he would cry later, alone, when there was no one to see.

"Let's go call your father. Let's get him back home. Your dad will take care of you boys, everything's going to be all right. You understand, Sean, everything is going to be all right. But while we're waiting, you both will stay with us until he gets home."

As they pulled up to the front of his house, he saw men from the sheriff's office; they were wheeling a stretcher out of the house. A black zipped-up bag lay across it. Another police car pulled up behind theirs. Joe Buck, Grandpa's friend, got out and walked up to them. "It's a crime scene, Burt. You can't go inside just yet. Take the boy home to your place. I'll be in touch."

"Come on, goddamnit, Joe. We need to get some stuff for the kids, we won't touch anything. It'll just take a minute."

"You know better than that, Burt. You know we can't let you anywhere near that house. Please, Burt, you know how bad we all feel about this, we've known that little girl all her life. This is personal. Let me do my job. I'm not going let anyone screw this up, not even you."

"Okay," said Burt. "Where is Jack? I need to get Jack out of there."

"The lady from social services is with him. I'll go get him."

Burt called after Joe, "Do me a favor; I need to get a hold of Jerry. His number is on the wall next to the refrigerator. At least go in there and write it down for me."

"Okay, Burt, I'll go get it for you right now. Here comes Jack."

Sean looked up to see a woman coming out of the house, wearing a bright blue dress. He thought that her dress was kind of short. He thought her dress should be longer. And then he saw that she was holding his younger brother by the hand. At first, he didn't see Jack hiding behind her. She had to drag him out from behind her, and that's when Sean reacted. He jumped out of the car and ran up to Jack, pulling him away from the woman. "Let go of him, that's my brother. Don't touch him."

The neighbors were out in the street, staring at him and Jack, whispering and shaking their heads. Sean turned around, ready to hit anybody or anything that stood between him and his little brother.

Burt grabbed Sean by the shoulder. "Don't worry, Sean, you and Jack will be okay; nobody is going to hurt you. You'll stay with me and Grandma until your father gets back. Everything will be okay, so don't worry, son." Sean looked up at his grandfather and saw the sadness in his eyes. Sean tried to hide his fear and anger. His emotions were running haywire—he was confused, mad, and sad all at the same time. "We'll be fine when my dad comes home, then we'll be okay," he repeated. The cop that his grandfather had spoken to came out of the house. Burt sent the boys to sit in the Cadillac while he and the cop talked.

"Burt," said the cop. "Look, I can't seem to find the number. I looked all over the place, even behind the refrigerator, but you know I have to be careful. Give us twenty-four hours and then you can come back."

"Joe," said Burt, "the fucking number is right on the goddamn refrigerator. I saw it last night. We were over there and I went and got myself a beer and there it was. There's a picture of Jerry in 'Nam with his buddies next to the contact number for emergencies."

"I'm sorry, I couldn't find it."

"Okay, forget about the fucking number. Why don't you give me an idea of what the hell happened? Was it some bastard looking for drugs or what?"

"Calm down, Burt, we don't know anything and we're not going to know anything until we do an autopsy."

"Cut the shit, Joe, you're a cop, you've seen this stuff before." Joe and Burt had grown up together, had played on the same teams, and even occasionally dated the same girls, which for them was just fine; in the end they were friends, and friends never betrayed a trust that had been forged over the years.

"Are you out of your mind, Burt? There hasn't been a murder here in ten years. I'm not used to this shit, I threw up my guts two times in the last hour. But it does look like she was strangled, maybe raped, I'm not sure. There is a mark around her neck. The place is a mess. It's like he was looking for something, the closets are a mess, maybe they were looking for money. Looks like Kate was in the wrong place at the wrong time."

"What are you, fucking nuts, she was in her home! Where the fuck would you like her to be?" said Burt furiously.

"Burt, you know what I mean. Kate's been spending a lot of time down at Tony's bar, maybe she met a guy and things got out of hand. You know that things have been different since Jerry went off to Vietnam. We need to look into every possibility. Maybe some guy was robbing the place and she surprised him. Give us some time. I promise you, I will find this guy."

"Yeah, sure, I've heard that shit before. You all say you're going to find the guy and a couple of weeks go by and all of a sudden the leads dry up, and the next thing you know, I'm calling you and you're just giving me the runaround. I guarantee you, I'll never stop crawling up your ass until that bastard is caught."

"Burt, I know you're upset. Look, I need for you to bring the boys down to the station tomorrow; we need to know what Jack saw and maybe Sean knows something. Come down around nine tomorrow, is that okay?"

"Yeah, we'll be down there in the morning. Sorry for being an asshole. Boys just lost their mother and my son is off in that fucking bullshit war. I don't know what I'm going to do."

Burt got into the car with the boys and drove away from the house. They pulled up to the light on Main Street. Sean was holding Jack's hand and looking straight ahead. A car pulled up next to them at the light and Sean and Jack both turned. The two men in the car stared over at the boys. To Sean, they looked exactly like all the guys in the pictures that their father sent home from the war. The men smiled and then drove off as the light turned green. There was something about their eyes that sent a shiver up Sean's back. He slipped his hand over Jack's shoulder and pulled him in close. "Jack," Sean said, "I know you're scared, but don't worry, Dad's coming home and we'll be okay. Jack, do you hear me? Jack, say something."

"Sean," his grandfather reached over and held Sean's arm. "They think that Jack saw the whole thing. Give him a little time to sort things out." Jack sat there silently.

"Maybe he was upstairs sleeping," Sean whispered.

"Maybe. The cops believe he saw something, that's why he hasn't said a word. They think that he has been traumatized. So we're just going have to give him some time."

Sean looked over at his brother and said, "Okay."

Sean felt that it wasn't right that it should be such a nice day. The winter had been bad—cold and raw, with a lot of snow—but today the sun was shining. It would be a great day to play baseball on the high school field. *It just wasn't right*, he thought.

The three of them walked into the house. Grandma Doris met them and hugged the boys. She led them over to the sofa. She wanted to sit between them, but Sean wouldn't let go of Jack. Some men came into the room, and one was talking.

"Hi, Sean, you remember me? I worked with your grandpa at the paper. I'm real sorry for what happened to your mother, but you guys are in good hands until your dad gets back. I know that they're looking for him, I'm sure that he's all right."

Sean looked up. "What do mean they're looking for him? They don't know where he is?"

"John," Burt said, "what are you telling the kid?" He stood up.

"Nothing, Burt, just that everything is going to be fine when Jerry gets home."

"Look, Sean, just hang in there, things will be better, I promise you." Sean worshipped his grandfather. He would sit in awe as Burt retold stories that had been told countless times before. But this time was different, nothing was making sense and for the first time since he could ever remember, he instinctively doubted his grandfather.

"Grandpa, how come my dad hasn't called?"

Burt tilted his head to the side and closed his eyes for a second. "I don't know what's going on, but I'm sure everything will be okay, as soon as they can locate your dad."

"They don't know where my dad is? Stop saying it is going to be okay, nothing is okay." Sean's words tore at Burt's heart. He had grown accustomed to an unquestionable trust that is rare outside the

29

realm of grandfather and grandson. He struggled with the deception and felt an unfamiliar sense of shame. He had no choice. For the sake of Sean and Jack, he would hold fast to an optimism that had no place here.

That night, Sean and Jack slept together in their dad's old bed, Jack whimpering quietly, Sean holding him. Their grandfather sat with them all night on the old desk chair.

CHAPTER 4

Selinsgrove, PA 1970

To Sean, it all seemed like a bad dream that never ended, a dream that had a life of its own. Jack and Sean stayed with their Grandpa Burt. They wouldn't have minded staying with their other grandparents, but their mom's mom was crying so much and her dad was just sitting there on the sofa getting drunk. Going home with them didn't seem like a great idea.

The following morning Burt told Jack and Sean to get ready, he was going to take them down to the police station.

"Burt, can't it wait till next week? Let these poor boys bury their mother first," their grandma told him, while everyone was still sitting at the table eating Rice Krispies.

"It won't take too long, and Joe asked me to bring them. I'll take them downtown after to get them suits for the ceremony. I don't know if the police will even let me in to go look for good clothes."

Grandma just shook her head. Sean looked over at Jack who was quietly eating his cereal. He didn't seem to be listening to anything.

The police sergeant behind the desk looked up when the three of them walked in the front door. He stood up to tell the boys how sorry he was about their mom.

"Boys," he said, as he put his hands on their shoulders, "we need to talk to your grandfather for a little while. How about you both just sit out here for a few minutes. We can fix you up with some hot cocoa and maybe even find you a donut or two. Hey, Tom," said the sergeant to a young guy walking by, "do me a favor and fix these boys up with a little hot cocoa and a donut."

"Sure thing, Sergeant," said the other policeman. "Come on, boys, you like glazed donuts or chocolate?" He kneeled down slowly in front of Jack and gently put his hand on his arm, looking up at Sean. "He still not talking?" he asked quietly. Sean nodded.

They both nibbled on their donuts for a little while until Grandpa came to find them. "Okay, boys, come in here with me. Officer Joe wants to talk to you for a little while, and I will be right here with you."

The boys followed him into a dark office with a desk in the middle and some chairs around it. "Do me a favor, Joe," Grandpa said, "go easy on the little one. The poor guy hasn't said a word since they found him sitting there next to his mom. Jack has been traumatized. We just need to make him feel safe and hopefully he'll get back to being the happy kid he's always been. Right now, I got to find Jerry and get him back home. I'll tell you, Joe, I think the Army is giving me the runaround. I keep asking to speak to somebody about getting Jerry home and they can't even get in touch with him. I know that it's dangerous over there, I'm no fucking idiot, but Jerry was working for some military newsletter. He wasn't doing any fighting. I just don't get it."

Grandpa Burt looked over at Sean; it seemed as if he'd forgotten that the boy was standing right there and could hear everything.

"Look, Burt, I'm sure he's all right," Joe said. "I hear what you're saying, but I can't do anything about Jerry. I got a job to do right here, and I need to talk to these boys now."

"Just please go easy on them."

"I know who I'm talking to, Burt. As God is my witness, I get it, but I need to get some answers. Did they see anything strange or unusual? Did they hear their mom talking about anybody new, or to anybody they don't know? Was she fighting with anyone? Was there ever anyone in the house that made them feel uncomfortable?"

Burt slumped back into the chair opposite the desk and said, "Look, I'm more concerned about Jerry right now. You do your job and find that bastard, and I'm going to do my job and take care of these kids and get their father home."

Sean didn't want to hear any of this. He knew his grandpa couldn't fix anything. His dad was missing, what did that mean? Jack might never talk again, what had he seen? How was Sean supposed to help? He just looked at the desk in the middle of the room and waited. He wished he had something to tell them that would help. Jack couldn't do it. It was his job, Sean was the oldest, but he didn't know what to say.

Joe told Sean and Jack to sit down, and he sat on the other side of the desk. "Boys, want you to know that I am really sorry about your mom, and I can tell you both I won't stop till we find the person who did this." Sean wanted to cry then, and he wanted Jack to cry—why wasn't his brother crying? Jack used to cry about every little thing and now he was just sitting there, powdered sugar around his lips from the donut. Sean thought to himself: Mom would have licked her finger and rubbed it off. He didn't want to, was he supposed to now that she was gone?

"Maybe if you try real hard," said Joe in a quiet and cautious tone, "you'll remember somebody. Maybe there was someone hanging around your house or maybe one night you were watching TV and you noticed your mother with somebody?"

Sean just shook his head and wondered what he was talking about. Her friend Sandy came over sometimes, and the neighbors came sometimes too.

Sean cleared his throat and said, "You mean like Mrs. Kauffman from next door or mom's friend Sandy? They used to come over. Do you think they did something to our mom?"

"No, Sean, I mean like some man, maybe some man that came at night or talked to your mom on the phone?"

"Did you notice any strange guys coming over to the house, Sean?" his grandpa asked.

"NO," Sean answered forcefully and truthfully.

Sean knew that their mom was lonely ever since Dad went to Vietnam, but no men came over. Joe and their grandpa showed pictures of guys to the boys and asked if anyone looked at all familiar. All morning Sean and Jack and their grandfather sat there while they asked the boys questions and showed them pictures.

Jack was the only one who had been there, thought Sean, the only one that could help the cops find whoever killed their mother. But Jack said nothing, just sort of sat there with his head on their grandfather's shoulder. He was making a little moaning sound when he breathed, nothing more, just that faint whimper of a six-year-old boy.

The police were acting like they thought that it was somebody that their mother knew. They asked again and again if their mom had ever brought anyone into the house, maybe late at night when they were sleeping or during the day when they were off at school. Were they blaming her for getting herself killed? Sean got tired and put his head on the table and finally felt the tears roll down his cheeks. He didn't want to answer any more of these questions. He just wanted his father to come home and take care of them. It seemed like everything had gone wrong with them since their father had gone to Vietnam.

Finally their grandfather said, "That's enough, can't you see that the kids don't know anything? Look, I got to get Jack to a doctor."

"Okay, Burt." The two men stood and shook hands.

After they left the station house, they went downtown and bought clothes. Grandpa picked out white shirts and clip-on ties and black pants for both of the boys. Sean got a jacket too, but they didn't have one small enough for Jack. Grandpa said it was okay. The lady who helped them was really nice and quiet.

Once outside Sean asked their grandpa about their other clothes, his baseball card collection, and the rest of his stuff. Couldn't they go home to get their stuff?

"Yeah, Sean, we'll swing by your house and get your stuff," said Burt.

Their grandfather turned on the radio when they got back in the car. The Phillies were playing and they sat for a moment listening to the game. For a few minutes life felt normal to Sean, the way it was supposed to be. Philadelphia was playing the Mets. Sean hated the Mets. He didn't know exactly why, except that in his house you rooted for the Phillies and you hated anything New York: Mets, Yankees, Giants, Knicks.

As they drove up the street to their house, Sean look around—it seemed like they were having a block party. All the neighbors watched as they turned into the driveway, then quickly turned away.

There were police cars parked in the driveway and on their lawn. Sean thought about how angry his father would be when he found out that the cops had parked their cars on the front lawn. His father was proud of the lawn and every Sunday after breakfast he would go outside to cut the lawn and trim the hedges. Sean remembered, after he would mow the lawn, Dad would stop the mower, get up from the seat, and survey what he had done. He was proud of the lawn; he would have been furious to see the cars on it. Sometimes he would let Sean cut the grass, but he had to wear goggles and earplugs so he couldn't hurt his eyes or hearing. Sean went slowly, not wanting to miss a blade of grass. All he wanted to hear was Dad saying, "Good job."

Sometimes it got so hot, Sean would sweat just sitting on that old tractor, he remembered. It was more of a sit-down lawnmower than a tractor, but his dad loved to call it a tractor, made him feel closer to the land. His mom would come out with a big jug of lemonade, and Sean and his dad would stop and sit under the elm tree, just the two of them, and drink that lemonade down with one big gulp, and then they would burp the loudest burp a person could burp and they laughed and laughed. Sean's mom would smile and say, "You men are just a bunch of rude pigs," and Sean and his dad would look at her and just keep on laughing until she started laughing with them.

"Let's go, boys," said their grandfather. Sean looked out of the passenger window. He knew most of the people gathered in front of the house.

"Jack, come on, son, it'll be all right. Just a few minutes and then we'll get you boys back to Grandma." Jack didn't move, he sat there staring straight ahead.

Grandpa Burt stood at the open door and waited, and then slowly leaned into the car and gently took hold of Jack's arm to pull him out of the car. Jack took hold of the door handle and wouldn't let go. Their grandpa let go of Jack's arm and slid into the car next to him. He put his arm around his grandson and said, "Don't worry, son. It's okay, you don't ever have to go in there again, I promise." He turned to the older boy.

"Sean, please go get what you need for a few nights and get some clothes for your brother."

Sean stood there, not moving. He could see the people staring at them, then looking away.

"Sean," said Grandpa. "Go ahead, son, it'll be all right. I got to stay here with Jack."

Sean walked slowly toward the house; it was only a few steps from the curb to the front door. Lots of people were standing on the lawn. Sean knew his dad would have been pissed.

Sean felt a hand on his shoulder and looked up; it was Andy Dorfman. "I'm so sorry, son. Tell your grandpa that if you need anything, just give us a call. You got our number… Never mind, I'll give it to Burt. You want me to go with you?"

The Dorfman family had been in the house next door long before Sean and Jack moved in. Their dad and Andy Dorfman were good friends.

Sean looked up and said, "I'm okay, Andy." Andy Dorfman was the only adult that Sean ever called by his first name; he had insisted, and eventually, Sean got used to it.

"Okay, Sean, you go ahead. If you need anything, just call."

Sean stood in front of the steps to the porch; he and his dad had painted the porch last May. They called the paint color Seagull Gray, and he remembered they argued about the color, that actually Dad didn't want to paint it at all. He wanted it to be natural, to just stain the wood. His mom got her way in the end. He walked into the house, the front door was already open. The couch in the living room had been covered with a white sheet and men in suits were walking around looking everywhere. He stood there for a few minutes and tried not to cry, but he couldn't help it. He felt light-headed; he remembered feeling this way once. It was hot, so hot, and he and his brother were playing catch. Sean felt light-headed, and the next thing he knew, he was lying on the couch, his mom fanning him with a magazine. "Sean, drink some water, you'll feel better," she said.

Sean sat down on the bottom step. He couldn't go up the stairs. He couldn't imagine passing by his mom and dad's room. He closed his eyes.

"Sean, drink some water, son." His grandfather was suddenly there next to him. He sat down on the stairs and handed him a glass of cold water. Once Sean drank it down, he felt better.

"Come on, I should have never let you go by yourself. Andy's watching your brother. Let's get this over with."

The house hadn't felt the same since his dad had left, but now it was worse. It felt empty and cold and dark. Sean couldn't stand being there. They collected some clothes as fast as they could.

"When is my dad coming home?" Sean asked his grandpa as they drove away from the house. Burt didn't say a word, just continued driving. Sean asked again, "Grandpa, when is my dad coming home? Didn't you call him and tell him to come home?"

Their grandfather looked at the boy with a sad expression on his face and said, "I tried to call your dad, but they said that he was on a mission and couldn't be reached. As soon as he gets back they'll have him call us, and then the army will send him home as soon as possible."

"When?" asked Sean. "Who are we going to live with?"

"You'll live with us until your dad gets home. Me and your grandmother will take good care of you both until your father gets home. So don't worry, okay?" Sean turned and looked out of the window as they stopped for a long freight train to pass by. They sat in the car at the railroad crossing and watched the train go by, and every once in a while you could see the tranquil Susquehanna river just beyond the tracks.

The day of their mother's funeral was bright and sunny, not a cloud in the sky. Sean thought that it should be a rainy and cold and damp day, but it wasn't. It was a great day to go swimming or fishing. He didn't understand why his father hadn't even called.

Sean and Jack stayed with Grandpa Burt and their grandma. Sean tried not to be mad at his dad for leaving in the first place. He remembered his father saying, "A man's got to do what a man's got to do," but no other kid's father had gone to Vietnam, so why his dad? Sean's dad had told him that he was simply reporting on the brave actions of the troops and sending back stories so their families would be proud of them. He told Sean, "Don't worry, son, I'll just be reporting on the fighting, not doing the fighting," and then his dad would smile and put his arm around his shoulder and tell Sean that he was going to be the man of the house until Dad got back home.

Since his father had left and Sean had become the man of the house, his mom told him that he had become self-reliant. At the time it seemed like a good thing to be, except that Sean had no idea what being self-reliant meant. He wanted his father to be the man of the house again.

At night, he tried to keep all the good memories alive, but he couldn't stop thinking about the bad stuff, missing his parents, his old life. He missed sitting on the couch in front of the TV with his dad, watching John Nelson explore the dangers of the sea. *Sea Hunt* was Sean's favorite show; he could slip into a world of danger and excitement. John Nelson was his hero; there was nothing that could keep him from finding the truth and getting the bad guys. Eventually he would fall asleep and his dad would carry him upstairs. Then, almost like in a dream, his mom would be standing over him, smiling down, kissing his head,

"Oh, big boy," she would say. "Sleep tight."

Sean thought about his father and what he had told them, about doing his duty to serve their country in a time of need and that they should all be proud of him. His dad had told him that he needed to go there to find the truth, and that he would explain everything when he got back.

They would get letters almost every day from his father. Some letters Mom would read to the boys, but there were a bunch that she put into a big box in the hall closet.

"This is Daddy's work, so just leave them alone and don't tell anybody about them," she said. Every night they would sit in the kitchen after dinner and listen to their mom read about what their dad was doing and thinking and seeing in Vietnam. Sean missed playing ball with him and fishing on the banks of the Susquehanna River. When would his dad be home?

CHAPTER 5

Selinsgrove, PA

Jack McGinnis strolled slowly up the porch steps. He stared at the tattered welcome mat that said "Welcome to Joe and Patricia's Home." For a moment, he tried to think back but the memories had always been cloudy and vague. Everything had gone straight to hell. The three years in the hospital, then Grandma and Sean moving out to California, leaving him behind to spend the next eight years with Joe and Pat in this house.

Over the years, Jack had kept in touch with some of his old buddies from high school and had heard that Patricia Smith had died. He remembered feeling bad, but not too bad. Not bad enough to take the time to go to her funeral. After all, he thought, she was there all those times her husband came home drunk. Sometimes she tried to distract Joe, sometimes she didn't. The welcome mat was bringing back the memories, some good but most not so good. *Fuck it,* he thought to himself, and pushed the door open.

He had sworn that he would never set eyes on this house ever again and sure as hell would never set foot in it. Not after all those hard years in this old, battered house. He stood there frozen in time and the memories, the memories that he tried so hard to drive out of his mind seemed to flow back, stronger and more vivid than ever before. The house, the porch, the swinging rocker, and the ancient welcome mat brought back them all back.

He felt a moment of fear and anger, but an instant later, those feelings, the feelings that he had felt so many times over those years, seemed to drift away and were replaced with a sense of strength and power. He walked into the house and heard the TV going in the kitchen down the hall. Jack walked toward the sound and stopped when he saw the old man standing with his back to Jack. He was waiting for the toast to pop up from the old toaster. Joe Smith grabbed the toast and turned and stared at the man that stood in his kitchen. At first he didn't say a word, and then, just like Jack wasn't there, walked toward the kitchen table and sat down.

"Well, well, well," said the old man in a matter-of-fact tone. "Look what the cat's dragged in, or should I say what the rat's dragged in." Then he laughed in a gravelly tone, like he was laughing and choking at the same time. "Don't just stand there like a fucking jerk, grab a beer and come sit with your old dad."

Jack walked over to the refrigerator and pulled a beer out before he sat down across from Smith. He had never wanted to call him dad. Joe Smith would never be his father. It had been a long time and Jack could hardly recognize him. He looked so old. His thick black hair had become thin and white, and those dark blue eyes seemed to have lost some of their shine. He had gotten thin and frail over the years, but those eyes still had that glitter, the twinkle that could look caring and warm but was also there when the beatings began.

Jack sat quietly and finally said, "You're not my dad, you never been my dad and you sure ain't never going to be my dad. You're just an old beat-up son of a bitch sitting here having a beer with your toast."

Smith looked up and said, "That's the best you got, after all these years? I thought you would come with something a little more original, but you were never too bright. Anyway," said Joe, "nothing changes. What have you been doing with your life? I hear that you've really made a name for yourself. That doesn't surprise me, always knew that you'd become a real productive citizen," he said sarcastically. "So tell me, Jack, how were things up at the VA? Must have been a blast cleaning up all those bed pans."

Smith took another bite of his toast and took a swallow of beer. Jack sat there and said nothing. Finally the old man said, "What are you doing here? I don't have any money, so if that's what you're looking for, you're wasting your time."

He reached for the beer when Jack reached out and grabbed his hand with a firm grip.

"I don't want your fucking money. I don't want anything from you," said Jack angrily.

"Than what the fuck do you want? And take your goddamn hands off of me before I give you a smack."

Jack let go of the old man's hand and stood up slowly and put both hands down on the table. Staring at Smith, he said, "Your days of beating up little kids are over."

"I never beat you," said Smith in a defensive tone. "Sure, I might have been a little harsh, but you needed it, you were like a wild fucking Indian. You needed a little discipline. If I got out of line, my father would take one of those electric cords from the old Remington electric razors and go to work on my back. Now that was a beating,

43

but you never heard me complain, I took it like a man, not like a little girl, not a little crybaby. Is that what you are, a little girl? I always thought you were a little fag, now I know for sure."

Jack sat back down at the kitchen table. He slowly slid his hand over the surface of the yellow linoleum table, his fingers moving over the smooth aluminum strip that covered the edges of the round kitchen table. Jack took a breath to calm down and said, "Look, Smith, I don't want any trouble. I know there are some boxes of my father's down in the basement. I'll never see you again, what's done is done. I just need to get those boxes down in the basement."

The old man stared at Jack and said, "What's in the boxes?"

"Papers, journals, notebooks. Just some old useless shit, but it's my dad's last words. It's important to me; I'll take the boxes and get out of your life."

"Well, well," said Smith, "If they're that important to you, then maybe I should be collecting a storage charge. I mean, those fucking boxes have been cluttering up my basement for, like, twenty fucking years. I figure a hundred dollars a year, that's a goddamn bargain. Two thousand bucks and you can have your fucking boxes."

Jack jumped from his chair. He grabbed a knife that lay on the table, butter still on it. He took hold of the old man's hair, pulled his head back and put the knife to his throat.

"You child-molesting motherfucker, I should slice your fucking throat open and let you slowly bleed out. Just give me the key to the basement." The old man didn't dare to move with the knife pressing hard against his throat.

"Yeah, no problem, Jack. It's right up there next to the clock, hanging on the handle of the wooden desk light that you made when you were in the hospital. Remember you made it for me in that woodworking class up at the children's hospital in Williamsport. It wasn't all bad, Jack, there were plenty of good times, don't you remember, son? Now why don't you be a good boy and put that knife down." Smith's voice was suddenly frail.

Jack stood up, dropped the knife on the floor and pushed Smith to the side. He walked over to the mantel and grabbed the key.

"You better pray real hard that what I'm looking for is here."

"Okay," said the old man. "Take it easy, there's a lot of old shit downstairs in the basement."

Smith took notice of Jack's eyes. They seemed different, and he suddenly felt a sense of unease. Jack wasn't the frail, slender boy he had smacked around. Sometimes Smith would haul off and give Jack a slap across the back of his head for no reason, and sometimes he would ask, almost joking, "Which arm?" permitting Jack to make a choice, and then punch the boy in the chosen arm. Sometimes Jack would cry, but over time, he learned to bear it silently. That's when Smith would become enraged, but Jack tried not to give in to the pain and eventually he got good at hiding the hurt.

Joe said with a tone of grudging respect, "I got to admit it, you grew up pretty nice and tall. You over six feet?"

"You enjoyed it, didn't you, that turned you on, right?" said Jack.

"I don't have any goddamn idea what the fuck you're talking about."

"You son of a bitch, you just loved smacking me around. Well, I'm not that little kid anymore." Jack picked up the knife again.

"What you doing with that, boy? Now look, kid, put the knife down, you're making me a little nervous. You don't need the keys, the door is open. I'd help you bring them up, swear to God, but I can hardly make those goddamn stairs. Got emphysema now, after four packs of Chesterfields a day. Oh well," he said, "got to die of something, right, but you go ahead and get your dad's boxes. I'll have a nice cold beer for you when you get them up here." Smith smiled and nodded his head in a friendly gesture.

Jack stared at the old man for a while, then pulled some rope out of his pocket and said, "Put your hands behind your back, I don't trust you for a second."

The old man stood up and stared at Jack and said, "Who the fuck do you think you're talking to, you little shit? I beat the shit out of you before and you can bet your tight little ass I'll do it again."

Jack hesitated, a smile on his face, and then in the next instant, his right hand drew back and his fist flashed forward, smashing into Smith's right cheek. The old man stumbled into the wall, reaching for the counter next to the sink to steady himself. On the counter was a sharp knife.

Jack moved forward toward Smith, grabbed him by his arm and pulled him around—revenge, hate, betrayal. This time it would be Jack who won, let Smith see how it feels to be the punching bag.

Smith lunged up and to the right, the knife coming out of nowhere. Jack saw the flash of the blade and moved back as Smith plunged the knife toward Jack's stomach. Jack grabbed Smith's arm just as the tip of the blade sliced through Jack's right side. He reached for his stomach, instinctively protecting his body.

Smith had gotten thin and frail; he may have lost much of his quickness, but years of working in the wood shop, lifting all those heavy planks of wood, kept him strong enough. With all his strength, he brought his right elbow crashing down on Jack's head. Jack fell back against the kitchen table; he steadied himself, moving around the table to keep some distance from the knife in Smith's hand.

"You're a worthless piece of shit. You think for one fucking second you can come into my house and push me around? I should have strangled you while you slept, and buried you in the backyard with the dog. I'll tell you what, here's what I'm going to do with your precious fucking boxes. I'm going to build the biggest bonfire you ever saw with your dad's boxes. Then, I'm going to call the cops and have your worthless ass arrested for breaking into my house and coming at me with a knife. This time there will be no pansy-ass judge to go easy on you. You'll go straight to the prison in Allenwood, where you belong."

Jack smiled, gently nodding his head, and said, "You fucking devil."

The two men stood on opposite sides of the round kitchen table. "Come on, son," said Smith, sounding almost sincere. "Look, Jack, I know that I made mistakes. I know that I lost control. It was a tough time for me and Pat, and as God as my witness, I am truly sorry. I swear we did our best." He put out his right hand toward Jack.

Jack gently nodded his head and with a slight smile reached forward to shake Smith's hand. Smith grabbed hold of Jack's wrist, twisted upward and pulled him forward, while Smith lunged toward him, knife in his other hand. Smith didn't see the big black iron skillet that Jack had grabbed from the kitchen counter. The force of the blow from the pan knocked the old man to the floor, the knife went flying, and the old man lay face down and motionless.

Jack stood over him and said, "Nice try, asshole, nearly brought a tear to my eyes." Jack dragged Smith into the den and threw him onto the wooden chair next to the couch.

Jack found the rope that he had bought earlier in the day. He wrapped it around Smith's hands, tying them to the wooden legs of the chair. Smith was in a daze; he couldn't move, his right jaw felt broken, and some of his teeth must have shattered in his mouth. Jack looped the rope around Smith's upper chest and each leg, and tied the ends to the back legs of the chair. Jack pulled the end of the rope around the old man's neck and tied it down tightly.

Smith finally opened his eyes and looked up at Jack and said, "I knew I should've beaten you to death when I had the chance."

Jack slammed his fist into the old man's face one more time and said, "Shut the fuck up, you piece of shit."

Jack turned toward the stairs that led to the basement and walked down the narrow stairs. At the bottom, he found the light switch on the side of the wall. The 110-watt bulb hardly lit up the basement, but Jack saw a pile of boxes in the corner that looked like they hadn't been touched in years. The box on top had two words on it: "Jerry's papers." Jack brought it up the stairs. His foster father was staring avidly as he tried to turn his head around to watch Jack as he put the box on the wooden dining room table.

"You got what you want, now get out of here and I'll forget about this whole thing, okay? Just go," Smith said in a pleading and shaky voice.

Jack sat there at the table for a moment staring at the box, mesmerized. He moved his hand slowly over the dusty top. It had been sealed years before with brown tape that had all but disintegrated. He carefully opened the top of the box and stared at the files full of papers and letters.

"Make yourself comfortable," said Jack. "You know what, being down there in the basement brings back lots of fond memories. When you got good and drunk, I would go down there and crawl over and under those pile of boxes. I hated that dark, damp basement, but it beat the hell out of getting a beating. Yeah," he continued, "it was a pretty damn good place to hide. Who would have thought that those goddamn letters from Dad were down there all the time."

Jack went up and down the stairs to the basement to bring up nine boxes, all dusty and all marked "Jerry's papers." *All these fucking years...it's all here*, he thought, *the truth, the fucking truth. Maybe I can finally get my life back. Sean got raised in a fucking "Leave It to Beaver" family and what did he get?* Jack turned around to face the old man in the La-Z-Boy in the corner of the living room. He smiled, but it wasn't a happy one.

Jack stood up slowly, holding the knife. He found a roll of duct tape in a drawer in the kitchen. He walked over to the old man and sat down next to him, as if they were sitting down on a Sunday afternoon to watch the Eagles play the Giants. He pulled a length of tape off and wrapped it over Smith's mouth. He had heard all he ever wanted to hear from the son of a bitch. He pulled on the rope around his neck to make sure it was tight.

"I would just relax if I was you. The more you struggle, the tighter it will get. Just some friendly advice."

Smith sat still, staring at Jack; he quickly understood that moving and struggling seem to tighten up the rope around his neck, just like Jack had warned. The duct tape over his mouth magnified the heavy breathing from his nose. He could feel his nasal cavity start to fill up; his nasal spray dose was beginning to wear off. For years, he had been addicted to NTZ nasal spray. He couldn't live without it anymore, or his nose would become so blocked up it felt like concrete had been poured into his sinuses. The fear was building: if Jack didn't pull off the tape over his mouth, he would suffocate. Smith tried to shake his head back and forth, but every time he moved, the noose around his neck seemed to get tighter and tighter. He begged with his eyes, staring at the grown boy sitting just a few inches away. The boy he had abused – physically, emotionally, spiritually, and sexually. He wanted to plead for his life, he wanted to say that he was sorry, he wanted to beg for forgiveness, but he couldn't do anything but moan.

Jack could feel a slight breeze from the open window on his left. It was getting cold, and he leaned over the couch and closed the window. A fire would be nice, he thought. He sat down and put his legs up on the wooden coffee table that sat between the couch and the La-Z-Boy.

Jack sat there, looking at Smith, the old man sitting still, just blinking his eyes. Jack smiled ruefully and spoke to him, knowing that he couldn't answer. "Are you trying to tell me something, old man? Maybe you want to ask for forgiveness?"

Smith blinked again and again, as if confirming what Jack had said.

"Okay, well, maybe it wasn't all bad; you did take me in after all. Maybe I will let you live." Jack stood up. "Be right back. This fucking bladder infection is driving me crazy. I got to pee all the time, and when I do, it burns like hell. It is always something, right, old man?"

Jack walked out of the room and went down the hall to the bathroom. He stood over the toilet and unzipped his fly. He could feel the burning sensation in his lower stomach and his groin as he held onto the sink to his right and strained with all his might. A dark red liquid poured into the toilet turning the clear water a dark red. Jack gripped the sink and pushed out as much of the blood-red piss as he could. He felt light-headed as he pulled up his zipper and reached down to flush the toilet. His head started to spin, his vision became a blur; this had happened before, he knew the feeling. He held on to the sink and lowered himself down to the cold tile floor.

In the other room, Smith sat still. He couldn't move, he couldn't scream, he could only wait for Jack to come back and pull the tape off his mouth so he could breathe. He looked up at the old clock that sat on the mantel over the fireplace; it was a few minutes after three. He felt the fear rising up in his gut. He knew that it would only be a few minutes before his entire airway would be blocked completely. And then he would suffocate in the middle of the fucking den. Tears came to Joe's eyes, and he asked his Lord to forgive him.

He breathed in with all his strength, but suddenly no air came in. He struggled against the ropes, his head shaking back and forth in a panic, the rage flooding back in. He lurched in the chair. The noose around his neck was tightening and he could feel his lungs exploding.

"Fuck," Jack said, as he woke on the bathroom floor. He slowly stood and walked out of the bathroom. He felt clammy, cold, and still a little light-headed. He had been feeling this way more and more lately. Jack walked into the den. Smith's head tilted to one side, his eyes wide open, staring up at the mantel toward the cross that Jack had made in art and crafts.

"Hey, shithead, staring at that little cross is not going to wash away your sins." But Smith did not look up. Jack reached down to touch his face, it felt damp, cold, and the man did not respond. Jack felt for a pulse, but couldn't find one. "You son of a bitch, what the hell happened?" The ropes around his neck were tight, but not tight enough to strangle him; there was no way in hell he could have strangled to death. But Smith was dead and Jack had been denied the pleasure and the satisfaction of watching the old man die slowly.

Jack pulled the tape off Smith's mouth and untied the old man. He sat down on the couch opposite the dead man. He didn't know how to feel. The shithead who abused him all those years finally got what was coming to him. Jack didn't understand why, but instead of feeling good, he felt sad and empty.

Jack picked up the pack of cigarettes from the coffee table next to the couch.

"And you thought you were going to die of lung cancer. You can't always get what you want."

Jack stood up from the couch with a cigarette in his mouth and walked back toward the old and battered kitchen table. He sat down slowly, as if it hurt to sit, and took a long swallow of the beer and pulled in a long drag on the cigarette. *I got to get some rest and some food*, he thought. *Then I will deal with him*. He felt so tired, but hungry too. More often lately, Jack didn't feel hungry, but right now he did. In the refrigerator he found six eggs and half a package of bacon. The large black pan was still on the floor; he reached down and put it on the stovetop, turned on the flame, and put a slab of butter in the pan. Jack cracked open each egg into a large glass bowl and stirred. The bacon in the smaller pan began to crackle, and he dropped some bread in the toaster.

He ate slowly, savoring each mouthful. He looked up at the small clock that sat on the windowsill; it was just before 8 p.m. It had gotten dark outside and he moved to the screen door that led out to the front porch. Jack looked up and down the street. It was quiet and he could see the TVs on in most of the neighbors' windows. Jack's car was parked on the street; Smith's car was parked in the driveway, next to the house. The old man's keys were hanging on the rack that Jack had made while he was in the hospital. It was supposed to look like a big deer with antlers, but it didn't.

He needed to get Joe's body out of the house and bury him someplace. No one would miss the son of a bitch. The old man had lost a lot of weight, but the dead weight of his body was still too heavy for Jack to lift. Jack eased him to the floor and dragged him to the back door of the kitchen. He used Smith's car keys to open the trunk and laid an old bed sheet down carefully to cover the bottom. Making sure nobody could see, he carried the old man's body out of the house and put it in the trunk.

Jack drove slowly through town, turning north on Route 23 up toward Williamsport and the dirt roads that led to hunting cabins only used during deer season. When he was almost to the cabin, he pulled to the side of the dirt road and got out. There was a chill in the air. Jack stood beside the car and listened; it was quiet, no sounds other the rustling of the leaves. He opened the trunk and stared at the old man's body, barely visible under the starlight. He didn't know quite how to feel. He hadn't really intended on killing the old man, but maybe it was meant to be.

The cabin he remembered was just up the road, but he wasn't sure if anyone was there. There could be kids up there drinking and smoking pot. Jack closed the trunk lid and walked up the road to the cabin, turning the flashlight off so that he wouldn't be seen. He knocked on the door, there was no answer; he looked into one window, no one was there. Joe had taken him up to the cabin a few times during the summers. He remembered there was a shed in the back with tools and a wheelbarrow. He also found shovels and a pick. Jack put a shovel and the pick into the wheelbarrow and started back down to the car.

Jack slid the old man's body into the wheelbarrow. The ground was uneven and covered with tree limbs and rocks. He pushed and pulled the wheelbarrow deep into the woods, moving for more than an hour with only the flashlight to light the way in the moonless night. He was exhausted, sweating and shaking in the cool night air, but he had no choice. The ground was soft where he began to dig. It seemed like two or three hours of digging when the grave was deep enough. He pulled himself up and out and dumped the body in. Smith was facing down. Jack wanted to roll him over, but he couldn't manage it. He stood over the grave; he thought he should say something, but no words came.

Over the years, he had fantasized about revenge for the years of abuse. "Burn in hell, you bastard," was what he had planned to shout after killing the old man, but now it felt different. All the rage, all the hate seemed to drift away, and he felt the tears well up in his eyes. All he could think was *Why?*

Jack picked up the shovel and pushed it into the mound of dirt, but then hesitated. He went to gather up as many stones as he could find. He lined Joe's body as best he could with smaller stones. He gathered larger stones to cover the old man's body. Jack stood, stretched; his lower back was killing him. "This will keep the animals away, I think."

He picked up the shovel and began filling the grave; it took forever. He flattened the dirt then walked over the grave to push the soft dirt farther down. Last, he put a large tree limb over the grave, spread out some random stones and brushed over the spot and around the area to make it look as undisturbed as possible.

He could feel his heart pounding in his chest. *I'm dying of thirst,* he thought and wiped the sweat off his forehead.

He sat on a fallen limb, took a deep breath and said in a quiet voice to the fresh grave, "I'm not the bad one here, I'm not a violent man. I didn't mean for this to happen, I just wanted to find out the truth. I just wanted to find out what happened to my family, I didn't mean for you to die. I'm sorry, I'm truly sorry."

The sun was coming up; he'd been working through the night. The morning sun's dim light was filtering through the leaves and he could feel its warmth, it felt good. He pushed himself up from the fallen tree branch; he looked around, it still didn't look quite right. He broke off a small branch from the fallen tree, the leaves dried up and mostly dead, but still useful. He tried to brush away the signs of a freshly dug grave. He began retracing his steps, bringing the wheelbarrow and tools with him. He used the branch to sweep as he walked, wiping away his footprints and the wheelbarrow track.

After he put the tools away and closed the shed door one last time, he fell exhausted into the car. He sat there for a few minutes; he knew that he had to head back to town before anyone came by. His hands were shaking and he shivered all through his body. He could feel the exhaustion in his bones, his teeth rattling in his head, his headache was blinding. He took a deep breath, started the engine, and pulled forward until he found a spot where he could turn around and headed back to the main road.

The sun felt good, he could feel it through the open window. He leaned his head back and let the early morning warmth of the sun clear his head. Jack turned the radio on as he began the short trip back to Selinsgrove, and was surprised that it was only 5:38 a.m. It was another peaceful morning in central Pennsylvania. *Well, maybe a little more peaceful if you ask me,* Jack thought, smiling. He turned to a country music station. That's all they listened to in the cafeteria up at the VA. He had never been into country-western music, but lately he had become a real fan. He loved Willie Nelson and Merle Haggard. The music took him back to the hospital ward where he first met Tony Ramo.

It was still dark, the streets were empty, and he turned slowly and pulled Smith's car up the driveway. Jack turned off the engine quickly. He didn't want to wake anyone up; you never know who is about at six o'clock in the morning, letting out the dog or getting the paper. Jack sat for a few minutes, trying to come up with a logical answer to the question: Where's Smith? That's a question that his brother would surely ask. *Hunting, that's it. The son of a bitch went up to the cabin to go hunting or fishing or whatever the fuck he does up there.* Jack reached over for his jacket before getting out of the car, his nametag almost glowing in the hazy morning sun. *Funny how shit happens, if that old bastard at the hospital hadn't seen my nametag, I never would have found out about the letters.*

The old house seemed quiet, peaceful; there was nobody around. He opened the door and walked inside. He sat down at the kitchen table, staring at the dusty boxes. He wanted to hear his father's voice in his head before he got some sleep, but he couldn't keep his eyes open. He stood up, feeling dizzy and faint, and stumbled to the couch in the den. He let himself fall onto the soft cushions, his eyes closed, and he slept.

The pain in his side woke him up hours later. He felt cold and clammy, the nausea coming from nowhere. He stood up, balanced himself on the side of the couch, and stumbled to the bathroom. Diarrhea poured from his bowels; he couldn't tell if he was peeing or shitting, and he grimaced in pain. The sweat on his forehead dripped into his eyes, and he wiped his brow with the bathroom towel that lay on the sink next to the toilet.

I've got to get something to eat, maybe some soup, he thought. He stood up, balanced himself against the sink, and took a few breaths. He stared at the bloody stool going down when he flushed.

He walked back into the kitchen and found a can of Campbell's soup. Jack had lost track of the time, he looked up at the small clock that sat on the windowsill. It was almost 8 p.m.

Jack felt some strength come back as he sat down to his food. There was a package of Wonder bread on the counter and butter on the kitchen table. He spread the soft butter on the white bread and dunked the piece of bread into the soup. It burned as the soup and the soggy bread went down his throat, but it felt good to eat.

After almost ten hours of sleep and the food, he felt better. He went down to the basement one last time to check. Even with the lights on it seemed dark and hazy in the corner; at the back lay one more box. He remembered hiding behind all those boxes; he never had any idea what was in them, and never cared. It was as good a hiding place as he could find.

Jack wiped away the dust on the last box, written on the top were the words "Jerry's stuff." The light was too dim, the box was heavy; when he picked it up, the bottom fell out and everything fell down. He stood there with an empty box in his hands. He cursed and threw the broken box against the wall. On the floor of the dirty and dimly lit basement were notebooks, letters, and random sheets of paper; he didn't know where to start.

By midnight he had the contents of all ten boxes in piles on the kitchen table. *I can't remember your voice*, Jack thought. *I just want to hear you talk.*

He picked up one of the letters on the top.

Dear Dad,

I know what you're thinking, you're thinking that I lost my mind. What could have ever possessed me to give up a great job, leave my wife and boys, enlist in the army, and end up in Vietnam. Well, it's been a little more than three months, I guess it's about time I tell you the real reason I came over here. I know you're real upset with me, but please just hear me out.

It all started with an interview that I did with my old high school friend, Chuck Harris. You remember Chuck. His family owned the funeral parlor in town. I went up to Williamsport in February to see my old friend and interview one of the few soldiers wounded in Vietnam from right here in Selinsgrove.

I got up there around ten in the morning, there was a light snow that morning. Visiting hours didn't start until 2 p.m. I figured that maybe they would be a little flexible with family, so I told the volunteer that I was Chuck's cousin and that I had just got back from 'Nam myself. These old vets are a sucker for any hard luck story, especially from a fellow vet. So of course, they let me up.

I was surprised that there wasn't anyone in the waiting room area. The news was on. They were talking about Westmoreland requesting another 200,000 troops. I asked the nurse on duty what room Chuck Harris was in and told her that I was his cousin.

Chuck was really out of it. He was all drugged up, and barely could keep his eyes open. I pulled up a chair and sat close to him. I forgot about the interview and just tried to talk to my old friend. I sat there and held his hand. I figured the best way to bring him back was to just talk about when we were back in school, bring back some old memories, like when he saved my life. Suddenly, I felt his hand grab my wrist, and he was looking straight into my eyes, not blinking.

Jack put his father's letter down and got the last beer out of the refrigerator. He opened the flip top and took a drink, cringing at the burning sensation. The urge to pee was suddenly overwhelming. The doctor at the VA told him that this would pass, the almost uncontrollable sensation to pee. He stumbled to the bathroom. *Maybe,* he thought, *I should go see another doctor.* When he was done, he walked back to the kitchen table to finish reading his father's letter.

Chuck started yelling. He was talking crazy stuff, about kidnapping and killing and stolen equipment. He wouldn't let go of my arm, talking about a black market gang over there called "The Unit." I knew that something serious had been going on over there.

The nurse on duty comes running in and said, "You're supposed to calm him down, not rile him up!" She told me, "You'll have to come back later, visiting time is at two. I'm sorry, he's been real agitated these last few days."

Dad, I know you're upset with me and maybe disappointed, but look, you always taught me that if there was truth to be found I needed to go looking for it. I found the truth here, Pop. I'm going to document every goddamn thing that's going on, put it all down on paper. I'm sending home two copies, one to you and Mom and one set to Kate. When I get home, I'll have all the proof I need: names, places, dates, and then, I'll bury the bastards. The American people have a right to know, and Chuck's family has a right to know.

I hope I haven't hurt my family too much. I'll be home in no time and then everything will be fine. I'll be careful. But if something does happen to me, then take the letters I've sent over to Bill over at the paper. He'll know what to do, and don't forget, Dad, keep all these letters out of sight.

Take care, Love you Dad...Jerry.

Jack put down the letter. There were more than twenty other letters, hidden for more than twenty years in the brown boxes.

The letters will finally clear everything up, Jack thought. *As soon as Sean sees the truth, he'll want to be here with me.* Jack said out loud, "He better help me. Oh yeah, 'cause if he won't..." *Stop thinking so much, Sean won't let me down. He owes it to me, owes it to Mom and Dad, and owes it to himself.* Suddenly it seemed like all the emotion of the last twenty-four hours put him over the edge. Jack put his head down on the table slowly, both hands clamped over his ears. He realized he was shouting, sobbing, screaming out, "Why did this happen to me? Why me?!"

The room was dark but he knew all the places he could go and hide in this house. He had gotten good at hiding as a boy, behind the couch, the chair, even under the kitchen table, but mostly he would hide in the basement, behind the boxes. The boxes had always been there, protecting him from the man who was supposed to protect him. Maybe his father had sent the letters home to build a fort, a fort of boxes to keep out that evil bastard. Even though he knew it wasn't true, Jack smiled.

His eyes closed, and for a moment, Jack was at peace, even in here, in this house.

CHAPTER 6

Los Angeles, CA

Sean sat at the table against the wall in the hotel room and stared at the closed curtains that had kept the room dark. He thought about Jack. The guilt washed over him and he said aloud, "It wasn't my fault. I didn't know what was going on, someone should have known, but how could it have been me?" He shook his head, trying to jolt the dream he'd just had. It was always the same dream. He was back at home, staring at his mother, his father, and his brother. It was before everything changed, before his father enlisted. Why had he decided to enlist in the army and volunteer to go to Vietnam anyway? His mother hated the whole idea. At first, she would calmly try to reason with his dad, and then the reasoned conversation would disappear in a moment and turn into a screaming match. He could never forget.

If you watched the news in the sixties, it seemed like every draft-age kid in the country was trying to get out of the draft. The reality was that a substantial group of patriotic young men were willing to fight for what they believed was the survival of freedom in Southeast

Asia. All those young men, barely out of high school; how could they know what they were doing? And then his father, with a wife and kids at home, walked into an enlisting center and signed up to go to that godforsaken hellhole on purpose. Was it the stupidest fucking thing anyone has ever done or what?

Maybe Jack figured something out, he thought. *Maybe he's got something. Maybe we could finally get some fucking answers. What a horrible fucking day.* His plane wasn't leaving LAX until three that afternoon; he had hours to kill before the flight back to Philadelphia. He thought about calling his therapist, just to talk things out, to help clear his mind.

Sean was brought up believing that therapy was for losers, for weak men that just didn't have the inner strength to stand up to adversity. Back then, especially in small towns like Selinsgrove, asking for that type of help was admitting to a personal weakness, a real character flaw. But Sherman Oaks, California, was nothing like Selinsgrove. Everything changed when Sean and his grandmother moved out west. Grandma's sister, Hillary, was a bona fide hippie, a borderline revolutionary with a deep distrust for government agencies, from the CIA to the local police. She was convinced that Sean's mom's murder was in some way connected to their dad. "There is no way on God's green earth that your father voluntarily goes to Vietnam, then a few months later your mother is raped and murdered, and then coincidentally he disappears off the face of the earth," she would say. "Sean, as God is my witness, they know something. There are too many roadblocks. You have got to find a way into their system. Go to law school, work for the Justice Department. That's where you'll find the answers, but you've got to be on the inside, you've got to find a way to work for the MAN."

He wondered what Jack had found. Perhaps it really would lead them to the answer of what happened. For years, he had fantasized of the moment when he would take that sweet revenge, settle the score, using his own brilliant detective work to find the answers to the mystery that the police had never been able to solve. So four years at Stanford, three years at Georgetown Law, and then almost fifteen years with the Philadelphia District Attorney's office. But the doors remained shut.

Jack wasn't the only victim. The guilt of not being there for his younger brother, the guilt of leaving Jack back home had consumed Sean his whole life. He tried to keep up with his brother's life, through his old high school friends, but after a while Sean stopped asking. Not knowing had made it easier to live with. But now, in an instant, a phone call from his brother brought it all crashing back.

Sean remembered the letters his dad had sent home—about how far he was from the action, how they shouldn't worry, and that he would be home real soon. He said he was stationed in Saigon, safe in an office building, writing for the military news information unit. He was writing stories to support the troops.

He had been so confused about his dad going to Vietnam. Sometimes Sean felt proud and would tell his friends about his dad, but inside, he was always angry that he had left them alone. Sometimes his father would put quotes from President Johnson in his letters. One in particular he remembered.

Johnson had said, "We can never again stand aside, prideful in isolation. Terrific dangers and troubles that we once called 'foreign' now constantly live among us." Was his dad there to save the world from the North Vietnamese, the Russians, and of course, the Chinese?

And then just months later he lay in bed in his grandfather's house, looking over at Jack as he lay motionless in the small bed in the corner. Jack couldn't sleep in a room alone and would just lie there crying, so he stayed with Sean. Sean stared at his brother hoping he would say something, anything, but the younger boy just lay there and slept and cried and then slept some more.

Sean remembered that Dad would gently knock on the bedroom door and peek into the room with a smile on his face and say, "Rise and shine, sleeping beauties, time to get ready for school."

Sean's father used to say, "If you want something bad enough and you work for it, then nothing is impossible." So, Sean had tried it: he closed his eyes and then when he opened them, he hoped there would be the gentle knock on the door and there his Dad would be, with that smile on his face, and he'd say the same thing that he said every morning: "Rise and shine, sleeping beauty, time to get ready for school."

But there was no knock; instead the doorbell rang. Sean pushed himself up on his elbows and listened. Who would be coming to the house so early on a Sunday morning? He tried to concentrate on the voices from downstairs, but they were low and quiet. Sean got out of his bed quietly and slipped to the door of his new bedroom. He slowly opened the door and walked down the stairs to the kitchen. There were two strange men sitting at the long wooden table; one man was dressed in an Army uniform and the other was dressed in regular clothes with a white priest's collar. When they saw Sean, they fell silent. For just a moment, nobody said a word and then Sean's grandfather slowly walked over to him.

"Son, they can't find your dad. These men are telling us that maybe he has been taken prisoner by the North Vietnamese and is being held as a POW."

Sean stood there silently with a blank expression on his face.

The man with the collar around his neck stood up and said, "Son, I want you to know that the Army is doing everything it can do to bring your dad home just as soon as possible. I know that you need him now more than ever and I know that he would want you to be brave and look after your brother."

Sean looked up into the eyes of the older man and said, "My father went there to write stories about the soldiers, not to fight. He told me that everything was going to be okay when he gets home. Grandpa, I don't think everything is going to be okay anymore." He turned and walked out of the kitchen and up to his bedroom and lay down on his bed and sobbed in his pillow.

Burt knew that something wasn't adding up. He could feel it in his gut, and for the next two weeks he called the Army trying to find out more about his son. He even tried to call the White House. All he was told was that they were looking. They assumed he had been captured; they were sure he was alive, because they didn't have the body. He wasn't assigned to any kind of dangerous duty, and they thought it possible that he had been following a story on his own. They were investigating his disappearance and told Burt that they were doing all they could.

In the meantime, the investigation of Kate's murder was getting cold; all the leads were leading nowhere. The days were turning into weeks and the weeks into months, and the family was getting on the best they could. But instead of Jack getting better, he just seemed to get worse.

Doris McGinnis had taken the young boy to doctors in Harrisburg and Philadelphia. They all said the same thing: that the boy was traumatized by whatever he had seen and may not come out of this silent state for years. They said the best place for him would be a hospital for people suffering from trauma.

In the winter of 1970, their grandparents Burt and Doris took Jack up to live at a rehabilitation home in Williamsport. Sean missed his brother, and his father and mother, but after a few months of this new normal life, Sean found that he was able to block out portions of what had happened to his family. Getting back to school helped, and his young mind was able to adjust to his new life. Burt and Doris tried their best, but they were going through their own personal hell. Without Jack around, they seemed to be able to forget at times, even if it was just for a few moments.

Every morning Sean would get up, get washed and dressed, and go downstairs for breakfast before heading off to school. He found that the harder he studied, the easier it was to forget, so he immersed himself in school and slowly his life fell into a pattern of a normal eight-year-old kid.

The weather that next April was crazy. One Tuesday they predicted seven to ten inches of snow beginning just after lunch, and the middle school principal decided to send everyone home at noon.

There was a sense of excitement in the air as all the kids climbed into the buses for the ride home. Sean didn't feel much like horsing around with the other kids. When he got to his grandmother's house, two really tall men were knocking on the door. They seemed surprised to see him. Both men were wearing formal army uniforms; one of them wore a white collar around his neck. Sean felt a knot in his throat.

Doris opened the door before they said anything to Sean.

"Burt," she called, her voice tight. "Sean, what are you doing home so early, and who are these men?"

"I'm sorry, can we come in?" said one of the men.

She continued to look at Sean. "Burt, where are you? Come out here?"

She put her arm around Sean. "What happened?"

"We got out of school early because of the snow storm coming. What do these men want?" He asked the last part quietly.

Burt came to the door and looked at the men, his wife, and Sean. "What can I do for you, gentlemen? Can I help you with something?"

"May we come in, sir?"

Burt stepped aside and everyone followed Burt into the living room.

The men sat, Sean and his grandmother standing next to Burt. No one spoke at first. The men came with bad news, Sean knew, but if they didn't say the words, he could still hope. Those few moments of silence were going to be the last moments of hope, and no one wanted to let them go.

The chaplain spoke first and Sean hated him for the words he was going to say. "You know that God has his plans for all of us, for you and for me and for your father. Sometimes those plans are not clear, sometimes the answers that we look for are just not there, but what we all know for certain is that God is always with us, you and your dad." He stopped, took a long breath, and continued, "The Army can't find your dad. Officially, they have classified him missing in action and presumed dead. It is true that he is possibly still alive and you should never give up hope, but I urge you to get on with your lives the best you can. Do you understand what I'm saying, son?" He put his hand on the young boy's shoulder and said, "There's always hope and you can keep on praying that someday you'll stand next to your dad, and surely you will, in this world or in Heaven. Someday you will see him again, that I know as sure as I am here with you."

Burt sat down slowly and took out the heart pills he had been taking the last few years and placed one on the tip of his tongue with one hand, and picked up a pack of Chesterfields with the other.

"We will be in touch with any news we receive." Burt looked up, then nodded his head and watched the men walk toward the door. Sean went upstairs.

And that night, like every other night, Burt, Doris, and Sean sat around the big table outside the kitchen and didn't talk about what they were all thinking.

A few days later, another man came in the evening.

Grief had a way of keeping Burt up at night. The clock on the nightstand was hidden from sight, buried deep beneath the socks and the letters from the Department of Defense. His occasional sleep had become less and less frequent. The fatigue and the exhaustion had taken its toll. Burt could feel his heart beating in his chest. Every night, lying close to his wife, he could hear her breathing. At least she is sleeping, he thought, but she wasn't.

The knock on the door woke Burt at 6:30 p.m. from his early evening nap and brought Doris in from the kitchen. Unexpected visitors had become the nightmare they were always expecting. Doris took a breath and walked to the door, always hoping for the best. It had been six months since her son had first been reported missing in action.

The smile on the young man's face confused them both and then in what felt like an instant, a serious look replaced the friendly expression. "I'm Jay Donald. I'm here to talk to you about your son, Jerry. May I come in?"

Burt hesitated and then said, "Sure, where are my manners?"

"Can I bring you a cup of coffee, or a beer?" added Doris.

"Water would be nice."

Jay Donald reached into the pocket of his well-tailored blue suit. Burt took the business card, which read: Attorney at Law, Jay Donald, partner.

Burt's confused expression lingered. "Are you with the military?"

"May I sit?" asked Donald.

"Of course," said Doris as she put the glass of water on the table next to the couch.

Doris and Burt sat opposite the young attorney. "We're listening, young man."

"My firm represents a group of organizations who have charged us with the care of children of MIA or KIA active service personnel that served in Vietnam and who were members of a special clandestine unit." Burt and Doris sat stiffly, saying nothing. Jay Donald hesitated, took a sip of water. "Beginning now, your two grandchildren will receive financial support, until their eighteenth birthdays, when it will end, unless they're enrolled in an accredited university. In that case, they would continue to receive support as is deemed necessary and appropriate. Checking accounts will be set up with both of you as guardians. Your family will be assigned a trustee who will monitor this case."

Burt stood up and said, "What the hell are you talking about? Who in hell asked for your care and support? I don't know you, or any fucking organization. I don't know where you come from, young man, but we take care of our own in this part of the country."

"We know that, and we know the sacrifice that your family has made. We are honoring your son's service to his nation, so we want to subsidize the boys' upbringing. We are taking any money issues off the table." Jay Donald stood, and handed Doris an envelope. "This is a letter from your son explaining everything. He set this up, he made the arrangements. One more thing before I say goodbye. There is also a short nondisclosure agreement that you and your wife must sign. Please read it. If you decide to honor your son's wishes, then simply call me." Jay Donald put out his hand to say goodbye.

Doris came between her husband and the young man and said, "If my son has chosen a path, then we'll walk on that same path. We'll sign now and never speak of this, you have our word, and our signatures. And know this, Mr. Donald, our word is worth ten thousand signatures." Jay Donald smiled and said, "Please read your son's letter, then read the agreement. I'll stop by in the morning."

CHAPTER 7

Selinsgrove, PA

On Sundays after church, Sean, Doris, and Burt would drive to Williamsport to visit Jack. Driving north on Route 11 from Selinsgrove to Williamsport had to be one of the most scenic drives in the country, with mountains on the left and the Susquehanna on the right. When it snowed, the pines along the river came alive, covered in snow.

There was little conversation in the car. Each one lived in their own isolated hell. Sean looked out the window and watched the river meandering through the countryside, navigating between the giant boulders crashing forward. His grandmother sat knitting a scarf or sweater for Jack or Sean, Burt intent on the road, cigarette dangling between his fingers, puffing and then flicking ashes out of the little side window.

When they arrived, the nurse on duty was always so friendly and seemed happy to see them, as if she hadn't expected them to come. If the weather was nice, Jack would be outside on the lawn around the back. "He likes to sit under one of our old maple trees," she would say, and then under her breath would add with a weak smile, "We think he does. Have a nice visit." They found him and Doris was ready with a small gift, candy or a new scarf, bending down to kiss his head. She spoke to him as if he could understand her. "I swear you have grown since last week, hasn't he, Burt? And that hair. Next week I will bring scissors to give you a little trim. That's how the boys are wearing their hair now, isn't it, Sean?" Sean couldn't look at him; he would sit on the grass and pull it out or find a stick and dig in the dirt.

Doris would bring sandwiches she had made and they would eat a picnic there on the grass. Then they would kiss him goodbye and drive home. The ride home on Route 11 seemed even longer than the one going up. There was always hope on the way to visit Jack, but none on the way home.

The spring of 1971 seemed like all the others, except that they never once went down to the banks of the Susquehanna. It didn't seem right to Burt to go down there without Jerry.

School was almost out for another year. A long summer lay ahead. Sean couldn't keep his mind on the homework he was supposed to be finishing or the upcoming tests. It was still light outside, and it would have been a perfect time to hang out on the river. Sean left his books and walked down the stairs toward the kitchen. "I wonder how come Grandpa isn't home yet?"

Doris turned around from the pasta that she was stirring. "Must be traffic on 17. Did you finish your homework?"

Sean shook his head. "I'm hungry."

"Go ahead and finish up, I'll call you when Grandpa gets home."

Sean turned and walked upstairs to his room and returned to his homework, but the history lesson couldn't keep his attention.

He gazed out of the window; the glare of the late afternoon sun was a sure sign that summer wasn't far off, a long lonely summer. The sound of the phone ringing brought Sean out of his sleepy trance, and then he heard the crash of something hitting the floor, and then he heard the scream. He jumped from his desk and ran down the stairs. His grandmother was standing in the kitchen, a blank stare on her face, the bowl of pasta splattered on the floor.

"What's the matter, Grandma?!" asked Sean. Doris stood there for what seemed like a long time, then looked at her grandson and said, "Your grandfather had a heart attack. Get your coat on, we have got to go to Harrisburg."

Doris picked up the phone again and called Pat and Joe Smith, their best friends. "Burt's in the hospital, in Harrisburg. They told me he had a heart attack, please come over. I need for you both to come with me. I can't handle this myself."

The Smiths lived only two blocks away and were at the house in just a few minutes. The four of them drove down to the hospital, the Smiths in the front seat and Sean and Doris in the back. Doris leaned forward and put her hand on Pat's shoulder. "I need to ask you both something. I wouldn't ask if it wasn't important to me and I know that you won't let me down."

Pat turned her head toward her friend and said, "Doris, we're best friends, anything you need, we're here for you."

"If Burt doesn't pull through this and if something happens to me…"

"Stop talking like that. Doris, Burt's going to be fine, it's just his first heart attack. He's strong, he'll pull through this and what are you talking about? If something happened to you, what do you mean?"

"Look, I'm sure you're right, but I need to know that if things don't work out, I have to know that Sean and Jack have a good family to take care of them."

"First of all, none of that is ever going to happen, and besides, have you forgotten Kate's parents? They would be the boys' guardians, their blood relatives."

Doris said in a low voice, "Just tell me that you'll be there. You don't have to worry about the money, you can sell the house and Jack and Sean have a trust fund set up by the Army unit Jerry was in. Burt has all the papers in the house. I will find them."

"Sure," said Pat. "Of course we will do right by the boys, don't worry."

"Joe?" said Doris from the back seat.

"Sure," said Joe Smith. "We will take care of the boys if you need us."

Pat put her hand on Doris's hand and squeezed hard. "Don't worry, everything is going to be all right, just don't worry." She turned back and stared out the window. Sean seemed not to hear. He was lost in a world that made no sense and where everyone he loved seemed to die.

They were led to a waiting room and told to wait for the doctor. Sean sat down and stared at the old TV that was in the corner. "Bowling for Dollars" was on, but he couldn't concentrate. After about twenty minutes, an old man in a white coat walked into the waiting room and asked for the McGinnis family.

He sat down next to Doris. "Mrs. McGinnis, your husband suffered a massive heart attack. We did everything we could, but I'm terribly sorry to tell you that he passed away a few minutes ago. Your husband never regained consciousness and died peacefully.

I'm so sorry. Please see the nurse; she'll help your family with all the arrangements."

Eight-year-old Sean closed his eyes tightly, contorting his forehead as if fighting off the pain, unable to will it away. An out-of-place smile came to his young face for a moment. He was thinking of happier times, the four of them, his father, his brother, his grandfather, and him, all snuggled up under the same old blanket that had kept them warm and safe from the chill of the river.

Now gone, all gone. Jack in his silent prison, his dad lost, and his grandpa gone, gone forever. Of the men in his life, only he was left. Sean felt his grandmother take his hand firmly. "Come with me, we need to say goodbye." Both hesitated outside the room where Burt McGinnis lay. She slowly pushed the door open, Sean clutching her hand tightly. Burt's eyes were closed, a serene peacefulness had settled on his face. Doris turned slowly, kneeling down to look into her grandson's eyes. "Your grandfather was a good man. I know that he will be proud of the man you will become." Sean pulled away and walked cautiously to the edge of the bed. His young mind was trying to process this moment. Tears welling up, and he leaned down to whisper into unhearing ears, "We'll be okay, Grandpa, we'll be okay."

Burt had been the glue that kept what was left of the family together. With him gone, Doris lived in a shallow trance. Sean went to school in the mornings and she would still be in bed, when he got home she would be sitting in Burt's old recliner watching TV. Pat finally convinced her to get a simple office job, taking calls and writing up orders at a coffee business in town.

It wasn't that Doris and Sean needed the money. They had the money coming in from the Army lawyer and the insurance money, and the house was paid for, but it gave Doris a reason to get up in the morning.

For the next two years, she worked at the coffee company and every Sunday she and Sean would drive up to Williamsport to visit Jack. Slowly things were getting better; he would talk a little now. Never about what happened or what he had seen, but he would talk about people at the hospital and ask when he was coming home. The doctors said he was making progress, but then he would backtrack and go into a trance-like state, often found rocking and staring into the far-off woods that surrounded the hospital grounds.

One day, almost three years after Burt had passed away, Doris walked into Sean's room and said, "Sean, we're getting out of here, we are moving to L.A. to live with my sister."

It was so sudden. He had met his great aunt only when she came out for Burt's funeral. She and Doris used to talk on the phone every Sunday night after visiting the hospital. Doris often cried to her sister, telling her about Jack, how hard it was to see him, how lonely she was with Burt gone. How she worried that she was all that Sean had left. It scared her that he would eventually be left all alone.

Sean was scared, then mad. He didn't want to start over in California. All his friends were here, but his family was gone. Everyone in town knew what had happened to him; maybe it *was* a good idea to start over. He had heard the rumors around town, about how some guy killed his mother, that maybe she was fooling around and the guy she brought home probably killed her and that his father was still alive, but didn't want to come home. He didn't believe any of the talk, but after a while he got tired of fighting. And he hated going to Williamsport every Sunday.

Doris's sister came out to help them get packed up for the move to California. Hillary lived in a town called Sherman Oaks, which was about twenty minutes from downtown Los Angeles. Sean liked his aunt Hill. She had a warm smile and her long brown hair looked just right with her deep tan. Her husband had died a long time ago, but she wasn't the kind of person who dwelled on the sad times. She had a good attitude about almost everything and seemed to find the good in things, even when everything seemed to be nothing but bad.

Doris was very conflicted about what to do with Jack. He was really making progress now. The doctors thought that if she were to take him out and move him to a new hospital in California it could set him back. Doris convinced herself that he would be okay until she and Sean got settled in and then she would come and get him. He would be ready to come home with her by then. She went to talk to her best friend.

"I've got to get out of this town," she told Pat. "Everywhere I turn, I see Jerry, Kate, and Burt, and it's driving me crazy. We both need a new start and I need to ask you for two things."

Doris had poured her heart out countless times to Pat, and this didn't come as a surprise. Doris told Pat everything and always felt that Pat listened well, but she knew that Pat had a history that she didn't like to talk about. Doris respected that. She never asked the hard questions. She knew there was more to their story; she knew there was a reason why Pat and Joe had left upstate New York. The one time she asked what had made them leave their home upstate, Pat simply said, "Nothing, it was nothing. We just needed a new start. There was nothing holding us up there and besides, if we didn't move out here, I never would have met my best friend." And Doris had left it there. Until now.

"Pat, you've been my dearest friend for more than twenty years. What happened in New York?"

Pat looked up. "You want to know why we left? Okay. Joe and I worked in the middle school up in Gloversville, he was the head custodian, and I worked in the kitchen." She was silent for a few moments, taking her time to go back all those years ago. "It was late in the evening sometime in February, cold as hell. The knock on the door surprised us. Who could that be on a night like this?" Pat paused, seemingly frozen.

"Who was it, who was at the door?" asked Doris.

"It was a friend, a childhood friend, one of Joe's best friends. A local cop, actually, the chief. He told us there had been an accusation made against Joe, by one of the eighth graders. Joe didn't say anything."

Pat told Doris that John Davis had been on the force for fifteen years. He was a good honest cop, but he had always looked the other way when it came to Joe. There had been rumors, Pat said. Some parents complained but never had any proof. No one ever made a formal complaint. Maybe it was just a brush up against a kid, a remark that was just a little bit inappropriate. Pat knew that John had spoken to Joe about the rumors, and always got the same response: "What the fuck are you talking about?"

Pat told Doris about the rest of the conversation. John had said, "Listen to me; I can't brush this one under the rug. This time you crossed the line, you took a kid down to the boiler room and gave him a drink."

Joe had turned to Pat and told her to go to the kitchen and get them a couple of beers. She left the room but still stood by the door and listened.

She heard John say, "The kid doesn't want to talk about it, just said that you asked him if he wanted to see the boiler room. He smelled of cheap liquor and his parents had to smack him around until he told them where he got it. He told them that you said it was the coolest thing, said you had a bottle of liquor on the desk, that you told him he could have a little drink and be just like the boys and then you touched him, told him it would be a secret. The kid's parents wanted to come over here and string you up, press charges, but I convinced them it would be worse for their son. But you can't work at the school ever again. You've got to get out of town, Joe, that's the deal."

Pat took a long breath, then stood up and went to fill a glass with water. She came back and sat down with Doris without taking a sip.

"I haven't spoken of this for more than twenty years," she continued. "They couldn't prove anything happened down there, but kids had seen the two of them going downstairs, and the teachers had claimed that something was odd with the youngster. They weren't sure what it was, but it was something. Anyway, we were told that if we just left town and never came back, that we'd make this whole nasty rumor just go away." Pat looked up, this time staring at her friend. "So that's it. It was rumors, just rumors, so we packed our bags and left."

"Okay," said Doris. "Okay." Doris raised her eyes and looked right into Pat's soft green eyes, tears threatening to spill over their lids. "Has anything like that happened since? Please tell me the truth, Pat, do you trust Joe around kids now?"

"Joe is no saint as you know. Sometimes I feel like I should just walk out that door, but honest to God, I never believed he was capable of doing something like that to a boy. I just don't believe it."

"I came over here tonight to ask you a huge favor, Pat, and I know that you will be honest with me. You're my best friend," she said and paused. "These last few years have been hell. I don't understand why this is happening to us, but through it all, you've been there for me and for Burt and for the boys. But if we don't get out of this town, I swear I'm going to lose my mind. I want to take Sean and move out to L.A. to live with my sister. We're both getting on, she needs me, and God knows that we need her. I guess when it comes down to it, family is what matters the most, but leaving you breaks my heart. It just breaks my heart."

Doris hesitated, looked around. "Pat, listen to me, if you ever decide to pack your bags and get the hell out of here, you have a home, you know that. Never forget what I'm telling you."

Pat smiled, wiped away the tears and said, "Oh Doris, how am I going to go on without you? You know I'm a good Catholic girl, married to the end, even if I have to put up with him. But who knows, maybe that son of a bitch out there will jump into the Susquehanna and float downstream..." The two women smiled and sat for a moment in silence. Then Pat finally said, "What do you need?"

Doris stared at her friend. She could not find the words that she needed to say. She took a deep breath. "I've spoken to the doctors, they tell me that taking Jack out of the hospital and bringing him to an unfamiliar place could set him back for years. The best place for him is right there in Williamsport. I'll come back as often as I can to see him, but if anything happens to me, I need you to look after Jack. I know it's a lot to ask, but I wouldn't ask if there were any other way. I know what you're thinking, what about Kate's parents? But they are both sick. Neil has stage four prostate cancer and Barbara has colon and breast cancer. I'm here with their blessing and their gratitude.

"I know what everyone's going to say, but I don't care, frankly I don't give a shit. I've got to put this nightmare behind us. I'm ashamed to say this, God forgive me, Pat, but I need to get Sean away from here and away from his brother. He'll never move on with his life otherwise. I've got to save one of the boys. I know that people will say that I'm a horrible person, but I have no choice. I've spoken to Father O'Neil. He's told me straight out that what I'm doing will be condemned by most, but sometimes the sacrifice we make can only be understood by God: He will judge you, no one else."

"Okay," said Pat. "I understand, but what happens when Jack starts to recover? He will recover, right, and what do we tell him then?"

"Let's take one step at a time. I'll deal with that when it happens, okay?" Doris paused; there was no good answer.

"Okay," Pat said.

"What about Joe?" asked Doris. "Do you think he'll put up a stink?"

Pat looked out at the porch, turned back to Doris, and said in a defiant manner, "Fuck him!" Both women laughed at their uncharacteristic language.

"There is one other thing I need you to do," said Doris. "Only a little favor, I swear," she said with an uncomfortable smile. "When Jerry was in Vietnam, he sent home boxes of letters and journals about stuff that he was doing over there, and he made me and Burt swear that we would hold onto all of them until he got home. Now I know he's most likely never coming home, I realize that, but I can't go back on my word. It's the only hope I have left. I need you to keep the boxes for me. There are only about ten of them, and you can just throw them in the basement. If something happens to me, burn them and say a prayer for my family."

"Sure," said Pat. "If that's what you want, then I'll have Joe put the boxes downstairs."

"Oh no," said Doris. "Tell him I'll have them brought over and put down in the basement. I'll pay some of the boys on the block, I don't want your husband lifting a finger."

Pat put both hands on her friend's shoulders and said, "You take Sean and don't worry about Jack. We'll take care of him. You go out west, live with your sister, make a new start. You're a strong woman, a survivor."

Doris looked up at Pat and said in a soft voice, "Thanks for being a good friend. Thanks for being there for me and Sean and for Jack."

"Don't worry," Pat smiled. "You go home, start packing. What about the house?"

"I spoke to Joan over at Century 21, she told me that this isn't the best time for selling, prices aren't great, but what else is new? My luck ran out the day that Kate was killed."

Saying goodbye was the toughest part of leaving, but it was a new start. There was the promise of better days and always the hope that someday they would be together again, if not in this lifetime, then in the next.

That last Sunday, Doris, Sean, and Pat and Joe Smith drove up to Williamsport to see Jack. It was a beautiful sunny day and the nurses had most of the patients out on the lawn, getting some sun and fresh air. The four of them walked over to Jack, who sat on the grass. They sat down in a half circle facing the young boy. Jack didn't look up, just sat there playing with the grass, running the soft green blades through his hands, deep in his own little world.

Doris put her hand gently on his knee and spoke softly to her grandson. She told him that she and Sean were taking a little trip, but they would be back soon, and he would be fine and Pat and Joe would be coming up to see him all the time. Jack looked up with a far-off expression and then turned his head back down, brushing his hand over the warm grass. For a moment there were no words, as tears crept into the corners of Doris's eyes, and then she said, "Let's go."

CHAPTER 8

Selingrove, PA 1971

There seemed to be a dreary mist crawling over the banks of the Susquehanna. Joe Smith noticed it, as if it were a premonition of decisions gone horribly bad.

The Smiths made a real effort to visit Jack, almost every weekend. Joe Smith had never really liked Burt's family and now he was saddled with the boy. Joe hoped the little shit would spend the next ten years at Holy Spirit. But he didn't.

The psychiatrists at Holy Spirit decided that Jack was making some real measurable progress and that it might be best, finally, to send him home. Familiar surroundings could make a real difference in his recovery, the doctors said. It was time to leave Williamsport.

Jack was only six, and he couldn't understand why he was going to live with the Smiths and not with his grandmother and Sean. Over and over Pat told him that in time his grandmother would come back and take him out to California.

Doris called every week to check in on how Jack was doing. "I've got to bring Jack out here, the boy needs to be with family, especially now, more than ever," said Doris, pleadingly.

"Doris," said Pat. "I know how you're feeling, but the doctors were insistent that Jack is better off being close to the hospital. I think he's becoming more and more comfortable with the therapist. They tell me that he's making real progress and I don't think it's a good idea to take him away right now. I know you love him and miss him, but this is for the best." Pat was still taking him up to therapy twice a week. Familiar surroundings were supposed to help him adjust and learn to live a productive life.

Doris accepted it, even though she felt in her heart that the right place for Jack was with her and Sean, in California. Every week she spoke to Jack on the phone, and told him that soon he would come to live with her and Sean. For just a little while longer he needed to stay with the Smiths and be a good boy. She told him that she loved him very much.

Doris and Hillary made plans to move to a larger apartment so they would have room for Jack. Doris pre-enrolled Jack in Encino elementary school and planned a trip back east to pick him up. But another unexpected tragedy hit the McGinnis family. In midsummer, Doris was diagnosed with stage four breast cancer. She knew in her heart that the last years of terrible stress had damaged her body; maybe it had caused the disease to develop. She had no more fight left in her. She called Pat and asked if they could become Jack's legal guardians; Hillary would be there for Sean. Once all the agreements were made, she lost her will to survive. A month later she passed away with Sean and Hillary by her side. In the minutes before she closed her eyes for the last time, she smiled at Sean, held his hand, and said, "You take care of your brother, don't ever forget your brother."

Jack's six-year-old coping mechanism couldn't handle the death of his grandmother. The new trauma left him powerless and disoriented once again. The nightmares were relentless, and he woke up drenched in sweat, with the images of his mother haunting his mind. He felt confused and angry. One moment he was happy and content and then, in a snap, he'd be weeping uncontrollably. He sent a barrage of relentless questions Pat and Joe's way, always ending with "Why am I here?" They didn't have the answers.

Joe Smith pushed the door open to Jack's room. Shots of liquor and beer had taken its toll that night. He stood with a cold smile on his face. "Supper's ready, wash up and come down." The boy rolled over and buried his head in his pillow. The force of the clenched fists hitting him shocked the boy and he felt his body being lifted off the bed and hurled across the room onto the hardwood floor. "Now get your ass downstairs, before I throw you out of the fucking window."

Downstairs, Jack sat in silence as he stared at his plate. Pat gently stroked his back and he winced in pain. "You better keep your shirt on in school, I don't need any questions." The young boy turned slightly toward Pat, and he could see the compassion in the eyes of his grandmother's dearest friend. He asked again, "Why can't I live with my aunt and Sean?"

Smith lurched out of his chair and grabbed the boy by the back of his head and unhesitatingly slammed Jack's head down onto the edge of the linoleum table. Smith didn't mean to crush Jack's front tooth, but the damage was done. Smith grabbed Jack by his hair and threw him to the floor and screamed, "One more time, you ask that one more time, and you're gone to the upstate home with the other orphans."

Jack looked up from the floor and started to cry. Joe leaned down as if to lift the child up, but instead he slapped Jack across the face with all his strength. Pat Smith looked up from her meal, said nothing, and continued to eat, as Jack ran upstairs to his bedroom.

It was the last time Jack asked why he couldn't live with Sean and his aunt, but it wasn't the last time that Joe Smith would beat the boy and send him to his room with no dinner. He was always careful when he beat Jack, never on the face, especially after the incident with the tooth. Instead he made sure to only hit him on the back, sometimes with his hand and sometimes with the cord from his electric razor and sometimes with a wire hanger. As time went by Jack began to know when the beatings would come and would run downstairs to the basement, hiding in the darkness behind a pile of boxes that had been there for years.

As the years went by, Jack grew into an angry young man. He joined the local gang, did poorly in school, and eventually dropped out of high school. He worked odd jobs for more than a decade until he was arrested for minor drug charges and was given the choice of spending ninety days up in Allentown or six months serving as an orderly up at the VA hospital. The judge had been an old friend of the family and believed that justice would be better served to send Jack to help veterans.

In the meantime, Sean grew up in Sherman Oaks, an affluent neighborhood not too far from downtown Los Angeles. He grew up with his loving aunt in a nice co-op on Laurel Canyon Boulevard. Sean went to Stanford, got his BA, and then went to law school at Georgetown. He and his girlfriend Joan moved east after they both graduated from Stanford. They rented a townhouse on Commonwealth Avenue in Alexandria, just down the street from the Metro. Joan taught seventh grade Earth Science at Langley High School. Sean graduated at the top of his class and had work published in the law review and *The Georgetown Law Weekly*. It was a surprise to his friends and Joan when he told them that he was signing up with the

District Attorney's office in Philadelphia. He had met Joan during his freshman year at Stanford; they got married the summer after he finished law school.

Sean had told her a bit about his childhood; mostly he talked about his time in Southern California. He told her that moving to L.A. was the best thing that ever happened to him; he was able to block out the horrible things that had happened to the family. But even with his successes in life, Sean was prone to fits of anger and depression. He knew he was angry but wasn't sure with whom to be angry. It wasn't his mother's fault that she was killed, and his father was just a void in his life. He went to therapy on and off to try to deal with his past, but they could never answer the questions that plagued him. None of it made sense. He knew the facts: that his dad enlisted in May of 1969 after getting an Associate's Degree at Penn State in journalism and also in accounting. Sean knew his father got a job at the local paper right out of college with the help of his father, but had big-time dreams.

The war in Vietnam was heating up in 1969 when his dad went over. In those days the polls taken in the U.S. said that eighty percent of citizens agreed with the military involvement in Vietnam. There are a lot of different reasons why young men go off to war, his grandfather would tell him. Some guys just like to fight, to do battle on the field of honor, to be a patriot like George Patton.

For Jerry, it was not about fighting communism, it was a way for him to get out of the small town and the small job. He believed that going to Vietnam would give him the step-up he needed. His father had loved to write. He sent long letters home, and as a child, Sean sat and listened to those letters when his mother read them out loud. He had tried to understand his father's frustrations. Sean had known that enlisting also had something do with his dad's friend Chuck Harris, who had been injured over there and sent back home, only to end up dead from some terrible mistake. Sean's grandfather had told him that his father was driven to find the truth, no matter where it was and no matter what he had to do to get it. So many things back then didn't add up, and although Sean tried to put the pieces of this riddle together, he always came up with a big blank page.

Over the years Sean had learned to keep his past in the past. In the beginning, Joan tried to open him up. She knew his anger and solemn moods were caused by his childhood trauma, but her husband was good at keeping his life under control most of the time. She learned to leave it alone. When things got really bad, she insisted he see a therapist. It seemed to help. Joan had become pregnant soon after they married and life moved along.

When Sean called her from L.A. to say he had received a call from his brother, Jack, she was pleased. She agreed he needed to go back to Pennsylvania and spend time with him, to try to reconnect. She hoped it would help him come to grips with what had happened. She suggested that he bring Jack back home with him, so she and the kids could meet him. Maybe they could give him the family he had lost.

CHAPTER 9

Selinsgrove, PA

Jesus Christ, nothing changes. It's been thirty fucking years, but it's like I never left, thought Sean, as he drove down familiar streets and past homes of childhood friends. He tried to concentrate, tried to stay focused on the present, but the memories wouldn't go away. His emotions were swirling, one moment filled with guilt, the next with fear. It was just before 10:30 a.m. when he pulled up to the old home of Pat and Joe Smith. Jack was standing on the porch, his hands resting on the rails. He smiled a small smile as Sean slowly got out of the car. Sean took a deep breath, smiled back, grabbed his bag from the car, and started walking up the flagstone path toward the porch. Not a word was said. Sean stared at his brother, and he could feel his tears welling up. He came close to Jack, and neither moved.

Sean finally said, "Hi, Jack." He slowly reached for his brother to hug him, and Jack moved away at first, unsure, but then let his brother put his arms around him. It was awkward, but it felt necessary. Jack broke away first.

"Let's sit down. It's a nice day, you want a beer?"

"Sure," said Sean. "I could use one right about now." Jack turned and walked into the house, returned with two bottles of Budweiser, and put them on the table that separated the old chairs that had been on this porch for more than twenty years. For a moment, the two boys sat there, not making any eye contact, and then at almost the same time they each took a long swallow.

"I needed that," said Sean, as he turned toward his brother. "Jack, I'm not sure exactly why I'm here, but it is good seeing you after all these years."

Jack looked at Sean and said, "I know that it wasn't easy for you to come out here when you don't even know exactly what I found. I figured that you had a right to know what happened to Mom and Dad, because for me what happened to them also happened to me. I'm sure your life is one pretty picture, but when we lost them, my life went into the shitter. Now that I found out what really happened…" Jack took another long swallow and continued, "I figured that maybe, once you see what I've seen, well, maybe you'll want to come along for the ride."

"Why don't you just start from the beginning." Sean looked around and said, "Where are the Smiths?"

Jack took another long swallow and put his beer down. "I'm getting another one, you ready for another?"

"Nah, I'm good," said Sean.

Jack stood up slowly, turning toward the screen door, and casually said, "Pat died a few years back. Joe went turkey hunting; he told me that he'll be staying in the old cabin. He told me to make myself at home. God knows we had plenty of issues, but tell you the truth, it was okay seeing him. We actually caught up a little. I told him that I was sorry for not making Pat's funeral. I think he understood. I've been pretty fucked up these last few years. Anyway," continued Jack, "he said he would be up there about a week. He told me that he had nothing to come home to. Life can kick you right in the gut. It happened to him, and it happened to me."

"Come on in here," said Jack. "I got something to show you." Sean followed Jack into the kitchen where piles of papers and letters were all over the kitchen table. Jack turned to his brother and said, "You want to know what happened? It's all right here, all the letters from these dusty old boxes." Jack walked over to the refrigerator and took out another beer and said, "You hungry?"

"Yeah," said Sean, "I can go for a cup of coffee and some eggs. How about we go downtown, grab some breakfast, and you can fill me in on what this whole thing is all about." He walked over to Jack. "First, I need to say something."

Jack shook his head slowly. "It's okay, Sean, water under the bridge."

"No, Jack, just hold on for a minute." Sean hesitated and then continued, "Look, I was just a little kid. I didn't know what was going on and I'm sorry that I never reached out to you, but I guess it was my way of putting what happened to us out of my mind."

Jack said, "It's cool, don't sweat it, man. No sense digging up the past. Fact is, you seem to have done all right for yourself and I'm happy for you, man, I swear to God. It wasn't your fault, I just got fucked, that's all. Sometimes, you eat the bear, and sometimes the bear eats you. So, look, let's just put the past behind us and let's go get something to eat, I'm fucking starving."

The two brothers got into Sean's car and drove toward a café on Route 15. Jack leaned back; he felt worn out. They drove the ten minutes without saying a word. Jack looked around at the town that he had grown up in. For some reason he couldn't take his eyes off the river.

"Things don't change as much as you would think. The river's still here, just where we left it." Jack turned to his brother, put his hand on Sean's shoulder, and smiled. Sean smiled back, holding back the tears.

They walked into the café and sat down at a table next to the window. Sean ordered two eggs over easy and Jack told the girl that he'd just have coffee.

"Thought you were hungry?" said Sean.

"It's weird," said Jack. "One minute I'm starving, the next I can't get anything down, and when I do, I feel like shit. I don't know what it is, I'm just not feeling right."

When the waitress brought the coffee, Sean picked up the cup and held it toward Jack, as if making a toast, and then said, "Here's to learning the truth."

"You sure about that, big brother? You know what they say, you better watch what you wish for, you might just get it."

Sean looked at his brother as Jack put sugar into his coffee, and said, "I wouldn't be here if I didn't want to find out what happened to Mom and Dad. No matter where it takes us, this time I'm staying," he said in a firm voice.

Jack stared down at the half-empty cup of coffee. It really bothered his stomach lately, but he was damned if he was giving up coffee, no fucking way.

"What's going on?" said Sean.

Jack looked up. "Nothing," he answered. "I was thinking of filling you in on my life story since you left for sunny California and never looked back."

"Come on, Jack," said Sean. "Let's do this another time... Please, I know what you think of me and Grandma."

Jack shook his head gently and said, "You're right, Sean. We'll have this talk another time, not now."

Jack started. "You know I've been in and out of trouble over the last few years. Nothing big, small-time drug stuff, and the judge gave me a choice: I could work at the veterans hospital up in Williamsport or do my time in Allenwood. I took the hospital. It was disgusting work, but I figure it was better than a cell. I was working in one of the wards." He took a sip of coffee. "I'm giving this old guy a bath." Jack smirked. "Can you believe that, a fucking sponge bath. Then the vet grabs my name tag and looks me straight in the eye and says, '*Jerry.*'

"It hit me like a goddamn thunderbolt. This son of a bitch thinks that he's back in Vietnam talking to Dad. Starts talking like a mile a minute. I just shut up and tried to make sense of what he was talking about."

Sean stared at Jack and asked, "What's his name?"

"Tony Ramo. He said they use to call him Big Hands, cause he's a little wiry-type guy with these huge hands." Jack sat back and continued. "He's so out of it, he thinks he is back in 'Nam. I get that he was tight with Dad. They were in some special secret unit together. I couldn't follow most of what he was saying but I couldn't get him to shut up. But then he said something that rang a bell. He mentioned all the letters, journals, and notebooks and what a mistake it was to send them home. He kept saying, 'You shouldn't have written all the shit down, Jerry.' And I remembered there were boxes down in the cellar at the Smiths' house. Eventually I decided to go back to the Smiths and look for them. I found them just where they had been for all these years. I started to read the papers. That's when I decided to call you." He signaled the waitress to bring the check.

"So, I was looking through all this shit that Dad wrote and I come across the name Tony Ramo; they definitely knew each other. I couldn't fucking believe it. Come on, let's go back to the house, I want you to see some of this stuff."

Back at the house, Jack took a notebook from the top of one of the piles and handed it to Sean. Sean recognized his father's handwriting immediately.

Tony (Big Hands) Ramo
1969 Vietnam

From a distance, Tony Ramo looked like the average big guy, except he was short, not more than 5'6". Tony and I connected right away. We were tight since we met on the bus to basic training. We formed a bond that could never be broken, a brotherly relationship, borne of mutual pain and suffering at the hands of a ruthless Master Sergeant. Tony looked like a refrigerator without a neck, but when you first met him, his eyes were the first thing you'd notice. He looked at you with those gray eyes, like he's sizing you up, and then, before you know it, he reaches out to shake your hand and yours just disappears. One moment your right hand was securely attached to your right wrist, the next second it looked more like it was Tony's hand attached to your wrist. His hands enveloped yours, like a vice, squeezing harder and harder, and just when you felt your hand going numb, he'd let go and smile. "Nice to meet ya." His thick Brooklyn accent revealed an attitude that small dogs must have when they blindly go after a dog five times their size. No fear, no hesitation, and certainly no remorse, no matter what the outcome might be. You can't teach attitude, you can't practice attitude; you either have it or you don't. He had it. You could feel it a mile away, or a barstool away. If you were about to get in the middle of a brawl at one of the bars in Saigon, Tony Ramo was who you wanted to be standing behind. Usually, it never got that far; Tony would stand slowly and then there was that stare, like looking down the barrel of a 12-gauge automatic shotgun. The other guy would back up and back down, live to fight another day, and most of the time, that was that. Sometimes the other guy had too much to drink, or maybe he needed to prove to himself or his buddies that he would never stand down. Tony was fast and vicious. His immense right hand would slam into the other guy's face and he'd crash to the floor, and that was that.

Sean put down the notebook and looked at Jack, who had been dozing on and off while Sean read.

"Hey Jack, you okay, man?" Jack looked up.

"Yeah, yeah, I'm feeling worn out." He moved his hands over the edge of the table, feeling for that slight nick, made years ago by the impact of his front tooth. "Joe Smith smacked me around you know. This one time I ducked away and hit the fucking side of this table right here. Broke my front tooth...could you believe that?"

Jack had altered the true story, a habitual coping mechanism he used to forget the past. He ran his tongue along the jagged edge of the broken tooth. "You want to know what that son of a bitch said? *That's what you get for not taking it like a man, little girl, serves you right. And who the fuck is going to pay for the dentist? Not me, goddamnit, no way, you little bitch. You better call your grandma, the one that abandoned you and ran off to California.*" Jack went silent, lost in the memories.

Sean reached out for Jack's hand, but Jack pulled away. "I don't need your pity, Sean, I just need you to help me find out what the fuck happened to us."

Sean nodded and said, "Go on, Jack, I'm listening."

Jack reached out for the bottle of Bud and slowly gulped down the last half of the bottle.

"Once I figured out that Tony really did know Dad, I spent the next few weeks with him, as much as I could. I became his personal caregiver; the doctors were fine with the arrangement. They thought that it was a good idea. I started paying a hell of a lot more attention to Tony. This guy could talk nonstop for three hours. I don't know how, but he remembered every last fucking detail. I got the feeling that this guy Ramo really cared about Dad. I think they were as different as two guys could be, maybe that's what drew them so close. Ramo didn't know anyone like Dad, and I guess Dad never met anyone like Tony Ramo. I think they became best friends."

Sean put down his beer and asked, "Jack, what's this got to do with Mom and Dad?"

Jack smiled and said casually, "Our dad was a fucking gangster."

That got Sean's attention. He looked up with a confused expression. "What?!"

"I know," Jack said with a smile on his face. "Could you fucking believe it, Jerry McGinnis was a fucking criminal! Now I know where I got all my talent, I inherited it. Not my fault that I'm always in trouble with the law, it's in my DNA. Out of control, completely out of control, and it's all Dad's fault," said Jack, shaking his head.

"Get to the fucking point, Jack, you're killing me," said Sean in an irritated tone.

"Yeah, I'll get to the point."

Jack continued, "So I would listen to Tony at work, even though sometimes it wasn't easy to understand. Little by little things started to fall into place. They were both stationed just outside of Saigon. Dad was a photojournalist with *Stars and Stripes*. Ramo was just another grunt. Sometimes he rambled on about missions that these guys went on, it wasn't just about going out and shooting the gooks. That's what he called them, he loved that fucking word. He talked about missions where they would kill the parents just to grab the kids who would be sold off for adoption or other stuff. And then all of a sudden he would stop and stare out the window, or he would fall asleep and I would have to leave it there till the next day."

Jack stood up suddenly, "I've got to take a piss."

"You okay?" asked Sean, noticing the sweat on Jack's forehead when he returned.

"Yeah, I'm okay," said Jack. "It burns when I pee, and I can hardly get more than a shot glass full of pee out."

"You should go to a doctor. I mean you're in the fucking VA hospital."

"I did. They told me that it was some kind of urinary tract infection. They gave me penicillin and said stop jerking off so much. Look, Sean, I know this is a long story, but stay with me. I'll fill in the blanks." He sat back down, and with the sleeve of his T-shirt, he wiped the sweat from his face.

"Tony called me Jerry most of the time, and one day he grabbed me by my shirt and said, 'Jerry, Jerry fucking McGinnis. I swear to Christ I missed you. How you been, Jerry? I can't tell you how bad I feel about what we done to your wife and you, will you ever forgive me, Jerry? It wasn't my idea, I swear, it was John. I was just following orders.'

"Fuck, Sean, when he said that I almost shit myself. What the fuck did he know about Mom?"

Sean leaned forward. "What else did he say? What did he mean?"

"I don't know, or I didn't then. Just listen, I'm telling it the best I can. I tried to get him to talk more but he was gone again. He would say something and then get lost in his head again. I tried all kinds of stuff, I even got music from the sixties and played it, trying to get his head back there. Then two days later he says, 'The letters, you asshole, you shouldn't have sent those goddamn letters and notebooks and diaries. What were you thinking, for Christ's sake? John didn't have a choice, he had to do what he had to do and I had to do what I was ordered to do, I swear Jerry, I swear I had no choice.'"

Sean listened as Jack walked him through what he had pieced together so far. As the days passed, they ordered pizza and drank lots of beer and slept in the same house for the first time in over thirty years.

"Tony told me that around 1955, the U.S. government started sending consultants, military advisors, medical staff, military personnel and, of course, billions of dollars in economic and military aid. The old bastard could talk as if he were narrating a documentary. Over the days and the weeks, I learned a little more. He told me that Dad had sent home letters, journals, and diaries, written evidence describing an illegal and vicious band of military personnel and civilians who had found a way to profit from the war in Vietnam.

"The Unit was a well-run organization with branches throughout Southeast Asia, the United States, and into the Caribbean supported by a huge number of troops, both civilian and military, whose mission was to carry out the duties of this clandestine operation. It had been going on for generations: military personnel and military contractors finding ways of profiting from war.

"I even went to the library to do some research. I wanted to understand why we were in Vietnam. Did you know that in 1961, John Kennedy sent in 100 Special Forces troops along with millions of dollars in aid to support and train the South Vietnam regulars?" Jack continued.

"The founders, a group of both officers and enlisted men and women, quickly understood the potential that awaited anyone with the vision and the strength to carry out the primary mission of the Unit.

"The Military Industrial Complex, all the big companies like Northrop Grumman and Lockheed Martin, were making a fortune off the wars, off the blood of soldiers. This Unit was an informal alliance of folks in the military and other government departments that figured they ought to be able to profit from the wars they were fighting as far back to the very beginning of the U.S. Through the worldwide network of arms sales, military advisors, medical supplies, and enormous amounts of economic and military aid, the ability to divert goods and sell them to the highest bidder was the primary function of the Unit. Then they filtered all the money into savings accounts for those that gave their allegiance and life to the Unit.

"The Unit ripped off the military and economic aid that was supposed to go to building schools, hospitals, and sending supplies for the troops fighting the war. A black market was set up to sell to the highest bidder: so much food, drugs, and building materials that were sent over there to help the Vietnamese people and support the American troops."

Jack told Sean that Tony Ramo had described the bodies of dead soldiers that were cut open, organs replaced by every drug you could imagine, heroin, grass, pills, whatever, and then sewed back up and shipped to very select funeral homes, where the bodies were cut open and the contents handed over to 'our colleagues in the States.' Tony would smile, recounting his old conversations. He thought that was funny, calling them "our colleagues." But that was nothing, said Jack; soon Tony told him about the most lucrative part, that these scumbags were into child trafficking. Unit soldiers would kill the parents and grab the kids, sending them all over Southeast Asia, particularly to Bangkok. Jack stopped talking. Sean waited, then finally said, "What does this have to do with Mom?"

Jack looked up and said, "Mom wasn't murdered by some fucked-up drug addict looking for money so he could score some dope. She was murdered by a couple of Unit soldiers looking for the information that Dad had sent home."

"What?" said Sean. "What the fuck are you talking about?"

"Dad didn't go over there to fight a war. He went over there to find a story, this was all about a fucking story. He originally went over there to find out what happened to Chuck Harris. He got involved in this organized crime outfit, in the Unit. He became a full-fledged member, and every day he sent home letters and all his journals and notebooks with the real story about these guys. I think his plan was to gather up all the evidence and eventually write the story for the papers, get famous and rich. Unfortunately, it didn't quite work out the way he planned. They found out, and sent two guys over to the States to get the papers. Tony Ramo told me about it.

"So that day, when I was six, while you were at school, they came over to the house and instead of just getting these fucking papers and journals and notebooks and getting out of there, they raped mom and killed her. And there I was, upstairs, sucking my fucking thumb. And then after that, they went back to Vietnam and must have murdered Dad. That's it."

"Are you shitting me?" said Sean. "That doesn't make any goddamn sense at all."

"Look, Sean, I think all the proof we need is in the papers that have been sitting downstairs in the Smiths' basement for the last thirty years."

"So, if they killed Mom to get the papers, how did they end up here?"

"I don't know. Grandma gave these boxes to the Smiths to hold for her. Maybe Dad sent an extra copy of everything to Grandpa and Grandma, just in case."

Sean sat at the table with a blank expression on his face and said nothing. He stood and walked to the window and stared at the river as it moved through the countryside. Then he spoke. "Grandma wouldn't give up, she never did. That's why she kept those boxes, that's why she moved them to the Smiths' house. It makes sense. All those years you were sitting right over those boxes with the whole secret."

"Over the years, I spent a lot of time in the basement, hiding from that son of a bitch so he wouldn't beat the shit out of me. I would look at the boxes and I never knew what was in them, just that they were Dad's stuff. It made me feel good to be near something of his."

"I didn't know what was happening to you," said Sean. "We were a long way away and I never guessed."

Jack stopped him and said, "Hey, Sean, forget it, that's in the past. And don't you worry, that bastard will get his, trust me on that."

"Okay," said Sean. "Let me see if I understand this. This guy Tony tells you that there were letters that our dad had sent to Mom that spelled out everything that had happened over there, and he tells you he knew how Mom died, and then suddenly you remember that there were boxes of stuff down here and that's how you found out he was telling the truth?"

"Basically, that's it," said Jack. "But I haven't read it all yet, I just read some of it. I figured that I would wait for you. I haven't been feeling too good and, well, I'm pretty sick. I'm having a hard time concentrating. I think the whole story is written in these letters and journals from dad."

"What do you mean pretty sick?" said Sean. "I haven't seen you in a lot of years and, tell you the truth, you look like shit. What's the matter with you?"

Jack looked up and said, shaking his head, "I haven't been straight with you. Right now I have a urinary tract infection, but that's because I got that virus that kills my immune system. There is no cure, it's bad. I'm taking medicine. I feel pretty good sometimes, and sometimes I feel like I'm dying."

Sean reached out to his brother, but Jack pulled away. "Shit," said Sean.

"Sean, listen, none of this was your fault, you didn't know anything about what was happening to me. We lost touch, it happens all the time. Let's just find out what happened to our parents, and then let's find out who the motherfuckers were that wasted them, 'cause tell you the truth, big brother, I ain't got a lot to lose."

"What do you mean, Jack, you got nothing to lose?"

Jack turned to his brother and said, "Don't worry, bud, I'm not crazy. I just need to know what really happened, before I die."

"Who said anything about dying so soon?" said Sean. "You said you were taking the medicine."

Jack looked down and said, "Look, man, let's get real, it's just a matter of time for me. Are you going to help me, or do I have to do this all on my own?"

"No, man, I'm with you, I owe that you that much."

Jack turned and grabbed his brother's arm and said angrily, "You don't owe me shit. If you do this, you do it because you want to do it, you got it?"

Sean looked at Jack and nodded and said, "Yeah, I got it."

"Let's get the hell out of this house for a while, get some dinner and stop at the store on the way home. We have a lot of reading to do; we're going to need food."

"When was the last time that you were here in town?" said Sean as they drove home after shopping at the A&P. "I can't believe you would want to set foot in that house after all the shit you'd gone through, I mean, after what that bastard did to you."

"I don't know," said Jack. "It's been a long time, maybe six or seven years."

"Good thing he didn't throw out the boxes," said Sean.

"That lazy motherfucker," laughed Jack. "He wouldn't lift his finger, unless it was to pick up a cold beer and give me a whack."

Sean nodded and then asked, "How was it when you came here and asked him about the boxes?"

"Not too bad, the old fuck just sat there and told me that he hadn't touched a thing and that I could stay here as long as I wanted to, just like the old days. He said he was going hunting and would be back in a week or so. It was just like nothing had happened. So, he took off after an hour or so, and I went downstairs and started to bring up all the boxes."

"Okay," said Sean. "Let's get to work."

The two brothers started arranging the piles of letters and journals by the dates written on the tops and front covers. By the time they had gotten things sorted out, it was around eleven o'clock and Jack said, "I'm tired, I'm going to bed. Let's get back into it in the morning."

CHAPTER 10

S ean woke up in the Smiths' house. The years had done their damage on the shredded curtains, and the wallpaper was peeling off the walls. He remembered lying in his grandparents' house, which had looked a lot like this room.

The radio clock that sat on the small table next to the bed said 6:15 a.m. He stretched, got out of bed, and put on his shorts and shirt. He looked into the bedroom next door, Jack was still fast asleep. Sean decided to let him be. It would be best for his brother to get as much rest as possible. It would give Sean a chance to organize his father's papers. It was dark in the kitchen, the shades blocking the rising sun. Sean found a can of Maxwell House; he'd make himself a pot of coffee and get to work. He was determined to find out what had happened to his parents. Before he got started, Sean took a cup of coffee and walked outside to the porch and sat down in the old rocking chair. This was his favorite time of the day, the sun just coming up and a clean, pure smell to the air. He thought about his mother and father, sitting on a porch just like this one, planning their future together and raising a family. Sean took a sip of the coffee and then said out loud, "Why am I doing this, what's the point?" He hadn't noticed that Jack was awake and standing just inside the screen door.

Jack stepped out onto the porch and leaned against the rail. For a moment neither brother said a word, and then Sean stood up and walked over to Jack and put his arm around his shoulder and said, "All this was almost thirty years ago and nothing we do now is going to bring them back. And even if we find out exactly what happened, what are we going to do about it?"

"I don't have all the answers. I don't even know half the questions," said Jack. "Let's read everything and maybe we'll figure it all out. It's the least that we can do for Mom and Dad."

Sean said, "All right. Let's get to work. What the hell, maybe we can find a way to bring these guys to justice. Jack, do you know what I do? Do you know what I've been doing over the last thirty years?"

Jack turned and faced his brother and said, "Yeah, I know exactly what you been doing for the last thirty fucking years. But you know what, you didn't accomplish shit. This may be the first time in thirty years that you've seen me, but guess what, I've seen you plenty of times. I've seen you walk in that building in Center City plenty of times. I've known for a while that you work at the District Attorney's office. But I kept my mouth shut. I didn't want to burden you with my shit, so I just loaded those fucking vending machines and kept my mouth shut."

"What the hell are you talking about?" said Sean.

Jack turned and placed his hands down on the weathered railing and said in a sad voice, "I worked for a vending company in Bensalem. Penn Square was one of my stops. It doesn't matter. Look, Sean, I don't for one second doubt that you've been trying."

Sean grabbed his brother firmly around his shoulders, feeling Jack's thin body underneath the baggy clothes. He said in a sympathetic voice, "Jack, I swear to God, I've been trying. I joined the District Attorney's office so that I would be on the inside. I figured that I could spend time on the side investigating what happened to Mom and Dad. My boss just thought I was working on an old child abuse case. But every direction I turned, there was a dead end. It was like somebody put up a roadblock. So, fine, I spent half my life trying to figure this out, and you stumble on it like a drunk in a fucking alley."

Jack stared at his brother and then hesitated, before he smiled and simply said, "You asshole."

Sean smiled and said, "I guess."

Both turned to walk back into the kitchen when Jack said, "Hold on. I need to ask you something."

Sean turned to his brother and said, "Sure, what?"

"After you left and went with Grandma out to California…" Jack hesitated for a moment and continued, "I mean, I understood why you left, after Grandpa died. I guess you guys just needed to get away from this shithole, but why did you leave me behind? Why did she leave me here?"

Sean sat down again on the porch and said, "Jack, I barely remember those first months, I was only eight. Grandma wanted to bring you but the doctors advised against it; they thought it was better for you to stay close to the hospital and continue your therapy. She had all the plans made to come and get you that next September, but then she got sick. What was I supposed to do? When she died I just wanted it all to go away. I was just a kid. I'm sorry, Jack."

Jack saw the tears running down his face. He sat down in the chair next to him.

Sean turned to his brother and said, "I didn't know, Jack. We all thought that you were doing fine. Grandma told me that she had heard from the Smiths and that everything was just great."

"Yeah, great, my ass. I found out years later that Pat and Joe Smith took all the money that was left from the sale of Grandma's house and spent it on themselves. Goddamnit, Sean. That money was mine, and there wasn't a fucking thing I could do about it."

Sean hesitated and said, "I got money. They told me that Dad had set up a fund for us. I got money up until I was eighteen, and then they even took care of school. I just assumed you got exactly the same thing."

Jack stood and leaned up against the porch railing. "They let me have some spending money at the beginning, but then it stopped when I was around fourteen or fifteen. I was pretty fucked up those days. Anyway, I just thought it ran out, that there was no more money. So, I just let it go. You telling me that you kept getting money even for college. Where did all that money even come from?"

Sean sat, looking at the floor, while Jack spoke. He looked up at his brother and said, "Maybe the answers are waiting for us right here."

The two brothers walked into the house and began sorting through the papers.

"Jesus Christ," said Sean. "Look at all this shit, it's going to take a fucking month to go through all of this. What did he do, chronicle every fucking minute of his life?"

Some of the letters and journals were dated and some weren't. There were letters and notes and stories, as well as day-to-day diaries.

"I don't have any idea how to figure out where the beginning is, so let's just start here," Sean said looking at the page in his hands.

"And just out of curiosity, what's the plan? I mean once we find out the truth, what are we supposed to do with it?"

"I don't have a fucking plan," said Jack. "We will figure it out as we go."

Sean looked at Jack and then down at the notebook in his hands. He opened to the first page and began to read his father's words out loud. The brothers both smiled for a second. It was nice hearing their dad's voice after thirty years.

My Diary 1969

I grew up just a few miles outside of downtown Selinsgrove, Pennsylvania, not that it was much of a downtown. The house sat on the top of a small mountain, the highest point for 100 miles. A long winding road came up the hill and ended in front of our house. We had a small barn where we kept tools, bags of fertilizer, and a big old red tractor. The house had been in the family for more than fifty years. We had more than ten acres of pristine farmland and could grow almost anything during the summer and spring. The crop of choice on the farm was Christmas trees. Every winter, just before Christmas, folks from all over the county would drive or hike up the long driveway to the McGinnis Farm, where the families would search for the best Christmas tree they could find. Miraculously, every family always found just the right tree, and then, ceremoniously, each and every member of the family, the mother, the father, and the kids, would participate in cutting it down. It seemed like they all knew they had a special hand in making Christmas perfect. It was my favorite time of year. I was a tour guide on the property, leading new friends down row after row of small pine trees that would soon end up in living rooms throughout central Pennsylvania. "This one, this one!" the kids would cry out, picking out their favorite tree. I would hand over the saw. Cutting down the chosen tree made it feel so much more like a traditional old-fashioned Christmas. It was a special moment for the family, and I was happy to share it.

I loved sitting on the front porch, rocking back and forth, watching the families walking through the Christmas tree orchard. This was a special place, drinking a cup of hot cocoa, enjoying the Pennsylvania countryside.

Steps from the back door was an old fence that had become a beat-up, broken-down eyesore over the years. There was no gate, and the fence had one simple purpose: to keep you from falling off the edge of the mountain and tumbling down the steep and narrow dirt path that led treacherously down to the banks of the Susquehanna River. I would often look out of my window and listen to the river below. Grandpa had put up the fence just a few days after Chuck Harris slipped down the hill and broke his leg. Could have been worse, but Chuck took it in stride, as did his parents. Chuck was my best friend till they moved away; we went through a lot together. We thought the sky was the limit, and we had such plans for our lives.

I wonder how old you need to be before you give up those childhood dreams. When you're in your twenties the world is yours to grab onto. It feels like you have no limits. Maybe ten years down the road, you begin to sense that life is not going exactly the way you planned it. Maybe reality is starting to set in and that's when you start giving up, even the dreams become a little less frequent. After college, I still believed I was on a path headed out of small town USA. My first job was working for the local paper, nothing more than a brief stopover on the way to the New York Times or the Washington Post. But the years started to slip by, adding marriage and kids, which was all part of the plan of course, but my career was going nowhere. I shouldn't be complaining. It's not that bad. There are worse things than a quiet life in central Pennsylvania, a good job on the local paper, being a big man in a small town.

Yesterday, driving home from work, I felt the winter chill from the river go right through my bones. I rolled down the window and took a deep breath; the air had a fresh smell to it. The river was high on its banks. I thought back to junior high school, reading Mark Twain, about Huckleberry Finn and Big Jim drifting down the river on a raft. It was dark by now, and the light of the full moon seemed to glance off the sparkling water as it made its way across the rolling landscape. The weather reporter on the radio said that there was a 50 percent chance of light snow. What a job, a weatherman. I thought about a line in a Bob Dylan song about, "You don't need a weatherman to know which way the wind blows."

The drive from Harrisburg to home seemed to be getting more unbearable lately. I'd been getting this feeling that I just need a change, something to get me out of this same old routine. I don't want to end up just like everyone else. Living in this small town in the middle of PA and working for the same paper, doing the same job and reporting on the same small town stories. Dad always knew just what to say; when I was feeling sorry for myself, he would say, "You don't have to be me, but you have to be somebody; and whatever you do, do it the best you can."

Maybe Dad had bigger dreams but reality has a habit of getting in the way. Those kids, they've got to eat every day of the week, and you have responsibilities, and a real man never walks away from his responsibilities.

"You got a really good head on those shoulders, Jerry, make a life for yourself. Working for the paper is a noble profession. Stop dreaming about what will never happen and get to work on making a life for yourself and your family." Truth is I have heard these words so many times before, and so once again I put the dreams out of my head, switched the channel on the radio to my favorite music station and headed home to Kate and our boys.

It hadn't been more than four months since we bought the house off of Carey Street. Deb from Century 21 showed it to us on the first day we started looking and we loved it. "It's a fair price," Deb said. "They're asking $27,000, offer them $25,000, maybe they'll come down a little. But I've got to tell you, they priced this house to sell, not to show, so if you don't pull the trigger, you'll lose this one in a heartbeat."

Dad walked around the half-acre lot before we made the offer. "Great house to start your family, nice quiet street, school's okay, you should know that, you went there." I wouldn't have done anything without talking to Dad. We understood each other; sometimes we finished each other's sentences. So Dad lent us $5,000 and the bank lent us the rest. I was living the American dream: marry your high school sweetheart, have kids, get a good job, and buy a home.

It was just before six o'clock when I pulled into the driveway. Kate smiled from the kitchen window. The frustration and anxiety I was feeling just a few minutes before seemed to vanish as I got out of the car and walked up the path toward the front door. Kate walked over and opened it for me, her light brown hair seemed to glisten in the early evening light.

My wife, Kate, also grew up in this town, and we were girlfriend and boyfriend since elementary school. Before long we were planning our future. As I walked in, she gave me a kiss and said, "The baby's taking a nap and Sean is playing. You want a beer? I'll have one with you on the porch, and we'll have dinner in about half an hour."

"That's fine, let me just get out of these clothes and wash up." I gave her a kiss on the cheek and told her I could use a beer.

We sat for a while and then I told her about Chuck. She remembered him from elementary school and that right before we went to high school, he moved up to Williamsport. His parents owned the funeral parlor in town, not so easy to forget a kid who lives in a funeral home.

Chuck got drafted, I told her, and was sent over to Vietnam the summer before. From what I'd heard, he was over there working on an airfield when Viet Cong guerrillas attacked their camp. Eight of our soldiers got killed and Chuck, along with about 150 other guys, got wounded. They sent him home after a month in some German hospital, and now he was finishing up his recuperation at the VA hospital in Williamsport. It seemed pretty cool to me. The papers were calling him a hero, and when he got out, they were going to have a parade and a party in his honor. My editor at the paper wanted me to write about him, and I wanted to go up there and see him. "We were real good friends," I said. "It'll be good seeing him after all these years. If I write a good story on him, maybe some big shot will offer him a great job, instead of ending up at the funeral parlor." She thought it was a great idea and made me promise to say hello, and she wanted to know if he ever got married.

On the news that night they were talking about the U.S. air strikes against the Ho Chi Minh trail. It was the road that the North Vietnamese used to send soldiers and supplies from the north. The report continued that every time we bombed the trail, the NVA would send female construction crews out to make the repairs. I pictured a bunch of old ladies running around with brooms and mops cleaning the place up.

Kate sat next to me watching the news. She has the best of her parents: the heart and kindness of her father and the tenacity and spirit of her mother. These are the characteristics I fell in love with way back in grade school. She had it all: looks, personality, and she was smart as a whip, but there was one thing we didn't share. I wanted to get out of this little town and get a job as a journalist with a big city paper. I didn't care what paper, just as long as it was away from here and in some big city, like Philadelphia or maybe even New York. But Kate didn't share my dream. She was as happy as a clam staying right where we were, and we often fought about this.

She saw I was in a pensive mood and asked what I was thinking about. I told her I was thinking about that interview with Chuck. It could get picked up by the national papers, look great on my resume, and maybe even get me a shot at one of the big papers.

She got angry. She said I was always looking for a way out of here. I told her, "I love you and I love the boys, but I've got dreams, and I can't get them out of my head. I've tried to just be *satisfied with what we have, but I just can't help it. You want to spend the rest of your life here, I understand, but I'll tell you right now, Kate, I'll never stop dreaming of getting out of this bullshit town. There is so much more out there."*

The news that night also covered a story about the Gulf of Tonkin Resolution that had been passed by Congress, which basically gave Johnson the authority to deploy troops to Southeast Asia without having to declare war. Within three years, the number of Americans in Vietnam went from around 15,000 advisors to over half a million, many of which were in combat. Before this, I had never thought much about Vietnam, and lately it was all that we were hearing about. There wasn't a day that went by that there wasn't a newswire about the pending military involvement in Vietnam. It had been almost a year since those eight American soldiers were killed by Viet Cong guerrillas in some compound at Pleiku in the central highlands.

I had never been outside of Pennsylvania except for a high school trip to Washington, DC. Southeast Asia seemed like a long way away, and sending American boys over there, even if they were supposed to just train and support the South Vietnamese, made no sense.

I sat and listened to the president talk about the need to continue to send troops to protect South Vietnam from the communists, but all I could think about was my old friend lying up there in the hospital in Williamsport. And what if I got drafted? I had kids, a wife, and house payments. I knew I sure as hell was not one of those draft card–burning hippies running off to Canada to avoid serving his country. I read about Johnson signing a law that made burning your draft card a crime. If those hippie bastards didn't love this country, they should leave it. Maybe if I enlisted, I could get assigned to an administrative unit where I could work as a reporter. But how could I even think of leaving Kate and the boys?

When Kate had gone to bed, I looked out into the dark night. Below the window just 100 yards away was the river that I had grown to love over these many years. It always calmed me down to feel the river close. I could smell the river and feel its power as it surged down the Pennsylvania countryside, constantly moving and rising but always moving forward. For millions of years the river had found its own way, meandering around any obstacle that got in its way, avoiding anything that blocked the path. It always found a way and I needed to find my way.

Sean put down the notebook his father had written in so many years before. For the first time he felt like he was beginning to understand a man he could hardly remember. Jack sat silently.

Sitting across the table from his brother, Sean picked up another notebook and started to read out loud again.

CHAPTER 11

Selinsgrove, Pennsylvania

My favorite place in the world is a big boulder that sits just on the edge of the river on my parent's farm. The perfect spot, right at the bend, protected from the harsh winds of winter and the blistering days of summer. There's always a cool breeze in the heat of the day or a feeling of warmth on a cool morning that seems to be generated from the rock. The giant boulder might have been in this very spot for a million years. There was a smoothness to it, almost like it had been purposely designed for my dad and me. There was even a hollowed-out space for us to sit with a backrest that was most likely the result of a million years of rain and wind and a relentless river pouring over the same stone for millennia.

When the river was high on its bank after the heavy snows of the winter, we would sit there in awe of the power of the water. Sometimes we fished and sometimes we just sat there and talked. The steam from the hot cocoa warmed my cold fingers. I remember one time watching the ducks heading south for the winter months. They fascinated me with their almost perfect formation. I asked my father why they flew like that. He smiled at me and said, "I don't know, son, but maybe you can find out why. I sure would like to know. It's something I've wondered about all my life."

I promised him I would, and I spent the next few days asking around and finally one of my teachers explained it to me. That night as I was sitting on the porch with my father, I carefully explained the nature of the birds and why they fly in such a perfect pattern. I had learned about the wind drag and how the head bird takes all the wind for those who follow, then they change places. It felt so good to explain something to my dad. I had never been as proud and happy as I was that night.

Dad tried to convince me not to enlist. He believed it was a terrible idea to leave Kate and the kids. But I hope that he will be proud once he reads what I have written, when my story is published.

I thought back to Chuck and why I was here in Vietnam. Mostly it's about that one day by the river. The story started with a man named Joe Bentley and his two sons who had come down from Elmira, NY for a canoe trip down the Susquehanna River; we didn't know him, but he changed my life. The heavy snows that winter caused the spring runoff to swell the river particularly high that year. The water was cold and the rapids were strong and violent. One afternoon Chuck and I had been hanging out at my house when we heard a man screaming from the river; it was an awful sound. We called to my dad to help, but then we took off toward the river. We were twelve years old and we knew the river pretty well. I remember my dad screaming at us to not go into the water, that he was calling the police.

When we got to the bank, we could see two people in the water, wearing life vests, desperately trying to get to shore. The current was dragging them downstream, and we knew they didn't have much time. I tried to hold a branch out, Chuck holding onto me to anchor me, but the next thing I knew, I was in the water up to my waist. It was cold, so cold it made me dizzy. I couldn't reach the man and his son, they were too far out. I tried again and then the icy current snagged me and I was moving fast down the river. Chuck told me later that he ran as fast as he could, following me in the water, trying to find a place to help me out. We both knew Kramer Falls was just around the bend, and every year some dumb boater in a canoe would die going over those falls by accident. The rocks were huge.

Right before the drop-off, Chuck waded out in the water. He knew he had one chance, and he held onto a branch sticking out over the water. He waited for me to come up for air one more time and managed to grab me, and drag me, half-frozen, onto the bank. Joe Bentley and one of his sons were almost to the falls, and Chuck leaned back out into the freezing water, and managed to pull them out too. My dad was there to help by then, and soon the cops arrived. The river divers spent the afternoon searching, but Joe Bentley's other son hadn't made it. He died in the river that day.

Chuck and I were friends for life; that day forged a bond that could never be broken.

Sean looked up from the mildew-stained notebook. He gently placed it back on the kitchen table.

"That's the end of that notebook," said Sean, as he stood and walked over to the coffee maker on the counter and poured himself his third cup.

"What a story," said Jack. "Dad and Grandpa were pretty close, weren't they."

"I guess so. Grandma used to tell me about Grandpa all the time. Tell you the truth, after a while, I got tired of hearing about him." Sean stretched his arms above his head and arched his back. "Grandpa loved to write, that was his passion, Grandma used to say. Just like Dad, I guess."

"I guess," said Jack.

"When did you say Smith was coming back?" Sean asked.

"I don't know, after hunting season, I guess. Who cares, I'd just as soon never see that scumbag again." Jack looked away as Sean picked up another notebook, labeled "My Youth."

"I tell you, man," said Sean. "Dad was bizarre. How many people sit down and write so much about their youth?"

Jack poured himself a cup of coffee, sat down, and started to read aloud from the notebook Sean had found.

I was born April 19, 1942, in Selinsgrove, PA. My parents, Burt and Doris McGinnis, moved here looking for work in the early thirties. My dad got a job working for a local newspaper, and they settled down to raise a family. Growing up an only child in a small town tends to make you pretty independent. I didn't have any big brothers to look out for me or teach me the stuff that only an older sibling could teach a kid.

We belong to the Wesley United Methodist Church, down on Rhoads Ave. The Methodists were serious about the mission and the ministry. God and country, nothing complicated: work hard, go to church on Sunday, be as good as you can, we're all sinners just trying to move closer to God's glory.

My dad had been in the Navy during WWII and served in the South Pacific. I remember getting dressed in a little sailor's outfit. I had the whole uniform, with dark blue pants, the tie, and the open collar sailor shirt. I'd put the uniform on and we would go to church every Sunday like clockwork. After church, we'd go fishing, me and my dad.

My dad still works for the Harrisburg Times. He's a copy-editor, checking all the stories for accuracy, or as he used to say: "The Truth." There was nothing in the world more important to my dad than the truth. He was a simple man with simple values, like "You're only as good as your word." If you break your word, it's a mortal sin, simple as that.

My senior year I got the editor job for the high school paper. I loved writing but I got tired of putting out the same old stuff, and I wanted to shake things up a little. I reported that Mrs. Kramer was seen leaving BJ's Steakhouse with Mr. Evans around eleven one night. All hell broke loose and I got thrown off the paper and suspended for a week. My father hit the roof, even after all those years talking about the truth. I learned my lesson and went to college and studied journalism.

In 1960 Kate and I got married, and I got a job at the local paper with a little help from my father. My first important story was President Johnson's speech about Vietnam. The paper wanted a young man's opinion of what was becoming a controversial situation for the country.

"We can never again stand aside, prideful in isolation. Terrific dangers and troubles that we once called 'foreign' now constantly live among us."

I totally bought into everything Johnson was saying. I wrote about the pride in serving your country and that we all had a moral and ethical responsibility to save the world from those godless communists. If we allowed North Vietnam to overrun the South, then the communists would keep on going throughout Asia, and evidently they would soon be at our back door. We needed to draw a line in the sand and Vietnam was that line.

Sean slapped his hand on the kitchen table and said in a frustrated tone, "For Christ's sake, Jack, just skip to where he goes to Vietnam."

Jack looked up, "Fine, but this is the closest I've been to him. I want to get to know him before..."

Sean reached over and grabbed Jack's wrist, Jack looked down at his brother's hand. "What do you mean, before what? You got something more important to do with your time?"

Jack pulled his hand away. "I got that disease, that virus. I know that if you get it, you're most likely going die. I don't know where I caught it, maybe at the hospital, or doing drugs. I did some stupid shit. So yeah, I would like to know before I run out of time."

"You look like shit, I've got to admit," said Sean. "That sounds really bad. What do the doctors say?"

"They don't know much, they just gave me all kinds of drugs. The meds make me sleepy, spaced out. I get sick to my stomach and don't feel like eating. Let's just keep going, okay, Sean? Please."

Sean looked into his brother's eyes, sunken deep in his head and bloodshot. Jack looked away.

"Okay, Jack, sure. Keep reading."

I got really good feedback on my first article and started to think that this little town and half-assed paper were not going to hold me back. I wanted more, I wanted a byline on a big city paper. I wanted to make a name for myself, and it was not going to happen here. Problem was that Kate loved Selinsgrove. For her, life was about as good as it could get, and if this place was good enough for our parents, it was certainly good enough for us. Kate had it all planned out: four kids, two boys and two girls, right down to the white picket fence that would surround our home near my parents' farm on the top of the mountain that overlooks the Susquehanna River.

So the boys were born and I tried to make it work, put in my time and wait for the opportunity to move up. I figured she would come around.

Jack put the notebook down. His eyes were feeling heavy.

"You okay, Jack? You want to take a break for a while?"

Jack didn't answer for a while, then he said, "You know, if we were just like everyone else, I wonder how different my life would have turned out. I sometimes lie awake in the middle of the night, staring into the darkness, thinking about what it would have been like to be normal, just a regular family. You know, where our dad went to work every morning, our mom stayed home and took care of us, we grew up, met girls, got married and lived happily ever after. But not us. Dad went to Vietnam and got involved in some fucked-up crime organization, disappeared off the face of the earth and because of it, our mom got raped and murdered."

"It's the cards that we were dealt, you got a bad hand. I'm sorry," said Sean, more to himself than to his brother. "Why did you stop reading?"

"I think we should start looking for notebooks from the late sixties. That should be the right time, right before he went and while he was in Vietnam." Jack got up from the kitchen table and walked over to the refrigerator. "You want a beer?"

Sean looked up and gave his brother a nod. "Sounds like a really good idea."

Jack put the beers on the table and began to rifle through the papers until he pulled out a notebook with the date 1969 across the front cover.

"Let's start here," said Jack.

Sean reached out and took the notebook from his brother. "I'll read for a while."

CHAPTER 12

*J*an 14, 1969. Maybe, if I had to do it all over again, I would have thought twice about getting out of bed that morning. It was a cold and snowy winter that year, not at all like the last two years. I had started to think that maybe winter in Pennsylvania isn't so bad after all and then this winter came in like it was fixing to make up for the last two mild ones.

I was thinking about the talk I'd had with Bill Mullen, my boss at the paper. The day before he told me about a story he wanted me to follow up on—a wounded Vietnam vet at the VA hospital in Williamsport. I wasn't that interested in the long drive in bad weather until Bill mentioned the soldier's name: Chuck Harris. That was how I found out about the attack he had survived, and how serious his injuries were. I was ready to walk out the door before my boss was done giving me the assignment.

That morning I sat at the table over my coffee staring out of the window. Even when they moved up to Williamsport, Chuck and I had kept in touch. It's hard when you're not right next door to hold onto a friendship, but we tried to talk every once in a *while. Sitting next to Chuck with blankets wrapped around us that day long ago, watching the police divers look for that dead boy, that kind of thing cements a friendship. The Susquehanna River was high on the bank again; the water is freezing cold this time of the year. I remember the Bentley boy that died in the river, I remember Chuck pulling me out.*

It was one of those bone-chilling mornings; the mist coming off the river seemed to meet up with the clouds, turning the countryside into a huge fog bank. The fields were barren, picked clean, harvested of the feed for the cattle during the long winters in central PA. Nothing changes around here. There's a war going on over there, call it anything you like, police action my ass, but nobody seems to give a shit around here, life is just fine and dandy. I have a friend in the hospital, and I'm going up there to get the interview. Maybe it'll be the one that will get me out of here.

The drive up Route 44 to Williamsport shouldn't take more than an hour, but not today, because of the fog, and I always seem to end up behind an old lady driving slow. As I drove up with the river on my right, I couldn't help thinking that I had some big decisions that I needed to make. I long ago stopped questioning where I planned to go, I knew exactly where I was going. The problem was, how to get there without hurting my wife and young boys, but I knew it was for their own good. I used to think that good things come to those who wait, but I wasn't getting any younger, and I started to realize that the only thing that comes to those who wait is a dead-end life. I was determined to make my life have meaning, and that meaning wasn't going to happen in this little bullshit town.

I had always thought about how at a particular moment in a person's life, what may seem at the time to be an insignificant and meaningless event can forever change the direction of their entire life. A simple thing like stopping to kiss your wife goodbye, that brief moment can mean the difference between watching the guy go through the stop sign and getting hit by someone else, or maybe getting killed yourself by that same guy. Maybe it's all fate, maybe the direction your life takes is predetermined, or maybe you can take control of your own destiny and determine the path that you travel. I had been having these thoughts more and more lately.

All I knew is that I didn't want to spend the rest of my life regretting the road that I seemed to be traveling.

For Kate, this world was all she could have ever dreamed of, but for me it was becoming a prison. I needed to make that right turn and find what I was looking for. The problem was, I wasn't sure exactly what I was looking for or if I would even know it when and if it ever stared me in the face. As I pulled onto Route 44 I switched on the radio just in time for the 8 a.m. news. I didn't start to listen until the reporter started talking about Vietnam and the enemy body count. It seemed to make people feel better about this far-off war, to vindicate the loss of American life to hear how many of the enemy had been killed.

I was brought up in a family that was proud to serve their country. If I were called up, then I would be ready to go. I'm not saying that I wanted to go to some little country that I had never even heard of before, but if I were called up, then I would go. We should round up all those fucking draft dodgers who ran off like cowards and hid in Canada and send them to the front lines.

The traffic was light that morning and I pulled into the hospital parking lot a little after 9 a.m. The wind was blowing, and the snow on the ground whipped around the almost full lot. I found a parking space in the back and walked toward the main entrance. The volunteer at the information desk told me that visiting hours started at 1 p.m. I took out my press ID card and showed it to the old guy, hoping maybe he would either be impressed or maybe a little intimidated by my credentials.

"Like I said, son, visiting hours don't start until one." He looked down and continued to read the paper. I stood there, just for a moment, but it seemed like forever. In the end I told him I was visiting a true hero, my childhood best friend who had fought in Vietnam. The guard at the info desk was a vet, and he softened up when he realized what I was there for and told me to go on up to the fifth floor, room 523. I didn't know that this was one of those moments that would change my life.

I took the elevator up to the fifth floor and found my way to his room. As I turned the corner there was a nurse coming out of 523.

"Excuse me, I'm looking for Chuck Harris." She asked if I was a relative and I told her that I was his cousin.

"Only immediate family, I don't make the rules," she said in a matter-of-fact way, "You'll have to speak to the doctor."

"Please, I drove up from Harrisburg to see my cousin, just for a few minutes."

She looked at me and said, "He probably wouldn't even know you're there. He's been in and out of a coma since he got here, and I just gave him a sedative. He's going to be fine someday, but he needs to recuperate."

"Can I ask, if he's in a coma, why do you have to give him a sedative?"

"Because when he does come out, he comes out yelling and extremely agitated. It must have been hell over there. You can look in on him, but not for long."

She walked away without another word. I pushed the door open slowly and parted the curtain surrounding the bed. It didn't look like Chuck lying in that bed, hooked up to two IVs, his eyes closed and looking peaceful. I pulled over the chair that was in the corner to sit by the bed. There were get well cards everywhere, and the room was full of flowers. There was a picture of his family by the bed. Outside the snow was falling softly, light and fluffy.

I sat there for a minute and stared at the person lying in the bed, for a moment not even sure it was the same Chuck Harris that I grew up with. He looked different; his face had an ashen tint to it, and an uneven and scrubby beard covered his once smooth and clean-cut face. All in all, he looked like shit. What happened to my friend? I reached out slowly and touched his shoulder, and spoke softly.

"Hey, pal, how you doing? It's me, Chuck, it's Jerry. Can you hear me?" I sat there for what seemed like forever and just stared at my old friend. "Chuck, remember me? I used to be your best friend." The monitors above the bed showed his heart rate and blood pressure, both holding steady. I reached out and touched his hand; it felt cold and clammy.

I thought back to when we were kids together back in Selinsgrove. Chuck was a real superstar in school. He was one of those kids that did everything and did it well. He played football, basketball, baseball, he was good at everything. He was always the captain and no matter what, when it came to picking teams, he always picked me first. That's the way it was and everybody knew it. If Chuck was there, then I was there, and it was no surprise to anyone that when I went into the water to try to save that father and son, it was Chuck who pulled me out and saved my life.

Chuck was my best friend, the kind that would be there for you in the good times and the bad times. There's a special friendship that's like no other when you're in your early teens. It was my fault that we lost touch, I should have tried harder, and I decided right then that I would try harder. I pulled my chair closer and put my mouth close to his ear.

"Chuck, wake up, sport. It's Jerry."

It scared the hell out of me when suddenly his eyes opened and looked directly at me. But it was like he didn't really see me. He started to turn and squirm, and it seemed like he was going into a minor convulsion. As suddenly as he started moving, that's how suddenly he stopped. That's when I noticed a strange tattoo on his upper arm. He lay there, eyes still open, looking at nothing and breathing fast and shallow.

I turned his arm gently and pushed up the sleeve of his shirt to get a look at the tattoo. It looked like a butterfly. I thought that it was strange that a guy like Chuck would ever get a tattoo of a butterfly, but as I looked closer, I noticed that the butterfly had teeth and claws. I sat and looked at Chuck and thought about how different he looked; it had only been about four years, but his eyes looked different. They weren't the happy, carefree eyes that I remembered. I always thought that it was fascinating how much you can tell about a person when you look into their eyes. There was no brightness in Chuck's eyes anymore. His eyes looked mean, or maybe just sad. He was sweating, his skin was clammy, and then his eyes focused and he looked at me and said, "What the fuck you looking at?"

I was startled and said the first thing that came to mind. "Nothing, Chuck! I just came to see how my old friend was doing. I heard that you were home and I figured I'd come on up and see you."

Chuck just kept staring and then he said, "Who the fuck are you anyway?"

"Chuck, it's me, Jerry, you remember me from Selinsgrove. We were best buddies. You saved my life in the river, remember?"

He closed his eyes and his body starting twitching. He was scratching his skin with his left hand almost like his skin was crawling with ants, and he was sweating like crazy. I sat next to my old friend and tried to remember the way it used to be. Good friends are hard to come by, and I felt a tear rolling down my cheek. I don't remember ever crying before; in my family men don't cry. What had happened to my friend? I just sat there staring at him, not knowing what to do. After a few minutes, I figured maybe it was time to go. I got up and started for the door, but turned when Chuck groaned, a low sound. I walked back. His eyes were wide open and staring into space and he started talking. I thought he was talking to me and went to his bed.

"No fucking way, I'm not going shoot the guy because he won't sell you his fucking daughter. There's thousands more young girls out there, this one's not so special. I'm not going to kill him because he won't give up his kid."

His eyes closed right after and he lay there unmoving again. I sat there, looking into his face. I didn't understand what he meant. The door opened and the nurse came in.

"Time to go, son," she said, as she walked over to the bed.

"Sure," I said. "No problem. How's he doing?"

She looked at me like I was an idiot and said, "As good as possible while going through drug withdrawal and recuperating from getting shot in the back of the head. I guess he's doing great. It's really time for you to leave."

"Just a few more minutes, please."

She looked at me, shook her head, and said, "I'll be back in five minutes, then you're gone. You can come back at one, during visiting hours, like everybody else."

The nurse left and I reached out to hold Chuck's hand. At first there was no response and then I felt his strong grip and then suddenly, my friend was back, really back. He smiled at me and closed his eyes as a tear formed in the corner of them.

"Jerry," said Chuck. "I can't believe you're here. They fucked me up, they forced me to do some really bad stuff. I didn't want any part of their shit. They wanted me to kill the parents and grab the kid. I'm okay with the other shit, but not this. I got into some deep shit over there. They promised me so much, told me everything was okay and by the time I figured it out, it was too late and they wouldn't let me out. It was John, that bastard. I know that it was him that tried to kill me. Don't let them get away with this, Jerry. You got to help me stop those guys."

"What guys are you talking about, Chuck? Who wouldn't let you out?"

"Big John. I'm going to tell everyone what's going on over there, I've got to stop them. We're supposed to be over there to help people."

Just like that, he fell back to sleep again. His eyes closed and he was gone. I sat there trying to understand what I had heard, and then the nurse walked in and told me I had to leave. I walked out of the room and toward the elevators. I knew that something unbelievable had happened to my old friend.

Chuck had been a deeply religious kid. He was an altar boy and never missed church on Sundays. This kid would sooner die than take the Lord's name in vain; there's no way he would shoot someone in cold blood. Why would you kill a guy for his daughter? The whole thing didn't make any sense to me. Must be the drugs they had him on in the hospital. What did the nurse mean when she said that he was going through withdrawal? Chuck was as straight as they come when we were kids.

As I walked down the hallway, the nurse was coming out of another room.

"Thanks for letting me spend some time with Chuck, I really appreciate it," I said to her, and turned and left. I was coming back to talk with Chuck at 1:00. So many questions and only my old friend had the answers.

The snow had been falling for more than an hour, and the path leading to the parking lot was covered with the bright pristine early morning flakes. I stopped and leaned my head back. The cool snowflakes fell on my face. I got to my car and turned on the windshield wipers.

It was then that I noticed the two military guys standing a few cars away. Instinctively, I smiled and nodded as I put the key into the ignition. The car started up and I turned my head to back out of the space. When I turned around the two men were gone. I didn't give it a thought, after all this was a VA hospital. I headed into town to grab an early lunch and do some thinking.

I planned to go back to see Chuck at 1:00 and find out what the hell he'd been talking about. I was going to get that interview. Then I thought: the hell with the interview. This wasn't about getting an interview with my name on it for the paper, this was about finding out what happened to my childhood best friend. I went into a diner and found the pay phones next to the men's room. I called my boss to tell him that the story was deeper than we'd thought, and I was going to stick around for the day to talk to Chuck Harris some more after visiting hours began. I killed time by going back over happy memories from our youth.

The waiting room was on the fifth floor, down the hall from the rooms, and I could hear talking and some crying as I walked past. I figured somebody must have just died and I looked straight ahead; I didn't want to interfere with their grief. I asked the nurse what was going on and she told me that Chuck Harris had died that morning.

"What are you talking about? I saw him this morning, not more than three hours ago! He was okay; he seemed okay. What happened for God's sake? They told me he was stable. What could have happened in three hours? How's this possible?"

"You were here this morning? Who are you?" asked the nurse.

"What do you mean, who am I? What's that have to do with anything?"

"Just wait here a second," she said. "I have to go get somebody."

I walked over to the waiting room and leaned against the door. I saw Chuck's mom and dad and Brian Harris.

Brian was Chuck's younger brother, a couple of years younger. Brian walked over to me at the door and said, "You're Jerry, Chuck's friend. I remember you." We shook hands. "You work for the newspaper, don't you? Can we talk for a second? I need to tell you something."

"Brian, I am so sorry. What the fuck happened? I was just here this morning."

I noticed then that everyone in the room was looking at me, but pretending not to, staring out of the corners of their eyes. The two military men that I had seen in the parking lot were now talking to Chuck's father. I felt a tap on my shoulder.

"We need to talk to you." It was a man in a suit standing in the hallway, the nurse right behind him.

"Who are you?" I asked.

"I'm the guy with the badge, Detective John Brown. I need your name and address, just for the record."

"Hold on," I said. "Why do you need my name and address? What's going on here?"

The detective looked up from his notepad and smiled coldly. "So that's the way it's going to be. I ask the questions and you answer back with another question."

"Fine," I handed him my card. "I'm a reporter with the Harrisburg Times. I was sent up to interview Chuck Harris. So now that you know who I am, could you please tell me what it is that we have to talk about?"

Brian was still standing there with a strange expression on his face. I turned toward him and said, "We will talk later, definitely." Brian just nodded and walked back into the waiting room.

"Let's go over here and sit down," said the detective. "I need to ask you some questions." He sat in a chair in the hallway.

"Fine, ask your questions."

"Let's just start from the beginning," said the detective. "Why were you up here this morning? Visiting hours were in the afternoon. You told the nurse that you were a cousin, but we know you're not a cousin. What's going on here?"

"I'm a reporter for the Harrisburg Times, *I was sent up to interview Chuck. And in case you don't already know, we were good friends. I came here to see my friend and to talk to him about what happened over there. The nurse told me I had to leave and come back at 1:00. That's it, there's nothing more to tell, I swear. Now please, what happened?"*

"Look, kid, this is what I know. You walked into Chuck Harris's room about nine this morning after telling the nurse you're his cousin from Harrisburg. But ten minutes after you leave his room, the nurse comes to check on how he's doing and finds him dead. She sees that the IV with the morphine drip is turned all the way open but he's been in a coma most of the time or totally out of it. He's dead from a morphine overdose, and we think somebody killed him. We need the autopsy to complete the investigation, but that's what we think happened. So why don't you save us a lot of trouble and go easy on yourself and tell me what really happened."

"Detective, I don't know what the hell you're talking about. I work for the Harrisburg Times, *I was sent up by my boss. Call him and he'll tell you. I figured Chuck would be okay talking to*

me, we were real close friends. I had to tell the nurse that I was his cousin or she wouldn't let me in."

Detective Brown seemed almost understanding, even sympathetic in a way, and he put his hand on my shoulder. I shrugged it off and said, "All I did was try to talk to Chuck, and I swear that's all, nothing else. Look, if you're accusing me of killing Chuck Harris, then go ahead and arrest me, because if you're not, then I need to go back to work. I have a story that needs telling."

"Fine," said Brown. "Just stay close to home. We're going to find out what happened here today and we're going find out fast."

I thought of going to pay my respects but didn't want to intrude. I was anxious and confused and a bit overwhelmed. I couldn't believe Chuck was dead. I figured it was better to head home and try to get my head around all of this.

I started down the hall, when I heard someone calling me. "Jerry, hold on." It was Brian. "I need to show you something, but not here, not now. How about later today, back home. I'll meet you at the Friendly's in Selinsgrove."

"Sure, Brian, no problem, how about 4:00 p.m.?"

"Okay, good," said Brian. "I'll see you at 4:00. I got to get back to my family. I'll see you later."

I grabbed Brian by the arm and said, "You know that I had nothing to do with this. Your brother was the best friend I ever had. I'm sorry."

Brian looked at me and said, "You don't have to tell me that, I know that. I got to go. See you later."

Walking out to the car, I looked toward the sky and let the fresh snowfall on my face. Just as I put the key into the car door, I felt a sharp blow across my right shoulder. I fell against the car, sliding down, and somebody grabbed me under my arms, pulled me up, spun me around, and threw me against the car. The door opened, and I was tossed into the back. The two soldiers I had seen earlier got in the car with me.

"Relax, if we were going to kill you, you'd already be dead, so just calm down and relax. We're not going to hurt you, just want to have a man-to-man talk."

"What the fuck do you want?" I asked. I was breathing hard.

"Look," the bigger guy said. "We're going to ask you some really simple questions. You can handle a few simple questions, can't you?"

"What the fuck? What's going on? Who are you guys?"

"We're friends of Chuck Harris, and we want to know what you were doing there this morning and what you told that cop."

"I told the cop that I work for a newspaper and was sent up here to do a story, but that Chuck was totally out of it. Like in a coma, that's why I came back to get the interview this afternoon."

He looked hard at me and said, "Okay, kid, makes sense. Sorry about the slap on the back. I get carried away with my emotions, got to work on that. You know we're real sensitive about Chuck Harris." He turned and moved closer to me, and said in a low voice, "Be careful what you write. You go ahead and tell a story, but it better be about a young kid from central Pennsylvania who went off to fight for his country. It better be about a hero who came home to be with his family and friends, and paid the ultimate sacrifice. Are you reading me loud and clear?"

"The cops think I had something to do with Chuck overdosing."

"Don't you worry about that, Jerry, old pal. You didn't have anything to do with it. Chuck turned up the morphine himself. Even wrote a goodbye note. You write your story, but make damn sure that the story you tell will make his parents proud. Do we understand each other?"

They got out of the car, then the one who had been doing all the talking leaned back in and said, "You can go. This little visit is just between us, right?"

I managed to nod my head and he slammed the door. I watched them go and then moved to the front seat and started up my car and got the hell out of there. How did they know my name? What hell was going on?

I needed to get home. My hands were shaking on the steering wheel. I had wanted action but not this much.

The drive back to Selinsgrove took forever, the traffic slowed down to a crawl going down Route 44. I didn't go straight home, I didn't want Kate to see me like this. She would know something was up, and what could I tell her? I pulled into the parking lot at Friendly's and waited for Brian to show up.

When I saw him walk up to the entrance, I got out of my car.

"Hey, Brian. God, I'm sorry about your brother."

"Yeah," said Brian. "Jerry, I need to ask you a question."

"Come on, Brian, I told you that I had nothing to do with what happened to Chuck."

"No, no, of course I know that. But did Chuck say some strange things to you this morning?"

"What you mean?"

"Did Chuck say anything to you this morning?"

"Yeah, but he was delirious, he was talking crazy."

"Maybe. What did he say?"

"Something about two guys wanting him to kill somebody for his daughter. It didn't make any sense to me."

"What else did he say? Come on, please, man, what else did my brother say?"

"That's it, Brian, I swear. The nurse came in and threw me out. What's going here?"

"I don't know, but I'm telling you, man, something is very fucked up here. They're telling us that Chuck overdosed on purpose, turned off the safety switch on the IV. There's no fucking way that happened, man. Chuck loved life. There's no fucking way he would kill himself. Something happened in 'Nam. My brother was with some real badass guys. He wrote me about this unit that he got himself involved in and about this guy, someone named Big John. Look, I'm no goddamn detective, but my brother was into some heavy shit, and I got a feeling that this was no accident. My brother didn't kill himself, no fucking way."

I stared at Brian and for a moment thought about simpler times, better times. "Brian, if Chuck didn't kill himself, then who do you think did?"

"I'm not sure, but I think it must have been those two soldiers. Who else could have done it? All I know is, Chuck didn't kill himself."

"You still got those letters, Brian?"

"Yeah, I got them."

"You think maybe I could take a look at them?"

"I came right here from the hospital, they're at my house. I got to get back, my mom is real bad and my dad just sits there, *doesn't say a word. I'm worried about them. I'll bring the letters down in the morning, how about 7:00 a.m. at Dunkin' Donuts?"*

"Look, I think you're right about those two soldiers, something is up with those guys. I don't know who they are either. I think you should stay away from them. They roughed me up in the parking lot a little after I left you. They are two dangerous motherfuckers."

"What do mean?" said Brian.

"It was no big deal, but you should still stay clear of those two. It's been a long day for everybody, you should be with your parents right now."

"Okay, I'll see you in the morning," said Brian, and we both left.

I didn't want to tell Kate much about what happened, and after a lousy night's sleep, I pulled into the Dunkin' Donuts parking lot just before 7:00 the next morning. I got a cup of coffee and waited for Brian. By 7:30 I was getting disappointed and a little nervous. Maybe something had come up. I'm sure his parents were a mess. I understood, but I figured that Brian would call me when he could.

Eventually I gave up waiting and went outside. I heard a distant sound; soon it got louder. It was a siren.

"Must be a big accident on 44, those crazy kids come flying down that road, still slippery from the snow last night," some guy standing next to me said.

"Yeah," I answered and walked to my car.

Jesus Christ, something's wrong here, my gut was telling me. I headed the opposite direction of the sirens, toward Harrisburg.

Better just to get to the office and see if I could do a bit of research on the story I was now going to write. See if I can make sense of what Chuck said, or tried to say. But what if the answers to my questions were what got Chuck killed? What if I was next?

First things first, track Brian down. I called the Harris house.

"Mr. Harris, this is Jerry," I said, when a man answered.

"No, son, this is Father Jonas."

"Hi, Father, I'm Jerry McGinnis, a friend of Chuck's. Is Brian around? I was supposed to see him this morning, but I guess something came up. Is he there?"

"Jerry," said Father Jonas in a halting and sorrowful voice. "Brian's dead, son. He was killed in a car accident on the highway this morning at around 7. I'm sorry, son. I'll give John your regards."

I could feel my hand grip the phone, staring straight ahead, seeing nothing, feeling nothing; a sense of numbness came over me. I sat there in shock.

"Can I speak to Mr. Harris, Father? It's important."

"I don't think that I can get him on the phone right now, I'm sorry. Why don't you call back this afternoon and maybe he'll talk to you."

I put the phone back in the cradle. Fuck, the poor Harris family, two sons gone. A sense of guilt started building in my gut. How could I help fix this nightmare? What happened to Chuck in Vietnam? Was Brian's death connected to Chuck's? The answers must lie in Vietnam, where it all started. My mind started turning. I could go there. I should go there. There was one hell of a story here, and it fell in my lap. I could find the truth, and find out what killed my childhood best friend.

143

I needed to talk to someone who would understand it all and help me figure this out. Bill Mullen had been a great boss at the paper, and I wondered if he was still an active Lieutenant Colonel in the National Guard in Harrisburg. He could help me join up and get assigned to a specific job in the army, and then get shipped over to Vietnam. I couldn't even think about what Kate would say. It seemed like I had only one choice.

Sean put the notebook down and looked at his brother.

"This shit is getting real," he said. "What the fuck was going on? I can't believe this story."

Jack looked exhausted, but he wasn't ready to stop. "Keep reading. What's next?"

CHAPTER 13

*T*he next day, the four of us drove down to Harrisburg to go to the wake, my parents joining Kate and me. My dad remembered Chuck well from our childhood. I stood at the entrance to the main room and for a moment I couldn't move. I stared at the two mahogany caskets, brothers side by side. Wakes for older people are very different than for young people. Children are not supposed to die before their parents, and I could hear the sobbing. The grief in the room was smothering and after a while I couldn't bear it.

"Dad, I need to talk to you. Mom and Kate are talking to the Harrises, let's take a walk."

"Jerry," said my dad. "You okay?"

"To tell you the truth, no, I'm not okay, I'm not anywhere close to being okay. I don't know how and I don't know why, but those two boys are dead and I think that somehow I played a part in this."

"Hold on, Jerry," he said. "I don't know what the hell you're talking about but you didn't have a thing to do with those boys' deaths."

"Dad, listen to me for a few minutes and I'll tell you what I'm talking about." We both stood up and walked out of the chapel. There was a bench outside the office. I told my father the whole story. There was a chill in the air as the sun went down and dusk was moving over the Pennsylvania countryside.

"So, you're going to the cops to tell them what you just told me, right?" asked my dad. "That's what you do, and then you're done, you're finished with this shit. You aren't responsible for their deaths. Look, son, I want you to stay clear of those guys."

"Dad," I said, "forget about it. They probably wouldn't believe me, anyway, they'd think I am making it up to get a story out of this tragedy. They are local cops, they won't care what's happening halfway around the world. And even if they do take me seriously, it is only going to upset the Harrises and that's out of the question. Dad, I've given this a lot of thought and the only way I'm going to find the answer is to go to Vietnam myself."

Dad stood up and turned to look me dead in the eye. "Look, son, I know you're upset, you just lost your oldest friend and his brother and you're not thinking clearly. You and I are going back into the chapel, pay our respects to the Harrises, and then we're all going home and that's that." He turned and headed for the chapel. "Are you coming?"

"Yeah, I'm coming, Dad."

Tom Harris sat in the first row just a few yards from the caskets of his two sons. On his left was Father Jonas, on his right was his wife. I could feel their grief. It was hard to breathe as I knelt down in front of Tom Harris. "Mr. Harris," I said softly. "Mr. Harris, it's Jerry, Jerry McGinnis." Tom Harris sat there with his head bent into his hands.

I couldn't get any more words to come; I just knelt there with my head bent low feeling the tears in my eyes. Tom Harris softly put his hand on my head. There was nothing to be said right then. I stood up and held onto Mr. Harris's hand and said, "Mr. Harris, I sure would like to come up and visit you and Mrs. Harris, would that be okay? Things don't make sense. Chuck said some things to me before he died."

"Jerry, listen to me, please." He grabbed hold of my wrist like a vise grip. "Jerry, Chuck was out of his mind, he was talking crazy. It was nothing, you hear me, Jerry? I want you to forget whatever you heard. Now please, go home and forget it." I said goodbye and left, thinking hard about what had happened in the last two days.

The morning after the wake, I got out of bed around 5:30 to make a cup of coffee. I sat at the table trying to understand what had happened and what I was supposed to do. Maybe I should just mind my own business; maybe I should listen to my father.

Maybe this is going to be the biggest fuck-up of my life, but it was my life and this was my chance to do something that really mattered. I put my cup in the sink, grabbed my coat and keys, and walked out of the house, leaving Kate and the boys asleep.

I drove straight down to Harrisburg. Brian's car didn't go off the road by itself, this was no accident. I didn't know why, but my gut told me that somebody killed Chuck and Brian and I was sure that those two soldiers had everything to do with their murders. I was as mad as I had ever been. This had become more than a story; it was now about revenge. They killed my best friend.

Bill Mullen sat behind the old mahogany editor's desk that every editor since the founding of the paperback in 1926 had sat behind. He'd been a friend to our family for years. Mullen had been the editor of the Harrisburg Times *for just two years and had been brought in to make significant changes in the paper's format. He had always seen himself as a bit of a maverick, and pissed some folks off. He didn't give a shit. If they didn't like the way he was running things, they could just kiss his ass and get the fuck out.*

Bill was going over copy that came in over the wire late Sunday; he looked larger than life sitting behind his desk, even though he stood only 5'6". His trim and fit body, the result of his days in the Army and an obsession with working out, gave you the impression that this man was driven.

Bill looked up, took his wire-rimmed glasses off, and said, "Shame about those two boys. I don't know how a parent can go on after losing both sons."

"Bill, I need to tell you something and I need your help." I wanted to get right to the point.

"If I can help you, you know I will. What's on your mind, Jerry?"

"I knew Chuck Harris, he was an old friend. I knew his brother, Brian. Bill, those two guys were murdered and the answer has to be in Vietnam. I need you to get me there working as a reporter. I need to find out why they were murdered."

Bill put down the red marker he was using to edit the copy he was working on and said, "Hold on, sport. I don't know what the hell you're talking about, but if you want to start from the beginning, I'm here to listen."

I sat down in front of that big editor's desk, and told Bill the whole story. Bill leaned forward but said nothing. He always said, "You can't learn a damn thing by talking, only by listening."

I stood up and paced back and forth. "But there is something else. When I was leaving the hospital, in the parking lot these two military guys grabbed me and threw me in the back of the car. They asked me what Chuck had said to me. They told me that Chuck had killed himself and I shouldn't get involved. I had seen them in the morning as well, even before I went in to see Chuck the first time."

Bill finally had a question. "What did you tell them?"

"Nothing. I told them that I was sent up here to interview Chuck, but that he was totally out of it. I told them that he didn't say a word. Then they told me that I better keep my mouth shut about Chuck. Then Brian told me later about the letters—I believe that there's something really serious going on here."

"You've got to get your hands on those letters. You have any idea where they are now?"

"I'll get my hands on those letters." I sat back down. "But really, the answers to all this shit are in Vietnam, not here. The police aren't going to do anything, there's no way in hell they're going to investigate this. One soldier dead from suicide, and one more kid killed in a car accident. Look, I got my personal reasons for finding out who killed Chuck and Brian, but besides that, this could be the biggest story of the year. This isn't about two brothers getting killed, I think this is about some really bad shit going on in Southeast Asia."

"Look, kid, I know you're upset. This guy was a good friend, and I'm sure you feel bad. Listen to me, Jerry, I think you're sticking your head in a fucking bees nest and you're going to get stung. In any case, I can't just send you off to Vietnam to write a story. What do you think this is, the New York Times? You

want to go to Vietnam, then sign up, serve your country. Tell you what, if you sign up and go over there, I'm pretty sure I can get you assigned to an administrative job writing a newsletter and reports. This could be real dangerous. Whatever you do, you've got to be able to prove it, all of it."

I walked over to the window that looked over the Susquehanna and stared. I couldn't take my eyes off the river, it brought back memories. Bill walked over and put his hand on my shoulder.

"Jerry, please, think about this. You have a family and a good job."

"I appreciate what you're saying, boss, but this is something I have to do. I only got one real serious problem." I turned from the window and looked at Bill and said, "How the hell am I going to tell my wife?"

Bill smiled at me. "Tell her that you got some inside information that you were getting drafted soon and that if you enlisted first, the paper could see to it that you got a job that would keep you far away from the front lines. She'll never know. But you still have to talk to your dad. I can't imagine that he is going to be all right with this. If you get him to agree, then I will back your decision."

I left Bill's office and headed down the hall to my dad's office. He was city editor and although he would never make editor in chief at this point, he was well respected and ready to retire.

I knocked on his door and went in. He looked up and asked, "Did you talk to Bill about the Harris boys? What does he think?"

"He thinks he can get me assigned to an office job as a journalist if I enlist."

"Are you seriously thinking of going to Vietnam to investigate what happened? You understand the risk you are taking; you have a wife and kids. Jerry, I'm asking you, please don't get mixed up with whatever is going on here. It's starting to scare the hell out of me."

We sat down on the couch in the corner of the room and Dad put his arm around my shoulder. "Dad," I told him, "I had something to do with what happened to Brian and Chuck, I'm sure as Christ, but I don't know what." I stood up. "I've got to go."

Dad grabbed my arm. "Jerry, you need to get your head back to work. Pray if you like, that's about all you can do for the Harris's."

"I'm past the praying stage," I said as I left the office. I wanted to go sit by the river. It would calm me down, it always had. The river just keeps on flowing, no matter what happens. Chuck pulled me out of that river.

I drove home and pulled the car into my parents' driveway and made my way down to our boulder. I sat and silently made a promise to Chuck. I would find out what happened to him and his brother. I wouldn't just walk away.

I walked into the U.S. Army recruiting office later that morning. Bill Mullen had already called and let them know I was coming. I was enlisting with a request to be a public relations officer. Two hours later I walked out with a stack of papers. I was told I would be receiving information in the mail in about two weeks. I would be leaving for boot camp in North Carolina in about three weeks and then off to Vietnam. I wasn't sure about the timing but I was sure of one thing and that was how Kate would react when I told her what I had just done.

There was a time, perhaps a simpler time, when a drive home from the office was nothing more than a drive home from the office. As I headed up Route 44 toward Selinsgrove, I was wrapped up in what I had just done and the impact on my family. A sense of guilt at first ran through my mind and then excitement about what I would find out there.

The traffic was slowed to stop-and-go for the last mile and I pulled off the main road and parked the car and sat there looking at the river. For a moment I wished I could take it back; too fucking late now. I needed time to think, time to figure out what I was going to tell Kate.

The sky was gray when I pulled up at the house and I knew it would get dark early. I walked up to the front door. It was unusually quiet; the kids weren't there to run up and give me a hug.

"Kate, are you home?" There was no answer. I walked into the small den and stood there looking at Kate lying on the couch, fast asleep. I reached over and touched her on her shoulder and said in a quiet voice, "Kate, honey, are you all right? Where are the kids?"

She woke up to my touch. "The kids are at my mother's, I have a terrible headache. Why don't you go get the boys? I'll have dinner ready when you get back."

"I'll take them to the diner, don't worry about dinner."

I turned and walked out and got back into the car. When I pulled up in front of Kate's parents' home, the boys were playing in the front yard. I got out of the car and the boys ran to me. I knelt down and hugged them to me. I couldn't let them go; I felt the tears welling up and slowly sliding down my checks.

After a moment I said, "Where's your grandmother?"

Before they could answer, Kate's mom opened the door and said, "Hi, Jerry. Want to come in?"

"No, that's okay. I'm going to take the boys out for dinner. Kate's got a little headache and I figured I'd give her some rest."

I ordered food for the boys and a coffee for me at the diner. I didn't feel hungry; maybe Kate and I would have dinner later while Jack and Sean were watching TV. Then I could tell her. I rehearsed the lines over and over again in my mind while the kids ate their fries and grilled cheese sandwiches.

I knew that during the last few years things had changed between us. Of course, I loved Kate, but a deep void had opened between us. I wanted something more, she didn't. Why should she? Kate was complete and content with her life, I was the one always looking down the road, still searching.

On the way home we passed Christ Methodist Church, where we were married. Life seemed so simple in those days. I was sure I loved Kate, but I also knew that it had always been a love of convenience and routine. Getting married right after high school seemed like the natural and expected thing to do. Now I had done something unexpected. Now I just need the courage to tell Kate.

I pulled into the driveway, the two boys jumped out and ran into the house. "Why's mommy sleeping? It's so early," said Sean. I stared at Kate lying on the coach fast asleep again at 6:30 in the evening.

"Mom's got a headache, so why don't you two run upstairs and get into your pajamas and you can watch TV in our bed."

They did as they were told and I sat down in my chair. Only the glimmer of light from the TV cast shadows into the darkness of our small den. The national news would come on in a few minutes.

Kate was sleeping soundly; I sat there trying to find the words that would make this a simple and painless moment. I hoped she would support my decision, but knew that she wouldn't. The reporter was talking about Senator Robert Kennedy criticizing President Johnson's decision to resume the bombing in Vietnam and said that the U.S. was headed "on a road from which there is no turning back, a road that leads to catastrophe for all mankind." This war was going to be a turning point for this country and for me.

Kate lifted her head and smiled. "Hi, what time is it?"

"About 6:30," I smiled back.

"Where are the kids? Did you eat?"

"We went to the diner. They're upstairs watching TV. Kate, I need to tell you something."

Kate looked up, blinked her eyes to try to stay awake. "What do you need to tell me?" She smiled and said, "I know, you have another family on the other side of town and you finally got up the guts to ask for a divorce." I stared at her, bewildered. Then Kate broke out laughing. "I'm kidding, you jerk! Seriously," she said, "what's going on?"

"I've got to find out why Chuck and Brian were killed, I owe it to them." Kate stared at me. "I need to go out of town for a while and find out why Chuck and his brother were killed."

"What the hell are you talking about?" she said.

"Kate, I know that this is going to sound crazy, but the only way to get this story told is for me to go to Vietnam, so I signed up today. I'm going to Vietnam, but it's just for one year and besides I just found out that I was about to be drafted anyway. This way I'm able to get a job in the back lines away from the fighting. I have to go. It's the only way to find the truth."

Kate lifted herself off the sofa and stared at me.

"Is this a joke? Are you out of your fucking mind? You're not signing up to go anywhere. You'll find all the truth there is to find right here with your family, with us. Now please stop talking like this, you're starting to scare me. What do you want for dinner? I have some hamburger patties I got from the supermarket." She stood and I rose and went to her.

"I already enlisted. I'm scheduled to leave for Parris Island in about three weeks. I'm there for two months and then I'll be assigned to the Administrative Department of Public Affairs. Look, the guy told me I'd only be there for one year, maybe less. There's a story there that will change all of our lives—you, me, and the kids—and it's only for one year. Your parents will help you take care of the kids, don't worry. It will be fine."

Kate stared at me and tears welled up in her eyes. She put her face into her hands and began to cry. "Jerry, why didn't you tell me before you signed up? Why did you do this to us?"

"It's for all of you that I did this. I'll be back before Christmas, with what I think will be the biggest story of the war. I'm not going to spend my life in this small-time town writing stories about the local football team. This is our chance."

"You lying son of a bitch, this isn't about us, this is about you, it's always been about you. You found your way out, that's all you ever wanted, to find a way out." She was mad now, furious.

Kate ran upstairs. I sat back down. It didn't make sense to follow her now. It would be better to let things calm down a bit. Maybe she was right, maybe it was all about me. So be it. I got up and walked toward the stairs; the kids still needed a bath. This was my time with my two boys. I sat on the edge of the bath while Sean and Jack played in the bathtub. Kate would come to understand what I had done, why I needed to go to Vietnam. I would be home before Christmas. I wasn't the first father that went off to war to fight for his country, and I wasn't even going to do any fighting, and besides, there was a story that needed to be told.

Sean looked up and pushed the notebook to the side, his fingers moving slowly over the pages, feeling his father's thoughts and memories. He tried to concentrate, tried to feel what his father must have been thinking when he wrote this down. In almost a whisper he said, "Jesus Christ Almighty, I can't fucking believe what I'm reading here."

Jack had gotten up just before Sean had stopped reading and walked slowly over to the window. In the darkness, he could see his father coming alive on the pages of his notebooks. But he wasn't alive, he died over there, and his father was never coming home.

Jack turned from the window and walked back to the kitchen table where Sean was pulling out another notebook.

"This is the next one," he said. "Do you need a break? Feels like we are living in some time warp or something. Don't know what day it is, for Christ's sake. It is starting to feel creepy reading this shit."

Jack came back to the table and said, "I think I'm done for the night. I've got to get some rest. Yeah, I need a break."

The next morning after a light breakfast, Sean and Jack pulled out some old fishing tackle and went down to their old spot on the river. It was a bright, cool morning.

"What do you say we catch us some perch for dinner?"

"Sounds like a great idea," answered Jack. "I can hear him, his voice. I can hear him talking to us, just like we were back in our rooms. Can you hear him, Sean?"

Once they were seated on a rock with their lines bobbing in the river, they began to speak of the father they remembered and the man they were learning about. They were beginning to love their father again as they began to know him better. They had forgotten the feeling, but it seemed to be coming back, through his words. As boys, both Sean and Jack had wondered why. Why would he leave? Typed and handwritten words on old and tattered yellow pages could never make up for all the time they missed playing catch in the backyard, or watching the Phillies together on a Sunday afternoon, or sitting by the Susquehanna River, but right now it was all they had.

Jack said, as they sat on the river bank, "I don't remember much of those first years after Mom died. I remember you and Grandma coming up to the hospital, but the whole time I felt like I was in this thick cloud. I couldn't see your faces clearly, but I knew that you were there, and when you both left, I knew you were gone. After I went to live with the Smiths, I went through all kinds of crazy feelings. In the beginning I was always confused. I couldn't believe what was happening to me, I couldn't believe what had happened to me. After a while I gave up hoping that you guys would come back, and I just got mad and mean, all the time. Maybe that's why Smith beat the shit out of me. Maybe I wouldn't have blamed him. I was a fucking handful." Jack smiled.

Sean, staring at the river, said, "Anyone say anything? The teachers, the nurses, the neighbors—didn't anyone step up?"

Jack looked up with a puzzled expression on his thin, pale face, "No, I think they thought I was a troubled kid and they were glad it wasn't them that had to deal with me."

The two brothers turned back to the river, just as they had with their father and grandfather more than thirty years before. They sat for a long time, breathing in the mist of the Susquehanna; the smell, the sounds, the cool spray brought them back. At the same time, they turned to each other and smiled, a moment of solidarity together, as brothers.

"What do you want, Jack? To find the truth? And when we do, is it for revenge? 'Cause I got to tell you, Jack, that's one big fucking leap. I know I didn't go through what you went through, but I've thought about what happened to us and our parents all my life. But this is different now; we aren't kids anymore. What are we going to do?"

"I didn't go looking for this, trust me, Sean, it all found me. I'm heading straight for hell. I know that. You don't have to get involved, but I'm taking this to the end and if the end is nowhere, then so be it. I have to give it a shot, because I still remember the look on mom's face. It will haunt me till the day I die."

SECTION II

CHAPTER 14

Saigon, Fall 1969

Jerry McGinnis came out of Special Training Camp with a rank of Specialist 5th class. He was transferred to Fort Henry right outside of Philadelphia, and then on October 12, along with 200 other young men, boarded a chartered airline and began the flight to Vietnam.

Young men from all over the States, many who had never before been out of the town they were born and raised, strapped themselves in for the long flight that would change their lives. The first stop was in California for refueling. They weren't let off the plane. They sat there for almost four hours; maybe the brass figured if they let them off the plane, some wouldn't come back. They got under way around midnight, twelve and half more hours to 'Nam. They were heading for Tan Son Nhut Air Base, right outside of a town called Long Bin about sixteen miles north of Saigon. Jerry tried like hell to get some sleep; *the more you try the harder it is,* he thought to himself.

Some of the guys wrote letters, some slept; they were the lucky ones. The rest of the new recruits just sat there lost in thought. Those close to the small windows stared out as they glided through the dark and cloudless night over the vastness of the ocean below.

Jerry must have dozed off. The pilot's voice startled him from the comfortable familiar dream. He smiled to himself; it had felt so real, seeing the mist coming off the Susquehanna, even a slight chill.

"Buckle up, boys. We're landing in thirty minutes. Cabin crew, prepare for landing."

The sun was low in the hazy sky as the Air America charter plane began its final approach. Jerry strained to make out the countryside below, but the clouds were thick and gray; it almost seemed like you could land the plane on top of them.

Jerry looked around; he could feel the tension, the fear, mixed with a sense of excitement. Some of the young men held back the tears by putting their heads down into their hands, hiding the terror that they all felt, but not his buddy Tony Ramo. Tony looked like he didn't have a care in the world, as cool as a cucumber. Maybe he hid it better than everyone else, or maybe he just didn't give a shit. Either way, there was a smile that seemed out of place, but it was there nevertheless.

Jerry turned back to the small window. He strained his eyes, nothing but gray and dark clouds. Then in what seemed like a flash, the ground was there, maybe a thousand feet below.

You could hear the gasps as the young and frightened boys got their first glance of the country below. They all strained to peer out of the windows, leaning over one another to get a look at Vietnam.

The landing was smooth; he could feel the tires bounce on the landing strip and quickly come to a stop.

"Welcome to Vietnam," came the voice on the loud speaker. "Take your time, boys, get your gear, don't leave anything behind, and good luck. Godspeed, gentleman, we're all proud of you."

The land around the air base was barren and scorched, like somebody had taken a blowtorch to it. It turned out to be for security purposes, they didn't want some hidden gook taking down a C-51 with an M-16.

Jerry's orders were to report to the 23rd Artillery group in Bien Hoa, which was part of the 105th Battalion. Colonel John Ramsey would assign him to his unit and brief him on his duties and assignments while in the country. He got directions from the sergeant handing out assignments and made his way to the office.

"Morning, Colonel. Specialist 5th Class McGinnis reporting for duty," said Jerry as he handed over his orders to the colonel.

The colonel took Jerry's orders and glanced over them and then looked up at Jerry.

"Okay, McGinnis, looks like somebody is watching over your shoulder, so I'll spell it out for you. You report to Phu Loi tomorrow morning and report to a Colonel Benton. Look kid, Benton's not a bad guy, but here's a little friendly advice: watch your ass. Benton wants real bad to become a general, and the only way a colonel gets to be a general is to see some action and get some big-time recognition and awarded commendations. Point I'm trying to make here is, don't get yourself shot trying to make him look good. You understand, McGinnis?"

"Yes, sir, loud and clear. Appreciate the heads-up, Colonel."

"Okay, McGinnis, take off and good luck. I see you got a wife and two kids. Did you actually enlist?"

"Yes, sir."

"Try to stay alive then, kid." Jerry stood up, saluted then turned and walked out of the colonel's office.

Jerry grabbed a ride with a couple of medics heading for Phu Loi and reported to Company Headquarters 23rd Military Group. Colonel Benton waved Jerry into his office and said, "McGinnis, you got a real smooth job for the next year. You'll write stories about the soldiers over here and send the stories back to the States to the local papers so the folks back home can hear what a good job their sons are doing over here." He put down the cigar he had been chewing on. "You'll report on our soldiers working with the locals to build clinics and schools. And every morning at 900 hours, you come to me and brief me on what's going on out there. By the way, tomorrow at 0900 we're taking a little ride in an LOH just inside of Cambodia to inspect the troops. Make sure that you bring that Nikkomat 35mm camera with you 'cause you're going to take lots of pictures. Matter of fact, McGinnis, when you're not reporting on all the wonderful things we're doing over here, you stick close to me and make sure you get plenty of pictures, you got that?"

"Loud and clear, sir, I got it," said Jerry.

"Okay, Public Information is in a Quonset hut just outside the gate to the airfield. You can find a desk there and a room where you can buck down. So, get settled in and I'll see you in the morning."

Jerry walked out of the colonel's office and asked where he could find the Public Information office. He walked over to the hut and knocked on the door and walked in. Steve Jacobs looked up from his desk and smiled.

"Come on in, soldier, the water's fine."

"Sorry," said Jerry, "what water?"

Steve Jacobs looked up with a bemused smile on his face, "You kidding, right?" He stood about 5'7", little overweight at 200 pounds. Jerry noticed that he wore a Star of David on a thin gold chain. "I'm Jacobs from New York."

Jerry smiled. He seemed like a nice guy. "Where about in New York," asked Jerry.

"The Bronx, know where that is?" said Steve.

"Heard of it, never been there, never been out of Pennsylvania."

"Well," said Steve. "You're a long fucking way from Philadelphia."

"Not from Philly; Selinsgrove, it's in the middle of the state." Jerry walked up to Jacobs and shook his outstretched hand.

"What brings you to this godforsaken country?"

"Serve my country, just like you."

"Yeah, right," said Jacobs. "Where you from?"

"I told you," said Jerry with a smile. He knew he was being played with.

"Oh yeah, you did, small town north of Harrisburg, right? South of Williamsport, Selinsgrove."

Jerry looked startled. "How the hell you know that?"

"Working on a case, can't get into it, classified. I'm a lawyer," Jacobs said with a grin. "I would tell you but then I would have to kill you." Jerry laughed and threw his gear on the bed next to the wall.

"You must be the new Public Information officer. Got the camera, going to take lots of pictures of the colonel, right?" said Jacobs.

"How did you know?" said Jerry.

"Listen, McGinnis, there is only one way for a colonel to become a general and that's with lots of exposure and you're the one going to do the exposing. Watch your ass, that old bastard will do anything to get those stars, and I mean anything."

"Yeah, that's what I've been told."

"What's your first assignment?"

"He wants to go into Cambodia and inspect the troops. I thought that we weren't even supposed to be in Cambodia."

"Yeah, right," said Jacobs. "This isn't Kansas, Dorothy, you'll see. There's a lot of shit going on over here that's not supposed to be happening, but it is. Hey, I could use a beer. I'll show you beautiful downtown Phu Loi and introduce you to all the lovely young girls that frequent the local bars, and if you're really a nice guy, I might even take you over to the Steam and Cream club."

"Is that what I think it is?" said Jerry.

"Yeah, you can get anything you like, whatever gets your weird on," said Jacobs with a grin.

"I have no idea what the hell you're talking about. Besides, I'm an old married man with a wife and two little kids."

"That don't matter," said Steve, with his heavy Bronx accent. "It's not like you're fucking the girl, you're just fucking the pussy."

"I don't see the difference," said Jerry. "The pussy is on the girl; therefore, you are in fact fucking the girl, not just the pussy."

Steve smiled, Jerry smiled.

"I see your point," said Steve, and for a moment they sat staring at each other, and then almost on cue, started to laugh.

"Look," said Steve, "you're missing the point. The pussy is the great equalizer. Think about the scale."

Jerry looked up and said, "Jesus, Jacobs, you've given this a lot of thought, haven't you? What scale are you talking about?"

"You're putting me on, right? You don't know what I'm talking about? The scale by which all girls are measured! Ten being a fucking goddess all the way down to two; there's no number one, nobody can be that ugly, not possible. Anyway, no matter how pretty or ugly the girl is, the pussy is the same... It makes them all exactly the same. Pure unadulterated equality, the foundation of our democratic world."

Jerry looked at Steve and said with a grin, "You are one crazy fucking guy, you know that, right? You got pussy on the brain."

"I know," said Steve. "If you don't mind me asking, I mean, you've got a wife and two kids, you could have got off in a heartbeat."

"I have my reasons," said Jerry. "I'll give you the whole rundown some other time, not now. Okay?" Steve smiled. Jerry said, "What's a Jewish lawyer from the Bronx doing in Vietnam?"

"I fucked up. I had it made; good family, NYU Law, nice practice, hot wife, the whole nine yards. But no matter how much I busted my ass, it was never enough, so like a real fucking idiot, I start moving money from my escrow account into my personal bank account. I always meant to put it back, it got out of hand." Steve smiled ruefully. "So I was given a choice by the judge. A real genuine motherfucker, the son of a bitch rips into me right in front of my parents, it was fucking humiliating. He gives me a choice: sign up and do your duty or I'll disbar your chubby little ass, huge fine and six months in Danbury Federal."

Jerry nodded, then smiled and said, "So you decided to come here."

Steve looked amused and said, "Nah, I chose Danbury, not even close. Motherfucker sent me here anyway."

Jerry looked at Steve. "Well, I guess we all have stories. Where did you say we can get a beer?"

"Stow your shit and follow me," said Steve.

His black hair was cut short and his glasses sat on the tip of his small nose. Jerry thought to himself, *he doesn't look Jewish*, but then Jerry didn't really know any other Jews. *He seems like a good guy.*

They drove Steve's army jeep into the small town and pulled up in front of a bar. Steve said hi to a few guys as they were sitting down, but didn't introduce Jerry.

"So, what's a nice kid like you doing enlisting in this fucked-up war?" Steve asked.

"I'll tell you the whole story, but not now. Tell you the truth, I'm feeling like a real shithead right now, I must have been out of my fucking mind. But I'm here now, so I guess I should try and make the best of a bad situation. What does the army need a lawyer for out here?" he asked.

"You kidding, right?" said Steve. "There's more illegal shit going on over here than all the crime in the States. This place is fucking hell, they send over millions of dollars in aid and half of it winds up on the black market. Drugs, prostitution, you got to know, Jerry, this place is like Dodge City in the old west. The U.S. government wants me to be the fucking sheriff, can you believe it? A Jew from New York, and they want me to investigate and bring charges on these fucking crazy bastards. These guys are carrying M-16s and would blow my head off as soon as look at me. Anyway, since my momma didn't raise no fool, I'm keeping my head out of the real bad shit and just work on the cases that hopefully won't get me going home in a body bag. Hey, enough of this shit, tell me about your wife and kids. I could use some good old home and family stories."

They finished their beers while Jerry showed him pictures of Kate and the boys. "Ready for another round?" Jerry asked.

"Not now, sport, I got some work to do back at the office. You going to stick around or you want a ride back?"

"I think I'll hang out here for a little while, get the feel of the land."

"Okay, bud, don't get yourself in any trouble," said Steve as he got up to leave.

"Yeah, right," said Jerry. "See you back at the hut." Steve turned and moved into the crowd and was gone. Jerry sat there quietly alone with what seemed like thousands of people walking past him. He closed his eyes for just a moment and tried to imagine being back home, where he should be. He could see Kate on the couch. He could hear his two boys upstairs playing. He began to doze and then a voice broke through.

"You okay, soldier?" asked the bar owner.

Jerry looked up, startled, and said, "Yeah, I'm fine."

"Okay, want another beer?"

"No, how much I owe you?" Jerry paid his tab and stood up and walked back to his new quarters.

The rain here is different than back home, Jerry thought as he lay awake on his cot. He listened to it pounding against the metal frame of the Quonset hut that he shared with Steve Jacobs. He heard Jacobs move restlessly in his cot. Jerry turned to the wall, listening to the rain pound against the window and then gracefully move down the rigid side of their hut, finally splashing into large buckets. He thought, *I'm in a country where they need to collect fresh rainwater into buckets for drinking. I must have been out of my mind, but I'm here now. I need to focus, I need to do what I came here to do.*

Steve was awake next to Jerry; sleep had become elusive for him as well as Jerry. They both came here under unorthodox circumstances. Both for different reasons, none of which had anything to do with the war. Steve was thinking about how a young soldier from Williamsport, Pennsylvania, whose MOS was Ballistic Meteorology had ended up with a bullet in his head and two in his chest. It was a fucking miracle that he had survived. Anyone else would have been DOA and Jacobs would have been filling out forms specifying a mugging gone bad. Instead, he had the whole damn office looking into the attack on Chuck Harris.

Steve thought about the statements that Dr. Stephanie Weil had given. She had detailed Harris' rambling talk and almost incoherent cries. Something about a shadow unit that operated throughout Southeast Asia, with multiple operations in the States and Europe. Hundreds of millions of dollars in economic and military aid pouring into Vietnam, diverted and marketed to the highest bidders.

What's the connection? thought Steve. *Harris had been stationed in Bien Hao to study weather conditions and the effects on ballistic missions throughout the region. So, this kid is stationed in a non-combat area and somehow ends up in an alleyway in downtown Saigon with three bullets in him; stomach, chest, and head. Miraculously he survives, and on the way to the hospital he starts talking about this unit that is into some pretty heavy shit. If only he had the good sense to die when he got shot, I could be tracking down some U.S. aid that somehow ended up on the black market. But no, this superstar had to survive, tell some crazy story, get sent home, and then he still ends up dead in a hospital room in the middle of Pennsylvania. What the hell was going on?*

"Wake up, sweet boy," said Steve.

Jerry turned slowly to the voice and said, "I am definitely not your sweet boy."

Steve Jacobs laughed out loud. "Just playing around," he said. "That's what my dad used to say." Both men smiled for just a moment, then a brief expression of regret crossed each face. Both had disappointed their fathers.

When it came right down to it, Jerry's dad was his best friend, the one man in his life that no matter what would always be there for him. He thought about the times they spent on the river, the quiet times, the cold times and the hot times and the laughing times. The memory of the river blurred the moment with Steve.

Lost in thought, Jerry could feel the warmth of the thermos that held his hot cocoa. Jerry sensed the common bond that he and Steve shared. Jerry looked up at his new friend and said, "My father used to tell me that there are two types of sons, those that spend their lives trying to live up to the expectations of their fathers and those that are always trying to make up for the sins of their fathers."

Steve's expression turned somber, pondering the disappointment that both his mother and father must have felt. "I'm afraid that I'm not living up to anyone's expectations. I guess I'll just keep working on it. Anyway," he continued, "what time you taking off?"

Jerry said, "I don't know exactly. The colonel said to be ready at 0900 and to not be late. He said we're going for a ride, check out the troops, and that I should bring my camera and my notepad. That's all I know, besides, if I told you any more, I would have to kill you."

They both smiled. "You be careful out there. Don't get yourself shot for that crazy bastard on your first day," warned Steve.

"Thanks for caring."

Jerry put out his hand, which Steve grabbed with a firm grip and said, "Seriously, Jerry, be careful. That bastard will scarify your ass in a New York second, just to get a good shot of him blowing some gook into two pieces."

Jerry smiled, and said, "I'll be careful. Friends are hard to come by in this neighborhood, wouldn't want you to lose one." He turned to the sink and began to shave.

"Just keep your head down. See you this afternoon, we'll go have a beer." Steve let the screen door slam as he went out.

Jerry finished up and headed down the road to the colonel's office. He could hear the AH-1 Cobra attack helicopter before he saw it. Eight guys were already packed in, ready to go. One of the gunners was loading the ammunition into the magazine box, another just hanging on to his M-16. This was one badass piece of machinery. The blades began to swirl, dust and dirt was everywhere.

Moments before they took off, Colonel Bentley was told that his troops, 100 miles inside of the Cambodian border, were being shelled and that the U.S. artillery couldn't spot where the shelling was coming from. He decided to fly over the enemy, locate their position even though it would put his team in harm's way, and send back the location of the shelling to save those troops.

The colonel had been briefed on Jerry McGinnis. He knew Jerry was a news reporter with *Stars and Stripes* and would have access to materials inside Army headquarters in downtown Saigon. The colonel wanted to keep him close; he might be a good source of information and a way to leak exactly what he wanted leaked.

"Move it, goddamnit," he screamed and waved Jerry to jump into the 'copter. As soon as he jumped in, the 'copter flew straight up, and Jerry grabbed the bar and held on. He scrambled to strap himself in.

"I hope to hell you know how to work that thing," yelled the colonel as he was pointing at the camera that sat on Jerry's lap.

"Yes, sir," screamed Jerry. "Three months at Fort Bragg, know this baby inside out, Colonel." Jerry smiled at his colonel, but there was no smile on the colonel's face.

"Just make sure that you're ready to rock and roll. I don't want you loading that fucking thing with film when the shit hits the fan," said Colonel Bentley.

Jerry said with a confused expression, "I thought we were just going there to inspect the troops?"

The colonel didn't answer, just turned toward the window.

"One o'clock, Colonel," screamed the copilot. Holding on to the bar next to the hatch, Bentley looked down and saw his men. He felt a surge of pride and a chill ran through his body.

"Take her down in that field to the north. I'll call in the air strikes from the other side of the rice paddies."

The 'copter turned violently, first almost straight up and then a hard turn, as they headed for the field, which was surrounded by rice paddies. It seemed that the shelling was coming from the woods on the northern side.

"Get some pictures of the troops. I want their parents to see how brave their sons are. Get us closer to the woods; I want to make sure that's where the shelling is coming from."

"Colonel," screamed the pilot. "We can't get too close or we'll get shot down."

"Land here, goddamnit. Give me that hand radio, I'll do this myself. Specialist, follow me, stay low, and get some pictures."

As soon as the 'copter hit the ground, the colonel leaped out and hit the ground running. His men were on the other side of the rice paddies, pinned down by the Viet Cong.

Jerry knelt in the helicopter, holding onto the bar attached to the door. He watched as the colonel ran toward his men, all the while shouting out artillery fire instructions. The colonel looked back; Jerry was still inside the 'copter.

"What are you waiting for, a fucking invitation? Let's go and don't forget to get some good shots."

He could feel the hands on the back of his shoulders, "I got to get this baby off the ground. You going or staying?" shouted the pilot.

Jerry turned toward the pilot, shook his head, and jumped out. He ran toward the side of the road and jumped into the ditch alongside the paddies.

This must be a fucking joke. Of all the commanding officers in this entire goddamn army, I get the fucking lunatic of the century. What the hell, the son of a bitch wants pictures, he'll get his goddamn pictures, Jerry said to himself as he was running toward a dirt levee alongside the paddies. North Vietnamese regulars had the U.S. soldiers pinned down behind the mounds with small arms and mortar fire. The colonel had reached his men and was shouting out orders over the two-way radio. Jerry began taking pictures as he moved, holding down the button, and that automatic kept clicking.

The pounding in his heart reminded him of that day at the edge of the river, when he went in to save that guy and his kid from the cold water. But that had made sense. He was doing something dangerous for a reason then. Not this time, there was no good reason for this. The colonel could have called the air strikes from the air; all of this was about that fucking promotion. The son of bitch would be called a hero, Jerry would end up with a bullet in his head, and that motherfucker will get a medal and his goddamn star.

There is no sound like the automatics on a Black Hawk. The helicopters seemed to come from nowhere. Jerry turned his head toward the sky and watched three 'copters streaking across the sky, whirling toward the woods where the VC were embedded and taking cover.

Jerry watched as the 'copters moved in and thought to himself, *those motherfuckers are about to get their asses kicked.* He smiled; the fear that he had felt was gone. Now it was exciting, he was truly in the shit, no make-believe fantasy going on over here.

The attack helicopters opened fire with flamethrowers, napalm, and the 50mm guns. The woods turned into an inferno, no way in the world he was going to miss this. These pictures were his, he wasn't just taking them, he was in them. Jerry wasn't sure why, but he had a feeling that these pictures would turn out well. He got to his knees and starting shooting. He was whirling around, getting shots of every soldier; he got some shots of VC soldiers running through the paddies, trying to get away from the hell that had just erupted on their side of the tracks.

"Where's the colonel?" shouted the lieutenant who was standing up, surveying the area. He turned toward Jerry, who was snapping pictures.

"Hey, shithead, you see the boss?" shouted the lieutenant.

Jerry looked up at the lieutenant. He hadn't heard a word the man said. The helicopters were roaring and he couldn't hear a thing. "Is it over?" shouted Jerry.

The lieutenant looked down at Jerry and said, "It's not over till every last one of these motherfuckers is dead." Then he kneeled down next to Jerry and shouted, "You see the colonel?"

Jerry pointed to the last place that he saw Bentley, but there was no sight of him.

"Spread out, guys, stay tight. Those sons of bitches are still out there. We don't leave anyone behind, you got that?" the lieutenant shouted to his men. "That goes for you too, camera boy. You read me, soldier?"

"Loud and clear, sir," said Jerry as he got to his feet.

The stalks of the rice were high this time of the year, and unless you stepped on a body, there was no way to see anyone who was on the ground, so everyone in the unit began searching for the men that hadn't answered roll call.

Jerry wasn't really comfortable with a gun, but he sure wished that he had one right now. The men spread out, and before Jerry could move, one of the soldiers about thirty feet away, closer to the burning trees, shouted, "I got the colonel, he's down."

The men turned and ran over to the colonel. The Black Hawks had landed on a small dirt island that sat in the middle of the fields, like a raft in the middle of an ocean. Jerry stood between the 'copters and the men leaning over Bentley. The sound was deafening; the whirling of the blades turned the surrounding fields into a sort of horizontal waterfall. Two soldiers lifted the colonel up, carrying him toward the waiting helicopter.

Jerry lifted his camera and took aim. In the viewfinder was the image of the two soldiers half-carrying, half-dragging the colonel toward the helicopter with the other men right behind, running with their guns held out in front of them, and in the distance, almost as a backdrop, the fiery storm.

Jerry just kept on shooting as the men were piling into the first Black Hawk.

"Come on, you idiot," screamed the men carrying the lieutenant, waving to Jerry. "Get in the 'copter."

Jerry ran toward the 'copter and leaped in, almost crashing into the colonel. "How you doing, sir?" said Jerry. "You're not going to believe the pictures I got."

The colonel tried to pick up his head, but couldn't, and smiled slightly. "You're okay, kid," was all the colonel said.

The colonel's eyes glazed over and he went still. There was a smile that seemed strangely out of place, almost contentment. Jerry lifted the colonel's hand and felt in vain for his pulse. Then, he felt something warm touch his fingers. When he looked down, he could see it was blood. Jerry lifted the colonel slightly and saw the blood stain mark on the back of his shirt.

"I don't think he's breathing," said Jerry to the young lieutenant.

The helicopter moved south toward the base and radioed in for medical assistance and permission to land. Within minutes, the copter landed next to a Quonset hut that housed the MASH unit. The colonel was pulled out of the helicopter by a waiting medical team and whisked away into the makeshift hospital.

Jerry moved slowly out of the helicopter and stepped on the ground, when a young nurse rushed up to him and grabbed his arm. "You all right? Where have you been hit?" She started pulling him into the building. Jerry was covered with blood and soaked head to toe with the dirty water from the rice paddies.

"No, no," said Jerry, realizing that the nurse assumed that it was his blood and that he needed medical attention. Jerry turned to the nurse and smiled. "I'm fine."

"What the fuck happened to you?" gasped Steve as Jerry walked into their hut. "Jesus, you're covered with blood, and you smell like shit."

"Yeah, I've been told. I'm fine. Bentley got shot up pretty bad, think he's going to be all right. They got him in surgery, I just need a good hot shower."

"You are telling me that's Colonel Bentley's blood on you?"

"Yeah, I'll fill you in later." He patted Steve on the shoulder and walked toward the bathroom.

More than an hour had gone by since Jerry went into the bathroom, and Steve knocked on the door eventually to make sure that the guy was all right.

"You okay in there, Jerry?" he said through the door. At first there was no answer, he tried again. "Jerry?" Steve opened the door and saw Jerry in the shower scrubbing and scrubbing. Jerry turned.

"I'm okay, Steve, I'll be out in a minute. Just got to get this smell off my body. I can't seem to get this goddamn smell to go away."

"Take your time, pal. When you're ready we'll go out and have a couple of beers on me, okay?"

"Yeah," said Jerry, "that sounds fine." Jerry continued to scrub and let the hot water wash away the dirt and the smell and the blood and the thoughts and the memory of what he had gotten himself into.

Steve looked up as Jerry stepped out of the bathroom into the small room that they shared for the last two days. He jumped to his feet and saluted and bowed at the same time.

Jerry looked at Steve with a sly smile and said, "What's that all about, an officer saluting an enlisted man?"

"You kidding? You're a genuine hero, the whole goddamn base knows what happened out there! You saved the colonel's life, threw him over your shoulder and carried him to the helicopter. The SOB is going to get that star after all and you will probably get the Bronze Star for Valor under Fire. So, your majesty, the beers are on me."

Jerry looked at Steve with a confused expression on his face and said, "What the fuck are you talking about? All I did was take a bunch of pictures while these fucking idiots were getting shot at. I didn't save anyone from anything."

"Yeah, fine, but that's not what's going around the base. They got you down as a genuine fucking hero, so enjoy the moment."

Jerry looked at Steve and said, "Why are they making this shit up?"

"Don't be such an asshole, this war needs heroes and you fit the bill. So just shut up and smile for the cameras, and let's go get that beer."

"Okay," said Jerry, buttoning his shirt. "Let them think what they need to think, but let me tell you what really happened."

"I am going to have a Scotch," said Steve. "I got a feeling I'm going to need a real drink after I hear what really happened out there."

Jerry felt a soft hand on the back of his neck. He turned. She was beautiful, with incredible eyes, so big, so brown, innocent, yet determined. He smiled.

"Girls," said Steve, loudly and harshly, "not now, later." He shooed them away like they were bothersome flies.

"Okay, boys, we see you later, if that's what you want. We here to please, me and my friend, you and your friend, we all have really good time. Whatever you want, you get, okay, boys?"

"Yeah, now take off," said Steve.

Jerry turned to his friend and said, "Let's get one thing straight, I'm no more a hero than you are. Let me tell you another thing, Bentley is the craziest motherfucker that ever walked the earth. He didn't give a shit about anything, about me, about his men. All he cared about was getting those goddamn pictures. He was screaming at me to take pictures of him radioing in the location of the snipers while those fucking gooks were shooting at us. I could have been killed taking pictures of that idiot, just so that he could get his goddamn pictures."

Jerry took another drink. "I wouldn't have even got out of the helicopter if the pilot hadn't thrown me out, and then the idiot starts screaming at me to take some good pictures while he is running toward the action."

"You're shitting me," said Steve.

"At first, I didn't do a fucking thing. I hit the ground and stayed there, with my arms over my head. You think I'm going to get shot so some asshole can get promoted? Look, I was scared shitless. Then out of nowhere, the Black Hawks were flying overhead and heading toward the trees. I could hear some of the guys yelling, then all hell broke loose, and the woods went up in flames. It was surreal. I could feel the heat from the napalm on my face, and I could see men in the woods running for cover, some covered in flames. I was snapping pictures like crazy, I don't know what got into to me." Jerry looked straight ahead, finished his drink, and ordered another one. "You want another drink?" he asked Steve.

"Well," continued Jerry, "all of a sudden, everyone is looking for that fool. I'm still taking pictures. Must have looked like an idiot, but tell you the truth, I was getting into it, it was almost exciting now that the VC wasn't shooting right at us. I was getting caught up in the whole crazy moment. They found the colonel lying on his back like he was taking a nap. Some soldiers grabbed him and carried him toward the helicopters, and I was taking pictures the whole time. I got to tell you, man, I got some great pictures, the men carrying the colonel to the waiting helicopter with what must have looked like the whole world on fire."

Steve was listening avidly. "Then what happened?"

"They put him in the 'copter and I jumped in. I was sitting right next to him, and he stopped moving. I went to feel for a pulse and next thing I know, I'm covered in blood, and I realized I couldn't hear him breathing. Anyway, that's about it, we get to the MASH unit, they took the colonel in and checked me out, and here I am."

"Well," said Steve, "you may think that's it, but I guarantee you that's not it, because you're getting a medal and some serious recognition for what happened this morning and Colonel Crazy Motherfucker is getting shipped home and getting his star and probably assigned to some desk at the Pentagon. You really stepped into this one. I can't believe it. You're here for two fucking days and you get a medal. Go figure."

"There he is!" yelled a soldier. Jerry turned to see a group of men almost running toward them. They all gathered around, slapping Jerry on the back and shaking his hands and praising him for his bravery and for saving the life of their beloved colonel.

Beers were ordered and the rest of the night turned into a celebration for Jerry. As he sat there, for the first time he felt like part of a big family, part of a team; he'd never felt like that before, and he liked the feeling.

Even though it was just for a moment, he was able to put the other thoughts out of his mind, thoughts of his wife and two sons and even the reason he was here.

* * *

Jerry lies still in his childhood bed as he is slowly waking up. He can smell the bacon his mother is making in the kitchen. He can hear that crackly sound when the cold fatty bacon hits the hot pan. He gets out of bed and walks toward the kitchen and peeks in. His mother is standing at the stove, her back to him. She turns, a white mug in her hand. Jerry can smell the hot chocolate, he smiles at her, and she smiles back.

He looks out the window at the river. Something is lying on the bank of the river, it's the body of a boy. He is still and lifeless. Jerry stares and then realizes: it's his own dead body, and all of a sudden, there's Chuck, leaning over the body. Chuck turns toward Jerry at the window in the house, smiles, like a reflection in a foggy mirror, and then starts to disappear. Jerry feels his hand move forward and begins to wipe away the fog.

And then it was gone, and he knew he was waking up in Vietnam. He gently pushed himself up out of bed and steadied himself for a moment before walking toward the bathroom. He was careful not to wake Steve. He walked past the desk and looked down. There was a folder on the desk with a name on it: Chuck Harris. He shook his head, *What the fuck, am I still dreaming?* He couldn't believe it. The folder was labeled "classified." He checked that Steve was still sleeping and then he opened the folder. There was a photo of Chuck lying in a hospital bed with bandages around his head and around his chest. He had tubes down his throat and IVs in his arms. It was hard to recognize him with all the tubes and the bandage around his head. Jerry turned the page and began to read the classified report.

Corporal Chuck Harris, stationed in Saigon, was found by two Vietnamese men in an alley behind a dumpster between Mott and Hoi streets. The MPs brought him to the American hospital in downtown Saigon. Initially, the incident was reported as a mugging gone bad, but the injuries seemed to be inconsistent with that type of crime. The injuries from a mugging are usually random, and these gunshot wounds were precise. It seemed calculated. The report was signed by a Dr. Stephanie Weil. Jerry knew he needed to talk to this woman. She might know what was going on.

CHAPTER 15

Stephanie Weil was one of the few female doctors originally stationed with the 1st Medical Battalion in Da Nang, on the sandy beaches of Vietnam. In the early days of the war, they lived and worked in tents on the beach. After six months, the staff moved up to a rocky bluff overlooking the South China Sea. By the time she had transferred to the main U.S. Army hospital in Saigon, Lieutenant Weil had seen a lot of damaged bodies.

At first glance, Chuck's wounds seemed to be consistent with what was reported as a vicious mugging. But as she sliced through his shirt, it didn't add up. "Here's another one, this one in the stomach. This is the kind of shot that is meant to send a message. One in the stomach, two in the chest, and then one in the head, just to make sure he's dead." She looked up from the wounds at the nurses next to her. "Well, not this time. Every shot missed an organ and the one in the head just grazed him, it's a damn miracle. God was looking after this young man. It just wasn't his time." Her hands moved quickly from wound to wound, stopping the bleeding, getting him ready for more extensive surgery once he was stabilized. Stephanie was strictly triage at the hospital: sorting, allocating, trying to determine who was in the most need. Chuck was numero uno. "First to go," she called out.

She spoke to him gently as she washed the blood off his face. "I'm afraid we haven't met," she said. "I'm Doctor Weil, but you call me Lieutenant, or Stephanie, whichever suits you. It will be okay; you'll be home before you know it, fooling around with your high school girlfriends." She smiled; she knew that he hadn't heard a word. Chuck seemed at peace, and then suddenly, he began to stir in jerking and spasmodic convulsions. He was mumbling incoherently, and then a calm came over him again, but he was still talking. "I can't, John. I won't murder a father who is protecting his child. this is where I draw the line."

A sound came from behind her, and Stephanie turned. Two officers pushed the curtain back that separated Chuck's bed from the rest of the ward. They ignored Stephanie and stood over Chuck while he screamed, "NO!" Stephanie lurched up and grabbed the IV that Chuck had just pulled out while violently thrashing his arms. "I can't, I'm sorry, I just can't. No, I won't," Chuck kept saying, in a pleading tone.

Stephanie held on to Chuck's wrist while his eyes began to close again. She called for a corporal to help her restrain him. Soldiers were often agitated when they came in. But something about his words sent a shiver up her spine.

"What did he say?" one of the officers asked.

Stephanie glanced up and wondered why these guys were taking an interest.

"He didn't say anything, just crying out, 'No, no.' Why, what is your interest?"

"Ma'am, we're CID." Both reached into their pockets and pulled out ID cards.

Stephanie looked back down at Chuck with a feeling that she had felt before; her mother called it a premonition. She felt it here at this very moment. An uneasy feeling about these two men.

She smiled in a reassuring fashion and said, "If you like, I can keep a record of whatever he says, but most likely, it will be nothing but senseless gibberish. Now if you don't mind, we need to get this man up to surgery."

Chuck Harris was in and out of surgery multiple times over the next month, and although Stephanie wasn't assigned to him, she looked in on him almost every day. Most of the time he was unconscious, but some days he would wake suddenly, always agitated. Stephanie sat by his bed and listened, concentrating on every word he spoke. Mostly it was a rambling incoherent collection of sounds that made no sense to her. But there were lucid moments when he spoke clearly and with some degree of passion about the horrible abuses that were being carried out all over Southeast Asia. And then as quickly as he woke each time, he would slip back into a deep sleep. Chuck Harris seemed to sleep more and more over the last few weeks. Various CID officers had taken a real interest in Chuck's health, visiting him every day in the beginning. After the first week, always finding Chuck unconscious, they stopped coming.

Over the next four weeks, Chuck Harris was diagnosed with a traumatic brain injury. The team of doctors that had nursed him back to health all agreed that he would be better off going home. There was a VA hospital right in his hometown. The flight back would be dangerous, Stephanie argued, but she did finally agree that it was in the patient's best interests, even with the risks.

Dr. Stephanie Weil wasn't there to say goodbye to the man she had cared for over the last four weeks. She felt cheated; she wanted to say good bye, but the medical transport flight was leaving and every hour was important, especially to his family back home, who were all ready and anxious to care for Chuck.

Steve Jacobs's office was at JAG headquarters in downtown Saigon. The knock on the door announced his first appointment of the day.

Steve was gazing out of the window that looked over the busy streets of downtown Saigon. "Come in," he said.

Dr. Stephanie Weil opened the door. "I just can't get used to these streets. Between the motorbikes, the bicycles, and the rickshaws, I can't get across the street." Steve smiled. He wasn't sure why, but he'd always liked her. He had known Stephanie for a while; she was one of the good guys.

There was nothing average about her, her looks, her style, her personality. She was passionate about her family, her job, and the people that she cared for.

"You have to move with the traffic. If you stop in the middle of the street you get run down. There's a million accidents a day out there," said Steve. "Well, maybe not that many, but a lot. You get used to it. You step off the curb and just walk, and they go around you."

"If I am not used to it yet, I never will be." She smiled. She liked this guy, he wasn't like the rest of them. He didn't come off like a Marine, not tall or built like a body builder, somewhat average; just a nice Jewish boy. She thought, now this is the guy my parents would love me to marry, buy a house in Scarsdale, have kids, join the temple, and become a member of the Scarsdale Golf Club.

"What are you smiling about?" asked Steve.

"Oh, nothing," she said, changing the subject. "Where you from, Lieutenant?"

"The Bronx, Grand Concourse, right down the street from Yankee Stadium. What about you?"

"Just up the road from you. Westchester, Scarsdale."

"Oh, a rich girl."

"I guess," said Stephanie. "But here I am in Vietnam, my parents and their money couldn't stop that."

"Yeah, I can see that. It must have pissed your parents off."

"You think!" and she winked.

"What can I do for you, Lieutenant?" he asked in a business-like fashion.

Stephanie smiled. She had seen this tactic before, all business and official stuff.

"It's all here," she said as she handed Steve a folder.

Steve flipped it open, read for a few moments, then looked up and said, "There's a lot of info here. Why don't you give me the short version of what you think is going on?"

"It's not what I think is going on, it's what I know is going on. I've done what I can. This is way above my pay grade."

"Easy, Doctor, I'm not saying..." but she cut him off.

"Look, Jacobs, just read my report. If you don't think there is something there, then forget it. Something tells me to walk away from this and just do my job. Fine, that's what I'll do, right after you tell me there is nothing going on."

Stephanie said, "Listen, I'm sorry. I just get a little carried away sometimes, that's what my mother tells me, and maybe she's right. This kid just got sent home, after being in ICU for the last month. Tell you the truth, it's dangerous as hell for him to be traveling at all, but we figured that he would be safer in the States than he was here." Steve looked up from the file, tilted his head as if he had just seen something that only a moment ago wasn't there. "What do you mean safer?" asked Steve.

Stephanie hesitated and then said, "Almost every day for about two weeks, two CID agents would come by. They would march into his room, stand over him for a minute, and leave only after confirming Harris's unconscious state. It didn't take us long to figure out that they weren't stopping by out of care for Harris. They needed to make sure that he couldn't talk. And I'm as sure as I can be that if he ever did start talking, he would have been dead in twenty-four hours, no matter how many guards we put on his door. Harris was a member of some top-secret clandestine operation. He kept rambling on about using our dead soldiers' bodies to ship illegal drugs back to the States." The lieutenant hesitated, then continued. "Only you and one other doctor know this. If it got out, I think that we all would be in body bags with parcels of drugs shoved into our bellies." She continued, "Just to be clear, Steve, this was no mugging gone bad. It was an attempted execution. Only one problem: our soldier refused to die. Look, this needs to stay with just the three of us."

Steve stood slowly. "No one else has seen this file?" he asked.

"No, just you and the one other doctor." She stood to leave. "We have to trust each other, or all three of us are fucked. My contact information is on the first page. Call me if you want to talk."

He said, "I will look at it and get back to you, you have my word." He thought about the last thing she said: "Call me if you want to talk." He smiled, gently nodded his head. "Yeah, we'll talk."

Steve looked down at the papers in front of him and began to read.

The preliminary examination performed on Corporal Chuck Harris indicated four entry wounds, lower and upper abdomen, right thorax, and right side of the cranium.

The first few pages were medical reports written by Captain Tim Bennis, MD. What caught Steve's attention was a note written on the side of the report: "*This was no mugging, this was an attempted assassination. It's a virtual medical miracle that this man is not dead.*"

Steve leaned back in his chair and looked up at the clock. He had to get to a briefing. This would have to wait till tomorrow.

As Steve looked deeper into Chuck Harris's case, he could see that Stephanie was right, it didn't add up. Anyone with half a brain would see through this bullshit, but why the cover-up? It just didn't make any sense. But the more he looked into the Harris case, the stronger the pushback from his commanding officers; even the director made it clear that he was to move on. He was told to just leave it alone, and so he did. Fuck it, he thought, he had enough problems to deal with; the kid was back home as far as he knew, safe from whatever or whoever wanted him dead. Stephanie was disappointed, but she understood there were some powerful men pulling the strings, and if she didn't keep her head down, she would not be able to help anyone.

Steve kept the file she had given him in his barracks, and he looked at it once in a while, never really letting it go. And now this new guy Jerry shows up in the bed next to him, and he just happens to be from the same little town in Pennsylvania.

The morning after Jerry's big adventure, he reported to headquarters. He was told to write a detailed report of the accounts of the previous day. He turned in the rolls of film he had shot. The officer told him that he was being considered for a commendation and possibly a medal. "Hope for your sake the photos really show the action with Bentley in the center of it all."

"Bentley is a crazy motherfucker. He was definitely in the middle of it and the pictures will show that." Jerry left to write his report and decided to write a version for himself as well, a truer version that he would mail back home. When he was safe back in Pennsylvania, he had decided, he would sit down and use his notes to write a book about everything that was really going on over here.

That afternoon Jerry sat on the porch that looked over the airfield. The flies were relentless during the rainy season; thank God for the mosquito netting. Malaria was one of the biggest killers in this part of the world, and Jerry sure as hell didn't want to survive this bullshit only to get sick and die from some third-world disease.

For a moment, it almost seemed like home, sitting there on the porch. Jerry picked up the notebook that sat on the floor next to the wooden chair and began to write what would be the first of more than fifty letters he would send home in the fall of 1969.

For Jerry, writing was his passion and had become his drug of choice. Over the years he had become obsessed with daily diaries. But now he really had something to write about. This could be the best goddamn story of this war. He even knew the title: "The Innocents," by Jerry McGinnis, definitely a Pulitzer winner; it would be about the people who always paid the biggest price. He smiled. The fantasy distraction helped as he tried to explain to his father that this was exactly where he needed to be in order to find out why both the Harris boys had been murdered. The reasons were right here, under his nose; all he had to do was exactly what he had been trained to do: investigate and reveal the facts. Once he discovered those reasons, he would do all that he could to bring these bastards to justice, hopefully a fucking firing squad. And Jerry wouldn't mind a bit if he were one of the shooters.

His days drifted into a routine. He would report for duty every morning and write up stories from the reports that crossed his desk.

He would embellish a bit here and there, making it sound good for the folks back home. Everything went to a censor before being published, and over the weeks he had learned what things not to say and what should be emphasized. He asked questions; he had the perfect job for it. He never forgot why he was there and what the goal was. After reading Steve's file, he knew that the doctor who had treated Chuck was Stephanie Weil and he also knew that Steve had looked into the case with no results. He had done a bit of snooping and found more info in another file in Steve's cabinet in the barracks. The file left more questions than answers, but he was on track and was feeling pretty good about his progress.

Jerry seemed to do his best thinking and writing at a small café in downtown Saigon. The war was intensifying, with the U.S. now bombing NVA troops from altitudes of up to six miles high. The 100 bombs that each B-52 carried were also showering the Ho Chi Minh Trail winding through Laos. Stories about bombing mistakes, which often killed innocent women and children, were purposely left out of the newsletters to the troops and rarely saw the light of day in the States.

In August of that year, a South Vietnamese village was bombed by mistake, killing sixty-three civilians and wounding over a hundred women and children. Jerry had access to all reports, both classified and non-classified. He wasn't allowed to write about it for the paper, though.

It took some time to get used to the city, the people, and the culture. Jerry sat in that small café deep in thought, writing to his father and his wife and kids. He felt guilty over what he had done to Kate and the two boys, but he was also sure as his love for them that everything he was doing, the sacrifices that they all were making, was worth it. He was doing this as much for Kate and the boys as for himself.

Back home Jerry had been caught up in the almost fanatical fear and hatred that had been instilled in Americans for all communists. And he did believe that it was America's duty to stop communists before they took over the world. But he was finding that the reality on the ground was very different. The U.S. foot soldiers didn't know what the hell was going on, and most of them got stoned out of their minds whenever they could. The career guys were the officers, a bunch of lifers that lived for the war and didn't give a shit who got blown away while they were doing their patriot bullshit duty.

He knew that he was supposed to honestly report what he was witnessing, but he also knew that the support for the war back home was crumbling. Opposition to the war was building, especially among the colleges across the country. He hated those anti-war assholes, but now he was up close to the horrors of the war himself.

The civilian causalities were mounting and eventually even the Army couldn't keep the truth from the folks back home. Sitting at his favorite booth at the bar, he read over the day's report, which was now including the number of dead or missing. There was no way for him to really know the full truth. He would do his duty and report what was expected of him, but the real story was always lodged in his gut.

He was often expected to write human interest stories. Look for a specific soldier and tell his story or report on how the U.S. was here to save the Vietnamese people from falling under the control of the repressive government of North Vietnam. He read a classified report stating allegations that forty percent of U.S. economic aid sent to Saigon was stolen or ending up on the black market. He knew that the true story of what happened to Chuck was part of this war story;

by telling Chuck's story he would also be telling the folks back home what was really going on in this hellhole of a country.

As he sat there sipping his beer, a small child stuck his hand in front of his face, begging for a little money. Some of that aid should be going to help feed and care for these kids, the children of this war. *Jesus*, Jerry thought, *that's a good title, "The Children of the War in Vietnam." Maybe the second book.* He smiled and thought, *It's worth it, definitely worth it to be here.* The city was filled with homeless and parentless children that were desperate for the smallest handout. Jerry handed the child some loose change and went back to his work. But he couldn't get the face of the child out of his mind, the children of the war, the most innocent and vulnerable victims. There were so many families that had lost everything—their homes, their land, and their lives. Jerry had been in the country for only two months, but having been assigned a job on the military newsletter, he had access to the few agencies that served the thousands of orphans that this war had created. The military had no interest in the welfare of these children; it was more concerned about children born from military personnel and the potential responsibility the U.S. government had to them. This was just one more story to tell.

"Hey, shithead." Jerry looked up, startled, and saw Tony Ramo standing over him with a bottle of beer in one hand and a young Vietnamese girl on his arm.

CHAPTER 16

Jerry smiled. It was good to see Tony, it had been a while.

Tony pushed the girl onto the seat and he slid down next to her; he moved easy, like he owned the joint. He took a long swallow of his beer, gave the girl a kiss on the cheek, and smiled at his old boot camp friend.

It had been just a few months since Tony and Jerry left boot camp at Parris Island. Two guys, about the same age from different parts of the country. That's the way it was in the Army, a real live melting pot.

Jerry and Tony were as far apart as two men could be, but boot camp had made them into brothers. After a few beers and small talk, Tony leaned over to the girl and said, "Take off, Sue Ling, I'll catch up with you later. I got something's to discuss with my buddy Jerry."

"One beer, you promised!" she said. Tony grabbed her wrist and began to gently but firmly twist her arm. The young girl cried out softly, but she didn't want to attract any attention. "Go wait for me at the bar. The beers are on me, now go!"

"Okay, why so rough?" she asked, but didn't wait for an answer.

Tony turned to Jerry, "How you doing, McGinnis?"

"Pretty shitty. Sometimes I think I really fucked up coming over here. I mean, who in their right mind would leave a wife, two young boys, and a good-paying job for this?" The sun was still high in the sky at 5 p.m. on Dong Khoi Street in downtown Saigon. Every afternoon the streets were filled with thousands of locals on bikes, scooters, small cars, and hundreds of rickshaws, all trying to get somewhere. "I'm about to die every time I try to cross the street! If there isn't a soldier trying to direct traffic, maybe you'll make it to the other side, maybe you don't."

Tony laughed, "I know, these fucking people are completely insane. They don't give a shit about anybody or anything. But I do know how to cross the street."

Jerry smiled. "Really, so tell me, how do you cross the street?"

Tony pointed to an old woman standing at the corner. While they watched, without a moment's hesitation, she walked into the traffic as calmly as if she were sitting down for tea at a fancy café. She continued across the street in a steady and straight gait; she didn't deviate from her goal. The cars and the bikes and the scooters and the rickshaws rhythmically danced around her, coming within what seemed inches from her frail body. It was like she was moving in a specially designed bubble immune from what seemed to be almost certain death.

"What happens if she gets hit?"

"I don't know, never saw anyone actually get hit. They're pretty good at this. I suppose they been doing it all their lives."

Neither Tony nor Jerry said a word for a few minutes, then Jerry started talking.

"I think we're in hell. I came here to write stories, to send home reports with the truth, to let the people back home learn about what's going on over here. Gather support for what we're doing over here, maybe tell them some good things about what we're doing for the kids: building schools, hospitals, clinics in rural towns. But we're not doing any of that. This is an all-out fucking war. If we're not killing them, they're killing us, and if you ask me, somebody is ripping off half the shit that's being sent over here."

Tony shook his head, smiled slightly, and said, "Boy, ain't you one cynical motherfucker. Look," he continued, "what you need to do is get laid, my friend. How long has it been? It's the only way to release some of the goddamn tension and stress. It's all bottled up, you're going to explode. I'm serious, Jerry, your nutsack is going grow to the size of a fucking watermelon and then all of a sudden, it's going to blow up. You'll be dead in less than a minute. I'm serious, it's a medical certainty, no doubt." Jerry stared at Tony, an expression of disbelief on his face. Tony stared back blankly, and then he smiled, and they both laughed out loud.

Jerry picked up his beer and said, "What an asshole!"

The bar was full of young girls. If only he had a nickel for every time some girls came up to him and said, "Twenty dollar, make you holler, string bean." The first time it sounded pretty funny, and lord knows he wanted to. He was tempted, but he figured the least he could do was to be faithful to his wife. Christ, it was enough that he had left her at home; he couldn't start screwing some eighteen-year-old hooker, if she was even that old.

Jerry smiled at his friend. He noticed when Tony was around other guys, he came off like a real tough guy. When it was just the two of them, it was different. Tony talked in a softer voice; the wise guy look and language seemed to drift away. Being with Jerry made Tony feel calm. Back in boot camp Tony had told Jerry about his life back home, about his father who was Italian, born in northern Italy, and sent by his parents to New York when he was twelve or thirteen. Tony loved to tell the stories of growing up Italian in Brooklyn. Sometimes Tony would talk about life back home, about the gang he had joined back when he was in junior high school, and about the Friday nights, and the parties and the girls, drinking and getting laid.

"Well, it was nice shooting the shit with you, brother, but if you don't want to get laid then I am out of here. Can't keep little Sue Ling there waiting too long."

"Have another beer, will ya? I want to ask you something. The girl will wait or there will be another one to take her place."

"You're right, shithead. What do you want to talk about?"

"I hear a lot of shit, and I just want to know if it's true."

"Like what? If I know, I'll tell ya, maybe."

"Is there like a real organized gang that controls all the shit that I'm hearing about?" asked Jerry

"What shit?" Tony shook his head and continued, "Look, Jerry, keep your head down and mind your own business. You want to get home to the wife and kids, then don't ask so many questions. I swear to Christ, I never met anyone who asks so many goddamn questions."

"Just trying to understand how things work here." Jerry said in an offhand way.

Jerry was fascinated with Tony; everything about him was passionate and alive. Jerry had stuff going on in his life but nothing like Tony. Tony knew how to get things and how to get things done, and he didn't much care how it was done.

Jerry knew that Tony would have figured out what was happening within a week of landing in Vietnam. Now Jerry wanted his help. He waited now to see if Tony would answer him straight.

Jerry remembered the first few times he talked to Tony. He couldn't understand a word the guy was saying. It took some time before Jerry understood what Tony meant, when he would say something like "Hey, how you doing?" or "Fugetaboutit." *Fugetaboutit* was an all-encompassing word; it confirmed with attitude anything that was said. Could be as simple and casual as the answer to a question like "How's the steak?" Tony would reply, "Fugetaboutit," which meant "Fucking delicious!"

"What do you want to know so badly for? You're not getting involved in any shit. Just do your time and go home."

"Tony, I came here to get my hands dirty, I'm not afraid. I want to know and something tells me you are the man to ask."

"Okay, look, I got a date sitting right there so I am not going to talk about this now. Let's meet later. I will fill you in. Just be cool."

Jerry looked at the girl that was sitting at the bar giving Tony dirty looks. "Who's your girlfriend?"

Tony leaned his head in the direction of the girl watching him and smiled. He looked back at Jerry and said in a soft voice, "She's one of the girls we got working over here. A-1, clean as a whistle, they're all checked out." Tony put his hand up like a boy scout. "Swear to God." Then he waved the girl over. She got off the bar stool and walked over.

Tony stood up and said, "I got to take a leak, be back in a second. Take care of my girl and don't get any wiseass ideas." Jerry laughed, and then he wished he hadn't. Nothing funny about anything over here, including young innocent girls having to sell their bodies just to survive.

Jerry looked at the young girl and smiled, "You speak English?"

"Not too bad. I am taking classes and I am getting better. My name is Sue Ling. What's yours?"

Jerry smiled. "Jerry McGinnis," he said as he put out his hand. Sue Ling took his hand and shook softly with a firm and steady shake.

She looked Jerry in the eyes and smiled and said, "Nice to meet you, Jerry. Are you from the same city as Tony? You two look like close friends, I can tell."

"No, I'm from a small town in Pennsylvania." He stopped and then said, "You look like a nice kid, what are you doing with Tony? I mean, where's your family? Look, I'm sorry, this is none of my business, I'm sure you have your reason. I just don't see a girl like you…"

Jerry stopped and took an uneasy swallow of his beer. "Look, I'm sorry, I didn't mean to insult you. You seem like a good person."

Sue Ling smiled at Jerry. "You don't have to explain, I understand what you mean. I take no offense to what you have said, and sometimes we do what we have to do. I will not be doing this for very long, but right now I must. Where did you say you were from?"

Jerry thought that trying to explain to this girl where he was from was like trying to explain the color blue to a man who's been blind all his life. But he smiled and nodded and said, "Just some little town. Not too far from New York."

"New York." A wistful smile played across her young and beautiful face, "New York. Someday, I'll go to New York, some day. When I can, I will go to America, and I want to know where to go. I know that America is a big place."

"I'm from Pennsylvania. You ever hear of Pennsylvania?

She had a strange look on her face when she said yes. "I have heard of Pennsylvania. I knew a soldier from there."

"Really?" said Jerry. "Do you remember his name? I probably don't know him, must be thousands of guys from Pennsylvania here, but you never know. What's his name?"

"His name is Chuck. I don't know his last name. He got shot and they sent him home. Do you know this man?" she asked.

Jerry looked up and said in a casual tone, "You don't remember his last name, do you? Lots of guys named Chuck from Pennsylvania."

"No, most soldiers don't want to tell us their last names. I guess they think we're going to follow them home and wreck their marriage." Sue Ling smiled and said to a grim-faced Jerry, "I am joking, just joking."

Jerry smiled and said, "I know, I was just thinking of something else," and then said, "Do you know what happened to him?"

"I heard that he was attacked in the alley just down the street from here. They said it was a robbery, he got shot, he was hurt badly. They said that the police thought he was dead, but he wasn't, and then I heard that they sent him home. I hope that he is okay. He was very good to me and my family. He tried to protect me and he made some soldiers mad, but he didn't care. I think that he maybe got into some trouble over me. I hope that he is okay. Maybe you can find out for me."

"Yeah, maybe, but since I don't know his last name it would be pretty tough. Besides, he's probably all right. I don't understand, why would this guy get into trouble over you and your family? Have you asked Tony to help you? He knows a lot of stuff that goes on around here."

Before she could answer, Tony appeared and sat back down at the table with two more beers and smiled. "Sounds like you guys are getting real friendly."

"Just making small talk is all. Wondering why a nice, intelligent, pretty girl like Sue Ling is hanging out with the likes of you."

"What can I tell you," said Tony, "the girl's got taste. Clearly, she's attracted to me, a charming fellow with refined taste and a witty personality." A big smile played across Tony's face. At the drop of a hat, he could switch from sounding like a low-life street thug to talking like an Ivy League snob. But then he got serious and said, "You know what I think, Jerry? Sometimes I think that you ask too many fucking questions. All you reporters are the same, always snooping around."

Jerry smiled. "You're right, it's going to get me in trouble one of these days. I'll try harder, but it's in my DNA."

Sometimes Tony acted like a dumb kid from the streets, but the fact was that he was as sharp as a razor blade. He didn't say anything unless he gave it some thought, and that's what he was doing now, giving it some thought. He learned that on the street: say the wrong thing at the wrong time and the price could be steep, and maybe deadly.

Tony hesitated for a moment and then said, "You think for one fucking second that it's easy to make a living in this town? It isn't, unless you break some rules. Everyone is doing what they have to do to survive." Tony stayed quiet for a few moments, as if thinking things over.

"Look, Jerry, you're my friend, right? You know what I mean. I mean if I were to tell you some stuff, you would keep your big mouth shut, right?"

Jerry stared back at Tony and said, "Tony, you know the answer to that. You know that we are brothers to the end," and they both grasped hands in a shake that seemed to last forever. Tony looked Jerry in the eyes and said, "Fucking right, to the end."

"Look, man," he continued. "There's more shit going on over here than in any goddamn city in the States. You have no clue the action that's over here, but you're better off not knowing, so just keep your little small town head out of this shit. Maybe if you're real lucky, I'll see to it that you get laid every once in a while, for free. Anyway, never mind this shit, tell me what's going on with you. What do these motherfuckers have you doing?"

Jerry smiled and said, "I'm working for the Army Public Relations Department."

"What?" said Tony. He turned toward the girl and said, "Hey, sweetheart, take a walk. Go do some business, you're not making any money sitting here."

"Okay, but I am not waiting for you anymore. If I find another GI, I just might go home with him." She walked out of the bar and went to stand on the corner across the street where three other girls were standing. Jerry and Tony watched her go. She looked out of place; she just didn't seem to fit in with the other girls.

"No shit," said Tony. "Sounds like a sweet MOS to me. How the fuck did you pull that off? Your father a fucking general?"

"Nah, no such luck, Kemo Sabe." Tony smiled at the reference to the Lone Ranger and his sidekick Tonto.

"So, come on, what do they have you doing, seriously?"

Jerry drank the last bit of beer and said, "Newsletters, reports, sometimes we give the journalists a bunch of horse crap, so everybody back home thinks that we're kicking Viet Cong ass and at the same time keeping the world safe from the communists. You know, lots of bullshit about how many of the enemy got killed and how much success we're having over here."

Tony picked up his bottle of beer and took a long drink and turned toward Jerry. He pointed toward the street in the direction of Sue Ling. "Pretty fucking cute." Tony put his hand down and smiled at Jerry and said, "Want a beer? I'm going to have another one."

"Sure," said Jerry. "I got nowhere to go."

Tony called over the owner of the bar and ordered two more beers. He looked down at the papers in front of Jerry and said, "Who you writing the letter to?

"My wife and kids, who else would I be writing to?"

"I don't know, maybe your parents."

"I write to my dad once in a while, we're close. He's pretty pissed at me right now, couldn't understand why I chose to come here. But he's a newspaper man and he gets why it's important that men make the sacrifice to leave their families and report on wars."

"Yeah, so how did you pull off getting such a cushy job?"

Jerry shrugged and said, "You know that I worked for the paper back home, so they pulled some strings and I got this plush job, pretty cool."

Tony smiled and said, "So you're hanging out with the top guys over here. Hear a lot of shit."

"Not really," said Jerry. "I mean, I see them and sometimes I'm around when there's shit going on, but I got nothing to do with those guys."

"You got clearance?" said Tony.

"Yeah, not secret stuff, but classified, yeah. Just low-level shit, nothing too hot, just basic stuff." Tony shifted in his seat and reached for his beer but didn't bring it to his mouth. He was thinking hard.

"What kind of stuff?" said Tony.

"Come on," said Jerry. "You know I can't get into that shit with you or anybody. Want me do hard time back in the States?"

Tony grinned, the way you grin when you're just a little pissed with what your buddy just said, but you sort of understand why he said it. "Yeah, okay," said Tony. "Forget about it. Hey, what's going on with your wife? She must be pretty mad at you for leaving her like that with two little kids."

"I think she's been drinking lately. I mean she always enjoyed a little cocktail before dinner but I think it's gotten a little out of hand. Sometimes I think I shouldn't have come, I should've never left. If she wasn't a fall-down drunk before I took off," he hesitated and then said, "she probably is now."

Jerry looked away, with a sad and far-off look on his face, and said, "I think she's all fucked up, not even taking care of the kids. Thank God her parents are taking care of things. I don't know what I would do if they weren't there."

"Would money help?" said Tony.

"Jesus, man, I send almost every fucking dime I get back home, but you know it doesn't mean shit. It's never enough, you know what I mean."

"Yeah, I know what you mean, and maybe I can help."

"Forget about it, Tony. I appreciate it, I really do, but I can't take handouts from you or anybody. I'll take care of this my way, I'll figure this out. I'll do my tour over here and then get back to my family and straighten things out. Thanks for the offer, but no thanks."

"Okay, take it easy, pal, I respect that. No charity, but maybe there's a way..." Suddenly Tony stopped talking, almost like he was about to say something, gave it some thought, and changed his mind. He said, "Look, I've got to get going. Take it easy, will ya? Don't do anything stupid, like getting shot."

Tony stood up and smiled at Jerry. "See ya, pal. Keep the faith."

Jerry watched Tony walk across the street to Sue Ling. He grabbed her arm and seemed mad as hell with her. She dropped her head as if to say, "I'm sorry." There was something about her, her smile, her eyes; they were soft and made Jerry feel warm. She made him forget about what he was doing here, and that he had a family back home. And she knew Chuck; he needed to talk to her alone, find out what else she knew.

He continued to watch Tony and Sue Ling; it seemed they were fighting. Then Tony walked away, leaving her where she stood. Jerry stood up, put some U.S. dollars on the table, and headed across the street.

"Can I talk to you for a minute, maybe buy you a cup of coffee?" he said to her as he came up next to her.

She smiled and said, "I can't. If I don't work my family doesn't eat." She looked down, perhaps ashamed to look Jerry in the eyes, and then looked up, with an expression of pride, and said in a strong voice, "I can't be selfish, I must do my job."

"Job," said Jerry, appalled. "What kind of fucking job is this? Look, I will pay you to sit with me, okay? No sex, just talk."

"I am done in two hours. Maybe we can have some tea in that shop over there." Sue Ling pointed to a small teashop down the road.

Jerry smiled. He knew that teashop well. He said, "Look, I'm sorry, I shouldn't be talking to you this way. I'm just trying to understand why you're doing this, I just don't get it. In two hours, I'll meet you at that shop and we'll have a cup of tea."

Jerry turned and walked away and just as he turned the corner, he looked back and saw Sue Ling walking away with a soldier. Jerry walked back to the small café and ordered another beer. Maybe this young girl had the answer to what had happened and why. There must be a connection between what Tony was talking about and this girl and what she knew. He got back to writing the letter he had started more than an hour before. The same letter that he had written to Kate so many times before, about how sorry he was that he left her and the kids. How he was safe and far from the action, just doing his job. That while he was over here, he was going to find out what had happened to Chuck and Brian, because he knew that the answers were here. He wrote that he loved her and that he would be home before she knew it and that everything was going to be all right once he got home. Then he wrote a special note to the boys and ended with love and kisses, Jerry and Daddy. That was his little ending to every letter he sent home, "Love, Jerry and Daddy."

Jerry wrote two types of letters. One was to his wife and kids, full of the usual things: "how are you doing, I'm fine" letters. The others weren't really letters at all; they were more like an ongoing journal, full of information on the investigation, concerning what he was now calling the operation. He believed Chuck's involvement in the operation had led to his murder and the murder of his brother. Jerry sent copies to both Kate and his dad.

He asked them both to store everything he sent home in a safe place until he returned home. Jerry understood from the very beginning that being casual about this search could turn out badly, so the journal entries were written only at night in the safety and security of his office and then sent home in diplomatic pouches. He sat back, stretched his hands around the back of his neck and peered down the crowded street, and thought to himself, *Maybe something good will come from this.*

CHAPTER 17

Jerry waited at Kim's tea shop for Sue Ling to show up; he wasn't sure she would. She was different, different than the other girls that came around. Not that he was an expert in anything Vietnamese, surely not its people. But he could see what Chuck had seen in her. There was a sweetness to her voice that seemed matched only by her eyes. Clearly, she was beautiful, but in the short time that Jerry was with her, he never felt that she knew it. Luck of the draw, he thought. If she were born in the States, she'd have been going to grad school at Penn. But here she's a ten-dollar prostitute.

Jerry was becoming a regular at Kim's. The proprietor, Mr. Kim, was as good as they get, and he made the GIs feel special, like they were home. It wasn't rowdy like the bars all along the street. He could sit quietly with a cup of tea and enjoy some peace and quiet. He even dozed off for a bit, and woke to feel a gentle hand on his shoulder. "Wake up, soldier," said Kim in a voice that was reserved for mothers and fathers. "You okay? Maybe I should get you a rickshaw."

Jerry smile. He missed the sound of a person who cared, even though he knew that Mr. Kim probably didn't. Sue Ling had never shown up. He put down two Uncle Ho's and walked out.

The street was dark and quiet at 2100 hours, but then he heard a sound from across the wide boulevard. At first it sounded like a whimper, and then it became a cry for help. He began to run, weaving in and out of the cars that were moving around him. There was a scream and all of a sudden he saw Sue Ling trying to pull away from a soldier who grabbed her and then slapped her across the face. She fell hard against the garbage cans that littered the alleyway. Jerry grabbed the soldier and turned him around, yelling as he did so.

"What the fuck do you think you're doing, you son of a bitch." The soldier was startled at first, but quickly turned on Jerry, pushing him away and pulling Sue Ling back toward the entrance of the hotel that rented rooms by the hour. Jerry grabbed the soldier from behind and spun him around to throw a punch that caught the soldier on the side of his mouth. The soldier barely flinched, more stunned than hurt.

Jerry grabbed Sue Ling by the arm and pulled her away from the guy. "Come on, let's get out of here."

Before they could get to the street, Jerry heard the guy coming at them fast. He turned to see the soldier, a knife in his hand. Jerry fell back against the wall. The knife was coming down toward him. "Run," he yelled to Sue Ling, "get the hell out of here."

"I'll teach you to mind your own fucking business," the soldier said. Jerry tried to block the thrusting hand that held the knife, but he felt the blade as he tried to move away. It was all a blur, and suddenly there was someone else there, someone big and tall. The knife dropped, there was a groan, and Jerry fell to the ground. He opened his eyes and looked up.

Tony stood over the soldier who now lay on the ground not moving. Tony turned and grabbed Jerry by the collar and pulled him to his feet.

"You okay?" asked Tony.

"Yeah, I think so." Jerry's voice was strained, he could feel his heart beating violently in his chest, and he couldn't catch his breath. He turned quickly, looking for Sue Ling. She wasn't there.

"What the fuck you think you're doing?" yelled Tony. "What's the matter with you? You are going to get killed over this fucking bitch. Are you out of your fucking mind?"

Jerry couldn't answer. He couldn't catch his breath, he felt the pain in his side. He reached down and saw his hand was drenched in blood. Tony grabbed him around the waist. Jerry screamed in pain. Tony put one arm around his shoulder and the other around his knees and lifted Jerry into the back seat of the jeep. He was beginning to pass out, but heard Tony talking to him.

"You fucking idiot," said Tony. "I can't believe you would get yourself killed for that hooker. What's the matter with you? I got to get you to a doctor and get you stitched up. Listen to me, Jerry. You forget about the girl and the soldier. You tell the medic that you were walking around and somebody jumped you, stabbed you in the gut, and ran off with your wallet. You got that? You don't say a fucking word about the girl, you understand me, Jerry?"

Jerry shook his head and tried to answer but couldn't. He lay slumped over in the back of the jeep and stared out into the darkness. He didn't see Sue Ling in the street. They turned a corner; palm trees, a fountain in the middle of a roundabout that circled toward the entrance to the once splendid Victorian mansion that now served as the Saigon Central Medical Hospital.

"I don't think that it's too bad. You're going to be okay, kid. It's going to take more than that to kill you. You sure are one dumb bastard, risking your life for a ten-dollar hooker."

Jerry mumbled with what little strength he had and said, "Tony, please, stop calling her a hooker. She's a young girl, goddammit. That bastard was beating the shit out of her. You want me to stand there and watch him beat and rape her?"

"Okay, relax, pal. Save your strength." Jerry felt Tony's hand on his wrist. "I give a shit about people that give a shit about me and mine."

Tony pulled the jeep in front of the ER entrance and jumped out, leaving Jerry in the jeep. He ran inside and yelled, "Can I get some help here? I found this guy lying in the street, I think that maybe he got stabbed."

Two nurses rushed through the door toward Jerry, another came alongside the car with a gurney. They helped Jerry on and rolled him into the triage area of the ER. Tony held the door open and once they were through, he turned to leave.

"Hey, where you going?" said the nurse. "I could use a little info on this guy. You at least know his name?" Tony didn't turn, just walked out of the hospital and never looked back.

The sharp pain woke Jerry. He opened his eyes and reached down to where the pain was and felt a large gauze bandage around the left side of his stomach. He looked around and saw he was in the busy ER. He lay still, almost afraid to move, trying to understand what had happened. He could see the clock on the wall; it was 3:30 in the morning. He was hooked up to an IV, clear liquid dripping into the tube. Then he noticed the woman in a white coat next to him.

"It'll help take the edge off." A doctor stood at his bed with a chart in her left hand. He could read her nametag; it said Lieutenant Stephanie Weil. She lifted his wrist with her other hand and checked his pulse.

"You're a lucky soldier. Looks like you're going home. What happened, got into it with a couple of crazies at a bar? You guys will never learn, you all think this is one Wild West show, and you're all Billy the Kid. You're all a bunch of kids with big guns."

Jerry blinked, trying to focus on the voice, and said, "I didn't have much of a choice... This guy was trying to rape her, I couldn't just stand there and let it happen."

"Lucky for you he was there."

Jerry looked up and said, "What, what do you mean?"

"You don't remember a thing, do you?" said Stephanie.

At first the whole thing was a blur, and then it suddenly became clear as a bell. Jerry knew it was Tony who saved his life. Tony came from nowhere. It was dark in the alley, Jerry could hear the guy's jaw shatter from Tony's punch, and felt the soldier falling away. Jerry remembered Tony lifted him like he was a bale of hay and took him to the hospital.

How stupid to risk his life over somebody he hardly even knew. He had a family back home waiting for him and there he was lying in a hospital, stabbed in the side by some crazy son of a bitch trying to rape some girl. How did he get sidetracked from his main goal? *What's the matter with me*, he thought. *What am I trying to prove over here? When I get out of here, I'm going home to go on with my life, make a living, and watch my kids grow up, take them fishing with my dad, and that's it. No more of this trying to save the world from the bad guys. Fuck the bad guys and fuck the good guys. Let them have the goddamn world.*

"So you're finally awake. How you feeling?" said the doctor.

"I'm in a lot of pain. Is there anything you can give me?"

He watched as the woman filled a hypodermic from a small glass vial. She reached over and stuck the needle into the IV tube. "This will get you through the night." Jerry felt warmth come over his body and his mind and he drifted into a dreamless sleep.

A hand on his shoulder woke him and he looked up to see the faces of two soldiers standing over him.

"Hi, how are you doing, soldier?" The young MP leaned on the metal frame of the hospital bed. "We need to ask you a few questions. You okay?"

Jerry nodded his head, and said in a low voice, "Yeah."

"Why don't you tell us just what happened. And for the record, we'd like to know who brought you here, and why did they take off?"

Jerry stared at the two young MPs and thought to himself, *Christ, these guys look like they just got out of high school.*

"I was walking back to my quarters, and I guess I got jumped from behind and the next thing I know I'm here with this pain in my side. That's all I remember."

The MPs stared at Jerry and then looked at each other. The first one said, "Okay, if that's what you remember, then that's all you remember. The doc says it's only a flesh wound, and I guess we'll just let sleeping dogs lie. We'll report it as attempted robbery, is that okay with you, Specialist?"

"Yeah," said Jerry as if he were half asleep. "That's fine. I guess I'm lucky, I'm not on my way home in a body bag."

"You're right about that, I guess you're lucky at that. Listen, you have any idea who brought you in? It seems real strange that a guy brings you in and then splits. Why do you think he left like that? Do you know?"

Jerry looked up and said, "Nope."

Two days later Jerry was sent back to his quarters and was told that he would be as good as new in a few weeks. The wound wasn't life threatening and there was no damage to any internal organs.

Between the drugs and the painkillers, Jerry slept on and off for the next few days. He had no idea what happened to Sue Ling and there was no one to ask. Tony hadn't come by to see him either. He couldn't help but think of the pretty young girl; the whole thing was one big nightmare and he couldn't do anything about it.

Steve was attentive, brought him food and made sure he was okay before leaving for the day. On the third day, a knock on the door startled him. He got up slowly, his side still burned. He was in his boxers with no t-shirt. He thought to grab a shirt but the knock came again, this time louder. "Hold on, I'm coming. For Christ's sake, what's the fucking rush?"

Jerry opened the door. Two officers stood there. "You Jerry McGinnis?

Jerry nodded.

"We need to go over some details of what happened to you last week. I think maybe you might have left a few things out, and we just need to clarify a few details."

"Look," said Jerry, "I told the MPs at the hospital everything that I remember."

"Sure you did, but did you also forget about the soldier who was killed in the same alley that night? I mean, was that some kind of remarkable coincidence?" said the officer asked in a sarcastic tone. "You just happened to be there at the same time. Look, McGinnis, maybe it was self-defense but whatever it was, we need to establish just what happened and put this thing to bed. This is not going to go away, so why don't you just tell us what happened and we'll do everything we can to make this as painless as possible."

"How the hell do you know which alley I got stabbed in? I never said what alley because I don't know. It was late, and dark. I was walking home, this guy grabbed me from behind. Someone must have picked me up and brought me to the hospital. That's all I know."

"Yeah, okay," said one of the officers. "That's what is written in the report. But a soldier was killed that night and we are looking to see if these two incidents are related."

"Maybe it was the same guy that attacked me. I wish I could help."

The officers stood at the door, watching Jerry. "You know, I just don't buy it, it makes no sense. There's too much of a coincidence." One of the officers smiled and said, "We'll be in touch."

The two officers walked away. Jerry had to sit down again, his side was killing him. He walked slowly to the edge of his bed and carefully sat down. He had gotten himself into a real mess. How the fuck did that son of a bitch get himself killed? It must have been Tony. *Oh shit*, Jerry thought to himself. *I'm in a world of shit now. Christ, what the hell am I going to do now?*

Jerry looked up to see Steve Jacobs walk into the room. "Who were those two officers who just left? What did they want?"

"They said that another soldier was found dead that night and they think that maybe somehow I was involved."

"Why the hell didn't you tell me that? Are you fucking kidding me? You're in the country for a few goddamn weeks, and you end up in an alley, trying to save some hooker from some horny goddamn GI. You end up getting stabbed and some poor son of a bitch ends up dead. I got to tell you, Jerry, it's a good thing you got friends in high places."

"You mean you?"

"Yeah, asshole, me. I've got to get back to the office. I'll talk to some of the guys at JAG, see if they know anything." Steve went into the bathroom, threw some water on his face, picked up a briefcase, and walked out of the door.

Jerry sat down slowly and began to write. He left out the part about how he felt drawn to Sue Ling; he didn't need Kate reading that. But other than that, he left no details out. He had no idea what was going to happen to him. He wanted to talk to Tony, but knew he must be staying away for a reason. Better just to let him come to me, he thought.

After he healed, Jerry had been back at his desk for almost a week and no word from either MPs or Tony. It was like he became invisible. It reminded him of watching a log drift down the river, here one minute and gone the next, sliding around the bend and gone. He wrote in his journal: *I haven't heard from the JDs office, and the soldier who was killed was reported as having been killed in a local street crime. I came to this place to find the truth but it feels like I landed in Hell. This is where you go to kill or be killed.*

Jerry checked to see if the carbon copy was clear underneath the original. The original journals were going to his father, the copies in letters home to Kate. He needed a fresh sheet of carbon paper. He decided to give it a rest for the day.

CHAPTER 18

The streets of Saigon were always filled with people on foot or on bikes, but at 1700 with everyone heading home, the street took on a life of its own. There were countless people going somewhere, all in a hurry to get wherever they were going. Jerry headed for Kim's tea shop; it was his favorite place to head after work.

One of the waiters came over, a small man, with jet-black hair and a mustache that curled around his nose. He had a nice smile, calm and gentle.

"I'll just have a cup of tea." The waiter bowed turned and walked toward the kitchen.

Tony Ramo was suddenly standing behind Jerry and put his hand on his shoulder. "Well, well, so you're back from the dead, alive and well, just where we left off."

"Hey, Tony," said Jerry. "I thought you died and went to heaven."

"Me?" said Tony with a surprised look on his face. "You were the one that got stuck, not me. Anyway, if and when I do get whacked, going to heaven may not be in the cards for me. Being a good practicing Catholic, you never know: a couple of Hail Marys and maybe I'll get eternal bliss. Anyway, enough of this bullshit, we need to talk."

"Sure," said Jerry. Tony raised his hand to call over the old man, who came running over to take his order.

"What's that on your right arm?" Jerry asked, distracted for a moment from the questions that had kept him up the past few nights.

"What's what?" said Tony.

"Your arm, what's that on your arm?"

Tony looked at the spot Jerry was pointing to and said, "You never saw a tattoo before?"

"Yeah, I've seen plenty of tattoos but a fucking butterfly? No offense, but you don't look like the butterfly type of guy, if you know what I mean. And you didn't have it when we got here."

"Yeah," said Tony, "I know exactly what you mean, don't be a smartass. First of all, if you look close, it's a butterfly with teeth and claws, you get it, asshole?" Tony smiled. "Silent but deadly. You know, like Cassius Clay, move like a butterfly, sting like a bee. We're soft and quiet and then when you think everything is going to be all right, we take a bite out of your neck and rip your throat out." Tony laughed and gave his friend a gentle slap on the back. "Seriously, how you feeling, man? I need to tell you some stuff."

"Yeah, what the fuck happened that night?"

"Those guys from the JDs office who came to pay you a visit were preparing a case against you, maybe second-degree murder or maybe manslaughter, but there was no way in hell, as far as they were concerned, that you were going to just walk away from this. Somebody was going to go down, and they were going after you big time. Your blood was at the scene."

Jerry looked confused and stunned and said, "So what happened? Why didn't they come back? I don't get it."

217

Tony took a long swallow of his beer and said, "They didn't come back because we cleaned things up. Because some guys that you don't know put in the word and pulled some strings and made the whole thing go away."

"I don't know what the hell you're talking about. I didn't do a fucking thing, it was you that…"

"Yeah, you're right. You didn't do a fucking thing except jump in between a soldier and a cheap hooker and get yourself stabbed in the process, and guess what, the soldier ended up dead. Perhaps you might consider that if I didn't knock the knife out of his hand, you would be in a body bag right now, heading home to your sweet little wife."

Tony put his beer down and said, "Anyway, that's all over now, and as long as we keep things the way they are, then you'll be just fine."

"What are you getting at, Tony? I don't have any idea what the hell you're talking about."

"I'll spell it out for you, pal. We did for you, now it's going to be your chance to do for us."

"Who the hell is us?"

"Us is a unit, let's just say an undercover unit, sort of top secret. More like a shadow unit that has special interests and deals in special activities."

"What's this got to do with me?" asked Jerry. "What kind of special interests and activities?"

"I really can't give details. I have to leave that up to the top guy. He's the only one that can bring you in. I can tell you that it involves some activities that some people would think were a little over the line. Look at it this way: all of us guys are here, not home, we're here.

In this totally fucked-up country, getting blown away—for what? You getting where I'm going with this?"

"No," said Jerry. "I have no idea what the hell you're talking about."

"Okay, we're on the front lines sacrificing everything, family, health, future, while a bunch of old white guys, who sent us here in the first place, are lying around their fucking pools playing with their grandkids. In the meantime, our families are shoveling shit just to put food on the goddamn table." Tony stopped talking and waited for some reactions from Jerry.

"I'm listening. Go on, you got my attention."

"Okay," said Tony. "What I'm going to tell you could get a lot of people in some serious shit, so you need to give me your word that this stays between us, okay?"

"Yeah, of course." said Jerry.

"Before we were here, they were here. In the beginning, way before the ground troops got sent over, there were military advisors and a shitload of military contractors that were working with the advisors. Mostly they were in charge of distributing all the military and economic aid that started flying into this country in the late fifties. I don't know the whole story, but these guys figure out one day that maybe it's time for them to reap some of the riches, if you know what I mean." Tony put his beer down and looked at Jerry. "You see where I'm going with this?"

"I think so," said Jerry. "I'm still listening."

"Good. So these hardcore guys decide to put together this unit, and they name it Delta Unit. They run it like the military, with a command structure, not based on military rank, but on your individual contribution to the Unit. At first, they diverted a small percentage of the stuff that was coming into Da Nang and Hai Phong. Didn't matter what it was, tools, guns, food, cigarettes, liquor and drugs, medical equipment, X-ray machines, everything you could imagine. Nobody was watching, and the Unit would divert maybe as much as ten percent, sell it here or anywhere for that matter. A lot went to medical facilities in other countries, like Cambodia, Laos, and Thailand. They would sell it for ten cents on the dollar... and this went on seven days a week. Anyway, that's the way it started. But soon they started getting into more serious shit."

"What's more serious than stealing from the U.S. government and the people of Vietnam?"

"Drugs, big-time drugs, like weed, heroin, cocaine. At first they just supplied the troops, but then they figured out how to get the drugs into the States. Guess how?" Tony stopped and waited, Jerry wasn't smiling but he was listening closely. "Smuggled with the bodies of dead soldiers going home. Seems kind of sacrilegious, not that I'm much of a Catholic. They would bring them in for preparation to go home, slice them up, take out all the organs, replace them with drugs, sew them up as good as new and send them to very specific funeral homes."

Jerry looked at Tony. "What the fuck, are you shitting me?"

"I know it's a lot to take in, buddy, but there is a hell of a lot of money to be made and someone is going to make it. You can share in it or you can sit it out, it's up to you."

"Why are you telling me this? What's this all got to do with me?"

"Simple. We need intelligence, and you have access."

Jerry was silent for a long time. "You know you could spend the rest of your life in prison for this shit. I'm not throwing my life away. The risk is just too high."

"That's the beauty of this. There is no risk, there is protection all the way to the top. You saw how they made your problems go away. Look," continued Tony, "don't overthink this. You work for army intelligence, you bunk with a JAG guy, so when you come across information that you think is important to us, you'll pass it along. You will be compensated and I don't mean chump change. What the info is exactly will determine how much you get. Good for you, good for the team."

Jerry looked at Tony with a strange and curious expression on his face and said, "Let me think about this. You can call this anything you want to, team, unit, Delta, but the fact is, you're just a well-run gang, only with uniforms... If I get caught, that's fucking treason. These are serious criminal activities, they'll put me away forever, if they don't hang me first."

Tony smiled. "Okay, Jerry, you give it some thought. You're right, if you get caught, you're fucked, big time, but when you walk out of this fucking cesspool of a country, you'll walk away with more money than you'd make in ten years. You go home, buy a bigger house, send the kids to private school. Look at it this way: a lot of people in the States are making millions on this war, don't you think that we deserve some too? Look, I cleared it with the top guys in the Unit and they know that I'm talking to you. But once you're in, you're in for good. You understand, Jerry? This isn't a social club, this is serious shit."

Tony reached across the table and grabbed onto Jerry's wrist, holding it down hard on the table, his sleeve rolled up, the butterfly tattoo flexing.

"Tony," Jerry said. "Can I think about this? I'm not really sure what you want. But I guess, as long as nobody gets hurt, what's the harm? I get where you are coming from. I know that you're putting your ass on the line for me. I just need to know what I'm getting into, okay?"

"Okay," said Tony.

Tony got up from the chair and patted Jerry on the shoulder and smiled.

"How's the shoulder, Jerry?"

Jerry looked at Tony and said, "Wasn't my shoulder, it was my side, and it hurts like hell, but I'll live."

"Yeah, I know, you'll be living a lot better in the next few months if you play your cards right, and maybe things will get better back home before you know it. So sit tight, relax, and get back to work. Here's a little welcoming gift. But just so we're clear, this stays between us. You say a word to anyone, we're both dead. I'm not fucking with you, Jerry."

"I read you loud and clear," said Jerry. Tony handed Jerry an envelope and started to walk away.

"Hey, Tony, hold on a second. Whatever happened to the girl, Sue Ling?"

Tony looked at Jerry and smiled, and said, "You starting to scare me, Jerry, sometimes I can't figure you out. Forget about that bitch. Wait, sorry," continued Tony. "I forgot, she's not a bitch, just a cheap gook hooker."

"Hey, look," said Jerry. "I almost got myself killed over her. I just want to know if she's okay."

"Yeah, yeah, she's fine, but don't get too emotional, because you're not going to see her anymore. She's being shipped out of the country. So just forget about her and let's focus on your future, okay, sport?"

"Where's she going?" asked Jerry.

"Goddamnit, Jerry, what the fuck you care where she's going? Forget about her."

"Tony, please, I don't understand why, but I feel like I need to see her before she takes off. Where is she, Tony? Come on, I just want to say goodbye."

Tony looked at Jerry with a strange expression on his face.

"You are one fucking weird guy, but fine," said Tony. "I think that maybe she's staying at a home for orphans in Moc Bai. It's a small town about twenty miles northeast of here. But you'll never see her, she's probably gone by now anyway. And if she's not, the two women that run the house won't ever let you near her. I can't deal with this bullshit, just forget about her. I'll be in touch, and don't talk to anyone about what we spoke about, you understand? I'm not kidding around, Jerry."

"Yeah," said Jerry. "I understand."

Tony had a way about him, the way he spoke, the way he walked, the way he looked at you when he was being dead serious. When he was kidding around it was like he didn't have a care in the world, but when he was being serious, you knew it was serious. That's the way he was at that moment, dead fucking serious. Jerry sat staring straight ahead thinking of only one thing, not about what Tony had said, but only one thing: the tattoo.

Chuck Harris had an identical tattoo on his right arm in exactly the same place. Jerry remembered the IV in Chuck's arm and right above where the needle went in was this weird little tattoo of a butterfly with jagged teeth and claws, just like the one on Tony's arm. He had to be closer to getting the answers to the questions he came with. He opened the envelope Tony had passed him and looked in. There were at least ten one hundred dollar bills. He folded the envelope and shoved it inside his shirt.

He closed his eyes and tried to picture himself and his dad sitting by the river back home, where the air had a clean and crisp smell. He took a deep breath, but instead of the smell that he had remembered, the foul smell of the Saigon streets filled his nose and the reality of where he was hit him hard and filled his mind with guilt. He looked down and started to write a new letter, not to Kate and the boys but to his dad. He would send the money to his dad and have him give it to Kate.

Jerry rubbed his side; the pain had eased over the last two weeks. As he sat there at the small tea shop in Saigon he began to think about what he had gotten himself into. He never forgot that he owed Chuck his life, but nothing he could do would bring his friend back from the dead. Jerry asked himself why he was doing this, why he was putting himself in harm's way. Already one soldier was dead and he had agreed to provide information to a secret criminal gang of thugs. Okay, he thought, the dead soldier wasn't his fault, but he could get into serious trouble if he got caught giving any classified information to anyone. Was this all about Chuck and Brian, or was this all about getting a story that would get him the national attention he needed to become a well-known investigative reporter?

"Hi, soldier, you want to go to a party?"

Jerry looked up to see a young girl dressed in tight shorts with an open blouse. Jerry smiled and said, "No, thanks. I have to write this letter home."

"I know," said the girl. "You lonely for your girlfriend, well, your girlfriend, she very far from here and right now, I the only one here."

Jerry looked at the girl and said, "Not my girlfriend, my wife."

"No way, honey, you much too young to have a wife."

"You speak English very well," said Jerry. "Can I ask you a question?"

"Sure," said the girl. "Maybe I tell you if I know, maybe I don't." She smiled and said, "What's your question?"

"You ever hear of a house where they bring in orphans, mostly young girls, I think it's in Moc Bai?"

The girl smiled and said, "I know the place you talking about, but I no information center. You want to know, it will cost you twenty dollars."

Jerry smiled and said, "Twenty dollars is a lot of money for a name."

"Yes, you right, but I know the name and you don't. You want to know or not?"

"Okay, here's the twenty, but how do I know that this is the house that I 'm looking for?"

"You don't," she said, "but it is." She took the money and slipped it into her tight shorts. "Mother and daughter run this house for young children, mostly girls."

"Why mostly girls?" Jerry asked.

"You want to know, you go there and ask, mother's name is Grandma Kim, her place is forty kilometers northeast, everyone there know her. That's all I know. Now you want to party, you give me twenty, another twenty, and I make you forget all about your wife and back home, you not be lonely anymore," she said with a warm smile.

"Thanks, honey," said Jerry. "I have to get back to my unit, maybe another time."

The girl smiled and said, "You're crazy, soldier," and turned and walked away.

Jerry sat there for a minute, picked up his pen and paper, paid his bill, and headed back to the Quonset hut. He had plenty of thinking to do, but not now. His head was spinning and he needed to get things sorted out before he took the next step. He thought about the path that he had chosen. He pondered his decision and questioned his judgment and considered the consequences. He believed that if he were careful and thoughtful about everything that he needed to do and say, then he would get to the truth about Chuck and Brian. He would write a story that would help a lot of innocent people and at the same time build a reputation for himself. *I just need to be careful and can't underestimate these guys. They're smart and they sound pretty fucking mean. If they would travel all the way to Pennsylvania to murder two innocent young boys, well, they must be a bunch of ruthless bastards who wouldn't give a second thought to cutting my throat and leaving me on the side of a road to rot.*

The following morning, he walked into the commanding officer's office. "Sir," he said, "you have a few minutes?"

"What's on your mind, McGinnis?"

"Sir, I'm thinking about doing a human interest story about how we are coming to the aid of the orphaned children in the country. Kids whose parents were killed by the NVA and we're helping to provide shelter and care. Anyway, I heard about a home in Moc Bai where a mother and a daughter take in young children and take care of them. I thought, if it's okay with you, that I would take a ride up there and get some information on the story. What do you think, Colonel?"

Bentley looked up and with his hand on his chin, said, "God knows we could use a little good press. Maybe we could get it in the national papers and get those fucking draft card-burning hippie bastards off the front page and get ourselves a little good publicity for a change. I guess it wouldn't hurt to go up there and ask some questions, but you don't print a goddamn word without my written approval. You understand, Specialist? Not one fucking word."

"Read you loud and clear, sir," said Jerry with a little smile on his face. "Sir," continued Jerry as he was about to leave the colonel's office, "You ever hear of these women or maybe we have some records or files on them?"

"Let me look into it, give me a couple of days."

"Thank you, sir."

For the next few days Jerry kept quiet and did his job. He made no inquiries and asked no questions. He would have to wait and be patient. Everything was coming together; things were beginning to make sense.

CHAPTER 19

The Children, Saigon

I   *walked into my office at the embassy in downtown Saigon, it was just 0800. The overnight papers from the States focused on the heightened scrutiny from the press regarding an increase in civilian casualties in North Vietnam. It was apparently the decision of the DoD that we admit that civilians may have been accidentally bombed with napalm along the Mekong Delta regions. At the very end of the year our troop levels reached almost 400,000 military personnel with close to 5,000 deaths and more than 30,000 wounded.*

Half the information that I would report in our newsletters was true and the other half was total bullshit and meant to keep the GI's morale from completely breaking down. The anti-war movement and demonstrations in New York and San Francisco with more than 200,000 strong are now claiming that poor white males and young Negro men are bearing the heaviest burdens both in Vietnam and at home. For every demonstration against the war, somebody like Johnson or Westmoreland condemns the anti-war demonstrators, saying that they are giving the North Vietnamese soldiers hope that they can win politically that which they will not be able to accomplish militarily. One minute, Johnson is talking peace, and the next minute, Congress authorizes more than four billion dollars for the war.

Jerry took a long sip of hot coffee. A yellow folder with the heading "Rainbow" sat at the top of the pile of papers in front of him. He put down his coffee mug and reopened the file. The first section was titled "Sexually Exploited Children." He began to read about children as young as eight years old, both boys and girls, taken from their families and sold into slavery. The statistics and the information in these pages were sickening. Slavery, abuse, rape, illness, and drugs awaited these innocent children. This was about money, about the commercial and economic value of children sold into forced labor or forced into sexual slavery. It all came down to money, and these innocent children had become nothing more than tools of the trade: they were the goods.

Foreign armies had been coming here for centuries, either for the value of the land or to alter the political process, and in the meantime, they destroyed the moral and ethical values of the people and their governments. Western soldiers had been coming to Southeast Asia to fight and to die, and left behind widows, wives, girlfriends, and children. Those children and their mothers were disowned by their families and were forced to live lives of shame and humiliation. Without any alternatives the mothers would have to turn to a life of crime, drugs and prostitution, and the children would be shipped off to homes that would sometimes care for them but others would exploit them in ways that made Jerry sick to his stomach.

The UN and the World Council of Churches were trying to bring this situation out into the light. It seemed that poverty, war, and ignorance continued to drive these children to be sexually exploited and trafficked.

On and on he read, and then he came to a separate folder titled "Sharing House." He sat back and rubbed his face and then his side. The wound itched, and every time he scratched it, a sharp pain would bring him back to the alley and the girl and the dead soldier.

He continued to read and realized: this is it, this is what I'm looking for. The file described a home for abused and orphaned children in a town just forty miles northeast of Saigon. Two women, a mother and a daughter, were operating it. The mother was known as Grandma Kim Hak-Soon, and she had been taking care of exploited women and children for years. Her daughter Lucy Hak-Soon had taken up the calling and apparently worked along with her mother. Jerry sat back and looked at the pictures of the two women in a press release from June of 1965. The army was concerned about bad publicity regarding American soldiers coming to Vietnam, getting the women pregnant and then leaving without a word or any support for the children. These women were working to help many of those children. He sat there and stared at the pictures. The old woman had a worn and tired face, with lines and wrinkles that spoke of fatigue and age. But there was a determined and forceful expression on her face, a look of defiance brought on by so many battles and so many disappointments. She was small, but stood straight and tall with her head held high, and her eyes—there was something about those eyes. Jerry stared at the old woman's eyes and then at the daughter's eyes. Their eyes were identical. He could see the passion and determination in their eyes, and at the same time softness or maybe a sensitivity that came with reaching out to those abused and forgotten people who have been abandoned by the rest of the world. These two women were special; Jerry thought about something Father Shannon had once said about people like this, they were God's Angels on earth.

The hand on Jerry's shoulder caused him to jump and spin around. "Relax, McGinnis," said Colonel Benton. "You find what you were looking for?"

"Yes, sir," said Jerry. "I really appreciate the information, and—"

The colonel broke in and said, "Never mind the appreciation bullshit. You want to write a story about how Uncle Sam is taking care of the little children over here, that's fine, but like I told you before, make sure that I see every word you write, you got that?"

"Yes, sir, loud and clear, Colonel. You'll see every word, sir."

"Fine, McGinnis, then get to it. We got a war to win."

"Right, sir," said Jerry as the colonel walked away. Jerry sat there for a minute looking at the pictures of the mother and the daughter again. If anyone would know about Sue Ling, it would be these women. And he needed to get to Sue Ling and find out what she knew about Chuck.

These women were doing good work. Of course, there were international organizations that also tried to help these traumatized victims, such as the World Council of Churches and the Christian Conference of Asia, but with a war raging on along with religious and communal conflicts, many of the abuses were being overlooked and forgotten. War kills, children suffer, and history repeated itself here in Vietnam. If he could help by getting the word out, then maybe he would be able to live with himself for all the dirty work he might be called on to do as a member of the Unit. He could help with one hand and take with the other.

It was a Tuesday morning and Jerry was finally given a pass to drive up north. He grabbed the keys to the jeep that was parked outside the gates of his quarters and headed out of Saigon. The streets were teeming with people heading to work, and he stopped, waiting for the traffic cop to signal that he could continue across the busy and crowded intersection.

Moc Bai was only about forty miles northeast of Saigon, but it would probably take him at least two hours to get there. Once he left Saigon, it felt like he had time-traveled back two hundred years. Nothing but rice paddies as far as he could see, farmed by what always looked like little old men and women with these huge sun hats to shade themselves from the blistering sun, stooped over, pulling the long stems from the water. The roads themselves were nothing more than gravel and dirt, and after a hard rain they were almost impassable.

The road to Moc Bai had been controlled by the South and was as secure as any road could be in Vietnam. The trip was uneventful and Jerry arrived in Moc Bai around ten o'clock that morning. The town was nothing more than some scattered huts surrounded by rice fields and manmade ponds where they raised fish. Jerry stopped by the market. He had learned a smattering of Vietnamese and asked the best he could where he could find the orphan house. The little bit of the language seemed to come in handy, and he understood that he needed to go another two miles up the road and then turn right after a large rice field. Self-doubt plagued his thoughts; he was tired of fighting the constant doubts. The guilt of leaving his wife and kids and the feeling that he might have had something to do with Brian's death, and Chuck's death too, gnawed at him constantly.

He made the right-hand turn leading to a long and narrow road to what looked like a large farmhouse on top of a small hill. Jerry pulled up to the gate in front of the house. He got out of the jeep, stretched, rubbed his side, and turned when he heard a voice.

"Can I help, soldier?" asked an old man as he bowed and smiled.

"Yes, you can," said Jerry. "I'm looking for Grandma Kim. I was told that she runs a home for orphans. Is this where she lives?"

"Yes, the woman that you ask for does live here, Please forgive me for asking, but what is it that you want to see her about?"

Jerry hesitated, feeling like he was being interrogated.

"I work for the Public Relations Department and we are doing some research on the orphaned children of the war, and I was told that Mrs. Kim was, well, the sort of the person that I should talk to."

"I see," said the old man. "Please wait here." Jerry watched him walk toward the house. In just a few minutes he came toward Jerry and opened the gate to the house and asked Jerry to please follow him. They walked the narrow cobblestone path up to the house and Jerry was shown into a small parlor. A large window opened out to a small garden filled with vegetables.

A cool morning breeze felt good on his face. He had been missing the brisk chill of the fall and winter months at home. There was a piano against the opposite wall. He walked over to look at pictures of young kids, neatly placed along the top. He lifted one of the photos. The child staring back at him had a hollow smile, as if there really wasn't anything to smile about. On the wall over the piano was a mirror. He looked into his face. He hadn't noticed how thin his face had gotten. He wasn't eating enough, too busy and occupied to spend a lot of time eating, and he didn't like the food anyway.

He turned to look around the room. It was sparsely filled with old and weathered furniture. He felt suddenly very sad.

"My name is Kim Mie Ky." Jerry turned toward the voice and looked up and then down to a tiny woman standing next to a table where a teapot had been placed. She stood no more than 4'11", with gray hair and a weathered face, but her eyes had a brightness and clarity that mesmerized Jerry. They were the same eyes that he had seen in the papers back at the office in Saigon. Grandma Kim smiled and she turned slowly to say, "Would you like a cup of tea? It's quite good, and good for you."

"That would be real nice. Thank you," said Jerry.

As she poured the tea into small white porcelain teacups, Jerry couldn't help but watch her hunched shoulders and thought to himself, *What weight have these shoulders had to carry? What pain and suffering had she seen over so many years? How many sad and lonely and abandoned eyes had this old woman looked into, and how much desperation and fear did she soothe with a soft touch and a warm smile? How many of those eyes had she pulled out of the darkness and brought into the light of day and given hope and optimism to?*

"Would you like sugar in your tea?"

Jerry snapped out of the trance that he had fallen into for a brief moment and said, "Yes, thanks, that's nice of you."

"It's no trouble." She looked up for an instant into Jerry's eyes. "The eyes are the windows into your soul," she said. "I read that, I can't remember where, but I always remembered that. I think that it's true. Do you think so?"

"Yes," he said. "I think they're right, the eyes are the windows into your soul. What do you see in my eyes?" asked Jerry in a soft voice.

Grandma Kim placed the china teapot down slowly as if it were a precious heirloom and said with a smile, "You look tired, come and sit down over here and have some bread. There's some jam. It's really quite sweet, we make it here."

Jerry walked over to the table, sat down, and took a sip of tea and took a piece of bread. Instead of taking a bite, he asked, "Are you the woman that they call Grandma?"

The old woman smiled and nodded her head. "Yes, I am that woman. Now maybe you will tell me who you are and why you have come out here to visit us."

"I'm so sorry. My name is Jerry McGinnis, and I'm with the Public Relations Department of the U.S. Army in Saigon. I'm here to ask you some questions about your work with the children. I have been looking into what this action has done to the children and I thought that maybe we could help."

"How could you help us?" asked Grandma Kim.

"With aid. We're not here just to fight the North Vietnamese. We're here to help your people build a future, and where better to start than helping the children of this country, and where better than here with you."

"Your words are noble and are filled with promises, but I must tell you, Mr. McGinnis..."

"Please," Jerry interrupted, "please call me Jerry."

"Okay, if you wish it, I will call you Jerry. Your words are good and we are happy to receive your help. But for many years, the words from soldiers have proven to be empty and unfulfilled. Your soldiers come here and they meet the young girls and maybe the girls fall in love with the soldiers or maybe the girls fall in love with the chance of getting away from here and finding a life in your country. Or maybe that's what the soldiers tell these young girls and of course they believe them. But then a child is born and then the soldiers leave and what is left is a ruined life. The families shun the babies and the mothers, who find themselves with nowhere to go and no family to turn to. So they find their way here, some of them. They come here and we care for them and teach them to support themselves. We educate them and their children and sometimes we are blessed knowing that sometimes we win and show these poor souls that they don't have to abandon their children on the steps of the church or, far worse, throw them into the river and return to a life of drugs and prostitution."

Jerry looked down.

"Please forgive me for being rude. You come here offering to help us and I question your intention and motives, please, forgive me." She bowed low and Jerry felt both humbled and embarrassed. He said nothing. What she had said, the accusations and the condemnation of the actions of so many U.S. soldiers were as right as anyone could be.

Listening well was one of his flaws. Jerry needed to talk, he needed to make a point or prove a point, to ask a question and get the answer.

"No," said Jerry, "please, I think that it is we foreigners who should be asking for your forgiveness. I think that maybe we have brought a lot of pain and suffering to this country. The price of freedom can be very high and the road to freedom long and hard." Jerry took a sip from his cup of tea and smiled as he spread the jam on the remaining piece of bread.

"How noble and kind you are to bring us your freedom," the old woman said in a sarcastic tone. Jerry sat back and realized what a fool he must sound like. The company line was to say just what the army tells you to say. What a jerk he had been. Jerry took a sip of tea and began to say something, but turned to hear somebody walking toward them.

"Who is our guest?" asked a young woman. Jerry turned around to see a tall slim girl enter the room. She was what they used to call a "tall drink of water." Jerry's dad used to say it when a tall, slim, attractive young girl would walk by, and now he understood exactly what it meant. A beam of morning sunlight glittered through the open window and cast a pleasant and serene light on the face of the woman. Jerry squinted against the bright sun and looked toward her. He could make out her long jet-black hair that lay upon her back and her long white dress clinging to her slender body. As she walked toward the table, the slit in her dress seemed to move up her thighs, and for a second Jerry followed the movement of her body as she walked across the room. He stood as she came closer and put his hand out. With the sun in his face, he couldn't see her features at first, and she stopped and bowed gently. When she was closer to him, he looked directly into her eyes. Her left eye was closed shut with a bruise the size of a man's hand. Her lips were swollen a deep purple. There was a smudge of blood that washing had not been able to wipe clean.

She smiled and before Jerry could say anything, said, "What is it that you are asking forgiveness for, soldier?"

"I think that if it weren't for the foreigners in your country there would be no reason for this orphanage to exist. And I am sorry for that and hope I can find a way to help."

"I see. Do you speak for your government? Because if you do, you have much forgiveness to ask for. But please, where are my manners? My name is Lucy Hak, and this is my mother." She gestured toward the old woman.

"I am pleased to meet you," Jerry said, as he bowed gently. "My name is Jerry McGinnis. I have come here not just to ask for your forgiveness, but to try and understand how we can help the children."

"I don't mean to seem disrespectful, it's not my intention to offend you, Jerry, but we have heard these words before. I guess it's possible that you are well intentioned, but the ones that have said these things are often those that exploit the tragedy that foreigners have brought to our shores. The exploitation and abuse of our children has been going on for generations, but war compounds this shame."

Lucy paused, and then said, "Good old American ingenuity. You bring war and tragedy to our country and then, like a well-oiled machine, you exploit those that are most innocent and fragile."

The old woman stood up and looked at her daughter and placed her hand gently on her face. The same brown eyes, the same air of confidence and spirit he saw in the older woman was there in the younger.

"What happened to you? Who beat you up?" asked Jerry. He had a hard time not staring and it seemed disingenuous not to mention the obvious.

"The parents of the girls can be most disagreeable when it comes to feeding their families."

"I don't understand," said Jerry.

"I know that you don't understand," said Lucy. "Maybe if you did understand then maybe, just maybe, I wouldn't have to fight for a nine-year-old girl who had been sold by her father to work in India, where she will surely become a child prostitute and end up dead in the streets before she turns twenty years of age."

Jerry sat down; this was way more than he had bargained for. He had come here to do some research, find Sue Ling, and maybe find out what the hell his friend and his brother were killed for.

The older woman said, "I have much to do and it's getting close to lunchtime. Please stay and have lunch with us, you seem like a good man. Maybe we can answer some of your questions."

She reached out and Jerry stood. "Come along," she said. They walked down a hallway into a much larger room, a dining room with children quietly standing by little chairs. He stopped. There were too many children to count. They stood and together bowed as Grandma Kim and Jerry walked in. A smile came to his face and he bowed back. Lucy led him to a chair and sat down on the other side of the table. She poured the tea without looking at him. "Do you take sugar in your tea?" Jerry could sense that there still remained an air of suspicion and misgiving.

"You look like a man with something on his mind, and since you are seated at our table, perhaps you'll give us the courtesy to tell us the real reason you are here."

"As God is my witness, I'll do what I can to let people back home know what's going on here, but I do have other questions. I hope you don't mind."

Lucy nodded.

"I need to speak with a girl named Sue Ling. Do you know her?"

"Sue Ling is a very common name. Where do you know her from, and what does she look like?"

"I met her in a bar in Saigon. She works there as a, well, as a prostitute." Jerry could feel his face redden.

"I see, you like this girl and want to see her again, maybe promise to take her back to your country with you. Is that why you come here, looking for a girl?"

"No, no, please, that is not it at all. She mentioned a man named Chuck Harris. He was a friend of mine and she knew him. I just want to ask her a few questions."

Lucy looked up from the tea and said, "I know Chuck Harris, he is a good man. He has a good heart, he was wounded and sent home. We haven't heard from him."

Jerry stared at Lucy. "You knew Chuck too?" He put his tea down. "Chuck was my friend, a close childhood friend. He was sent home, I saw him in the hospital. He died, but I don't think he died as a result of the injuries that he got here, I think that he was killed. I think that he was murdered and his brother as well. I need to know what happened."

A sadness fell across her face and she looked down.

"That's why I wanted to speak to Sue Ling, but perhaps you can help me."

Lucy shook her head. "Chuck is dead," she said as a way of confirming what she had heard.

"Chuck was my good friend. I owe it to him and his family to find out what happened to him. I need to find out why he was shot here in Vietnam and then killed at home."

"Killed at home, I don't understand," said Lucy, then she paused, as if she was thinking to herself. She slowly lifted her cup of tea and gently took a sip, before she said, "Is this why you have come here, to find out why your friend was killed? I can tell you why your friend was killed. You don't have to ask Sue Ling. Everybody knows what happens when you go against the Unit, when you refuse to do what you are told."

"Can you tell me more about this unit?" asked Jerry.

Lucy looked around the room and then back at Jerry. She eyed him with a bit of suspicion; she had learned over the years to be wary of Americans.

"I think maybe I should let you eat in peace and send you on your way, but you have a kind face and I can feel your pain for your friend. Let us eat our meal and I will tell you what I know of your friend, but first, tell me what you know."

While they ate, Jerry told the mother and daughter about his friendship with Chuck and Brian Harris, growing up together in central Pennsylvania. Jerry told Lucy and Grandma Kim about the last time he had seen Chuck in the hospital.

The two women sat and listened, picking at their food as Jerry spoke.

"That's it," said Jerry, as he finished his meal. "The simple truth is I came here to find out what really happened to my friend and his brother."

Lucy placed her chopsticks across her rice bowl and said, "We all have our reasons for doing what we choose to do. You have yours, I have mine. You leave the love of your family and join your military and come here to find what you say is the truth, the truth about what happened to your friend. Well, maybe there is more to your story, maybe there are reasons that you are keeping from us, but I am not here to judge your reasons. Chuck was a kind and good man. I saw it in his eyes, I heard it in his voice. I will tell you what I know, I'll tell you what I believe happened to him, and why. Let's take a walk."

Jerry thanked Grandma Kim for her hospitality and followed Lucy out a back door. There was a dirt path barely wide enough for them to walk side by side.

"It's not the first time I've seen this. The stories and the circumstances are always a little different but they always end the same way. Good men come here, with good intentions. They come here to protect us from the communists in the North, to help us defend ourselves, to secure our freedom. But after not too long some of these young men find themselves among others who feel differently about why you're here. The nobility of their intentions is soon poisoned by these other men who have very different agendas. But for some, like your friend, they finally hearken back to the values that they once held dear and they say: no more, I didn't come here to do this. I came here to help these people, not to hurt them. And then they feel good and warm and then one day, they're gone."

They walked in silence for a bit and then she continued.

"Chuck was one of those men. He came here and brought us food and medicine for the children. I don't know where he got these things or why he chose to help us but we were very grateful. We often talked for many hours. He, like so many others, came here to serve his country and help my people. At first he became one of them, but he would not talk of these men. He told me that he would not put us in harm's way, that's what he would say, 'harm's way.' He told me that he could no longer stand by and watch this happen and that he was done being one of their soldiers, and if it came to it, he would go to his superior officers.

"I asked him many times over the next few weeks to tell me about this secret organization that he called 'the Unit,' but he refused again and again. He told me that if I knew anything about the Unit, then the soldiers would come here and destroy everything. That they would not hesitate to kill my mother and me, and sell off all the children here as if they were nothing more than cattle."

Lucy stopped walking and turned to look at Jerry. They stood on a small strip of land that separated one rice field from the other. "We were supposed to meet in a coffee shop downtown and Chuck never showed up," said Lucy. "I thought that something important must have come up. I carefully asked around if anyone knew where Chuck Harris was. I told them that he was supposed to bring supplies up to the orphanage. Almost two weeks went by, and finally one day Sue Ling told me that Chuck had been seriously wounded and sent back to the States. I prayed that he would recover from his injuries, and now you tell me that he has been killed."

"Wait, so you do know Sue Ling?"

"It is a small country, Jerry. Yes, I know Sue. She helps us here when she can. She believed that someone from the Unit tried to kill Chuck, but we thought that once he was sent home he would be safe. I am sorry for him, for his family, and for you, coming all this way. But forgive me, Jerry, I don't really know who you are or what may be your true intentions. I feel there is more to your story, maybe you think that you are protecting us, maybe you are protecting yourself. I must think only of these children and the children that will follow. The men that flew all the way to the U.S. to kill a fellow American soldier are driven, committed to getting what they want, and it has been proven time and time again that they will stop at nothing to get it. I'm not here to solve your problems or to give you the answers. I'm here to protect these children, nothing more."

Jerry looked into Lucy's eyes again and said, "Chuck Harris was my friend, my childhood friend. We were born in the same town in the same hospital and went to the same schools. We dated the same girls and one day he saved me and two other men from drowning in the river. We were connected, almost from the day we were born. I owe it to Chuck, Brian, and their parents to find out what happened. I feel that in some way, I'm part of the reason that he and Brian are dead, and I'll go to my grave with this burden on my soul. But you're right, I do have other reasons. I came here for two reasons, yes, to learn the truth, but the other was to write about what's happening here. Maybe I can tell the truth of what happened to my friend and maybe I can tell the truth of what is happening to your people, the children of this war, maybe then I can really make a difference. I think that if I can do that, then maybe Chuck and Brian will not have died in vain. Maybe I'm kidding myself, but I've got to try, by telling your story and telling their story. It may bring some good out of this nightmare."

They walked slowly back to the house.

CHAPTER 20

Moc Bai, 1969

Afew days later Jerry met with Sue Ling and Lucy outside of Saigon, at a friend's house the women knew would be safe. Jerry was anxious to hear Sue Ling's story.

Sue Ling described how she met Chuck at the bars in Saigon where she was working. Chuck had fallen in love with her, and she with him. He had told Sue that he would find a way to take her away from this. They would live in Pennsylvania, raise a family, and live out their lives together in America. He had been so kind to her, she said, not like the others, the other men whom she had fallen in with. He told her how they recruited him. At first it had seemed more like a fraternity than a military unit. Chuck told Sue, "It all made sense. We're here fighting and dying, it seems perfectly logical that the boys on the battlefield should reap some of the rewards."

Chuck had also told Lucy Hak that he had become a member of a very special group of men and women who could get things, needed things for the children: "medicine, food, clothes."

Lucy continued the story. "So many good young men come over here filled with good intentions, but it doesn't take long before some of them turn. Chuck had become one of them, but in a short time he understood who they really were and what they were really doing."

There was a long silence and then Sue Ling began to talk again. "They paid him a great deal of money, with promises of a great deal more. We needed this money to start a life in America. So he became a trusted member of the Unit, at the same time supplying the orphanage with everything they could possibly ever need. The Unit was involved in the human trafficking and that included children. Some parents were willing to sell their young girls because they were desperate for money, but sometimes the Unit would steal children, even killing the parents if they would not cooperate. Chuck's conscience was getting the best of him. He couldn't sleep, couldn't even eat, and he wanted out. But he knew too much, they would never let him walk away. And then he was shot in an alley and left for dead."

"How do you know all this?" Jerry asked.

"I have many eyes on the streets of Saigon," said Lucy. "A network of people everywhere who hear things. A street vendor, shopkeepers in the markets, in the stores, and people working in the bars and tea shops throughout the city. We listen, and alcohol loosens the tongue. We hear when a child is being targeted, what village and the family name. We do our best. Most times we are able to convince the family not to deal with the Unit, but sometimes it goes terribly wrong.

"The families are offered money, more money than they can earn in a year. If money is not enough to convince a father, then there are always South Vietnamese police, who would have you arrested for collaborating with the enemy. But then there were those few brave fathers who would fight to the death to protect their children. For that brave soul, a bullet to the chest and then one to the head, just to make sure he's dead. In the end, his daughter is shipped to some hellhole in another country. Some are working in a place like a backstreet sewing mill, or even worse, a twelve-year-old prostitute working the streets of Calcutta. Chuck knew he couldn't stop this, so he decided to go to his CO, but Chuck never thought that his commanding officer could be one of them."

"I remember," continued Sue Ling, "Chuck told me that he had spoken to his CO, he said that he was a good military man that could be trusted. He wouldn't tell me his name, only that he was an egomaniac who was obsessed with getting recognition, whether earned or not. He told Chuck he would look into the whole mess. Don't worry, he told Chuck, I'll take care of this, don't say a word to anyone else, we'll get these bastards.

"A few weeks later Chuck came up here on a Friday evening around five p.m. He told me that the Unit was going to Lu Poi, that's a small town about ten kilometers from here, up north. They were going there to round up a couple of children to send off. They had never told him to go on these missions before, that wasn't his job. Chuck worked in a funeral home back in the U.S. He told me it was a family business. His job in the Unit was to prepare the bodies of soldiers to be flown home to their families. I think there was more to it than what he had told me, but he believed that keeping some things from us would keep us safe. But this one time they told Chuck that he was to be part of a mission that would take possession of one child in a village not far from here.

"Chuck told me that he agreed to go. He had heard of these missions, but had never gone on one. He needed the evidence that would help to bring down the Unit."

Sue Ling continued. "That night I traveled up to Lu Poi myself. I talked to the parents who had agreed to send their children off with these men. I told them the truth about what they would be doing. All of a sudden, the door to the house flew open, and the soldiers stormed into the small hut. Chuck looked scared when he saw me, but he said nothing. One of the soldiers came toward me, and when I stood up to him, he grabbed me by my hair and threw me to the ground.

"'You're that bitch going around making trouble,' he screamed at me.

"He grabbed my hair and pulled me up, threw me against the wall, where the other men were standing. They grabbed me and threw me outside of the small hut.

"Chuck tried to stay quiet, but he couldn't. He lunged out at the man who was dragging me behind the hut and threw the man to the ground. I fell against the hut, and two men grabbed Chuck. The tall soldier, they called him John, he walked up to Chuck as the others held him. I watched Chuck try to get free, but he couldn't. I couldn't get up.

"The tall soldier gave the orders. He was the boss, and he told them to take me behind the hut. I knew what was coming next. They pulled me up and started dragging me away, and I screamed, pulled loose, and ran as fast as I could. I ran into the jungle, and they didn't follow. I don't think they followed. I ran and ran, and then I stopped. I had never run away before, I was not going to start now. I started to run back. I got close to the village. I stopped at the edge of the woods where cattle were grazing. I used them to hide behind. I crept toward the hut, and then I heard a scream. I didn't know what to do, and then I heard a shot. I froze, I couldn't move. The door flew open, the soldiers came out, got into a jeep, and drove away.

"I waited a few minutes. I don't know why I waited, I just did. I think I was scared. Finally I went to the hut and opened the door.

Chuck was sitting in an old chair, his head was tilted up, his hands were tied in front of him, and the rope that tied his hands was looped under the chair and then tied to his neck. There was blood all over his face and his chest, his brown shirt seemed almost purple in the twilight.

"I ran up to him, grabbed a knife that was on a nearby table and cut the ropes. He dropped to the floor of the hut and I thought he was dead, but then I saw his chest move. I put my face down close to his mouth, I could feel a soft breath. He was still alive. I spoke softly, I asked him if he could talk. He said nothing, but his eyes were open. I could see the fear in his eyes. I had to get him out of there.

"I tried to carry him, but he was so heavy. I looked around for help. There was no one, or at least, no one that would help me, so I dragged him as best I could to my car.

"I knew that I couldn't take him to an American hospital, so I took him to a clinic that only my people use. The doctor told me that his wounds were very serious and he would surely not survive the night, but he would do the best he could. Before they took him away, I went to Chuck and I pulled his tags from around his neck and put them into my pocket. I'm not sure why I did that, but I knew that I had to do something to hide him, because I knew that they wouldn't stop until he was dead."

Sue Ling took a long drink of water. Jerry waited until she was ready to finish her story.

"I never saw him again," said Sue Ling.

Jerry slowly sipped his tea; it had turned cold.

"What happened to the girl that he was going to help?"

Lucy looked up and said, in a matter-of-fact way, "The girl, she was murdered along with her mother and father and thrown into a back room."

"What did you say the name of the boss was?" Jerry asked.

"Everyone called him Big John."

He couldn't hide the surprise on his face.

"You heard that name before?" Lucy asked.

"Yeah, I've heard that name before. When I went to see Chuck in the hospital he cried out that name."

Jerry realized something. "They needed him in particular. It was the family business, Chuck's parents were morticians."

Lucy looked up. "I don't know what that is."

"They needed his skills, to pull the organs out and replace them with the drugs."

"Oh my God," said Lucy. "I think that they are good at finding the value of a soldier and recruiting him with the promise of money, more money than he could ever dream of." She continued, "I think Chuck just got in over his head. We are all victims of this war, but the children, they are all so innocent, so precious, so vulnerable. For them it is even crueler, more heartless, and yet there are those that feed off the suffering of others. Chuck was trying to stop it, but he couldn't. He tried."

Jerry sat still for a moment thinking about what Chuck had done, and the children he hadn't been able to save. He could imagine the forced child labor and sexual abuse. The parents so desperate that they would sell their children in what they might have believed was for a noble cause, a good thing for the youngster and for her family, an honor reserved for only the best children. The sacrificial lamb.

These two incredible women were so brave. It was clear they would not give up the battle. He was feeling emotions he had never felt before; the more they spoke, the more mesmerized he became.

The time had slipped by and it was getting late. Jerry knew he had to get back to Saigon, but he still needed to know one more thing. "I just don't understand how they're getting away with it. And why have they left you alone? If they could kill Chuck, certainly you are in danger."

Lucy said, "This can't go on forever, and they know it. Soon this war will end, and when it does, so will the Unit. All that they have built up over the last few years will be gone. The exploitation of children has been here for generations, but there is a difference, now it is organized, controlled at the highest level of your military, governments officials paid off to look the other way. The police happily cooperate and look the other way when the South Vietnamese Air Force ferries drugs in from Laos, Cambodia, and Thailand to protected airfields for shipment to the preparation centers. I serve a purpose," Lucy continued. "I do everything I can to keep them away from the girls, but I don't go to the police. I keep as many children safe as I can so they can point to me and let the world think they care. I make a good news story for your Americans back home. Isn't that why you are here?

"I understand that in America, there is much civil unrest, demon-strations in your streets, men are burning their draft cards and even going up to Canada to avoid coming over here. The American war is coming to an end. I've seen this before, and it always ends the same. They see it too, they see the end is coming and they're becoming more desperate, and with desperation comes mistakes. So yes, this will end.

"Be careful, Jerry," said Lucy. "I'm sad to say, but you understand that you can't trust anyone. Money and power can move men and women to evil, and they won't hesitate to protect what they have for as long as they have it."

It was very late by the time Jerry walked out of the front door toward the gate. He got into the jeep and headed down the road toward Saigon.

CHAPTER 21

Saigon

Jerry walked up to his quarters around 1800; it had taken him three hours to drive forty-five miles. He had dropped the jeep off and walked back to the Quonset hut in the early dusk. He stepped onto the porch, not unlike the one back home, smaller, not as wide but nice. There were two folding chairs and an old folding table. The three-hour drive on a treacherous and usually unsecured road, after a difficult and emotional conversation, left him exhausted.

"Hey, Steve, you in there?" he called out. "Boy, could I use a cold beer."

Jerry walked into the Quonset hut. "Steve?" There was no answer. He wrote a quick note: "Steve, I am back from my little trip up north. A lot to tell you, going over to grab a beer, join me if you are around."

The streets were filled with a horde of people on bikes and motorcycles. There was a traffic cop up on a wooden box directing traffic as best he could.

Once safely in the bar, a beer bottle in his hand, Jerry found a table in the back and waited, hoping that Steve would show up. He wanted to talk to his friend about what he had learned from Lucy and Sue Ling. True friendships for Jerry were hard to come by. They needed to be earned. Chuck Harris had earned his friendship over the years. Steve Jacobs had earned it in only a few weeks. Time in Vietnam moved at a different pace. But either way, whether over many years or just a few weeks, Jerry valued them both. Jerry liked Steve. He often could make him laugh, but more precious was his way of listening, which for Jerry was a godsend.

A familiar laugh caused him to turn from the commotion just beyond the porch. Steve strolled into the bar as if he owned the place. He exuded an air of confidence as he asked politely for a bottle of beer. Jerry raised a hand and Steve walked over and slid into the seat opposite Jerry.

"Hey, man, glad to see you." Jerry smiled in relief; he had made a decision to tell his friend why he was really here and what he was doing. He'd been thinking about letting Steve in on his plan, even though he had originally promised himself that he wouldn't tell anybody. Jerry thought of this as his mission and knew that getting other people involved could be both dangerous for them and also for himself. But lately he'd realized he needed somebody to help him and that somebody was Steve Jacobs. Jerry decided to dive right in from the beginning.

"You know that case you're working on, Chuck Harris from Pennsylvania?"

"Yeah, what about it?" said Steve.

"I knew Chuck Harris. He was my best friend in high school."

"No kidding," said Steve, leaning forward as he put his beer on the table. "Why didn't you mention that before?"

"Well, let's just say, I had my reasons. Anyway, I need to tell you some stuff and maybe we can get on the same team and—"

Steve interrupted and said, "Hold on, Jerry, I thought we *were* on the same team. I don't understand what the fuck you're talking about."

"Steve," said Jerry, "just give me a second, and I'll tell you the whole story. If you don't want to get involved, fine. You can forget what I tell you and no harm done, okay?"

"Okay," said Steve.

"I didn't come here just to serve my country. I came here to find out what happened to Chuck Harris and his brother, Brian."

"Wait, what happened to his brother?" asked Steve.

He told Steve the entire story about the Harris boys and their deaths.

"So," said Steve, "how do you know that Chuck didn't just die from an overdose like they said? And how do you know that his brother didn't just have the bad luck to be in a car accident? It wouldn't be the first one."

"Because after I left Brian, right after I found out Chuck had died, I walked out of the hospital and those soldiers I told you about were waiting for me and they threw me into my car."

Steve looked up with a confused expression on his face and said, "What?"

"Yeah, they roughed me up a bit. They told me that if I knew what's good for me, I'd keep my big fucking mouth shut, otherwise, as they put it, I was going to be in a world of shit." Jerry continued, "Of course, I didn't tell these fucking nut jobs what Chuck had told me, but you don't have to be a genius to figure out that these guys had something to do with Chuck's overdose, and I think they also caused Brian's accident."

"So, that's it, that's why you signed up? You left your wife and kids, and got yourself shipped over here, because of all that? Let me tell you something, pal, you are fucking crazy. You came here to get justice for your two friends. You shouldn't be here, Jerry, you should be in a fucking mental institution."

"Wasn't the only reason," Jerry said with some hesitation in his voice. "I also came here to get a story. Tell you the truth, it wasn't just about Chuck and Brian. I mean, that should be enough, but I knew that nobody would believe me without any proof. So, I figured I'd come over here, find out what really happened to Chuck and Brian, and at the same time write the story of my life. Maybe it will get picked up by all the national papers and I get a fast track to the top."

"Fine," said Steve. "This isn't about justice, it's about fame and fortune."

"Hey," said Jerry, with anger in his voice and in his eyes. "You think whatever the fuck you want to think. The fact is, I'm here and I'm going to get those bastards, and yes, I'm going get that story while I'm at it."

"Okay, okay," said Steve. "Fine, whatever. But what's all this got to do with me?"

"I'll tell you," said Jerry. "I'm going to get all the proof, hand it all over to you, and you're going to move it up your chain of command and, in the end, put these motherfuckers away forever."

"Are you fucking nuts? Who the hell do you think I am, Marshal fucking Dillon? You want to guess what happens to guys like you? They get shot. I'm a nice Jewish boy from New York, I'm not looking to right all the wrongs and injustices of the world. Look, pal, I'm going to do my time here, and then I'm going home and start my life all over again, so just forget it. Take your shit to somebody else."

Jerry looked right at Steve and said, "I can't trust anybody else." He hesitated for a moment, then continued, "If I tell this story to anyone else, I'll be dead in an hour. You're the only one that can help me and maybe, for once in your life, help yourself. I know what you're thinking, but please, just listen to what I have just found out and maybe you'll change your mind and help me get these guys."

Steve said, "I guess it doesn't hurt to listen, but I'm not promising anything."

Over the next hour or so, Jerry told Steve about his buddy Tony and the young girls, about the soldier in the alley that ended up dead, and how Jerry figured he got set up. He told him everything he had learned about the Unit. He described meeting Lucy and her mother, and about finally getting more of the story about Chuck from Sue Ling. He continued with the truth about the child trafficking, forced labor, prostitution, drugs, and the stolen American aid and equipment.

"How are they getting the drugs out of the country?"

"Easy, the cocaine and heroin are flown in by the Air Force and sent to mortuary units all over the south. The morticians here prepare the bodies of the soldiers for transport to their hometowns, and they remove their internal organs and replace them with bags of the drugs. The reason it works," continued Jerry, "is because the body weight in the coffin is about the same. The bodies of the dead soldiers are shipped to specific funeral homes back home, where the drugs are removed, and the bodies are sewn up before burial."

Steve sort of smiled. "Brilliant, fucking brilliant."

"To tell you the truth, I could give a shit about the drugs. It's the child trafficking. They get orders, like you're buying a fucking car, only it's for a young kid; specific age, height, hair color, you would think that it's like ordering from a goddamn catalog. So they put the word out that they're looking for a village kid with these specific requirements. I guess you couldn't get away with this in the cities, but it works in the small villages.

"They give the local town bosses a commission for convincing the parents that their children will be getting these great jobs out of the country, that they'll be with loving families and taught a trade. They tell them that someday the children will be sending home money and gifts for all their brothers and sisters. And there is always a little something for the parents, who have a lot of mouths to feed; one less is no big deal, especially the girls. People hear what they want to hear, see what they want to see, believe what they need to believe. Half the time they can't put enough food on the table, and in case you haven't noticed, there is a fucking war going on over here."

Steve looked back at Jerry and said, "You're telling me that there is some super organized unit, made up of U.S. military personnel, that's connected to organized crime in the States, doing all this stuff."

"Don't be so naïve," said Jerry. "That's exactly what's going on here. There's big money here in slave labor, child prostitutes, drugs, stolen contraband goods, all in a fucking country that's gone crazy. Think about it, where else could you get away with this? Here, nobody cares, nobody gives a shit. Between the North Vietnamese and the Americans, we've turned this country into a Hell."

Steve had heard enough. "Fine, get me what proof you can. I think you are going up against some pretty heavy hitters, and trust me, Jerry, these guys won't go down easy. You can pretty much bet your life you aren't the first crusader that ever wanted to put these guys away. I guess your friend Chuck was thinking the same thing, and look what happened to him and his little brother. Proof, that's what you need, real proof. I'll do what I can. At least I can get it to the right people. But just for the record, I think you're insane, and I'm insane for getting involved in this crazy fucking crusade of yours. We're both going to end up in some ditch in the middle of the jungle."

Jerry shook his head then took a long swallow of beer. It felt good to share all this with someone else.

"What's next?" asked Steve.

"I need some information from you. Tony and these guys he works with want to know how far along you are with the investigation into Chuck's death. I'm supposed to get the info to Tony and he will send it off to this John Murphy guy and then I become a trusted source. Then I'm in, and then I can go after John and his band of lowlifes."

"Well, now I know why you want me involved, you figure you can get the information from me and then pass it along."

"It's not just that. I'm working at the embassy, so I do have access to a lot of stuff, but this information on Chuck will make me look totally legit. I don't have all the time in the world, because when this war is over, these guys walk away with nothing but boatloads of money."

"All right, already, I'll do the best I can, but I'm not promising anything."

Jerry shook his head and said, "Thanks for joining the fight."

Steve looked up from his beer and said with an incredulous expression, "What do you think this is, Casablanca? You're not exactly Humphrey Bogart. Look," he continued, "I'll do the best I can, but you need to keep my name out of this. Just tell them that you got the information from your source in the JAG office. I'll feed you what I can, but you need to protect my ass, are we clear? I'm not going to get myself killed over your crusade. It ain't mine."

Steve paused, finished the rest of his beer and stood up. He didn't look at Jerry, just asked, "I'm out of here, are you coming?"

The next morning while Jerry was working at his desk, Colonel Benton came over.

"How did it go yesterday? Did you get the information that you were looking for?" he asked.

"Morning, sir. Yeah, I got some of it, but there's a lot more I need to look into. There are a lot of kids running around this country with U.S. fathers who packed their bags and went home, leaving these woman and kids to fend for themselves."

"I know," said the colonel, "but you need to look into that shit on your own time, Specialist. Things are really heating up here and things are getting out of control back home. You see the report that the *New York Times* released, about how forty percent of U.S. economic aid sent to Saigon is stolen or ends up on the black market?"

"Yeah, yes, sir, I have that report."

"Well," said the colonel, "the chief of staff wants the military Public Affairs to play it down. Sure," he continued, "shit goes on over here, no doubt about it, but the fact is ninety percent goes to help the cause. That money builds schools, hospitals, roads, bridges, irrigation for their crops. Problem is that we got almost 400,000 U.S. troops over here and those anti-war demonstrators back home are giving the North Vietnamese hope that even if they can't beat us in the field, they might be able to beat us back home. So, I guess the bottom line is we got our hands full. The work that you're doing on the kids might make things worse, so just put it on the back burner for a while. I know what you're working on is important, but you've got to concentrate on the big picture. Are we clear?"

Jerry nodded.

Benton patted Jerry on the shoulder. "Don't screw up, kid. Something tells me you're better suited for a typewriter than an M-16. There are two wars going on, one here in Vietnam and one back home in the States."

"Yes, sir."

Over the next few days, Jerry got caught up in the job of reporting the war the way they told him to and writing newsletters for the troops. He didn't for one minute forget what he needed to do and why he came here in the first place, but he had to make it look like he was doing his job, or else he would be out of the loop and in no position to find out anything or to help anybody.

There had been increased scrutiny from journalists over the mounting civilian casualties in North Vietnam and the Public Relations unit had to find a way to admit that civilians may have been bombed accidentally.

Napalm and tons of bombs were being used daily in the Mekong Delta regions and the U.S. body counts were rising as well.

The day with Lucy and Sue Ling began to feel like an old memory fading away. The drugs that were being sent home and supplied to the troops in Vietnam began to feel more and more like victimless crimes. Nobody really gets hurt, they just get high, and in this godless country, getting high was the only thing a soldier could look forward to. The story of the children and the eyes of the young women were beginning to fade until Jerry was given a report of the death of a young soldier named Billy Andres. Billy had been a bunkmate of Jerry's in boot camp. They came from the same area in Pennsylvania and had become friends over the weeks down in Parris Island, North Carolina. The report indicated that his death was the result of a drug overdose, but Jerry was told in the accompanying memo to alter the details of his death for the sake of his family.

That afternoon Jerry felt a tap on his shoulder as he walked in downtown Saigon. He turned, thinking it was just another young kid begging for a handout. He had begun to keep a pocket full of pennies for the kids. It was Sue Ling. They walked together among the crowd of people heading home after a long day hot day. "Can you take some time and visit the orphanage? Grandma and Lucy have something that you need to hear."

Jerry said, "I'll try to get up there tomorrow afternoon. It's getting harder for me to be out of the office lately, but I'll make up some excuse. It's important, right? I can't make a three-hour drive to talk about the weather."

Sue Ling turned to him sharply and said, "You came to us, you are the one putting our lives in danger. Those two women have no interest in talking to you about the weather, as you put it."

"Okay, okay, can you let them know that I'll be there tomorrow afternoon? Sorry for being an asshole." Jerry smiled and added, "Forgive me?"

Sue Ling shook her head, but smiled as she touched Jerry on his arm and turned into the crowd.

The following afternoon, Jerry drove to Moc Bai. He pulled up to the gate around six o'clock just before dinner time and asked the old man if he could talk to Grandma Kim and Lucy.

Grandma Kim was waiting for him inside. "Jerry, it is nice to see you, come in. Have you eaten?"

"No, please, I don't mean to inconvenience you. This is the only time I could get away. Sue Ling said you had information for me."

"At least have some tea with us."

"Is Lucy here?"

Grandma Kim slowly poured tea and said, "No, Lucy had to leave this afternoon. She learned that a child's parents had arranged for her to be taken and sent out of the country. Desperate people will do desperate things. Of course, they believe that she will be well cared for and treated with respect. They were promised she would be learning a trade and this was her chance to get out of the country. But we know what it really means."

Jerry drank tea with Grandma Kim and the children. He had been distracted over the last few days, but this brought him back. Just a few words from Grandma Kim made him understand that his desire to avenge Chuck was turning into something much larger. This was going to be the story that would change not only his life but the lives of the children.

After tea Grandma Kim took him for a walk in the back garden. She explained that she was hearing from one of her many informants about where and when men from the Unit would be rounding up scores of children for transport out of Vietnam.

"This is the largest roundup of the war. If there was ever a time to take this information to your superiors, to people who can help, this is that time. We will do what we can," she continued, "but whatever you decide to do, be careful, and don't trust just anyone. I told you we have eyes everywhere, but so do they."

Jerry looked into her tired but serene face and said, "I'll do what I can. I just need to be careful, not just for me, but for you and Lucy."

Jerry got back to his quarters around midnight and fell instantly asleep. The sound of the phone woke him, and of all people, it was Tony. "How you doing, Jerry? You okay? You sound like shit."

"Just tired. They got me working my ass off. What's going on?" said Jerry.

"Meet me at our café this afternoon around 1700," Tony said.

"Sure, I'll see you then."

Jerry walked into the café just after five, but Tony wasn't there yet. He ordered a beer and sat down to wait for Tony to show up. Around 5:30 Tony strolled in and sat down next to Jerry.

"Fucking traffic, you'd think you were in downtown Manhattan. Can I get a beer over here, pal?" he said in his strong Brooklyn accent. The young man brought the beer and Tony took a long drink. At first, they talked about day-to-day stuff and then Tony asked how things were going back home with Kate and the kids.

"Not good," said Jerry. "Same as last week, nothing changes, same shit, different day. She's still pissed off that I'm here."

"Remember what we spoke about? About how maybe we could find a way to help you if you could find a way to help us?"

"Who exactly is us, Tony?" Jerry asked.

Tony looked at Jerry, picked up his beer, and said, "Yeah, okay, I trust you, so I'll tell you what I know, but this needs to stay between us, are we clear?"

Tony continued, "I already told you I've gotten involved in something pretty big. Remember the Unit? Everyone assigned to the Unit contributes a very specific talent, you get what I'm saying, Jerry? For me, I was here maybe two weeks before I got recruited to Delta Unit, commanded by Captain John Murphy."

Jerry didn't take his eyes off Tony. He had to listen carefully or he would get lost, Tony's Brooklyn accent was so strong.

"Anyway," continued Tony after a pause to take a drink, "they took me into this house outside of town, and that's where I met the man."

Tony smiled. "Son of a bitch was big. Jesus Christ, he must be 6'4", 240 pounds of pure mean. You got to understand, I don't tell this to hardly anyone, but I'm not even 5'7", so when I come face to face a with a guy that's like a foot taller than me, I notice. But I'm pretty sure I could kick his ass if I wanted to." Tony hesitated for a moment as if he were deep in thought, cradling his chin in his hand. "I know guys like Big John. You fuck with them, any little thing, and they will never forget. They'll shake your hand and tell you right to your face, 'no hard feelings.' Then one day, when you're not expecting anything, they'll stick a knife in your side, because they never forget, and they'll never let you forget it either. Anyway, that's Big John Murphy. He is one mean motherfucker you don't want to cross. So he tells me that I got real good credentials and could be a real asset to the Unit and I could make money, more money than I could ever dream of making back in the States. How long have we been here, Jerry?" asked Tony, before he answered his own rhetorical question. "Maybe three months, and before I know it, I'm in. Back in the States it could take years to become a made man, you know, a member of the family. Here it's totally different. In two stinking weeks, you're in or you're out. From what I'm told, between getting shot, sent home, or transferred, there just isn't that much time to really vet a guy. Within a few weeks, I start moving up in the family. I guess I got credentials, being that I'm from Brooklyn and come off like a real mob guy. Little did they know the truth, I'm nothing but a two-bit hustler. But here's the deal, once you're in, you're in. You fuck up or stray off the reservation, you're fucking dead. Two in the chest, one in the head, make sure he's dead."

"I get it, Tony, but I don't have any talents. What would I bring to the table?"

"It's not what you know, but what you have access to. Working in Public Affairs gives you firsthand information with real value. You are the link to the inside that they are missing."

They were both silent for a while. "Look, Jerry, here's the bottom line, I told you a lot of shit that could get us both shot and thrown into a ditch. I need to know whether you're interested or whether we end this right now."

"I told you last month after I got stabbed that I needed to do this. Look, Tony, I talk tough and I try to be like you, but the fucking truth is I am a pussy from Pennsylvania. And if I don't take care of my family, I'm not going to have a family to come back to. And besides, I told you as long as nobody gets hurt, I don't give a shit. A little harmless information and I get paid, is that the bottom line?"

"Yeah," said Tony. "That is the bottom line."

"Great," said Jerry. "When do we get started?"

"Big John will meet you tomorrow. Meet me here around 1500 and we will take a little ride up the river." Tony got up and said, "I got to take a leak, order me another beer."

Jerry knew he had crossed the line and there would be no turning back now. He would meet Big John tomorrow and make the deal. He would get the information that he needed to tell the story that would put these bastards where they belonged and at the same time do some good with his life. For a minute, he thought about what Grandma Kim had told him; he was taking a huge risk meeting this guy John. The whole damn organization could come tumbling down at any time and he didn't want to be caught with these guys. He promised himself that he would get in and get the information he needed and then find a way to get out. Shoot himself in the leg if he needed to, but he would get home to Kate and his family.

He wanted to see Lucy again and tell her what he was doing. She would be proud of him and for some reason that was important. But he understood that he needed to be careful now; more than ever he had to protect her and her mother and not get them involved in his mission.

Jerry looked up for a moment and suddenly there was a lovely young Asian woman standing in front of him. She smiled, Jerry smiled.

"Where's our boyfriend?" she said.

"Tony? He's in the bathroom. I'm getting a beer, you want one?"

She shrugged her shoulders, "Sure, just one."

He raised his hand to order three beers and gestured for the woman to sit down. She did, and the waiter quickly brought over three beers. Tony strolled back to the table. He smiled at Jerry and the woman, lifted his beer toward both, and said, "Salud."

"Where've you been? Haven't seen you around," said Tony.

"Busy," she said with a smile. "Busier than a one-armed paper hanger."

Jerry smiled. "That's pretty funny, never heard that one. You make that up? Hey, what's your name?"

"No," she said with a friendly warmth. "It's just a good midwestern colloquialism. I'm Connie."

Tony looked over at Jerry across the table and said, "Ain't she something?" Jerry just nodded.

Jerry tried to guess her age. Mid-twenties he thought, no more than twenty-seven, but no way of confirming this. Her jet-black hair just reached the back of her slender neck. They all have jet-black hair here, he thought. Her skin tone was slightly yellow; he realized she was part Asian and part Caucasian. She had big brown eyes that seemed to glisten in the half-light in the café. Jerry was drawn to her eyes. If you looked hard enough, they'd tell a story.

"Let me guess, you were born here but went to school in the U.S.?" said Jerry, instantly regretting his assumption. He continued, "Sorry for being so nosy, it's the journalist in me. Tony tells me I ask too many questions."

Connie smiled. "It's okay, I never mind answering questions, especially when they're structured to sound like something else. My father was a Master Sergeant in the First Infantry Division when he met and married my mother in the late forties. I was born in April 1945." Jerry quickly calculated her age: twenty-four, not bad, he thought.

Jerry asked, "What was your father doing in Vietnam in the late forties?"

Tony looked up from his beer and said, "Jesus Christ, you do ask so many fucking questions."

Connie looked at Tony and put her hand on his shoulder and said in a kidding-around tone, "He cares. And besides, like he said, he's a journalist, naturally just curious, right?"

Connie continued, not waiting for a response from Jerry. "Officially, there were no troops until the late fifties, but there were plenty of noncombatant military personnel working with the government troops, for training and intelligence. They were managing all kinds of economic and military aid. There was a lot of shit that was going on here long before you boys arrived."

Connie stood and said, "I've got to get back to work. I'll see you around." She turned and headed toward the door, surprising both Tony and Jerry.

"Hey," Jerry called. "What are you doing tomorrow night, maybe get a bite to eat?"

"Are you asking me out on a date?" she said as she turned.

"Yeah," Jerry said.

"Okay, don't forget, I'm not one of those girls. I come from a strict Christian home, and besides my father would cut your dick off with a butter knife if he found out that you got a little out of hand."

Jerry winked. "Hey, I am a married man, just want to enjoy a meal with a nice girl."

"Let's meet here at seven, we can have a drink and then," she hesitated and said, "figure it out."

CHAPTER 22

Saigon

Jerry moved slowly at the sound of the ringing. He consciously decided that it must be a dream, but then he heard a second ring. He picked up the receiver and said, "Hello." Tony's animated Brooklyn voice startled him all the way awake. "Yeah, Tony, what's going on?"

"Nothing much, just a little change of plans. Forget about this afternoon at the café, I'll pick you up in fifteen minutes. Don't keep me waiting, we got a date with the big man."

"Are you crazy? I got to go into work, I can't take the whole fucking day off. What I am going to tell my boss?"

"Don't worry, call in sick." Tony hung up without waiting for a response. Fifteen minutes later, he was outside.

"Jump in," said Tony, barely coming to a stop in front of the Quonset hut that Jerry shared with Steve.

"Where we going?" said Jerry as he jumped into the front seat next to Tony.

"You'll see soon enough," said Tony as he weaved through the narrow streets leading out of town into the Vietnamese countryside.

"Jerry," said Tony shouting over the roar of the jeep engine. "Let me give you a little friendly advice, okay?" Jerry nodded. "Don't ask so many questions, you know? Sometimes I think you ask too many questions, so just keep your big mouth shut and listen to the big man, you got it?"

Jerry smiled and said in a sarcastic tone, "Yes, sir, I got it, shut up and listen. Is that about it?"

Tony looked over and said, "Yeah, asshole."

Tony pulled the jeep into the middle of a large field where there was a helicopter waiting for them.

"Jump in," said Tony. "We've got to take a little ride."

There were two soldiers sitting in the Huey Cobra, manning 50-caliber machine guns. Tony got in and sat in front with the pilot. Jerry jumped in the back and strapped himself in.

"Where we going?" said Jerry.

"What the fuck did I just say? No fucking questions. Jesus."

Jerry looked down and recognized the road below. In what seemed like just a few minutes they landed on the outskirts of Moc Bai. Two South Vietnamese soldiers were standing next to the old man that Jerry recognized from Grandma Kim's front gate and next to him was a younger boy, in his early teens.

The soldiers grabbed the old man and the young boy and threw them both into the 'copter and jumped in after them. The soldiers handcuffed them to a metal post next to the large open door. The Huey lifted off and soon was over the jungle at about 3,000 feet. The old man looked at Jerry, but didn't say a word or let on that he knew him. He just sat there with a peaceful expression on his face. One of the soldiers moved to sit next to the old man and spoke in Vietnamese; the old man just looked down and said nothing. The soldier slapped the old man and shifted toward the young boy, who sat there shaking. The South Vietnamese soldier took the handcuffs off the young boy and held him at gunpoint near the open door that overlooked the jungle below. Once again, the soldier shouted a question at the old man, but again the man refused to answer. The soldier grabbed the boy's black hair and pushed him halfway out the open door. The boy screamed and was clearly begging the soldier to pull him back. The soldier smiled and shouted at the old man who was now on his knees, entreating the soldier not to hurt the boy. However, it seemed he still refused to answer whatever the South Vietnamese soldier was asking. Time seemed to stop for Jerry, the noise for the rotor blades was deafening, he could barely hear the boy crying to the old man, when all of a sudden, without warning, the soldier lifted the boy up like he was a rag doll and hurled him out of the helicopter.

"What the fuck?" yelled Tony.

Jerry stood up, holding onto the metal railing and screamed, "What the fuck is happening? I didn't sign up for this, we're the good guys, Jesus Christ." Grandma Kim's warning came back to him. He couldn't breathe. Nothing in his life had prepared him for what he had just witnessed. He wanted to jump after the boy, catch him somehow, make it not happen.

Tony grabbed Jerry's arm and threw him down onto the metal bench that ran from one side of the 'copter to the other. The old man, with his hand still handcuffed to the railing, fell sobbing against the side of the door; he was calling out what must have been the boy's name.

Tony stepped in front of the soldier and grabbed him and yelled in his face, "Now he'll never tell us a fucking thing. That was his grandson."

"He was never going to tell you a fucking thing anyway," yelled the soldier over the roar of the rotary blades. "He has a code, he has honor, he would rather die than betray the women he cares for."

"Well, then, why did you throw the kid out, what the fuck was the point?"

While they stood yelling at each other, Jerry was glaring at the soldier that had just thrown a young boy to his death for absolutely no reason on earth. In the corner of his eye, he saw the old man move. Jerry turned just in time to see the old man lunge forward and grab a machete that had fallen to the floor of the 'copter. Jerry was sure the old man was going to slash the soldier, but instead he raised the long blade and without a moment of hesitation, sliced off his own hand, freeing himself from the metal bar. In an instant, the old man turned toward Jerry and bowed, and then with the speed of a cat, he silently leaped toward the soldier, grabbed him around the waist, and lurched out of the helicopter. Still holding onto the screaming soldier, they both hurtled to their deaths, crashing into the rocky terrain more than 3,000 feet below.

Jerry sat frozen, shocked at what he had just seen. The expression on the old man's face as he bowed was almost serene, just before he leaped to his death.

"Son of a bitch!" yelled Tony. "John will kick our asses for sure. Jesus Christ, how the fuck am I going to explain this?"

Jerry sat back down, his stomach heaving. Thank god he hadn't had time to eat breakfast. He tried desperately to wipe the splattered blood off his face and arms. No, no, he couldn't be part of this. What would he tell Lucy and Grandma Kim? What the fuck had he gotten himself into? He wondered how these men had come to this point, how they were able to kill with no sense of remorse or conscience.

The 'copter banked hard left and headed up toward a long expanse of pristine beach, dotted only by random palm trees. Jerry felt ill, a sense of shock and regret clouded his thinking. As they landed, the dust and dirt flew everywhere and then settled down.

"Let's go," said Tony. Jerry jumped out of the 'copter, bent low, and ran behind Tony to get clear of the blades. What Jerry saw looked more like a resort than a war zone. There were American soldiers in shorts and bathing suits walking casually with young Vietnamese women on their arms, heading back and forth from the beach where they lay in the sun next to cases of beer and steaks on grills. Music was blasting from loudspeakers that had been set up on the beach. A radio somewhere was blasting "Light My Fire" by The Doors. Sand and dust were kicked up by the 'copter, and the smoke from the fires on the beach caused a faint haze that blurred his vision. Jerry stood still for a moment, then what he had just witnessed brought him to his knees, and he bent over and vomited.

"Jerry, come on, snap out of it, man. Get your head on, I want you to meet the boss." Jerry felt his heart pounding in his chest as he stood up, trying to catch his balance. He began to walk slowly and deliberately right behind his friend. His face was stoic and without expression. He felt numb. In front of them was a large tent set away from the others, about fifty yards off the beach. He felt eyes on him as he walked closer to the tent. A tall man sat in a rocking chair at the entrance. As the two men walked up, he put his book down and looked up at them. He smiled and stood and put out his hand toward Tony, but never took his eyes off the new recruit.

John Murphy stood about 6'4" with short brown hair and dark blue eyes that seemed to look right through you. He was dressed in Army boots, pants, and a white t-shirt that clung to his thin upper body.

"Pull up a chair and let's sit and talk. How was the ride?" John asked. Tony moved into the tent and soon came out with two chairs that he put next to the rocking chair. Before Jerry could answer, big John continued, "Nice here, isn't it? Almost peaceful, the ocean, the beach, almost like home. So where's your home?"

"Mine?" said Jerry, almost in a trance, like he didn't understand the question.

"Yeah," said John. "Where you from, soldier?"

"Pennsylvania, a small town about thirty miles northwest of Harrisburg."

"What did Tony tell you about our little operation?" John didn't look at Jerry, and Jerry stared at the ocean, the surf crashing onto the beach. He was lost in thought and then felt a hand grasp his arm and turned to see John Murphy looking into his eyes.

"I asked you a fucking question. What did Tony tell you?"

"Sorry, Captain, I was thinking about back home. He told me that I might be able to get some information for you and that maybe that info might be worth something."

"What kind of information can you get for us?" asked John. Tony stood up and walked to the table and grabbed a couple of beers. Then he turned back toward the two men sitting and handed Jerry and John each a can of beer.

"I work at Public Affairs in Saigon and have access to information that may be useful to you, and maybe if the information was useful, maybe you would be a little grateful..."

John stood up and grabbed Jerry by the arm. "Bring your beer and let's go for a little walk. Hang out here," he said to Tony. "We need to get a couple of things straight first."

They walked to the beach and when they stood at the water's edge, John turned to Jerry and looked him straight in the eyes. He said, "We've got two jobs, one is working for the U.S. Army and the other is working for ourselves. You've got a choice, the way I see it. One, you walk away right now and that's the end of it. You say nothing to nobody and everyone is just fine and dandy. But if you decide to walk away and later you say one fucking word to anyone, all that your pretty little wife will ever see of you is your fucking dog tags. Your other option is to become part of this team, part of this family, but if you make that choice, there is no walking away. Look, I know why you're here and I know what you bring to the table. But it's real fucking important for you to understand that we're not playing games here. This is heavy duty shit going on over here and you need to be real clear, because if you're not real clear in your head then you're going to be one sorry son of a bitch. Tony tells me you're a straight-up guy, a guy that we can depend on and a guy that knows the value of good friends and how to be faithful and trustworthy. He tells me that you do have access to all kinds of information that may be helpful to us and that you can use a little help. He tells me that your family situation is just a little fucked up and that maybe with a little help from your friends, things may work themselves out. Did I hear him right or was I dreaming? Because if I was dreaming then it would be a really good idea for you to disappear and get on that helicopter and forget that we ever had this little talk."

Jerry turned toward John to answer, but before Jerry could say a word, John bent down and grabbed a handful of sand and let it run slowly into his other hand and then filtered it back onto the beach.

"We're only given so much time, like this sand. It's running away, always moving away. Simple truth is that we only have maybe a few more years here before this whole thing is just one bad memory. Since we've been sent over here to fight some bullshit war, while those bastards are sitting home drinking gin and tonics, then it seems to me that we have a right to take care of you and me, and our families. You understand what I'm saying?"

"Yes, sir," said Jerry. "I read you loud and clear. I do need some help and maybe if I can get you what you want, then I can get what I want. But I need to understand what you need from me and what I get in return. What I mean is how can I tell you that I'm in if I don't know what I'm getting into?"

"Fair enough," said John. "Why don't you tell me what kind of information you have access to?"

Jerry turned back toward the surf. He had never been this close to the ocean. The sky was bright blue with just a few high clouds scattered around. He could smell the salt in the air, and he breathed in a full breath, filling his lungs, and then said to John, "Everything except top-secret, classified data, everything from troop deployments to ongoing investigations to upcoming operations."

"You have access to internal affairs investigations?" said John.

"Sure, my office is near those guys, we hang out."

"Okay, I get it," said John. "I know that I don't have to tell you this, but if they find out that you're passing along classified data, you'll be in a world of shit."

"I know, but it's not like you are the enemy after all. As long as none of our boys get hurt, why should I give a shit?"

John put his arm around Jerry and continued, "Let's go back to the tent and have a couple of beers and I will tell you how we get started."

Tony looked up, as Big John and Jerry returned to the tent like two old Army buddies that have been in the same unit for years. Tony stood, walked over, and handed each a beer. "Are we cool?" he said.

John glanced at Jerry, and said, "Yeah, we're cool."

Jerry smiled and said, "I'm in."

John stood at attention, slowly lifted his right hand to his brow and said in a military tone, "Sir, welcome aboard."

Jerry returned the salute and said, "Honored to be aboard, sir."

"Let's go get us a steak and a few beers and go down to the beach. I need to fill you in on the details of our primary mission and core values. We won't get it all done tonight," said John, "but we can start."

Jerry and John walked out of the tent, and John nodded for Tony to follow along. The three men walked over to a tent down the beach where they were grilling steaks and lobsters. The beers and sodas were in a large barrel.

"I'm going to ramble on for a while," said John as the three got settled on the beach. "You can ask questions, but mostly just listen."

Jerry nodded and said, "Okay."

"We run a military ship, with military procedures, operations, command structure, and military justice. We're made up of about fifty men, military both active and reserve, contractors and associates. The Unit's core values are loyalty, honor, mission, and personal courage."

Tony smiled, "He always starts off like this."

"Hey, are you doing this or am I? Because I'll just sit back and shut up."

"No, no," said Tony. "Sorry, go right ahead."

John looked at Tony with a bit of a smile. "Let's eat, I'm hungry," he said as he cut into the rare steak, took a bite, drank his beer, and sat back enjoying the beauty of the ocean. "I'm from St. Louis, not too many oceans in the middle of the country," he said as if he were telling a joke. "My father was military, my grandpa was military, and his father before him was military. You might say that I have the military in my blood, and I'm as patriotic as any living soul in the States. I come to realize way back that one simple rule applied to all the wars that we ever fought. You know what that one simple rule is, Jerry?" he asked and took another bite of his steak.

Before Jerry could answer, John continued as if he didn't care what Jerry might have answered.

"You know the one simple, undeniable rule in the war business?" John said as he chewed. "You run it like a business. Money is what it is all about. Period. You've heard of the Military Industrial Complex, haven't you? I know you're from the middle of Pennsylvania, small town, right, never been to the big city. A real live farm boy, probably a member in good standing at 4H. Look, Jerry." John reached down for his beer, but never took his eyes off Jerry. "I'm just fucking with you." John smiled and said, "How's the steak, and how about the creamed spinach, just as good as back home?"

Jerry looked up from his plate of steak and spinach and said, "I've never had better."

John smiled and said, "You stick with me and Tony, life can get much better. Look," continued John, "just remember what I'm telling you." Jerry ate his food and listened.

"There's only two types of people in every war: the ones that started it and the ones that fight it. Most of the time, it's old, rich, white men who for a myriad of reasons decide to go off and start a war. Most of the time they don't even need a good reason, could be total bullshit, or could be simple as you got something, and I want it. Might be land, oil, power. Doesn't matter, and here's the other simple fact. Guess who's sent to do the fighting?" said John, pointing at Jerry's chest. "You and me, and more than a hundred thousand boys and men just like you and me. Yeah, that's it, now you know the secret. Old, white, rich guys sending us poor slobs to fight their bullshit war. You think their sons and daughters are over here getting their legs blown off? I don't think so. No, I think those momma's boys are sitting by the pool, sucking down margaritas, and smoking pot, then running back to their Ivy League school to burn their draft cards and piss on the American flag."

Jerry sat silently.

"Okay, Jerry, my gut says that you're okay." John stood up from his chair, pushed away from the table and walked over to Tony and leaned down with his face right up against Tony's. "You vouch for him?"

Tony said, "Yeah, I do." John turned away from Tony and put out his hand to Jerry and they shook.

"Okay, welcome aboard. I'll fill you in on a little history. The more you know who we are, the more you'll know what's important to us." He pulled out a pack of cigarettes, knocked the back of the pack, and offered one to Jerry and then Tony. He pulled out one for himself and accepted a light from Tony, sitting back down at the table.

"Just before the first soldier set foot in this godforsaken country, huge amounts of economic and military aid started flowing in. In the first years, there could have been as much as eight billion dollars that poured into South Vietnam. Everything you could imagine, from tanks to washing machines, helicopters to operating room equipment. During the time when all this aid was being consolidated and ready for transport, eight enlisted men and four officers got together and devised a plan that would provide for them and their families for generations. The organization was simply called Delta Unit. The primary objective was to acquire, divert, and market a portion of all the aid flowing into Southeast Asia during the war. The founders understood from the beginning that there needed to be a clear understanding and methods for dealing with some of the unique challenges that they would face."

Jerry was silent but didn't take his eyes off John. He fought off his immediate reaction to the story he was hearing, the casual list of clearly illegal and fundamentally immoral actions of these men. His jaw was rigid, his teeth clenched.

Tony interrupted. "The thing is, we continually need to recruit personnel because of the constant flow of men in and out of Vietnam. Death, transfer to different locations, and of course being released from the military and sent back home."

John nodded in agreement. "We always need new men, men we can trust and who bring something we need to the table, because we have moved into various other lucrative markets, drugs and prostitution, both domestic and foreign."

They talked well into the night as the sun slowly faded and the darkness surrounded them. Jerry tried to take it all in. Many things shocked him, but now he was in and the ends justify the means, he told himself. He swallowed his many misgivings and nodded his head. Arrangements were made for Jerry and Tony to spend the night at the beach compound. The next morning while Jerry sat in the mess tent with a plate of eggs in front of him, John came up to him.

"How did you sleep?" asked John.

Jerry looked up and said, "It makes sense, it all makes sense. You guys are brilliant, fucking brilliant." He hadn't slept; he had gone over and over what he had been told. At some point he said to himself, what the fuck, these guys are making millions, why not me?

John sipped his coffee and said in a casual tone, "I've been here since '62, just kept on re-enlisting, and they always grant the request. Guess I have some pull. Plus, how many crazy motherfuckers like me want to stay in this shithole? For the last few years the turnover has been steady, getting killed or wounded, transferred or sent home." John put his cup of coffee down. "I been studying up on you, McGinnis, and I noticed that you also have a degree in accounting. I thought you were a journalist?"

"Journalism was my major, but I always loved numbers. There's something simplistically beautiful about them, pure and unambiguous. So I minored in accounting, figured if the newspaper trade didn't work out, I could always become an accountant. Anyway, believe it or not, accounting and investigative journalism go hand in hand. Follow the money and you'll find the truth."

John put his fork down. "I need someone who can be with me during the transition, this war is going badly and the end is coming sooner rather than later, and when it does, all our operations will end. For however long we have, we need to accumulate as much as we can, secure the funds and establish a care-taking and distribution team to funnel the money out to the team members in a fair and secure manner. The rewards for the care-taking team will be substantial. If you're interested, we can move forward with that mission in mind."

He got up and put his hand out. Jerry stood as well and saluted, then took the offered hand. "Your ride home is here. You will be hearing from us." John turned and walked out of the tent.

Jerry saw Tony by the door, shaking hands with John and waving Jerry to come. They both walked down to the clearing where the helicopter back to Saigon was waiting. They jumped in, buckled up, and held on tight for the ride back.

Neither Tony nor Jerry said a word. The doors were wide open; the air outside was so hot and humid, the noise deafening.

They turned south and followed the Red River toward Saigon. It was the same as the Susquehanna back home; Jerry followed the bank as it wrapped itself around the river, like a leather glove holding an invisible fire hose. He closed his eyes and thought back to when it all began. He thought about the choices he had made, the lives that he may be called on to hurt. He thought about the risk he was taking. About his kids, Kate, and how the money would change their lives. He thought about what he would say to Grandma Kim. He had no answer.

The helicopter landed outside Saigon and they both jumped into the jeep that was waiting for them and headed back toward the center of town.

"Meet me at the bar around the corner from the national theater tonight around 1800. I hope you understand what the fuck you've gotten yourself into, pal," said Tony.

Jerry turned and said, "What happens now?"

"Relax, Dick Tracy," said Tony. "I'll see you later. Go to work, just another day."

Jerry spent the day reading reports and writing his press releases. He tried to put the last twenty-four hours out of his mind. It seemed impossible for him to concentrate on the reports and newsletters that he was writing. *What do I do now*, he kept thinking, *what do I do now?* Tonight he was having a beer with Tony, just like any other day.

Just before 1800 hours, Jerry walked out of his office and strolled down Le Loi Street toward the center of Saigon. Jerry walked into the bar. Tony was there, sitting in the back, with his arm around a young girl. She couldn't have been more than sixteen, but he couldn't be sure, maybe younger, maybe older; everything seemed to blur over here. He hesitated. *What the hell am I getting myself into?* he thought.

"Hey," said Tony, "you waiting for a bus?" Tony waved him over, at the same time saying something to the girl, who stood and walked out of the bar. She smiled as she passed by Jerry.

"You want a beer?"

"Sure," said Jerry.

"You okay?" asked Tony.

"Yeah, just a little confused, I guess. Lot of stuff going on that I didn't see coming."

Tony nodded his head and said, "I know, it's coming fast and furious. Tell you the truth, I felt the same way, and I still do. Look," continued Tony, "something just came up and I've got to take off. I guess they require my unique talents. That's what it's all about, we all have something to bring to the table. I got mine, and apparently, you got yours. John was pretty impressed, he liked the way you listen. He said there was a quietness about you. He likes that, but I know why you were so quiet. It wasn't because you're a good listener, it was because you were freaked out about what happened in the helicopter. Anyway, he liked it that you never even mentioned what happened. He thinks that you are hardcore, his kind of a guy. Little does he know that you're just a little pussy who just about peed in his pants. Anyway, look, just lie low for a while, I'll be in touch. I guess I'm your handler, maybe because I brought you in. I got a feeling that pretty soon you'll be my boss, but right now, just be cool. I got to go. You okay?"

"Yeah," said Jerry. "I'm fine."

Tony looked serious. He felt it, that gut feeling that something wasn't completely right. He heard "everything is fine," but what he was sensing was that everything was not fine, not by a long shot. He got to his feet and then turned to Jerry before he left and said, "Please, do not fuck this up."

Jerry tilted his head slightly up so that their eyes met. "Don't worry, I got this." Tony turned and walked out of the bar.

Jerry watched Tony leave then blend into the crowd. He continued to watch as if he were looking for Tony to come back, and said quietly out loud to himself, "I'm not sure what the hell I'm going to do, but it can't hurt to write this stuff down and get it home. If anything happens to me, they got something to go on."

Jerry walked home. The street was far less crowded then it had been just half an hour before.

His quarters were quiet, and he was glad that Steve wasn't around so he could write in private. He looked up from the notebook when he heard the sound of footsteps on the porch outside. He closed the cover and put the book inside his desk drawer.

"Oh, it's you," said Jerry with a smile, as Steve Jacobs walked into the room.

"Who were you expecting, Marilyn Monroe? Speaking of which, where the hell were you last night?" He walked over to his bunk and sat down. "Did you meet with those guys?"

"Yeah, flew out to the beach, had one of the best steak dinners I have had in a long time. I'm in, not sure what that means but I am in," he smiled, somehow proud of himself.

Steve sensed a new level of arrogance from Jerry, and it concerned him. "You know, McGinnis," said Steve, "I've got a real uneasy feeling about this whole thing, and you know what really concerns me? I'll tell you just in case you're too stupid to figure it out. This isn't some bullshit crusade, and guess what, you are not invincible. You think for one second that these fucking animals haven't seen this rodeo before? They got more intelligence right here in Saigon than they do at the entire fucking CIA. They'll be watching you like a hawk. Look, asshole, you're into this shit, right up to your fucking eyeballs. This is one big game to you, you think you're some kind of goddamn superman, saving the world from the evildoers."

Jerry waved off Steve's concern and said, "Sit down, Steve, you're making me nervous. I'll fill you in. You are not going to fucking believe the shit I saw."

Jerry told Steve about the helicopter ride, the deaths of the old man and his grandson, about spending the day and night on the beach with the men from the Unit. He told Steve about meeting Big John Murphy and the sordid details and history of the Unit. He agonized over having to tell Grandma Kim and Lucy that he was there when the old man and his grandson got thrown out of the helicopter. He knew that what happened on the helicopter would haunt him for the rest of his life. What more would he have to see, what else would he be asked to do?

Steve sat motionless as Jerry finished up his story. He stood up after they had been silent a while. "Are you fucking kidding me? What the fuck have you gotten yourself into? You're out of your goddamn mind."

"Look, I'll be careful," said Jerry. "And besides, I'm putting everything down in these notebooks and sending them home to my wife and parents for safe keeping. This way when I get home I'll have everything at my fingertips, every last detail of what's going on over here. I'll have proof."

"What proof are you talking about? So far you ain't got shit. Matter of fact, all you've got is being an eyewitness in a helicopter while an innocent Vietnamese kid gets tossed out at 3,000 feet, otherwise known as murder. So right now, the only thing I know for sure is that you should be brought up on accomplice charges just for being there. Yeah, you're doing just great."

"Look, Steve, I trusted you when I told you all this. The only way to stop them is to get inside. I'm already in, so I got to run with it. This is my only chance."

CHAPTER 23

Jerry decided to lie low for a while. He thought about calling Lucy that night but decided that might not be a good idea. Maybe it was better this way. He felt a strange need to be with her; it was funny, he thought, he'd never felt quite this way with Kate. He loved Kate, he was sure of that, but this was different.

He continued to write half the night. Steve had gone to bed. In the morning, Jerry took the notebook to his office and made copies, put each set into a separate envelope, and used diplomatic stamps that he had taken out of the embassy. He sealed them up and put them in the classified diplomatic pouch for general mail to the States.

Jerry headed out around 5:45 and walked to the bar where he was sure to find Tony.

At first Tony didn't say a word, just sat there and drank his beer looking at Jerry. He finally said, "I just want you to know that my ass is on the line. You fuck up and I'm dead. I don't mean that I'm in trouble and that nobody will talk to me anymore. I mean that I'm fucking dead with a bullet in the gut and lying in a ditch somewhere in that goddamn jungle out there, and guess who would be lying right next to me?"

"Me," said Jerry.

"Obviously, you asshole, but your wife and kids would be next. You hear me?"

"Come on, Tony, aren't you being a little bit dramatic?"

"You don't know these guys. This isn't Pennsylvania, this is different, more different than you could ever imagine. John thinks you're okay, so if you're okay with him, then I guess you're okay with me. Anyway, your first job is to get some information about some internal affairs investigation, something regarding stolen kitchen equipment that was found missing in November. Get whatever information you can and meet me back here in two days."

Tony stood up and began to walk away.

"That's it?" said Jerry. "That's all you want?"

"It's a start. Just do it. I'll see you in two days, Wednesday at 1700 hours, we clear?"

"Yeah, we're clear. Hey, Tony, we got to stop meeting like this. People will start thinking that we got something going." Jerry smiled.

Tony turned and said, "Funny, real fucking funny. They're watching you, Jerry. Be careful, for your sake and mine." Tony turned and walked out of the bar.

It was the next morning that Jerry casually overheard two CID officers discussing an ongoing investigation about stolen kitchen equipment. From what Jerry could hear, they both thought that it was a waste of time to track down any idiot who would steal a goddamn refrigerator. "We have more important fish to fry," one said to the other. Before leaving that afternoon, he went in to talk to the colonel.

"Colonel, the interviews I had up there in Moc Bai were helpful, and I'd like to go back if that's okay. I think we can really get some good press, and I think that this would be one hell of a human

289

interest story. I'll meet with the village elders, tell them that their town has been selected as the site for the new children's hospital in the region. Maybe we can do a story on the two women up there who are running the home. What do you think, Colonel? I'll take the camera."

"It's fine, if you think there's a good story there. Christ Jesus, we could use some distractions." He paused to see if anyone was around and then said quietly, "I think we might very well lose this war."

Jerry nodded slowly, understanding what the colonel was saying.

"You've been reading all the press releases," said Colonel Bentley. "You hear what they're calling us. Baby killers, that's what they're calling us. Can you fucking believe that? They send us over here to fight this goddamn war, we do our fucking jobs, losing God knows how many men, and they call us baby killers." Bentley clenched his fist.

"Colonel," said Jerry, "we can't change what's going on over here, and we sure ain't going to change what's going to happen to us when we get home, but maybe we can do a little something good."

Colonel Bentley sounded resigned. "Maybe we can do some good. God knows we did so much bad."

Jerry placed his hand gently on the colonel's shoulder. For a brief moment they were just two guys talking. "I'll brief you when I get back."

"Be careful, Jerry, I don't want to write any letters to your family. Okay?"

"Yes, colonel, I'll be careful."

He pulled the jeep close to the main gate and looked around. He knew the old man was not going to be there and was filled with a sense of loss and then guilt. But it wasn't his fault, he had just been an innocent witness. Jerry walked up to the gate where a young boy sat just outside the entrance. The sound of Jerry's footsteps on the cobblestone path woke the boy. He stood, the sun blinding him for a moment. Jerry towered over the boy, and the boy stared at his uniform with an expression of fear, even while he tried not to show it. Jerry reached out. "It's okay," he said. Grandma Kim came to the gate, and she smiled and bowed.

"Hello, Jerry," she said, leading him toward the house. "How are you? It is so nice of you to come to visit." He stepped in as she held open the door for him.

"I was hoping to talk to Lucy. Is she here? I would like very much to talk to her."

"Lucy would be so happy to know that you were here. It's such a shame that she cannot see you, but I will tell her that you came."

"I must talk to her, to both of you, please."

"I'm so sorry, it's just not possible. You see, she's sleeping, there was a problem with one of the families of one of the young girls. Please, come back another time, I'm sure she will be feeling better. This happens from time to time."

"Hello, soldier," Jerry turned to the voice. Lucy stood next to the big table, and she put her hand on the chair to steady herself and sat down slowly. Lucy's mother moved toward her daughter to help her, and they spoke softly in Vietnamese. Jerry walked slowly to the table, pulled out a chair, and sat down with the two women. Lucy's long black hair hid most of her face; only her lips, bruised and swollen, were visible. From what he could see, her right eye was completely closed.

Finally, Jerry was able to get the words out.

"How often does this happen? Why do you put yourself in harm's way with these people? How many times do you need to get beaten up? It is just not safe for you to go out to these families alone." He had become used to seeing injured soldiers when they were brought into field hospitals, but this was different. He couldn't hide his anger and concern.

"Please," she said and forced a smile; it must have hurt to smile. "This is my purpose, Jerry. I don't expect you to understand. If you are going to come here and tell us that you want to help, then you will accept this situation. I will soon heal, and these scars will fade. Please, have some tea, and tell us why you have come."

Jerry stared at the cup of tea; he tried to smile, but even his weak smile seemed wrong. He reached for the cup slowly, brought it to his lips, and sipped.

"There's something I need to tell you." Mother and daughter looked up.

"I'm so sorry to bring you such sad news. Shun Lee and his grandson were both killed."

"We know," said Lucy. "We knew just a few minutes after they were murdered. When the helicopters fly low, we look up. This time it was Shun Lee and his apprentice. The villagers saw everything—they saw the boy get thrown out and his grandfather jump out, pulling the soldier with him. My mother and I are Roman Catholic in a country that is eighty percent Buddhist, but we believe that there will be a moment when we see our friends again. We're surrounded by death and despair and cruelty, and yet we go on. We have no choice; they depend on us. We're here, right here on this spot, because we were meant to be here. God put us here to take care of the children. Do you believe that we all have a purpose in life, a task?"

Jerry didn't answer; he realized he didn't know. Grandma Kim seemed to understand his discomfort.

"Let's not dwell on sad news, you had other things on your mind. Now would be a good time to tell us," she said in a soft voice.

"There are decent and good men here thinking that they're fighting for a cause that's bigger than they are. Most of them are just kids, right out of school. Mostly poor or middle-class kids, young black kids, a lot of Hispanics. It's not right what these powerful men—the ones running the war—are doing."

Lucy sat back in her cane chair, then leaned forward and put her hand on Jerry's arm. He hadn't realized it, but he had moved his hands out toward Lucy and her mother, reaching out in solidarity.

"You have your reasons for doing what you need to do, and I have my reasons for doing what I need to do," Lucy said. "Perhaps you are looking for justice and revenge. I'm here to try to save as many as I can. Each life is precious, a gift from God."

Jerry looked up. "Things have changed for me. At first it was just about Chuck and his brother, and about the story to advance my career. Now I want to tell this story to help people, to help these young and defenseless children. The American people have a right to know what is going on here, and I'm the one to tell them."

"Why are you telling me all these things? Now you are putting me and all the children in danger," Lucy said.

"I know, but I need you to help me look in the right direction. I am trying to help your people. We can work as a team, and you can save your kids. Look," continued Jerry, "I can help. I didn't start this war, it's not my fault we're here, but maybe, if you help me, I can help you. Maybe together we can do a little good, but I got to find out who the big guys are, not just the grunts that are doing the dirty work. There is no way in the world that this operation is not being directed from the States."

"How can I help you with this? What makes you think I have names?"

"You can tell me what Chuck was working on, who his contacts were, who I can trust."

"Okay, Jerry, I'll help you, but not for your story, not even to bring these men to justice. I'll do it for my children." Lucy stood up straight and said, "I'm tired, I need to get some sleep. I think that it would be very dangerous for us to meet here again. There is a town, just a few miles north of here, it's called Lai Khe. You'll find it just past a Michelin rubber plantation. There is a small shop that sells herbs. You can give a message to the shop owner; he's a friend. I'll meet you there, just let me know when."

Lucy looked into Jerry's face. "These men, they are very cruel, and you know they will stop at nothing. Be careful. What you do will help many, or it may hurt many, and there are eyes everywhere." She left the room.

It was late afternoon, still hot, and he could feel the wetness in the air. Jerry wiped the sweat that had formed on his forehead, got into the jeep, and headed down the road back to Saigon.

On both sides of the road were huge rice paddies; they all looked the same. He wanted to get back before dark, but the road was so bad that he could only drive a few kilometers an hour. He watched the people working the rice paddies. Men and women all wore what looked like black pajamas, with straw hats like a lampshade. Some carried two straw baskets, balanced on either end of a wooden pole that was supported on their neck. Others were so bent over their work that Jerry couldn't imagine the pain in their backs.

Jerry thought about how he was getting involved deeper and deeper and that there were now two more people who knew what he was doing. He could trust both of them with his life, and he knew that they would help him. Jerry hoped that in some way he could help them too.

He pulled his jeep up to the front of his quarters and looked around; it was quiet. *I need to put this down on paper, and I'll send it off in the morning mail with the cash for Kate.*

The next afternoon Jerry left his office around 5:45; it was just a few minutes' walk down the street to the café where he and Tony were going to meet. He walked in, looked around the small café, and saw Tony was sitting in the corner with another soldier, talking and laughing while they drank their beers. Jerry walked over to the two men. "Ladies," Jerry said with a smile.

"Sit down, smart ass," said Tony. Jerry sat down and said hello to the other soldier, who just nodded. "What do you have there, a little present for me?" said Tony.

Jerry handed Tony a large brown envelope and said, "It's all here, everything you wanted."

"We'll see," said Tony, as he took the package out of Jerry's hand. "I'll speak to you tomorrow. Why don't you take off."

"Okay, fine, I'll talk to you tomorrow." Jerry walked away.

Things seemed quiet for the next few weeks, and he didn't go see Lucy. He figured it was safer this way. Jerry fell into a normal routine, reporting on all the programs the U.S. military was carrying out to help the South Vietnamese people. They called it Vietnamization: programs meant to help the Vietnamese help themselves. The U.S. forces built roads, irrigation dikes, schools, medical facilities, and orphanages.

He was at his desk one day when someone called his name. "Hey, Jerry." And he turned and smiled.

"How you doin'?" That New York accent, three little words, but coming from Tony, it meant a whole lot more.

"Fine, where you been? Thought you forgot about me. I've got some information for you."

"Never going to forget you, man. Meet me in the café across the street from the National Theater."

"Sure, after work?"

"Yeah, 1800 hours, don't be late."

"Okay," said Jerry. "It sounds important. I got a busy day, but I'll do my best. We're making all the arrangements for the Bob Hope Christmas Show. This year it's with Raquel Welch, can you believe it? I might get to meet them. That would be fucking unbelievable."

Tony seemed impressed. "Yeah, that would be pretty fucking cool, no doubt. Anyway, 1800, see ya."

He watched Tony get into a jeep and drive away.

At just a few minutes before six, Jerry walked into the café, heading to the back where he knew Tony would be sitting.

Tony called the waiter over. "Two beers." Jerry sat down. Tony didn't bother saying hello. "There's this town, Lai Khe, with a big rubber plantation. Sometime next week we're sending out a shipment, there will be a few boats that will dock at Coco Beach, just north of the town. We need to know that it will be quiet, we don't need to be bumping into some fucking battalion on some sort of mission. You understand: Lai Khe. I will get you the exact time and date."

"Okay, I can do that, no big thing." He pulled out a small pad from his pocket and wrote down the name of the town. "Next week sometime?"

"Yeah, I will let you know. I almost forgot," he said, "John wants to talk."

"Sure, when and where?" said Jerry.

"Wednesday, I'll pick you up at 0700. Be ready, seems like you're being promoted."

Tony stood up, took a last swallow of his beer, and turned and walked away without saying another word.

Jerry sat there for a moment; he felt a sudden need to talk to Lucy. He wanted to tell her what he was doing and to let her know that a contingent of soldiers in the Unit would be in Lai Khe the next week.

After work on Tuesday he commissioned a jeep. He headed north toward Moc Bai, continued past the road that led to her home, and drove into Lai Khe. He stopped in front of the store she had described.

"Hello, soldier," said the man behind a wooden counter. His English was perfect, and he spoke with a British accent, which sounded weird coming from him. Jerry had met a number of soldiers from England, but wasn't expecting it from this shopkeeper.

"Hello, I need to leave a message for a woman who lives in Moc Bai. Is that possible?"

"Yes, I will take care of it for you. What is her name?"

"Great," said Jerry. "Her name is Lucy, Grandma Kim's daughter. Could you tell her that Jerry would like to meet her here tomorrow night, around seven?"

"Of course," said the store owner. "But if you prefer, you may tell her yourself." He pointed to a table at the far end of the shop.

The sun was fading in and out of the heavy clouds that had been threatening since early morning. Jerry looked in the direction the man was pointing as the room brightened. It was Lucy, who looked up and smiled at him.

It was as if no time had passed since their last visit. At first, they spoke of the war and the unbelievable transformation of good and moral men into truly evil ones.

"It is just incredible how war turns good boys into murderers. I believe we should look into the hearts of men and see the good that God has placed there," Lucy said. Jerry listened but had little to add. Then they spoke of themselves, their hopes and desires once the war was over. Jerry couldn't take his eyes off her; he felt numbness in his chest, almost like he was short of breath. He suddenly realized he was falling in love with her. Was this really happening? He slowly reached over and placed a hand on her arm. He couldn't look into her eyes any longer; the honesty was too real. He turned her hand over and took her palm into his own hand.

"Are you reading my palm?" Lucy said with a shy smile.

Jerry looked up embarrassed and said, "No. I mean yes, that's exactly what I'm doing, and do you know what I see? I'll tell you," he said without letting her answer. "I see a young girl who has seen too much suffering and pain. I see a young girl who has seen so little good and so much evil. I also see a woman who hasn't become bitter and hateful. Lucy, you still can see beauty in the world." They kept talking, and Jerry realized it was the first entirely honest conversation he had had since arriving in Vietnam.

She admired his strength and fearless drive in his quest to make a difference and right a wrong. He was tenacious and unflinching in his effort to find the men responsible for Chuck's death and determined to expose what was going on, no matter the risks.

It was very late by the time he got the jeep back to headquarters and himself into bed. He thought about writing about Lucy, but he couldn't tell the truth of what he was feeling, everything was changing. He needed to be clear what his goal was, what should go in the notebooks that were being sent home.

Tomorrow he would meet with John again. He would write only about the Unit and keep Lucy and Grandma Kim out of it. He was living in three worlds now: Kate and home, Steve and Lucy, and Tony and John. It was going to be a balancing act. He would figure it out as he went along.

CHAPTER 24

The sun was still high in the sky when Tony pulled up to the café. Jerry stood against the wall at the entrance.

"Get in, pal," Tony said, as Jerry walked up to the jeep. They were driving to the outskirts of town, where a helicopter was waiting to take Jerry to see Big John Murphy. The traffic was heavy, and it still seemed like pure chaos to him, like everyone was going in different directions at the same time.

"Pretty quiet. Is something wrong?" said Tony.

"Nah, just thinking, that's all," said Jerry. "Are we going back to the beach where we met with John last time?"

"You'll see," Tony answered and kept on driving. Tony turned toward Jerry and said, "You're thinking too much, you're going to end up in a world of shit if you keep thinking so much. I swear to Christ, stop asking questions, you will be told what to do. It's pretty clear to me they think you have a big-time role to play. Look at it this way: what you do over here will change your life and everybody you have something to do with. You get what I'm saying, Jerry? Please man, I'm begging you; don't fuck this up. Okay?"

Jerry smiled, "Relax buddy, like I said, I'm just thinking."

"About what?" asked Tony.

"What do you think, for Christ's sake? The last time I went with you to see John, a kid got tossed out of a fucking helicopter like he was a bag of garbage. I don't know where you were brought up, but in my town we don't do shit like that. So if you want to know what I'm thinking, that's it."

Tony turned away and then looked back. "It's different here, you become different here. I know what you're thinking, these are a bunch of tough guys, me included. But I'm not, or at least I wasn't until I got here. I mean, I was no pussy back home, but these guys are fucking barbarians."

Tony continued, "This is a business, there's a demand and there's the supply. We're the ones that are doing the supplying. Most of the time it's fine, nobody really gets hurt. You got skills. When you get out of here you'll go home and your life picks up where you left off. Have you seen what's going on back home? They're calling us baby killers. We're being treated like a bunch of fucking war criminals. There won't be any work for most of us, and that's if we're not in a goddamn wheelchair or dead. Maybe I'm exaggerating, but one thing is for sure: back home, safe and cozy, there are a bunch of old white motherfuckers making more money in a fucking week than we'll make in ten years. If you play your cards smart, you'll bring home some real money and then you can follow your dreams, instead of worrying how you're going to feed your kids. You know what I'm saying?"

Jerry just stared ahead and said, "Yeah, I think I do. But fuck, man, we *are* baby killers."

After about fifteen minutes they came to a clearing just outside of town, where a helicopter was waiting for them. Tony motioned for

Jerry to jump in; he did and they were off. The helicopter was flying low over the ocean. Jerry stared at the water below; it was so calm, peaceful. You could see the beach line stretching for miles down the coast. He could see small wooden boats just off the shore where men were in the surf, fishing.

They approached the beach head on. Jerry strained to make out the figures on the beach, but the sun was strong that day, and he had to shield his eyes from the glare. As they approached he could make out the soldiers, most with no shirts, just shorts, like they were lounging around on the Jersey shore on a warm summer day.

The 'copter landed on the beach; Jerry jumped out without being told, bent over, and walked through the soft sand to a clearing in the jungle. Tony came from behind him and put his arm around his shoulder and said, "You okay?"

"Where's the boss?" Jerry asked. Tony smiled and just pointed at the camouflaged tent that had been put up between two palm trees on a level patch of dirt just off the sandy beach. Two soldiers sat on either side of the open flap that led into the tent. There was a small metal table in front of the soldiers, like they were both sitting back home eating TV dinners and watching Steve McQueen hunting down the bad guys.

"I'm here to see Captain John Murphy." One of the soldiers smiled, and before he could say a word, John Murphy pushed his head through the flap of the tent. He nodded at Jerry and waved him inside the tent. Jerry bent down a little to push the flap open and entered the tent.

"If you need the bathroom, be my guest," John said, looking back down at the book he was reading.

"I'm okay," said Jerry.

"It's nice having your own shitter," John smiled. "One of the perks. Sit down. You want a beer, something to eat?"

"Beer would be good," said Jerry. John pointed toward the cooler. Jerry leaned over, lifted the top, took out a San Miguel, and sat down.

"Tony's been telling me that you've been doing a good job for us, and I've got a little something here for you, just a token of our appreciation." John pulled a brown envelope out of his pocket and handed it to Jerry.

Jerry took the package out of John's hand.

"Thanks," he said. "I'm sure this will come in handy."

John stared at Jerry for a moment, pulling his chair a bit closer to where Jerry was sitting. "You know the difference between small time and big time?" John didn't wait for Jerry to answer, John never waited for answers. "I'll tell ya, there are the givers, and then there are the takers. You, my friend, are a giver. It's all right," John patted Jerry on the knee and continued, "nothing wrong with a giver. Christ knows we need the givers, but then there are the takers, and we need them too. We all serve the greater good, makes the world go round." John sat back in his chair, took a swallow of his beer.

"I'm going to let you in on a little secret." John paused for a moment. Jerry just sat there; John liked that about Jerry, he listened. John spoke softly and Jerry had to lean in to hear what he was saying.

"You can have it both ways. You can give and take at the same time. We are here putting our asses on the line, we're the ones getting shot at, we're the ones that are getting our legs and our arms blown off, we're the ones getting called war criminals, we're the ones that are coming home to no jobs, no respect, no future." John stood up fast and startled Jerry, who leaned back in his chair. John continued in a more forceful tone.

"Are you hearing what I'm saying, McGinnis? Do you honestly think this war has something to do with fighting for democracy, fighting for the freedom-loving Vietnamese? Listen to what I'm telling you, because these are going to be the most important words you'll ever hear in your entire fucking life. It's all bullshit. You want to know what this is really all about? It's about money, it's about control, it's the Military Industrial Complex. You think for one goddamn minute that anyone back home gives a shit about us? Please. It's about power, who's got it, who keeps it. We're the Gung Ho obedient soldiers, killing and being killed, doing the bidding for those old white guys who are getting richer every goddamn day."

John walked over to the table in the corner of the tent, his back to Jerry, where there were bottles of four or five different scotches, vodkas, and gins.

"You ever taste a fifteen-year-old scotch?" John didn't wait for an answer; he took a small glass, poured to the middle of the glass, then put a splash of water in. He looked over at Jerry. "Just a touch of distilled water, makes it blossom."

John handed the glass to Jerry and said softly, with a warm and friendly smile, "You have no idea what the hell I'm talking about, do you? Well, someday you will. Here's to us, Jerry, here's to your kids; here's to my kids." They gently clinked glasses. "Every kid here has a mother and father, a wife or a brother back home, waiting for the phone to ring or the knock on the door. You know who's standing there? I'll tell you, McGinnis, it's the fucking chaplain and his little sidekick. There's a whole goddamn unit of chaplains and marines that do nothing but go to the moms and dads or wives, brothers or sisters. It's all the same, every day, the death squad. The message is all the same, and you think that this must be that nightmare that woke you up every other night, your heart beating and the blankets drenched in sweat. They would stand there almost at attention, their words would begin to blur, words like 'grateful nation' and 'the President sends his deepest condolences and regrets.'" Big John took a drink. "But I know one thing for sure. You know what that is, McGinnis? I'll tell you, they never visit the homes of those rich white guys I've been telling you about. You know why, Jerry? I'll tell you, it's because their precious children are safe and sound and all snuggled nice and warm in their beds. Here's the bottom line." John hesitated and then said softly, staring into Jerry's eyes, "There's us and there's them, and I want to be them. What do you want?"

This was the same line of bullshit that John threw down last time, always justifying what they were doing. Jerry was getting tired of the company line; it seemed so rehearsed. One thing for sure, John and his buddies were not suffering, they were living it up with fifteen-year-old scotch and porterhouse steaks. *Who did this maniac think he was bullshitting?* Jerry thought to himself. *He could tell me a hundred times about old white guys and us poor idiots dying just to make them rich. But he was the one getting rich and didn't give a shit who had to die.*

Jerry smiled, as if he was in all the way, 100 percent. But now he had a goal, a real reason for playing along. Jerry leaned forward, put his beer slowly down on the metal table, and looked up with an expression of thoughtful consideration and said, "I get it now, Captain. Truth is, I never understood before, but I do now. It's clear as a fucking bell. You'd have to be the stupidest motherfucker in the world not to see this, and now I do. Anyway," he continued, "I don't need any more time to think about it. I'm in, you can count on me. But tell you the truth, I'm not sure what more you want of me. I have been giving Tony the information he has asked for."

"I know," said John. "This coming Friday at 0500 there is going to be a delivery at a remote airfield about five miles outside of Moc Bai. You know where that is?"

"Yeah," said Jerry. "I know it. I was up there talking to a couple of women that run an orphanage there, doing a human interest story for *Stars and Stripes*."

"Really," said John, as if he were more amused than interested. "That's nice. Anyway, there is a planeload of heroin, weed, and cocaine coming in, about 500 kilos. There's lots of money riding on this shipment, so we need to make absolutely sure, and I mean absolutely sure, that there is nothing going on in that area, no troops, no MPs, no CIDs."

Jerry nodded. "I can do that. When do you need to know?"

"Wednesday, no later. We've got to let the South Vietnam Air Force guys know that they have the all clear." John smiled. "I guess they want to send their kids to those fancy colleges too."

John stood up and walked out of the tent. Jerry sat there for a moment, then stood and followed. John turned and said, "Going to get a steak. You in?"

"Sure, why the hell not."

Over the next two days, Jerry found out that a training mission was planned close to the drop area. Tony passed on the information that he had received from Jerry, and the incoming shipment was postponed. A few weeks later Jerry was heading for his office when a jeep pulled up.

"Hey," shouted Tony. "Get in, I'll buy you a cup of coffee."

"I got to get to work," said Jerry, as he jumped in the jeep.

Tony smiled. "Don't worry, this won't take long. John is in town and he wants to show you something."

Tony drove up to a large brick building. They got out and walked past two soldiers who stood guard. The soldiers nodded as they walked past.

"What's the most precious commodity we send to this country?" said John as they walked in. Jerry turned toward the voice. Before Jerry could answer, John said, "Our boys, right? And what's the most precious thing we send back to the States from here?" Once again John answered his own question. "Our boys, but the unlucky ones go home in body bags, the price of war." John stopped talking as he opened a large metal door, which was guarded by two soldiers. "I know you know about our system but it's time to see for yourself."

Jerry followed him into the room and stared at the bodies of dead soldiers laid out on tables. It was a makeshift morgue. He put his hand up to his mouth; the heat and stench were overwhelming. It took him a moment to figure out what he was seeing. Men in white coats were cutting open the lifeless bodies, removing their organs, and casually inserting bags of white power in the cavities. Other men were sewing up the drug-filled bodies. They were then placed back in the body bags with tags on the bags, ready to be shipped home.

Jerry tried not to gag. These guys were working on the fallen soldiers like they were pieces of meat, like they were just packing boxes. There was no emotion on their faces, cigarettes were hanging from most of their mouths, and they talked quietly among themselves.

"What do you think?" John was lighting up his own cigarette and handed the pack to Jerry. Jerry was glad to have something to do with his hands, but was afraid they would shake. He kept his eyes down, taking a slow deep breath.

"Pretty clever," he answered. "Who the hell would ever think to look or dare to look in the bodies of our dead soldiers? What happens when they get back to the States?" Jerry was beginning to feel dizzy; he wanted out of there, but managed to stay calm.

"No problem, the specially marked body bags get shipped to certain funeral homes all over the country. Once there, the bodies are opened up, the drugs are taken out, the bodies are sewn up and the caskets are closed and sealed and ready for burial. Every once and a while, we lose one, but that's the price of doing business." He turned and headed back out the door.

"What do you think?" said John, as they walked out of the building and got back into the jeep.

"Brilliant, never would have thought of that." The fresh air filled his lungs and he started to feel better. He was hoping John and Tony hadn't noticed.

"I know," said John, oblivious to Jerry's discomfort. "Look, Jerry, you are doing a good job, and people at the top have noticed. Fact is, you've proven to be a real valuable asset."

Tony put the jeep in gear and they took off. "Let's get out of here. I'll never get used to seeing that shit," he said as he pulled into the line of traffic.

He dropped Jerry off in front of his office, saying, "See you tonight. We'll meet you after work." Then Jerry walked into his office like it was just any other day.

After the workday, he met up with Tony and John at their usual spot.

"Three beers," said Tony as they sat at a table in the back of the café. The waiter bowed and said, "Yes, sir, Mister Tony."

"Look, Jerry," began John, "you can keep doing what you're doing and that's fine. We always need information and you'll keep getting paid for your services, unless, of course, you have interest in moving up the chain of command, if you get my meaning."

John took a long swallow from the bottle that had been placed in front of him and continued. "You're not like most of the guys here. Fact is, you're out of place, but we all got our reasons for being where we are, so between your talents, your access to certain information, well, there can be real big opportunities for you. So," John continued, "you let us know if you're interested."

Jerry didn't hesitate. "I'm in, I'm in all the way."

Tony looked hard at Jerry, then lifted his bottle of beer in a toast; so did John. Jerry lifted his bottle and clinked both and said, "Proud to be a member of the team."

"Meet Tony here tomorrow around three. I'll see you later," said John.

John and Tony stood up, both took one last drink of their beer, and then Tony casually handed Jerry a large brown paper bag and smiled and said, "Here's a little bonus."

Jerry took the bag and stood up as John and Tony walked out of the café and into the heavy traffic of downtown Saigon.

Jerry opened the folded bag and looked inside. It was filled with money, U.S. dollars, hundred dollar bills, lots of them. He closed the bag quickly and looked around; he felt like he was being watched, but nobody was looking, nobody was there. He folded up the bag and stuffed it in his shirt.

He couldn't keep sending this much cash to Kate, she would know he was up to something. He would need to open an account and funnel money to a Swiss bank. He would start to make inquiries.

Jerry hailed down a bike taxi. The drive to his quarters seemed like it took forever, and he had time to think, to ponder what he was

309

getting himself and his family into. This wasn't just about him, it was about Kate and the boys. He gave the driver two dong and walked into his hut. Steve was inside.

"What are you up to, buddy?" asked Steve. "You look spaced out. You on drugs or what, my friend?" He had a smile on his face.

Jerry smiled back at his friend and said, "Yeah, right, you know that I'm straight as an arrow. Long hot day. When the hell do you get used to the fucking heat?"

"Never," said Steve. "And with all the shit you are getting involved with, makes sense that you are feeling the heat."

"You are right about that. Truth is I guess I'm having second thoughts about what I'm getting us into."

"What do you mean, second thoughts?" said Steve with some irritation in his voice.

"I mean," said Jerry, "that maybe we're getting in too far. This is dangerous stuff, and I'm just not sure I should have gotten you into this."

"Well," answered Steve, "I'm in and so are you, pal. Look, for the first time in my useless fucking life I have a real purpose and maybe I can do some real good. Forget about your doubts and let's get to work and get these bastards. They're just a bunch of two-bit thugs. I'm going to get some shut-eye, I'm tired. You going to be okay?"

"Yeah," said Jerry. "I'm fine. Go get some sleep, we'll talk later." Steve patted Jerry on the shoulder.

Steve was a good guy. Jerry was wishing he hadn't gotten him involved. The guy only had a few more months in Vietnam. Jerry needed to back off and not let Steve get in too deep. He couldn't keep playing the good guy against the bad. And then he thought about the money and then about Grandma Kim and Lucy. He began to doubt everything about his mission and his big plans. *I'm fucked,* he thought. *I am totally fucked.*

Lying in bed, unable to sleep later that night, he came to a decision: at least for now he needed to protect Kate and the boys. The first thing he had to do was get in touch with her and tell her to destroy all the papers. She was a loose cannon. Who knew what she would do. Or maybe there was another way…

He got up and quietly, so as not to wake Steve, he opened his desk and pulled out the papers he had ready for the morning mailbag. The bulk of the information he'd been collecting and writing down had already been sent to both Kate and his parents, but these documents were full of details, specifics, names. He had more proof of just how extensive the operations were, how high the Unit members went in the chain of command, and some possible leads to the Unit's stateside associates. He sat on the edge of his bunk, the papers in his hands. Then a voice in his head said, *Fuck it.* He stood up, grabbed his lighter from the dresser top, and walked out of the room and over to a metal can outside. It was a damp night, and the small flame seemed to take the wetness out of the air. A blank expression was on his face as he watched the ashes drift into the wind and float off into the cloudy sky over the city.

CHAPTER 25

The gentle sounds of the surf rolling up the beach usually didn't keep Captain John Murphy from drifting into a deep and restful sleep. But tonight he moved restlessly on the cot. The flaps of the tent quickly shifted from side to side, giving a direction to the faint breeze as it filtered through the large tent that had been his home for the last three months. His headquarters had to be mobile and centrally located so he could closely monitor the large-scale activities under his command.

He awoke feeling anxious. It was still dark. He stood and walked over to look out the tent door. The moon lit the ocean. He could see the waves in the distance, smell them and feel their moisture seep into his bones. His joints felt better the closer he was to the sea. What a view, he thought, and laughed a bit; it was way different than rural Alabama.

What woke him was thinking about Jerry McGinnis. There was something wrong, but Christ, John knew it was almost too late now. Jerry had already seen everything. John realized he needed to find someone to get close to Jerry; someone to keep an eye on him. There was something he was hiding, John thought. Everyone was hiding something.

The following morning John put in a call to General Richard Kindred and arranged to meet that afternoon at the general's office. Kindred was the commanding general of the U.S. Military Assistance Command, which was stationed on Tan Son Nhut Air Base just outside of Saigon.

John was shown into the spacious office. The large mahogany desk was flanked by two chairs in front and one on either side. A large black couch sat at the far end of the room, with a coffee table and three chairs around the table.

"Hey, John," said the general in a friendly voice, as he motioned to a chair.

"Sir," John answered. Before he could step forward someone else entered the office. He turned. "Hey, Connie," he said. "Nice surprise."

Connie Kindred moved gracefully over to John and kissed him gently on his cheek. John smiled. There wasn't much that John Murphy would smile about, but the general's daughter was one.

She wore a long fitted dress with a light blue tunic draped over her shoulders. Her eyes were beautiful, dark brown with a clarity that gave one the feeling she was looking directly into your soul. Clearly all the best parts of a mixed union between a Vietnamese princess and an American John Wayne had created a stunning beauty. She was an only child and clearly had been doted on; her parents understood the challenges that mixed-raced children deal with. Connie had been sent to the finest schools wherever her father had been stationed. Her Vietnamese was flawless, her English had a faint British accent to it, and of course she spoke French and Italian.

"I didn't know that you were going to be joining us. It is a pleasure to see you," said John.

"Sit, John. Tell me what I can do for you," said the general.

John turned back to the general. "I told you a bit about this new guy, Jerry McGinnis. He's been getting us some really valuable information, and I think he could become a permanent member, maybe even after the war."

"Okay, remind me, what's his background? Where's he from? And if he is so smart, then why the fuck is he over here?"

"I'm not sure. I asked myself that same question. And I still don't have a good answer. I think it might be a good idea to look a little deeper. He's got issues with some of our operations, but sometimes those people turn out to be our best assets." John turned toward Connie. "Tony brought him in, and you have met him, I believe. I would love to get your read on him."

Connie looked at her dad then nodded her head. "Sure. I met him once. We haven't spent any time together, but I would be happy to make friends with your American GI. I'll find out what's going on with him."

The general stood. "Good, you two work out the details. Let me know what you think." He reached out a hand to John, who rose and shook hands. He and Connie walked out of the office together.

"How do you want to work this?" she said.

"I will have Jerry meet me at Yong Kim's one night next week. I'll let you know. You walk in and I'll leave you to work your magic."

"Sounds good. I will wait to hear from you." She kissed him on the cheek again and walked away. She was strictly business.

John arranged to meet Jerry the following week, he had asked for some info on troop movements. Jerry was to deliver the file to him directly, no need to bring Tony in on this.

Connie walked in just at the time they had planned. John watched her walk over to their table.

"McGinnis," said John in a casual tone. "Slide over, pal. I think you know Connie. She is General Kindred's daughter." Jerry stood; he'd been brought up with manners, respect, small-town values. Connie put out her hand; Jerry hesitated, and then took her hand.

"Connie works for the Department of Resettlement." Jerry still looked confused.

"It's not what you're thinking," said Connie, seeing the look on his face. She continued, "John told me that you work with *Stars and Stripes*, and I was telling John that I thought this would be a good story for the military." Jerry sat down and smiled.

"Listen, I have to run. Talk to Connie. See if you can help her out. Talk to me tomorrow." John took the folder that Jerry had given him. He stood and walked out of the café.

"Listen, I'm sorry, I remember we were supposed to meet for dinner the night after we met. I'm sorry I never showed up. I had a lot of work. So, anyway, what exactly does your organization do?" Jerry asked Connie.

"Well, when you heroes came over to save us, you created your own little exodus, maybe not by biblical standards, but close. Last count we've settled close to a million refugees from the north, mostly Catholics, and gotten them into government housing on the outskirts of Saigon." There was directness to this beautiful woman. Her eyes were big with an unusual tint, almost hazel brown, and her jet-black hair folded over her slender shoulders and crept down her back in an effortless form.

"Do you know my father?" she asked.

"The general, no," answered Jerry. "I've heard of him, of course."

Connie suddenly stood and said, "I have to be going right now, but let's have dinner. I'll tell you what I do, you tell me what you do. How about Friday, assuming you're not too busy with work? This Friday I'll meet you here at eight and then we'll go around the corner. There's a really great dumpling bar."

Jerry had no idea why Connie was suddenly so interested in spending time with him. He was attracted to her, of course, but this wasn't about that. She had something to do with the Unit, clearly, but he didn't know what. And did that mean her father was also involved?

His work over the next few days distracted him from his thoughts. The conflicts in his head were becoming acute. He felt himself drifting in and out of rationalizations that began to make more and more sense. He had come here with very specific intentions, but over the last few weeks, the lines between good and evil had become frighteningly unclear.

That Friday night Jerry and Connie met at the café as planned and then walked over to the dumpling bar just down the street. As they talked, he could see that their lives could not have been more different. He had been raised in a small town in Pennsylvania, she in the capitals of Europe.

She had confided in Jerry, and explained that she was cooperating with John's Unit in order to help with her resettlement duties. "I normally keep a very low profile. Not many members know to what extent I am involved, but I feel something with you. I like you, and for some reason I trust you."

Jerry just nodded his head. He couldn't take his eyes off of her that night. It felt like he was in a trance; he was mesmerized. There were many beautiful women in Vietnam, but she was different. Her hair was black and straight like all the other women, but hers was different, almost sculptured, the back of her hair aligned perfectly with the back of her neck. Her bangs perfectly shaped to her short and narrow eyebrows. There was a businesslike tone to her voice, and yet she seemed to always be smiling, just ever so slightly.

Over the next few weeks, Jerry and Connie's friendship deepened and transitioned into a strong connection. He had become the source for almost all intelligence information for the Unit's operations.

In addition to providing logistical information and whatever he got from Steve, he learned to work as part of the exit team. He would be setting up foreign accounts and organizing the distribution of funds to Unit members and their families. He had stopped writing to Kate and sending notebooks home, but he knew that what he already sent was potentially devastating to the Unit. He realized now that he had to come clean and figure out how to get rid of the information he had already sent home. He hadn't given up all hope of finding out what happened to Chuck, but he was sure the same thing would happen to him if the notebooks were found. He needed to talk to Kate. He could use the phone at the office, but decided it probably wasn't a good idea.

"Morning, uncle," said Jerry with respect and a tinge of genuine fondness as he walked into his favorite tea house. The elderly gentleman began to pour tea for him. "No, I just need to use your phone, I need to call my wife. I'll pay for it, no problem." Kim had heard these words, these tones, seen these expressions many times. How many marriages had come to an end by this latest conflict? Kim's expression changed from joyous to sympathetic; the change was imperceptible but it was there. Jerry smiled and then said, "I think I will take that cup of tea, thanks."

"Okay." Kim tilted his head toward his private office. "You can shut the door if you like, take your time."

Jerry stared at his watch; it was 6 a.m. here. What time was it back home? Eleven-hour difference, he mumbled to himself, so 8 p.m.

"Hello?" There was hesitation, then the young voice of Sean said, "Daddy, Daddy! Hi, Daddy, we all miss you, when are you coming home?"

"Soon, Sean, real soon. Where's your mom?"

"I don't know if I can wake her up. Mommy's always sleeping when we get home, but I'll try. She gets so mad, Daddy, please come home. I think Mom's been sick, but Grandma says she's fine, but I don't think so."

"Sean, please go and wake up your mom."

After a few minutes, he heard someone pick up the phone. "Jerry, is it you?"

"Kate, it's me. Why the hell are you sleeping at 7 p.m.? Who's giving the boys supper? Are you sick, for Christ's sake? Kate, what the hell is going on there?"

"We haven't heard from you in weeks, I thought you were dead. I can't deal with this anymore. I need you to come home, do you hear me, Jerry? I need you to come home."

"Kate, everything is going to be fine, I swear. I made a terrible mistake. I'll be home before you know it, everything will be just like the good old days." He could hear her breathing, "Kate, honey, those papers that I've been sending home, all of them… Kate, are you there?"

"Yeah, I'm here." Jerry could hardly hear her, Kate's voice and tone seemed so strange to him. He had never heard her sound like that, and he had known her since fourth grade. There was a change, a coldness, he had never felt before.

"Listen, Kate, I can't talk for very long. I need you to take all the notebooks, letters, journals, everything I sent you, put them in a metal can in the backyard, and burn them all. You can do that, I know you can. Kate, are you there?"

"I said I'm here." There was a pause. "Why on earth would you like me to destroy all your precious letters and journals and notebooks. I mean, maybe I misunderstood, but didn't you go over there to get all the stuff in those notebooks so you could avenge your friend? Then suddenly no more letters and now you've decided to throw it all away. I'll tell you what I'm going to do with all your fucking papers, I'm going to load them all in the trunk and drive them down to the newspaper office. Get them published, isn't that what you wanted?"

"Kate, will you listen to me? Things are more complicated than I thought, things have changed."

"What's her name, Jerry? There must be some little Vietnamese woman who has been turning your head. I am right, aren't I, Jerry? You son of a bitch."

"Kate, you are talking nonsense. You need to listen to me, you have to destroy those papers, they can get us all killed. Do you hear me for Christ's sake?" There was only crying now on the other side of the line. "Kate, relax, I told you everything is going to be fine. I'm going to put in for an emergency leave. I'll be home in just a few weeks, can you wait until then?"

Kate shouted, "You're lying, you're always lying. I am taking these boxes to the police. You can explain to them what you are doing over there."

"Kate, I need you to calm down, I will try to get home in the next few days. I need you to just trust me. Leave the papers. I will

319

take care of things when I get there. Just please don't do anything. Promise me, Kate."

"Please, Jerry, come home, I want you to just come home."

"You have my word. It is going to be okay, I will explain everything."

Jerry could hear her slam the phone down on the cradle. His tea had turned cold. Life had been simple. He wished he had never gotten that call. Life in Selinsgrove seemed so far away now that he was here, in Uncle's tea shop. *What a mess. Is there anyone that I haven't hurt or fucked over? Lucy and Grandma Kim, their mission, so pure and selfless. Connie, John, Steve. I've got to get this right. I've got to make a choice.* He sat in Uncle's chair, looking onto the street teeming with early morning crowds.

Jerry had to come straight with John, or everyone would be dead before the end of the month. If Kate took his material to the newspaper, it would blow up in all their faces. He needed to get home. He knew that John could arrange it, but he would have to be honest and tell him what he'd done. It was a terrible risk, but Jerry had to take it. He rehearsed every word in his head. *I have a problem, I fucked up. I'm sorry, but I can fix this. Everything will be okay, everything!* If they would just give him a chance to explain, Jerry thought. He could feel Tony's hands around his neck. There would be little or no hesitation from John or Tony. But maybe if he said it all just right, maybe he could fix it, fix everything.

* * *

When Jerry confessed the whole story from beginning to end, it required Captain John Murphy to call upon every ounce of that flexible personality to focus on the big picture as he saw it. He realized he had been betrayed, and from his narrow point of view, it was the worst kind of betrayal, by a friend. His ability to self-diagnose his own proclivities had served him well over the years. He understood his inclination to strike out at even the slightest provocation. What would have been a psychotic reaction was often replaced by a pragmatic view of the big picture. This alteration and merging of two distinct personality traits had vaulted him up to exactly where he wanted to be, a captain in command of what was now the most lucrative military structure in the U.S. military. Revenge and retribution would come later, much later, but not now. The war was coming to an end; it could be next week or next year, but the end was in clear sight. Protecting their assets was of paramount importance.

Up until now Jerry had not only proven to be a loyal and trusted friend, but more important, had also proven to possess the talents that only a college degree in journalism and accounting could offer. Those disciplines were essential in a post-war organization that would invest, manage, and ultimately distribute a vast array of assets to those who had proven their loyalty and their value to the Unit.

John had chosen in the moment of Jerry's confession to block out his fury at the betrayal of loyalty and friendship to focus on those other critical traits for the good of the founders and the Unit that they had created and nurtured over these many years. There was a way to salvage the situation, and he and Connie talked it over after Jerry's unexpected confession.

He smiled as Kindred's aide pointed to the couch where he could wait to see the general.

"Be about ten minutes, Captain. Can I get you anything?"

John smiled and said, "No, corporal, I'm fine. I don't mind waiting." The soldier turned back to the file cabinet marked MIA 1969. John slid his hand over the rich leather. The smell, the feel, brought back memories. Curled up with his head against an armrest. His father in the green La-Z-Boy recliner.

It wasn't so much that Jerry had almost shitcanned the entire operation, it was that he had so easily taken them all in. John thought he must be getting old and soft; back in the day, he would have seen through Jerry's bullshit in a New York second. It never made any sense, none of it. But for some reason or the other, John had looked past the obvious and just seen a guy he liked. That's what really pissed him off, that John liked Jerry. Soon Connie joined him in the office, as planned, so that they could all discuss the situation.

General Kindred stood as John and Connie walked through the door to his large and stately office in downtown Saigon. He walked from behind his desk, hugged and kissed his daughter, and shook hands with the captain whom he considered a friend and advisor.

John and Connie sat down in the two large chairs in front of the general's desk. John spoke first. "General, we have a critical situation but we believe we have a solution."

The general broke in. "Get to the point, John."

"Yes, sir," said John. "Jerry McGinnis has betrayed us. He came here with the intention to expose and bring us down."

The general sat expressionless and said, "Go on, John."

"McGinnis was good friends with Chuck Harris, and it turns out he came over here to find out why his friend and his friend's brother met such an untimely end. He has already sent home journals, papers, and letters detailing our every operation for the sole purpose of destroying all that we've built."

"Go on, John. I'm waiting for the solution part of this conversation."

John hesitated, then Connie said, "He's changed, Dad. He's become part of the team, and he realizes what he did was wrong and misguided. He tried to get the papers back from his wife, but she went crazy and threatened to send every last page to the papers. He had no choice but to fill us in on the whole story."

John continued, "We told McGinnis that we would send two very responsible soldiers to his house and, when his family was out of the house, retrieve the papers and then all would be forgiven and forgotten. We asked McGinnis to write down in detail every aspect of the mission, give us directions to the house, the neighborhood, detailing the house, and his wife and kids' schedules, and where the papers actually are in the house. But Ramo and I are the ones who are going. We're going to visit his wife, make sure the kids are in school, get the papers, take care of his wife, and leave behind the instructions that McGinnis gave us. A few days later, we'll break the news to McGinnis that there was a terrible accident, that his wife walked in on our guys, and things got out of hand, and that unfortunately his wife was killed. We'll tell him that she tried to fight our guys, and while they were trying to calm her down, she fell and cracked her head open. We're also going to tell Jerry that these idiots somehow dropped the note that he had given us, implicating him in his wife's murder."

The general remained silent. Connie said, "I'm going to tell Jerry that he needs to disappear. We can have him reported missing in action and, in a month or so, killed in action. We will give him a whole new identity and relocate him to Europe, maybe Switzerland, where he will manage our assets along with me for the next couple of years, or maybe forever, whichever comes first."

The general turned from the window he had been staring out of, moved closer to his daughter and John, and said, "Why the fuck don't you just put a bullet in his head? Isn't that your normal method of operation, Captain?"

"He's changed, General. He's not the man he was when he got here. This place changes you. He's what we need, and Connie will be there to watch his ass every minute."

"It's foolproof, Dad. We've given this some thought. This will work better for all of us."

"Okay," said the general. "Sounds like a reasonable plan. Let me know how he reacts, and we'll go from there. Now get the hell out of my office. You guys gave me a fucking headache."

SECTION III

CHAPTER 26

Selinsgrove, PA

*D*earest Kate,

It's late here, the pounding rain keeps me awake. My mind is racing, asking myself over and over, what have I done? What have I done to you and our boys? What have I done to my mother and father? My arrogance and my ambition have led me here. How can I ask you to forgive me? How can I make this up to you and the boys? I came here with what I believed were all good intentions. I deceived myself into thinking that I was going to do the right thing, the noble thing. I came here believing that I could find the truth and bring to justice those that murdered Chuck and Brian. I was wrong, Kate. This was never about Chuck and his brother; this was always about me. About being more than I am, reaching for a foolish and unrealistic prize. What a fool I am. There is evil here that I could never have imagined. I find that I am being drawn into the hell that I thought I was fighting against. I've met good and decent people here, people who are doing good. Men and women who sacrifice

327

themselves to save others. I'm ashamed that the temptation of money and power has blinded me and has drawn me into a life of greed and ambition. My eyes are open now, I can see the truth. I know now what I need to do. Please find it in your heart to forgive me, and please believe me when I tell you that I will come back to you and our family. Please know that I will put this terrible mistake behind me and live out my life as your husband and the father of our two boys...

Hug the boys for me, Kate, and know that I love you.

Jerry

"That's the last letter he sent home," said Jack. "I think we read everything. Goddammit, what a fucking mess."

Sean surveyed the papers and boxes that littered the floor and tabletop of Joe Smith's kitchen. He noticed a small piece of paper that looked out of place. They both had overlooked it. Sean reached down, pushed the papers aside, and held the small piece of paper up to the light. The name and the number had faded over the years. Jack held out his hand and said, "What is it?"

Sean placed the tattered slip of paper on the table and moved it across to his brother. Jack looked down and said, "Who's Jay Donald?"

Sean hesitated for a moment, lost in thought, and then he said in a quiet voice, "I spent a lot of time with Grandma while she was sick. I think she felt somewhat responsible for everything that happened. I mean, that's crazy. Like it was her fault that her son, our dad, would leave us the way he did. At the end, she began to fade away, and sometimes she talked crazy. But sometimes she was clear as a bell. She once mentioned a lawyer in Philadelphia. Apparently he had come to them after we heard that Dad had been declared MIA.

He had told Grandma and Grandpa that he and his firm represented an organization that must remain anonymous. He told them that a benefits package had been set up for those members who had died or were missing in action. He told them that at the discretion of the firm, funds would be doled out to the survivors depending on circumstances and need." Sean looked up at Jack, who seemed to be staring past his brother. "Jack, you following me?" said Sean.

Jack looked into his brother's eyes and said, "Yeah."

Sean began to say something, then hesitated before continuing, "Just before she died, she became alert again. I thought that maybe she was getting better. She said, 'Talk to the lawyer.' She died right after that." Sean took the small note from his brother's hand and said, "I think this is the name of the lawyer. We need to go and see this guy. I'll call in the morning; it's a Philadelphia area code.

"Anyway, now I know why I'm here," said Sean. "Now I under-stand." He stood up from the table and let the screen door slam as he walked outside. He went to the porch rail and leaned on it with both hands.

"What are you talking about?" Jack followed his brother.

"There's a reason for everything, Jack. You may not believe it, but I do. We're here for a reason. It's not some fluke that we're here together after all these years, sitting in this house, reading these letters and notebooks. I didn't get it at first, but now I think I've figured it out."

Sean turned to Jack. "Dad brought us here, he wants us to be together, and he found a way." He placed a hand on his brother's shoulder.

Jack pulled away and said, "Look, Sean, you got your reason, I got mine. Maybe you figure that everything was destined to happen, that this is God's plan. You get a sweet pretty childhood in L.A., and I get brought up by an abusive drunk. Tell you the honest truth, I don't give a shit whether this was God's plan or the devil's. The bottom fucking line is that I that I got fucked, and you and Grandma didn't."

"That's okay, Jack. I don't expect you to understand."

"Fuck you," said Jack with a snarl. "Don't talk to me like I'm some kind of fucking idiot. I understand everything you're saying. I'm just saying that for me, I'm going to find out what the hell happened to Mom and Dad, and if there is any chance in hell, I'm going to track down those motherfuckers and do to them what they did to our parents. It's not about you and me, not about long-lost brothers finding each other."

Sean hesitated. "Don't you get it? This isn't just about getting even with the bastards that killed our parents. This is about finishing Dad's job."

"What job, what are you talking about? Finishing the job, as far as I am concerned, is killing those bastards, period," said Jack.

"Look, Jack, almost thirty years ago dad went over to Vietnam to find out who killed Brian and Chuck Harris. Now we know something about what he found. There's more, I know there is. Maybe this lawyer can help us."

Sean walked back into the house. He looked up at Jack as he came back to the table and sat down.

"Look, the way I see it, Dad goes over there to find out why Chuck and Brian were killed and he ends up walking into what could be the biggest story of the war, and he realizes that reporting on it could turn him into a superstar overnight, and he hopes to get the Pulitzer.. And make some serious money on the side. He could work at any paper in the country, and besides, Dad said he thought that it was his fault that both brothers got killed. Maybe if he hadn't gone up to ask questions at the hospital, then maybe those two guys wouldn't have killed Chuck and wouldn't have killed his brother. Anyway, he figured that he owed it to Chuck after all they'd been through as kids. Look, all I'm saying is that he went over there for one reason, and that reason changed—the evil that he found started to swallow him up. But even so, it sounds like he was on a quest at the end, like a crusade or something."

"A quest for what?" said Jack. "He told everyone he went over there to get the guys that killed those two boys."

"Yeah, right, at first that's why he went over there, but after a while it turned into something a lot bigger, a lot more important, and maybe a lot scarier too. That's why we have to keep going, we've got to find out. We have to tell the story."

"Okay," said Jack. "Fine, maybe you're right. I guess you can say that Dad found a way to bring us together and to finish a job that he must have thought was important enough to risk his life for and to die for. Maybe you're right."

The next day, Sean called the number on the paper.

A young-sounding voice answered, "Law Offices. Where can I direct your call?"

Sean answered, "This is Sean McGinnis, I'm calling from the District Attorney's office. I need to speak with Jay Donald."

There was hesitation in the girl's voice as she said, "Please hold."

"Can I help you?" asked a new voice on the phone.

"Who am I speaking to?" said Sean in a firm voice.

"I'm John Bradley," he said and continued, not waiting for Sean to respond. "Did you say that you are looking for Jay Donald and that you're Sean McGinnis?"

"Yes, that's what I'm saying and yes, that's who I am."

"I have something for you, but I need to verify that you're the right Sean McGinnis," said Bradley.

"What do you have for me?" said Sean in a more irritated voice.

"I don't know, I never knew. Jay Donald died more than ten years ago. But he left a package and instructions that if ever a Sean or Jack McGinnis should come calling, to give them this. I've never looked in it. We've had it here for more than thirty years. I'm happy to give it to you, Mr. McGinnis. Tell you the truth, I'd be happy to be rid of it. It's part of a past that I would sooner try to forget. Do you know the Liberty Bell Diner in Philly? We can meet there," said John Bradley.

"Yeah, I know it. How about Sunday morning around ten?" Sean hung up the phone and turned to his brother and said, "We've got to see what's inside that package."

Jack was looking over the papers on the table. He'd taken refuge in the words of his dead father as he and Sean read through his notebooks and diaries. He'd gotten to know him; after all these years, it felt like his father was talking to him. He sat back and wondered out loud, "What would it have been like?"

Sean looked up from the scattered papers that littered the kitchen floor. "What?"

"You ever wonder what it would have been like if Dad hadn't gone to Vietnam?"

Sean stared at Jack and said, "Yeah, I thought about it about a million times. I'm tired of thinking about stuff I can't do anything about."

Jack stood up and walked to the window; he looked out into the backyard for a moment and then turned. "Look," he said. "The only way we're going put this behind us is to finish the job. I'm going to finish this one way or another. After reading all this stuff, we are left with more questions than answers. And now there's new information. We don't even know what it is. I mean, Dad got involved with this organization, that's clear. Obviously, he got himself killed for betraying them. And they killed Mom because she knew too much. The way I see it is he got greedy and tried to play both sides, and we are the ones who lost. Some of those bastards are still alive. We can't leave it alone. We need to go after these guys; we need the rest of the story. Maybe we'll find out our father was into this shit up to his eyeballs, but one way or another, we need to find the truth."

"Or maybe we should leave it the hell alone," Sean reasoned, playing devil's advocate.

"If we walk away, it was all for nothing. Dad's intentions were good, at least at the beginning. Something happened. What about these people, Steve and Lucy and Grandma Kim, John and Tony. Tony Ramo is still alive. We can start with him."

"I thought you said he died," said Sean.

"I never said that, least I don't think I did. Last I knew, he was still in the hospital in Williamsport. If the bastard didn't die since then, he'll have some of the answers."

Jack walked over to the phone that hung on the wall and called the VA hospital in Williamsport. He asked for Tony Ramo's room.

He waited. An old and gruff voice came on the line. "Yeah, who the hell is this?"

"Is this Tony Ramo?"

"Who wants to know?"

"This is Jack, Tony. Jack McGinnis, Jerry's son." Jack waited for an answer, but there was none. "I'm in town with my brother, Sean. We wanted to come up and talk to you. How about tomorrow?" For a moment, Jack thought that maybe he had lost the connection. He looked at his brother and shrugged at the silence on the other end of the phone.

"Get the fuck out of here," said Tony in the only way that Tony could have said it. "Jerry, is that you?"

Jack hesitated before answering, "Yeah, Tony, it's me. How about tomorrow?" Jack stood there in the kitchen, waiting for an answer.

"Yeah," said Tony. "It'll be good seeing you, pal. Been a long time."

Jack hung up the phone and said to his brother, "He still thinks I'm Dad. We'll go up there in the morning and get the rest of the story. Let's get something to eat, and we'll get an early start."

Sean and Jack ended up at the steakhouse by the river. Over dinner, Jack said, "Tell me about your family, your wife and kids."

Sean looked up at his brother and for a moment said nothing, then a smile came to his face. He said, "After we get through this little adventure of ours, you'll come up to Philly and we'll spend some time. I'd like my boys to get to know their uncle."

Jack smiled and took a long swallow of his beer. In that moment, Jack felt at home for the first time in a long time. He sensed a calmer time, a normal time. He hadn't felt normal or calm in a while. Sean noticed his brother's expression, it brought him back to the days before it all went bad.

"Jack," said Sean. "Why didn't you ever say something, you know, when you saw me in Philly?"

"I don't know," said Jack in an offhanded way. He hesitated, looking for the words. "Maybe because," he paused, "I think maybe, I didn't want you to see me. It's not that I didn't want to come up to you." Jack moved his hand slowly over the table. "I did, I wanted to come up to you and say, 'remember me?' And then I would put out my hand and smile. You'd look surprised, almost startled, but being a big-shot attorney, you would recover, and then you would say, 'Jack, Jesus, you look good.' But you wouldn't mean it, not for a fucking second. And then I would see it, that expression, the one I get all the time, disappointment. But then you would smile, and shake my hand, and tell me how good it was to see me, but I wouldn't believe it for a second, because I knew that the last person you wanted to see was me." Jack's voice seemed to grow louder as he said, "And you and I both know what you'd be thinking, 'This couldn't be good, he probably needs some cash, or a place to stay.'"

Sean shook his head as if arguing a case. But he knew that his brother was right, so he just said, "Let's eat dinner, go home, get a good night's sleep. We'll work on us later, okay?"

Jack looked deep into his brother's eyes; he could see the tears. Jack smiled and simply said, "Okay."

The next morning the two brothers headed up toward Williamsport. There was a slight chill in the air. Driving north, the Susquehanna was on the passenger side. Sometimes the road was so close to the water, you could almost reach out and feel the spray as the rapids smashed up against the rocks and the fallen trees that littered the banks. An occasional supermarket cart and a few tires lay in the river, but all in all, the river was looking pristine; how she must have looked a thousand years ago. One moment the thick fog would seem to swallow her whole, and in the next instant, there she was again, calm and serene, gently rolling through the countryside, like she didn't have a care in the world.

Nothing had changed over the last thirty years; maybe nothing has changed over the last million years. Jack turned on the radio and looked out the window. The traffic was light, and Johnny Cash was singing, "I hear the train a comin'." Jack smiled, turned to Sean; Sean smiled back. "Missed you, bro." Jack turned to the window.

"Yeah, me too."

Jack thought of his father, more than thirty years ago, heading north toward the same hospital. Maybe he had an idea of what was coming, maybe he didn't have clue.

Sean and Jack walked through the door that led to the information desk in the front lobby of the veterans hospital.

"Boy, I hated working here. I have done some pretty shitty jobs, but this is right up there with the worst. I wonder if anyone remembers me."

The girl at the information desk was new; at least Jack didn't recognize her. "Good morning to you both," she said, "What can we do for you this morning?"

"We're here to see an old friend of our dad's, Tony Ramo." Her smile seemed to glow for a moment, and she said, "What a character, that Tony Ramo. One moment he's a kid from Brooklyn and the next moment he's lost in his own personal hell. But when he is back home, he can bring a smile to your face. He's quite ill, you know."

"We heard that he was pretty sick."

"He loves company. I'm sure he will be happy to see you two good-looking guys. You say he was friends with your father."

"Yes, ma'am. Dad died in Vietnam, and we thought maybe it would be nice to visit one of his old friends."

"Sounds so nice. He is probably in the dayroom, take the elevator on the left," she said and pointed. "It's not quite visiting time yet, but I guess we can bend the rules a little. If he's not there, you'll find him in the solarium on the top floor. Tony seems to find some peace up there."

"Jesus," said Sean, as he and Jack walked into the solarium after not finding Tony in the dayroom. "Now I know why it's called a solarium," and they both shielded their eyes from the bright morning sunshine that flooded the large room.

Jack pointed. "Over there."

Tony was alone. He was next to a table with his feet on a chair and smoking a cigarette, with his back to the boys staring into the sun. Jack and Sean shielded their eyes from the bright glare and walked over.

"Mr. Ramo?"

Tony looked up, slowly took off his sunglasses, and asked, "I know you guys?" The voice was tired but the Brooklyn accent was strong and vivid.

"Sure. You don't remember me, Mr. Ramo, but I used to work here a while back. We were good friends, you used to tell me about your days back in 'Nam," said Jack. "You knew my dad, Jerry McGinnis."

"Oh yeah," said Tony, but he didn't seem to follow. "Well, why don't you boys pull up a chair and relax, and remind me. Don't seem to be able to keep track of nothing these days. There's some coffee in that pot over there. Tastes like shit, but tell you the truth, I can't taste much of anything anymore. Maybe that's why the food is getting better. I used to beg for some pasta and some real sauce, but now, who gives a shit."

Sean and Jack smiled and walked over to the table and poured two cups of coffee.

"He doesn't remember you," said Sean. Jack just nodded and turned back to where Tony was sitting. They pulled up chairs and sat down next to Tony.

"We've seen some pictures of you back in Vietnam with our dad, maybe you remember." Sean handed him a photo that they had found among the letters Jerry had sent home. On the back it said, "me and Tony."

He took the picture and stared at it awhile. "Oh yeah," said Tony. "That was a long time ago, lot of water under that fucking bridge. Who did you say you were? Did Murphy send you? Do what you have to do; I don't give a fuck anymore, haven't been able to take a shit in two weeks, so get it over with, sooner the better. You can tell that motherfucking boss of yours that Tony Ramo ain't no rat."

"No, Tony, nobody sent us. Do you remember Jerry McGinnis?"

Tony looked up. His tired and worn face seemed to take on a glow of defiance, his eyes seemed to brighten, his shoulders moved up and back, and his chest broadened. "Yeah, actually, there isn't a goddamn day that goes by that I don't think about Jerry." Tony put his folded sunglasses into his shirt pocket. "What's it to you?"

For a moment the two boys said nothing, and then Sean looked at Tony and said in a slow, loud voice, "We're his sons. I'm Sean McGinnis and this is my brother, Jack. We've come here to see you and to find out what happened to our dad."

The years hadn't been kind to Tony. His eyes were sunk deep into his face, and his skin had a yellowish tinge. His face was wrinkled and looked tired and weathered. His hands trembled as he reached for the cigarette in the ashtray. He put his sunglasses back on and slowly got up from his chair; he walked over to the edge of the building and looked over the rail toward the river in the distance. The brothers sat waiting for the answers they had dreamt of hearing for so many years. Then Tony turned and walked back and sat down and said, "How'd you find me? How did you even know about me?"

Sean pointed to the picture on the table of the two men back in Vietnam that his father had sent home for safekeeping so many years ago. Two happy young guys with so much future ahead.

Jack took hold of the book of matches that lay on the table and lit a match and put it under the cigarette that Tony held in his month. The old man took a long drag on the cigarette and looked up and said, "So you're Jerry's boys. Did you tell me how you found out about me? It's funny, sometimes I can remember thirty years ago like it was yesterday, and sometimes I can't remember what I had for breakfast this morning."

"Letters," said Jack. "We found the letters."

"What letters, what are you talking about?"

"Our dad sent home letters. We found them a few days ago and we've been reading them. He talked a lot about you, you guys were good friends. And when the letters stopped we figured that maybe you could finish the story. We've got lots of questions. Do you know what happened to our mother? There was never any word from my father after she died. No one knew anything. We'd really like to know what happened to our dad."

Tony moved restlessly in the chair and said, as he stared with a determined face at the two young men, "Sometimes it's better to let things go. That was a long time ago. Anyway, your dad was killed in action. Didn't the Army tell you that? There were no letters left, they got them."

The boys looked hard at the face of the old man. Living his life to excess had taken a toll on Tony. Jack stood up over Tony and said, "I spent the last thirty fucking years letting things go. I'm real tired of everybody telling me to get on with my life and let the past die." Jack stopped for a second, and then continued, "And what do you mean, '*they* got them?'"

Tony looked confused and rattled and said nothing for a moment; Jack sat down again and moved the chair close. He reached out his hand and placed it on Tony's frail arm and said again in a strong voice, "What do you mean, they got them? Who?"

"Please, Mr. Ramo," said Sean. "Don't you think it is time to tell the truth? Don't you think we deserve to know? Nothing is going to happen to you. Get it off your chest; just tell us."

Tony said nothing, just stared into space, and finally he said, "Look, boys, I'm getting tired. Maybe you can come back tomorrow and we can talk. It's good seeing you both. Sure Jerry would have been proud, looks like you both turned out to be swell kids."

"Cut the shit," said Jack as he stood up again. "I told you, we've been waiting for more than thirty fucking years to find out what the fuck happened to us." Sean reached out to his brother to calm him down and Jack flung his arm away from Sean.

"Are you kidding me? You threatening me? I would give my left nut, right fucking now, for you to blow my brains out." Tony picked up the cigarette and took a long drag. "Sit down, kid. I'll tell you what I know. Just relax, okay? I'm getting too old, besides you don't want me having a goddamn heart attack and dropping dead before I tell you what you came here for."

Jack sat down and said, "Okay, but before anything else, what did you mean when you said 'they got the letters'? Take your time."

"Fine," began Tony. "You're right, you need to know. Your father was one slick son of a bitch. I mean, he was smooth, he had me fooled, played me like a twenty-dollar hooker, and I'm a street guy from Brooklyn. Anyway, I come to find out, after he makes me look like a fucking idiot, that the whole reason that he comes over to the country was to find the guys who killed his friend and then he planned to write a story so he could get a big job on some national newspaper. You ask me, I think your dad, no disrespect of course, was one stupid bastard. So at the beginning he tells me he's down on his luck and his wife is going to leave him and take the kids and the only way that maybe he can save his marriage is if he can get his hands on some serious money and get back home and everything will be just peachy creamy, know what I mean."

Tony took a drag on his cigarette and continued, "But all the while, your dad is looking for a way to get in with the Unit, because he knew Chuck had been in the Unit."

"What the fuck does all this have to do with the letters?" said Jack in an anxious voice.

"Relax, sweetheart, I'm getting there. This ain't no ten-minute story, this is some complicated shit. It seems that your old man decided that it would be a good idea to send home the story and all the goddamn details. So he was playing both sides, you get it? He became a member of the Unit, all the while sending information about their activities back to his wife so he can write his story and become a hero and solve the murder of his friend. At some point things changed, everything got turned around for old Jerry."

"So what changed?"

"Look, a lot of guys go over there for a lot of reasons. I must admit that your father's reason was, without a doubt, the must fucked-up reason I'd ever heard." Tony continued, "Sure, Jerry probably figured that he had some noble reasons for leaving his wife, your mom, and going to the only place that had the answers. But that was all bullshit. He just wanted to get out of town, and Chucky boy was as good an excuse as he needed. Anyway, like I said, he turned."

"Turned how? What do you mean?"

"He met this girl. Stupid fuck went ahead and fell in love with the bitch. I mean, we had about a hundred babes better looking that would suck your dick for five dollars, and your old man falls in love with some gook bitch. No disrespect, of course, but he was nuts. I mean certifiable. Anyway, between the money, and I mean real serious money, and the girl, I guess he figures that life could be pretty sweet, so he turns."

"You telling us," said Jack, "that our father went over there trying to save the fucking world and after six months turns into one of you guys, a bunch of drug-dealing, pimping, murdering thugs?"

"Well, I wouldn't put it quite that way, but yeah, pretty much, that's exactly what he became. Sorry to burst your bubble, but your old man was one of the top guys in Delta Unit. What can I tell you boys, war and money can do some weird things to a guy's mind."

Sean stood up and walked to the window, stared outside. Everything he had believed, everything he had trusted, was tumbling down, and he turned back toward Tony and said, "Tony, what's this got to do with the letters? With what happened to our mom?"

"Well, to tell you the truth, I'm a little confused, there were not supposed to be any letters left. The joke's on me, or maybe him. The letters and papers that your old man sent over to your mom was his problem. If anyone found out about the letters, your dad was going to be fucking worm food. I would be lying right next to him. So, he told John about the letters he sent home to his wife. Someone had got to go to his house and find those papers and destroy them. Go over there when nobody's home and get the papers, make it look like a couple of drug addicts robbing the house looking for money and stuff."

Tony stopped, then continued, "Well, I guess things got a little out of hand. Turns out that your mom was home after all that day.

Look, boys, I'm sure nothing was supposed to happen to your mom."
Tony reached up and stroked his chin over and over again.

"Look," he said, "your dad fucked up. These guys, they weren't
right in the head, they became fucking animals. It must have been
like they were on autopilot or something. I guess, maybe she gave
them a little attitude, well, you know what happened. Needless to
say, Jerry heard what had happened and went fucking nuts."

Tony shook his head slowly and said, "After that, your father
changed. He got real mean, real nasty. You definitely did not want
to fuck with your dad, he became one diabolical motherfucker. I
used to like your old man, but in the end, he made me look like a
fucking choirboy, and trust me, I ain't no choirboy." He turned away,
shaking his head.

"That's it?" said Jack, staring at Tony. "You're telling us that our
father sent two animals over to our house to get the papers, and while
they were there, those guys decided to just go ahead and rape and kill
his wife? OUR MOTHER. That's what you're telling us?"

"Look, boys, I didn't make this shit up. You asked me what I
know, and I told you. Tell you the truth, I wasn't over there much
longer, so I sort of lost track."

"You got sent home?" asked Sean.

"Yeah, my tour was over, I got the hell out of there. But how
did you know about me?" asked Tony. "Didn't those assholes get
everything that was in the house?"

"They didn't get the ones that our dad sent to his parents. He
made a copy of everything he sent home," Sean answered.

"That doesn't make any fucking sense," said Tony. "Why would
he do that?"

"Who gives a fuck," said Jack, getting more and more irritated. "Maybe he figured he might need a little insurance. All I want to know is what the fuck happened to our old man."

"Look," said Tony. "All I can tell you is that I got sent home, got married, had two good kids, and for about two years, I kept working for the Unit. It was a pretty sweet gig. Didn't last too long, but I made a shitload of money. Me and my wife opened up a little Italian restaurant in Little Italy, did good, made a nice living, and then packed our bags and moved out here. My wife died a few years ago. Cancer. Then I got sick, guess it all caught up to me, and here I am."

Sean had been sitting quietly, listing intently, and then said, "That's a real nice story, Tony. Do you or don't you know what the fuck happened to our dad?"

"I sort of lost track of your father. I never really found out what happened. Sometimes you're better off not knowing. All I know for sure is that your dad disappeared. I just assumed that Murphy had him shot, one in the chest, two in the head, make sure he's dead. From what I heard, John Murphy had your mother raped and murdered and then killed your father and made it look like he had been killed by enemy fire."

"How do we find this guy?" asked Jack.

"For all I know, he's dead and buried."

"So you have no idea. Did he ever say anything about what he would do after the war?"

Tony looked up and said, "John was a Navy SEAL, scuba instructor, Master Diver, tough as nails, he was unbelievable. He always talked about some island in the Caribbean, going there when he retired. I don't remember the name, but I remember that it was a strange island, shaped like a fucking snow cone. He used to tell me it was an ancient volcano."

Jack looked over at Sean and then turned toward Tony. "Can you think of anything else? That's not much to go on."

Tony smiled. "King Kong, something to do with King Kong. I swear to God, that's all I can think of."

"King Kong, are you shitting me?" said Jack. "What the fuck does that have to do with some island?"

"Don't know," said Tony in a tired voice. "That's all I remember, I swear. Look, I'm real tired and I ain't feeling so good. Your dad didn't mean for any of the bad shit to happen, I mean, your mom getting raped and killed, but shit happens. I don't know if he ever knew that it was Murphy that gave the orders. Maybe he felt so guilty, thought it was all his fault. HHe couldn't face you; maybe he figured you two would be better off with your grandparents." Tony stood slowly, using his right hand to balance and push himself up. "Let me give you some fatherly advice, seeing that I'm old enough to be your father. Forget this. Forget the whole goddamn thing. Things were crazy over there. I mean, you go over there a decent kind of guy and before you know it, you turn into a fucking animal. People say there are some lines that nobody crosses, but over there, there were no fucking lines." Tony turned and stared at the two boys. "There are no more answers out there, so let it go. Just forget about the whole thing. Your old man went over there to do good, I swear to god, I swear on everything that I loved. Maybe some of what happened was my fault. I'm sorry, I'm asking you both for your forgiveness. Before I die, and I'm pretty sure it won't be long, but before I die, it would mean a lot to me if you two boys could find it in your heart to forgive me."

"Yeah, well, what are we supposed to forgive you for?" asked Jack.

"I might have had a little something to do with your dad getting involved with John and the Unit. I swear, I never thought it would turn out this way, not in a million fucking years could I ever imagine that Jerry would turn out the way he did."

Jack watched Tony walk out of the door and he sat down next to Sean.

"You don't look good," said Sean.

Jack turned to Sean, reached over, and held Sean's wrist tightly. "It's getting worse every goddamn day. I can't keep anything down, I'm still losing weight, and tired as a motherfucker. Am I the most unluckiest son of a bitch that ever walked the earth? So look, I figure I'm dead soon anyway, so you help me find out where this guy John Murphy is, and I'll take it from there."

"Let's get the hell out of here," said Sean. He stood and turned toward the door. "Come on, let's get something to eat, I'm starving. We've got to find something you can eat."

The two brothers walked out the front door of the hospital and said nothing until they sat down at the corner table in a luncheonette on the outskirts of Williamsport. "This was the place that Grandma and Grandpa would take me after we came up to see you every week," Sean remembered. "Do you remember, Jack? We would come up and see you almost every Sunday, right after church. We'd get in the old Chevy wagon, the one with the wood panels. It was so cool, like The Beach boys 'I got a '34 wagon and I call it a Woody, Surf City here we come, You know it's not very cherry, it's an oldie but a goodie.'"

Jack laughed. It had been a while since Sean had heard him laugh. Sean smiled at his brother and then said seriously, "It wasn't supposed to happen this way, but I know that you got fucked, big time. I don't know any other way to say it."

"It's not your fault," said Jack. "I'm tired, let's go home."

They started down Route 7 back toward Selinsgrove, Sean staring straight ahead as he drove. There was a light rain; the road was a little slick, and he occasionally glanced at the river. Jack was asleep, his head slumped over on the window. Sean tried to keep his eyes on the road, but kept glancing over at his brother.

Sean could feel the tears rolling down his cheek. His brother had lost everything, but he had not. It wasn't fair. But he vowed he wasn't going to abandon Jack now. Never again.

Jack stirred as they pulled into the driveway. "You have a nice little nap?" Sean asked, as Jack turned toward him.

"I remember that's what you used to say, when I was real young. I remember going to our room for a nap and you would always wake me up and say, 'Did you have a nice nap?' and then you would say, 'Rise and shine, sleeping beauty.' Remember, Sean?"

"Yeah, I remember," said Sean. "I remember. It's what Dad would say to us both."

The next morning Jack slept late, and when he did finally come downstairs Sean was on the phone. He saw Jack and finished up his conversation and hung up.

"I was just talking to my boss, telling him I need a little longer down here. I talked to my wife too, I told her what's going on. I told her you were sick. I think it's time we got you to a new doctor, get a second opinion, see what the hell we are dealing with."

"Forget it, Sean, I know what the hell is wrong with me, so leave it alone, okay? I know what you think of me, I'm a fucking worthless loser. Well, maybe you're right."

Sean broke in and said insistently, "I never said that! I never thought it for a goddamn second! I'll tell you what I do think, I think you got fucked, big-time fucked. I would try to make it up to you if I could, but first we have to get you better."

"I don't need you to do a goddamn thing for me except help to finish this, just get me to the end zone. I know that you got a family, and you can get back to them soon."

"Come on," said Sean. "That's not fair."

"It's plenty fucking fair, but if you don't mind we can fight that battle some other time. Right now I just want to find that fucking island. That's where the story ends. I want to know that we did everything we could do to find out what happened to our mother. She didn't deserve what happened to her. I saw every fucking second. I was there, you weren't. I saw the whole thing from beginning to end, and you want to know what haunts me every goddamn day of my life?"

Sean had stopped trying to get a word in. He just listened and then said, "What?"

"Her eyes, she spoke to me with her eyes. She told me to be brave, that she loved me, and that she always would. I tried to block out everything from that day, but I could never block out her eyes, and the tears, and then there was nothing there. Her eyes were wide open but she was gone. I was left alone, all alone then and for the next thirty years. Now together, we have a chance, small as it might be, to get to the truth. You say it's revenge, fine, call it what you like. I'm going to find that island if I have to go to the ends of the earth."

"I don't think we have to go that far," said Sean in a lighter tone. He smiled and said to his brother, "We'll find the island and try to get to the bottom of this fucking nightmare, and then as sure as hell, you're going to come home with me. If you go down the way you are saying, then I can tell you right fucking now, I'll be with you until the end."

Jack looked at Sean and they smiled at each other.

"Listen, there's this guy I know who works at the paper. He is like a research brain trust. I mean, if you're doing a story and you need some background information, you go to Brian Cox and you say, 'Hey, Brian, I need some data on the size of the average dick in fucking Tanzania,' and in ten goddamn minutes, he's got it down to the centimeter. I'll ask him what island has something to do with King Kong. After that, we'll just figure it out as we go."

CHAPTER 27

"Hi, Millie, it's Sean." The receptionist at the office had a pleasant, calming voice. She'd been there forever, long before Sean signed up to join the District Attorney's Office in Philadelphia.

"Who do you need, Sean?" He knew that at 9 a.m., there was just so much time for friendly chitchat.

"Brian."

"Okay, Sean. You take care."

Brian Cox was a walking encyclopedia, a trivia master with tournament-level credentials. "Hey, Brian, it's Sean," he said. "Hey, I need to ask you something. It's going to sound a little weird, but it's important."

"What is it, Sean? Stop being so fucking dramatic. If I don't know it, I'll find it."

"Okay," said Sean. "There's an island in the Caribbean that had something to do with King Kong."

"Saba!" said Brian almost before Sean could get out the last word.

"You sure, Brian? This is really important. Saba. Where is it?"

"You kidding me, that was your tough one? I knew that when I was four fucking years old. It's about thirty miles southwest of St.

Martin. It's a remote bullshit little island. It's shaped like a fucking snow cone, and there's only one road, one town, and a dive shop, with the best diving in the Caribbean: big fish, big coral, big currents. You want to know what that island has to do with King Kong?" You could hear the smile in his voice. Brian Cox was in his wheelhouse. He loved these moments. Showing off his skills. "The movie, you know, with Fay Wray, Bruce Cabot, 1933. You remember the scene where the boat is coming up on the island? The fog lifts, an island appears, but it's cut in half, the top shrouded in a heavy mysterious mist, almost unnatural. That's Saba, an ancient pinnacle from a more ancient volcano. That's it, Saba."

"Wow," said Sean, a little taken aback from the instant response. "You really do know everything. You know how to get there?"

"What am I, a fucking travel agent?" said Brian, in a tone that was not quite kidding around.

"No, Brian, but you are one knowledgeable motherfucker. Thanks, man."

"Hold on, sweetheart," said Brian in a casual yet serious tone. "I need a little favor."

"Sure, Brian, what's going on?"

"Well, I got a speeding ticket in a school zone. Can you take care of it for me?"

Sean hesitated, his initial response to these types of requests was no, but this was different. He owed Brian. "Sure, Brian, send it to me. I'll see what I can do."

"Thanks, Sean. I knew I could count on you."

Sean hung up the phone and walked outside where Jack was seated at the old iron table. He sat down and looked at Jack and said, "Saba. It's an island about thirty miles southwest of St. Martin, maybe not too far from Puerto Rico. It's the island King Kong came from in the movie. I don't know if that's what we are looking for, but it is worth a try."

Jack was nodding his head. "Hell yeah, it is worth a try. I could use a little vacation." He smiled. "I've got a good feeling about this. We are on the right track, I can feel it."

"Okay, but don't get ahead of yourself," Sean said as he took a sip of his coffee. "Tony, who I should point out is probably out of his fucking mind, tells us that our dad is really the bad guy, and maybe the one who had something to do with what happened to Mom. And maybe if we go to some island, and find this guy, Big John, assuming that the bastard is still alive, then maybe we find out why it happened and what happened to Dad. But maybe we don't and we've gone there for nothing."

"I have a good feeling, really, Sean. It's all coming together."

"What the hell," said Sean. "I'll probably lose my job and get disbarred over this if it goes badly. We don't know what this guy is going to be like. I know that my wife is going to kill me. But, like I said, we've gone this far, let's finish it if we can."

Sean put down his coffee and looked down at the river. It was the time of the year that the Susquehanna was at its lowest point, and she moved slowly and lazily through the Pennsylvania countryside. He thought about his father and his grandfather sitting on the bank of the river, always their favorite spot.

"Sometimes we would sit on the river bank, you were really young. Do you remember? We would go down there and sit and just talk." Sean glanced over at Jack, smiled. "You remember?"

"Yeah, I think so." Jack took a deep breath.

Sean stared into his brother's eyes and said, "I used to think the spot where we used to go and sit was a special place. I mean, sort of magical, like if you really want a prayer to work, you would go to church in the morning and then to the river in the afternoon. Or maybe if you had to make an important decision, a decision that could change your life, the river would help you decide."

"Look, Sean, if you are having second thoughts, I get it. You don't have to go, I can take it from here. You just get me on the plane. I've never been out of Pennsylvania, I've never even been on a plane. I'll go down there and find out the whole story, and then I'll come back and fill you in. This way you can get back to your life. And since I don't have one, it won't matter how long it takes. It may take a while. I doubt I'll find John Murphy in a phone book, assuming they got phone books. Bastard probably changed his name. It could take weeks, maybe months. I've got nothing to lose, you've got everything to lose. Nine chances out of ten anyway, Murphy is dead, and that ends everything. This could be just a stupid fucking waste of time."

"I appreciate what you're saying, Jack, I swear to Christ I do, but I'm tired of feeling the way I've been feeling for a long time. Probably nothing down there but a whole lot of bullshit stories, but maybe there's more. Worse case, we end up on this island in the middle of the goddamn ocean, take a vacation, hang out on the beach, maybe read a good book."

"I don't think I've ever read a book. Jesus Christ, I've got no life. Never been out of Pennsylvania and never read a book, no wife, no kids, no job, no life," Jack continued. "I think that maybe this is all I've got."

"You have a brother, you have a family, Jack. We'll get this done and then you'll come home with me. We'll get you to a doctor, and we'll figure it out. Let's just go to Saba, and we'll take it from there, okay?"

"Yeah, okay," said Jack. "Now, how the hell do you get down there?"

"I have a friend in Philly who's a travel agent, I'll call her."

Jack said firmly, "I need to ask you one more time. Are you doing this because you feel some guilt? If you are, forget it. Maybe you need to be forgiven and maybe you don't, but it doesn't matter."

Sean nodded his head slowly, "I'm doing it for us, Jack. For you and me. For our family. I'm going to call Deb and my family and let them know what we're doing. Then, tomorrow morning, we can make the travel arrangements."

The next morning, as promised, Sean called the travel agent next. "Rita, it's Sean McGinnis, it's been a while. How are you?"

"Sean McGinnis, how have you been?"

"Good. Hey, Rita, have you ever heard of an island in the Caribbean called Saba?"

"I think so. It's not a real touristy kind of island. I mean, there are no four- or five-star hotels or resorts, hardly even has a beach. Why?"

"My brother and I need to get there. Don't ask me why, it's a long story, and I'll tell you some other time."

"Okay, sure," said Rita. "I'll find out what I can. I'll get back to you this afternoon. Where do you want to fly out of? Philly or Harrisburg? You'll have to connect, probably though Miami."

"Not sure. Can you find out if my brother needs a passport? He doesn't have one, and maybe a driver's license will be enough."

"No problem. What's your number there?"

Sean hung up with Rita when they were done and finished making breakfast. Jack walked in and sat down.

"Did you call the travel agent?" he asked.

"Yeah. How'd you sleep?"

"Fair, between the sweating and the nosebleeds. Anyway, did you speak to her?"

"Yeah," said Sean. "I'll talk to her again this afternoon. I made you some eggs. Eat something, and then we'll go into town, get some clothes and stuff. We can't go there looking like this, we've got to look the part."

After lunch Jack went to lie down and Sean heard back from his travel agent.

"Hi, Sean. It's Rita. Saba sure is a weird little Island. I read up on it and asked a friend who runs a dive shop in Philadelphia. You want to hear about it, or just flight information?"

"Tell me as much as you know, I want to hear more."

"Okay," said Rita. "It's about twenty-seven miles southwest of St. Martin, in the Caribbean. Supposed to be beautiful, there's a mountain with a rainforest and magnificent blue water with great diving. Take pictures and let me see them when you get home. The tourists that visit the island come there for only two reasons: hiking through the rainforest and scuba diving. Apparently, Saba is one of the best-known diving destinations in the world. It has about 1,000 full-time residents and there's also a medical school there, with about 800 students."

"How do we get there?" said Sean.

"You can fly out of Philadelphia into Miami with a connection to St. Martin and then you take a ferry to Saba. There's an 8:37 out of Philly, arrives in Miami around 12:30 and then 2:47 to St. Martin. I need your return date."

"I'm not sure," Sean said in a hesitant tone. "Could be a few days, could be a week. Can we make those arrangements when we have a better idea? How many days does it take to get a dive certification? I think we want to do that too."

"Sean," said Rita, "what's really going on here? Sounds like you got yourself a little affair going and you want to get away to some exotic island and get laid."

Sean laughed at the thought of it. "No, nothing like that, I swear! No, just me and my brother trying to reconnect after about thirty years, and between you and me, he's pretty sick, so we just want to spend some time getting to know each other."

"Okay," said Rita. "I understand, sorry to sound like a jerk. We'll hold off on the return flights until I hear from you. My buddy recommended a place to stay called the Cottage Club, it's real low key. Everything on that Island is low key. I'll set up your flights and reservations at the Cottage Club. If you have to stay overnight in St. Martin, just get a cheap hotel at the airport," continued Rita. "You two should be all set, and don't forget your driver's license, they don't require a passport. Just go to the American Airlines ticket counter and they'll have your reservations."

"Thanks, I appreciate your help. I really do."

"Yeah," said Rita, "as soon as you get off the boat, just look right across the dock and you'll see a shop called Coral Reef Dive Center. Bob knows them, it's a good outfit. They'll have all the equipment you need. Have a good time. And hey, Sean," continued Rita, "be careful, I'm told that the diving down there is pretty rough."

"When are we leaving?" asked Jack.

"We have an 8:37 a.m. flight on Monday morning, so we've got all day today to get whatever we need. This weekend we'll head down to Philadelphia, get a room near the airport. We need to meet with that lawyer in Philly before we go."

"Okay, I'll follow your lead. It'll be nice to depend on someone besides myself. I'm tired of always watching over my shoulder; it'll feel good knowing that you'll be looking out for me!"

"You can lean on me," said Sean.

"Wasn't that a song?" asked Jack, with a wistful expression.

Jack and Sean were getting ready to leave for Philadelphia on Saturday morning.

"Hey," said Sean. "I thought Joe Smith was coming back. Where did you say he went? We should at least thank him for letting us hang out here for the last few days."

Jack threw his bag into the trunk. "Don't know," he said, "and who gives a shit? Let's get going. Should be a nice drive, just following the river."

"We're meeting the lawyer at the Liberty Bell Diner, you know it?"

"Yeah, I go there all the time, what time?"

"Ten," answered Sean.

"Why aren't we going to his office?" said Jack.

Sean shrugged and just said, "I don't know, he wanted to meet at the diner."

The Liberty Bell Diner on Frankford Avenue was as busy as always on a weekend morning. Sean looked around. He could spot a highbrow lawyer at five hundred feet, but he didn't see Bradley yet. The lawyer had suggested that they meet outside the office, and Liberty Bell was as good as anywhere. And besides the Jamboree, pancakes, eggs, and bacon was as good as any breakfast in Center City. Jack and Sean sat down at a booth with a window that overlooked the parking lot. Sean scanned the lot.

"Excuse me," said a friendly voice, "are you Jack and Sean?" Sean thought that he looked out of place with a jacket and tie. Sean and Jack nodded their heads. John Bradley placed the box on the table and said, "I just need to see some ID." They each handed their driver's licenses to Bradley. The lawyer looked up at both boys, looked back at the licenses, and then smiled. "We've been sitting on this for a long time."

Sean motioned for Bradley to sit down.

"I only have a few minutes. My grandson is waiting in the car. Look," he continued, "a long time ago this firm had arrangements with a client with whom we have since parted ways. But we were obligated to hold onto this one piece of property with simple instructions: hand over this box if you are ever contacted by either Jack or Sean McGinnis of Selinsgrove, Pennsylvania. So that's exactly what I'm doing, and now, I'm happy to say that I'm done with this. I've seen you in court, seen you in the papers. I never made the connection." Bradley put out his hand and said, "I don't know what this is all about, but it must be pretty important. I wish you both well." He turned and walked out of the diner.

The small box was closed with tattered tape that barely held the flaps down. Sean carefully pulled the tape off and opened it. Inside there was one large envelope.

Sean picked up a knife and sliced open the white envelope. He unfolded the letter inside and laid it on the table. It began, "Dear Dad."

Sean looked up and said, "It's to Grandpa." Sean got up slowly and slid into the banquette next to Jack and placed the one-page letter on the table for both to read together.

"I don't get it," said Jack. "If Dad sent this letter to Grandpa, then why is it here?"

Sean turned toward Jack and said, "I don't have a fucking clue. Let's just read it."

Dear Dad,

I hope you and mom are okay. I know you guys are pretty mad at me. I really screwed up, Dad. I was caught up in this crazy idea that I could be somebody more than just a small-time reporter of a little paper in Selinsgrove. I came over here to find out what happened to Brian and Chuck and maybe if I did, I could bring the bastards who killed them to justice. Well, turns out that I pretty much did figure it all out, but instead of turning them in, it looks like I've become one of them. I'm sorry, Dad, I know you'll never be able to forgive me. I don't think I'll ever forgive myself. But this is important: the papers I sent to you and Mom could get us all in big trouble. You have to make sure that they are all destroyed. I've made plans to take care of the copies that I sent to Kate, so you don't have to worry about them. I had to 'fess up to these guys over here, but it's okay, Dad, we figured out how to fix everything. I feel terrible about leaving Kate and the boys.

I'm sending this letter through the lawyers that we use. I'll explain everything later. Look, Dad, I'm gonna be out of touch for a while. But I'll try and keep in touch when I can. I'm so sorry, Dad. Please hug Mom. Please forgive me.

Love, Jerry

The last letter from their dead father lay before them. Jack and Sean read at their own pace, silently lost in their own private thoughts. The faded words had blended into the yellowish lined paper. Sean leaned back, absorbing the words, willing the obvious away, not wanting to hear his father's words from more than thirty years ago. It was him, it was him.

Jack turned to his brother, he squinted, the tears welling up, hearing the words that he had forced himself to avoid. Sean pulled himself from his brother's side, standing and moving to the opposite side of the booth.

Sean saw this message to his grandfather as an admission of guilt. Jack carefully ran his fingers over the frail notebook paper. Sensing a bond with his father, it was a sort of confessional from the grave. The proof of his father's betrayal turned his stomach, and he could feel his hands trembling. Still lost in the nightmare that had consumed his every waking moment. Never finding the diversions that his brother had employed to exist in a life filled and burdened with unanswered questions.

Sean reached across the table and put his hand gently on his brother's wrist and said, "Now we know. I didn't understand why all the papers hadn't been burned, but now I get it. Grandpa never saw this letter; he never knew to destroy the papers. Thank God this letter never got to him, it would have broken his heart. He died thinking that our dad was a good and decent man. Thank god he never knew the truth."

Sean asked the waitress for the check, then said to Jack, "Let's go, Jack. We've got a big day tomorrow. Let's go back to the hotel, they have a nice pool." Sean smiled at Jack and said, "You can try on that bathing suit."

Jack looked up at his brother and said, "I can't remember the last time I had a bathing suit on. I can't remember the last time I just felt normal."

"Come on, Jack." Sean put his arm over his brother's frail shoulders as they both walked out the door of the Liberty Bell Diner.

"The nightmares are back," said Jack as they drove to the hotel. "I thought that they were gone forever, but her face, I swear to Christ,

Mom's eyes, they were beautiful. Sean, that's all I can remember, her eyes, staring at me. He had one hand over her mouth and the other around her neck, but her eyes spoke to me. I know that sounds crazy, but I swear she told me it would be all right. I think she told me that she loved me, or at least that's what I'd like to think."

Neither brother said a word for quite a while; then Sean said, "Eyes say a lot, I heard someone say that your eyes are the windows to your soul. If that's what you think Mom was saying, then I'd bet anything, that's exactly what she was trying to say."

On Monday morning, Jack and Sean left Philadelphia. They connected easily to their flight down to St. Martin and took a taxi to the docks where the ferry to Saba and the other outer islands docked. The cab driver was a friendly native and gave the boys a bit of a tour of his island.

"What you boys going over to Saba for?" he asked in a deep and rich accent. "We got everything you boys could ever want here, you know, man. You just let Bobby know what you be liking, and just like magic, you got it."

"That's real nice, Bobby, but me and my brother are going over to Saba to go diving. We heard that Saba is the place to go for some really great diving."

"Well, got to admit it, the diving over at that little island is the best, but that's all it's got: diving, the med school, and the rainforest. Got some family over there, a cousin owns a little café right next to the dock, sits right on top of a dive shop, called Coral Reef Dive Center."

"That's where we're going, the Coral Reef Dive Center. We heard that there is a dive instructor there who's been around for a long time, named John Murphy. Have you heard the name?"

"Well, I'll tell you, the two boys that run the shop under the café is named Big John and Little John. Little John is a Jewish boy from the States, but Big John, I don't know anything about him. One day he showed up and been there for, well, got to be more than ten years. Anyway, when you get off the dock, head up toward the road and you bump right into their shop. Make sure you say hello to my cousin Alice when you get there, tell her that old Bobby boy said hello."

"Which road?" said Jack, turning away from the window.

The cab driver laughed and said, "Man, there is but one road on the whole island, going from the dock to the top. Not to worry, man, you won't miss it. Don't forget to tell John that I sent you."

"Sure," said Sean, "we'll make sure to mention it. Is there a place to get a bite to eat before we get on the ferry?"

"There's a little snack bar right next to the ticket window, food's okay, but you don't have too much time. Where you staying on the island?"

"Place called the Cottage Club," said Sean. "You know it?"

"Sure, it's next to the medical school. The view will take your breath away. Nice folks, natives, the family been on that island for three hundred years. When you dock, just go to the shop first, you'll have some paperwork to start, then just grab yourself a cab and head on up. They got a little pool and a grill; you can go shopping and get a couple of steaks and some potatoes, and have yourself a good old U.S. of A. barbecue."

Bobby pulled the cab up to a dock. "Okay, boys, this is it. Here's my card. When you planning on coming back?"

"A week from today," said Sean.

"Okay, call me when you get close, I'll come and get you. Don't worry about a thing, you boys have a friend on this island."

Sean and Jack got out of the cab, paid Bobby, said thanks, and headed for the window to pay for the tickets that had been reserved for them by Rita. They had about half an hour before the ferry left, so they went next door to the small snack shop and ordered two jerk chicken sandwiches and a couple of beers. There were benches along the dock, and the two brothers sat in the afternoon sun waiting for the ferry to take them to Saba.

"Sounds like we found what we were looking for," said Jack.

"Yeah, sounds like it, almost seems like we're being led right to the man himself."

"What do you mean?" said Jack.

"I mean…" Sean hesitated, then continued, "I don't know, maybe I'm just being a little paranoid. Forget about it. How's that jerk chicken, pretty fucking hot?"

"Yep," said Jack, "pretty fucking hot." They smiled at each other, finished their sandwiches, and followed them down with a long swallow of beer.

The sun was still high in the sky at five in the afternoon as the ferry began its twenty-seven-mile trip to Saba. It was a small ferry by Boston ferry standards, thought Sean, remembering the time he had taken the ferry from Woods Hole to Nantucket, a short day trip. This boat was sea worn, and the paint was peeling off the hull. There weren't many passengers. Sean noticed the various accents. There were a few North Americans and some people from England or Australia; it was hard for him to tell them apart.

One of the deckhands made an announcement that they would be arriving in about forty-five minutes, depending on the seas.

"When you disembark," the guy said over the loudspeaker, "go directly over to the customs officers that will be staffing the desks on the dock. You'll need to show your photo ID. Don't forget your personal property, and enjoy your stay on Saba. For all you divers, you'll need to stop off at the National Parks building, which is a shack at the end of the dock. The waters all around the island are National Parks, so you need to get a park pass before you can sign up at the dive centers."

The boat pulled out slowly past the buoys that marked the posted speed limit while they were still in the harbor. There seemed to be more cargo on the ship than people. The early morning trips were mostly local people coming or going from the small island; the afternoon trips were mostly for cargo. It was hauling tires, refrigerators, toilets, sinks, and lots of food: cans, fruits, and vegetables.

There was a cool breeze that seemed to skid off the water as the boat picked up speed and headed south. The sea was calm, and the two brothers leaned over the railing, looking at the coral reefs more than forty feet down in the crystal clear blue ocean. A school of dolphins came to the surface, following the boat as if it were a big play toy, but they soon disappeared under the surface.

"What are you thinking about?" asked Jack, as they both watched the water.

Sean hesitated for a moment, staring at the ocean, and said, "I was thinking of all the guys, I guess, just like me, no fucking clue, on a boat, like this one or not, but overlooking the same ocean, standing at the rail, sails, engines, whatever, looking down, wondering where they were going and what they would find at the end of their trip. I was thinking that some were looking for a way out, and that others were looking for a way in."

Jack turned toward Sean, "I don't know what we're going to find, maybe nothing, and maybe that's for the best. I've got a feeling that

I don't have a hell of a lot longer to live. I haven't felt good in a long time and I'm tired of feeling bad. Tell you the truth, Sean, I can't remember what feeling good feels like. But look, I admit that this is a crapshoot. Maybe he's on the island, maybe he's not. There's only one way to find out."

"Look," said Sean, "we can end this right here. Get to the island, turn around, and go home. Think about it: whatever this was, whatever brought us together, maybe that's enough. We found each other, and if that's all that it is, then that's not bad. Right?"

"It's not enough for me." Jack turned from his brother and stared out over the ocean.

Sean slowly put his arm around his brother as the two boys looked off into the distance, both dreaming of what could have been and thinking of what was waiting for them just over the horizon.

"I'm going inside," said Jack. "I've got to take a leak. Maybe I'll lie down on one of the benches for a little while, I'm feeling a little queasy."

"You okay?" said Sean.

"Yeah, yeah, I'm okay, maybe just tired. Haven't had a good night's sleep in months."

Sean turned and watched his brother walk into the cabin of the boat, then shifted his gaze back to the ocean. It wasn't so different from sitting on the banks of the Susquehanna, back in Selinsgrove, yet home seemed so far away. He stared into the water below; the strangest sensation seemed to be pulling him down, over the rail, into the inviting warm waters. He thought, *It's crazy, a week ago I was out in L.A., lying in bed with some girl I picked up at a bar, and here I am, on some fucking ferry to some godforsaken island in the middle of nowhere. Jesus, what the hell have I gotten myself into?*

The ferry slid through the water. The seas were calm and the winds were mild, the sun felt good on his face. Sean suddenly realized he was scared, more scared than he had ever been, even more scared than when his mother was killed and his father was lost.

"What are you thinking about?" said Jack. He touched Sean on the back as he came back to the rail. Sean turned; he hadn't heard his brother return. He was staring ahead into a deep dense fog that seemed to have just appeared. "What the hell is that?"

"Fogbank. Hope they have radar on this piece of shit boat." The ferry moved into the heavy fog, and there was a blast from the horn when everything went white. The brothers could barely see their hands in front of their faces. Sean and Jack could feel and hear the ferry slowing down to what felt like a crawl.

And then as quickly as it had come, it was gone, and the sun was blinding as it was drifting lower on the horizon and fading slowly as it passed behind the Island. A slight mist seemed to cover the smooth and tranquil water, like coming out of a shower with soap in your eyes.

As the ship drew closer to the island, the harbor and the dock came into sight. It was a small and narrow inlet that had been carved out of the side of a mountain. The two brothers said goodbye to St. Martin, and stood against the rail as the ferry pulled alongside the cement dock. A young boy caught the rope that was thrown to him by one of the hands on the ferry. Once the ship was secure, the gangplank was lowered and the passengers slowly stepped off and walked over to a desk that was set up at the bottom of the gangplank. The uniformed customs officers looked up at Sean and Jack as they came to the table.

"We were told that you didn't need passports."

The customs officer smiled. "That's right, but do you have some form of photo identification?"

"We have our driver's licenses," said Sean.

"No problem, where you staying?"

"Cottage Club."

The agent nodded, "You diving or hiking?"

"Diving," said Jack. "You know where the Coral Reef Dive Center is?"

"First you have to get a license to enter the underwater parks. The National Park office is over there." He pointed to the end of the dock, handed Jack and Sean back their driver's licenses, and said, "Have a nice stay."

Sean and Jack looked in the direction the officer pointed and saw a small shop that seemed to be cut out of the side of a mountain. In fact, it seemed to Sean that everything on the dock seemed to have been cut out of the side of this mountain. After they bought their National Park passes, they walked the short distance to the dive shop and noticed the café above the shop that the cab driver had mentioned.

"Hello," said Sean as the two boys climbed the three cement steps leading inside the small shop.

Behind the makeshift wooden counter stood a man about 5'8", slim with sandy blond hair. A Speedo bathing suit was all he wore, and a deep and weathered tan covered his body from head to toe. He had a boyish face with a friendly smile, and he looked up from the paperwork that he was going over and said, "What's going on, boys?"

Sean smiled at the man and said, "We want to learn how to dive."

The man took the glasses off his head and put them down on the counter. "No shit, you boys want to learn how to scuba, and wouldn't you just know it, we teach scuba! Ain't life funny. How did you end up here?"

Sean smiled and said, "Well, at first we were going to stay on St. Martin, but we were talking to some people and they told us that the diving in Saba was about ten times better. They said your shop was the place to go to learn how to dive. Anyway, we jumped on the ferry and here we are."

"Must be my lucky day. They call me Little John. You boys have come to the right place." He put out his hand toward Jack, who had walked up to the counter but still hadn't said a word.

Jack took his hand and said, "I'm Jack, this is my brother, Sean."

"Nice to meet you, boys," said John. He reached for a couple of forms and handed one to each of the brothers and said, "How long you going to be here?"

"We're here for five days, heading back Sunday morning and we have a flight back to the States out of St. Martin around 6 p.m.," Sean said, exactly as they had rehearsed.

"Where you staying?"

"We were told of a place called the Cottage Club, and we called and made reservations. You know the place?"

"Yeah, sure, it's a small island. Almost everyone knows everyone, except the med students. They mostly keep to themselves."

Sean looked up from the forms that he had begun to fill out, and said, "Yeah, met one of them on the boat. I thought he was pulling my leg about the school. Guess not."

Jack and Sean handed John their National Park passes. "They told you that this whole area is one big underwater park? That means no touching anything, unless you have to." John continued, "Sometimes the currents are pretty strong, and the only way to stay with the group is to hang on to anything you can, but try not to grab a piece of coral. Try for the rocks if you can."

"You'll start with some classroom work, then spend some time in the pool, and then do three open water dives. The whole package, including all equipment, comes to $550 each."

As Sean was taking out his credit card, a loud voice caused him to turn and look at a man walking in as he threw his fins on the floor.

"I swear to Christ almighty, these fucking Germans are going to drive me crazy. I tell them: stay with the group, you follow me, I don't follow you. What do they do, they see a little turtle and off they go, get caught up in the current down there by the Pinnacle and they're gone, like a fucking runaway truck barreling down a fucking mountainside with no brakes."

John looked up and said with a calm and casual smile on his face, "Did you at least recover the equipment?"

"I'll tell you, if it wasn't for those new BCs, I would have let them swim back, but they were grabbing onto everything down there. They broke off a piece of coral, and of course I have to report it, probably get a fifty-dollar fine. Fucking assholes."

"John," said little John, "these boys are taking the open water with us. You got time to do some classroom work this afternoon? I'll do their pool work in the morning."

"Fine," said John. He turned to Sean and Jack, stuck out his hand and said, "John. You do what I say, you follow the rules, and maybe you don't drown. I sure as hell don't want to be calling your mom and telling her she lost her boys. You two read me loud and clear?"

"We read you loud and clear. You don't have to worry about calling our mother, she's dead," said Sean.

369

John said, "Sorry to hear that, boys. Lord knows, we all got our stories, you got yours, I got mine. Anyway, I'm going upstairs to get a bite to eat. You hungry? Come on, I'll introduce you to Alice, the best goddamn jerk chicken on the island, and the conch chowder is outrageous."

Sean's heart was pounding as he looked at this man he and Jack had come to find, the man responsible for his mother's death. It took him a moment before he could answer. "Sure, we can eat. Sounds good."

"Good, come on, first round is on me," he said as he brushed past the boys and turned right to head up the concrete stairs leading to the café that sat atop the dive shop.

"It's him, Jesus and mother Mary, it's him, it's him. What the fuck do we do now?" asked Jack quietly as he slowly walked toward the steep steps leading to Alice's café.

Sean took Jack by his arm and gently turned him around and said, "Jack, just be cool, let's just play along. 'Cause I got to tell you, I have no idea what the fuck we're going to do. Are we straight on this? You say nothing and you do nothing." He could feel Jack's arm shaking. "Get it together."

Jack in turn took Sean's arm and pulled him closer to his face and said in a soft but firm voice, "Relax, bro, no big thing. Let's go have lunch with the SOB that killed our parents and ruined my life. I can handle that, no big thing."

Jack began to walk up the stairs when Sean grabbed him again and said, "Jack, listen. We get the evidence and turn it over to the cops, right?"

"Here's the deal, pal, you can take your evidence, and you can take the cops and stick them all right up your ass. I'm not leaving this fucking rock with that motherfucker alive, and I don't give a shit whether I leave here walking or in a fucking body bag."

Sean began to say something in response but Jack cut him off as he grabbed both his brother's shoulders and said, "Relax, Tinker Bell, I didn't come this far to blow it, we have all the time in the world. Let's just go along with the story and figure out the next few steps. I'll guarantee one thing, Sean, and I'm serious. I won't do anything that will put you in harm's way, I swear."

Jack and Sean made it to the door to the café, when Big John stuck his head out and said, "You boys need a written invitation?"

He was standing on a step higher than the boys and towered over them. He stood about 6'4", wearing a red bathing suit that reached to his knees and a T-shirt that said, "Divers go deeper." He must look very different than the man their father had known. But he'd be about the same age as their father if he had lived. Would Jerry have looked like this man, graying at the temples, lines etched into leathery skin? Sean always thought of his father as tall and strong, and he felt short and weak in comparison. The pictures that they had found were deceiving, showing Jerry always in a group, like a college fraternity. They all seemed to be laughing it up, like they were having a big old beach party.

Both boys looked up at John. They studied his face for just a moment. They were trying to see John and the other men from the photos standing side by side thirty years ago. The pictures they had were worn, faded on the edges, and thirty years old. People change, but not that much. Big John turned to walk back into the café.

Before the boys walked in, Sean said to John, "Just need to talk to my brother for a few minutes. Why don't you order us a couple of those chicken sandwiches and some soup? Be there in a minute."

John smiled and said, "Cool, take your time." He went into the café.

Jack turned to his brother. "Look, Sean, I don't have all the answers, and you're right, I don't know what the fuck we're going to do. All I know is that we're about to sit down and have lunch with the guy that ruined my life, maybe not yours, but he definitely fucked up mine." Jack took a deep breath and continued, "Sean, I'm not trying to pull you down with me. I called you and you came, more than thirty years down the road. And then we spent a few days reading the papers that should have been destroyed a long time ago, but guess what, they weren't, I found them. So here we are, and if nothing else, I'm not leaving until I find out exactly what happened. I need to know why they killed our father, but mostly, I need to know why he did that to Mom. Christ, Sean, it was barbaric and cruel. I mean, he could have just shot her quick, painless, you remember: 'one in the chest, two in the head, make sure he's good and dead.' But that's not what he did, Sean. He raped her and strangled her and he did it with a grin that will haunt me to the day I die. I think it was his face I saw that day, when I was just a kid. And until I get to wipe that grin off his face, I'll just continue to live and relive the nightmare."

Jack was sounding a bit unhinged, but Sean was committed to helping his brother. "Okay, Jack, I'm with you."

The sound of the door to the café startled them again. John was standing there. "You girls coming up or what? We got a lot of shit to go over, so let's get your sorry asses up here."

"Coming, boss," answered Jack.

The café was one big bar with small tables on an outside porch that overlooked the harbor and the inlet to the ocean.

"Over here, boys," said John. "Since we're not doing any water stuff, just classroom information, we can have a couple of beers."

John ordered three drafts and said to the woman who ran the café, "Alice, my girl, want you to meet a couple of friends of mine. This here's Jack and this is his little brother, or big brother, I don't know," he said with a smile, "Sean."

Alice smiled at the boys, and said in a strong island accent, "No matter, whether you're a big or little brother, the only thing that's important is that you're brothers. Nice to meet you, boys. Now let me tell you the special of the day." Alice had a ready smile; she was a large woman, but not fat, just big. Her face was round, and the smile just seemed to go with her face; her large white teeth shone in the bright afternoon sun.

"Okay," said John. "Here's the way it works: you do about four or five hours in the classroom. We'll give you all the books, they come with the package, plus the dive chart, the whole enchilada. Then you do three open water dives, and we'll do some dives in the pool. Last thing, you'll take a written test and a skills test in the water and that's it, you're certified. Open water divers, piece of cake. One thing," John continued with all seriousness, "it's a bit rough out there. So being new to this wonderful sport of ours, I would very much appreciate it if you would stick real close to me. I mean to say if I stop swimming, you better be so fucking close that you just about swim right up my ass, we straight on that? I almost lost two crazy fucking Germans this morning, but who gives a shit about them. I lose one of you boys and I'll feel bad about that for two, maybe three days. Okay, we understand each other, good," said John waiting for no answers. "Let's eat and then get to work."

Sean looked up at John just as Alice was putting down a bowl of seafood chowder and said, "So how long have you been doing this?"

"Doing what?" asked John, as he added dashes of salt and pepper in the soup.

"Diving, how long have you been diving?"

John took a spoonful of soup and said, "About thirty years." He took another sip, turned toward Alice, and said, "This fucking soup is hotter than a devil's asshole."

Alice said with a big smile, "And just how would you know how hot a devil's asshole is?"

At the very same time as this little banter was going on between two good old friends, Jack and Sean sat on the opposite side of the small table and stared at each other. A thousand questions were silently moving back and forth between them. They sat there, seemingly enjoying the camaraderie and the apparent carefree good humor of the moment, but nothing could be further from the truth. The truth was that both Jack and Sean knew they were coming to a curve in the road. Sean was scared to death of what was waiting on the other side of that curve. Jack knew it too, but he was determined to push his foot right through the floorboard. He was done being scared.

During the next half an hour, the three talked, easy and relaxed, like they had been doing it for years. John was a friendly guy, with an animated personality; he could be as crude as a sailor, and then as sweet and charming as the guy next door.

"I'll meet you boys across the street, at the building where you got your passes, in two hours. Give you a chance to go to the hotel and settle in. Don't be late. We got a lot of work to do and I want to get you guys in the water as soon possible." John stood up, not waiting for the check, and headed out the door.

CHAPTER 28

Saba

On the other side of the island, the Saba School of Medicine was located on the most beautiful site for a university one could imagine. But it was not the first choice for many aspiring doctors to head to an unknown Caribbean island to attend medical school. They were there because they couldn't get into a school stateside. If they failed on Saba, there was no place else to go. So once or twice a year, with too much alcohol or too many drugs, a distraught young student would find the only way out, leaping to his or her death off the cliffs to the rocky shore more than six hundred feet below.

The job of director of security was created to deal with the aftermath. After all, nothing else much happened on the sleepy island. Of all the challenges the Board of Governors needed to address, the biggest was changing the public perception about the school of medicine—proving to the world that this relatively unknown island in the middle of the Caribbean housed a quality institution and was a reasonable choice for those who needed the option, in a safe and secure environment. So, it was considered a stroke of luck when an

American with a military background applied for the job. He and his Vietnamese girlfriend had settled on the island a few years earlier, after they had lived in Europe on and off for almost thirty years.

It was here at this quiet and peaceful post on this remote Island that Jerry McGinnis found some peace with the choices he made. The guilt and the nightmares still plagued him. Regret and remorse were his constant companions, and with little or nothing to do from day to day, daydreaming dominated his days. It had always been his intention to make everything right. Sending somebody to retrieve the notebooks he had sent home was the biggest mistake of his life. It was never supposed to end that way. He had planned for some guys from the Unit to go to Selinsgrove, sit and wait 'till the kids and Kate left, break into the house and retrieve the notebooks, and make it look like a couple of drug-crazed kids looking for money or stuff to buy drugs. It was never supposed to end up with Kate murdered and little Jack traumatized. He had left the other set of copies with his father, but he'd asked his father to destroy them in the end. He was probably the only one who still knew the truth; there wasn't anyone to set him free, to set the record straight. Somehow it all got away from him and the years past.

Jerry found some peace over the years with Connie, and he was sure the boys, men now, had been better off with his parents. He couldn't have faced them then. Someday he would go back, he always believed that.

He strolled out of the small wood-framed building that acted as his office at the university and walked down the wooden ramp to his motorcycle to head up the mountain to his home.

When he walked in, he went first to the refrigerator to pour a beer, then opened the back door and walked out onto the balcony, which overlooked the ocean more than three thousand feet below. He closed his eyes and thought back to the time he had spent in South Vietnam. And then the quick exit after the terrible news about Kate reached him. They shipped him out with Connie to Switzerland, and he found himself living a life he could have never imagined.

The Unit had amassed close to a billion dollars from its menu of operations, and he and Connie managed the money, moving it from country to country, creating corporations and distributions for the members of the Unit.

As the war dragged on, the Criminal Investigation Department ramped up its investigations and was actively indicting and court-martialing those who were proven to be involved in illegal activities. Certain activities, especially those enterprises that involved human trafficking, started getting a great deal of notice by the human rights organizations and the agencies within the UN whose mission was to bring an end to such activities.

Jerry immersed himself in the management of the Unit's mone-tary funds and, with the support of Big John, successfully convinced the founders back in the States to ban all human trafficking in the future. Trafficking in stolen economic and military aid had surged, the drug trade had exploded, and while there was always a demand for female companionship, Jerry knew that it was smart to only deal in goods and money.

Jerry and John teamed up to become the Unit's eyes and ears. They figured out who the CID was focused on, what materials or evidence it had acquired, and the timing of the potential raids. This invaluable information became vital to the continued workings of the Unit. The intelligence that Jerry provided had been critical.

By the end of the war, the primary objective was to secure, preserve, grow, and distribute the wealth that had been amassed.

Each and every member of the Unit would share in the wealth based on their contribution to the overall success of the Unit's enterprises. Bank accounts were set up in the member's name and distribution established. Jerry's primary responsibility was to funnel all proceeds from all activities to foreign banking institutions, to be distributed to the members in a gradual and secure fashion. And now, after almost thirty years of managing the money, Jerry and Connie retired to Saba with John.

Life has a way of taking you for a ride, Jerry knew, and the latest, and most likely the last, stop for him was this little island in the middle of nowhere. He and Connie had had a good run. They understood each other, and although they never married, they lived as an old married couple and both seemed content with that. He had after all been declared MIA and had taken on a new identity with the help of the unit. Marriage licenses were an unnecessary risk.

"Rise and shine, sleeping beauty, got some news you might be interested in hearing." John sat down in the wicker chair next to Jerry on the deck; he often let himself in.

Jerry stirred, opened his eyes, and said, "Hey, John, what brings you up here?"

John smiled, making Jerry feel sort of queasy in an unusual way. "I'm not sure, 'cause there's no way I could be sure, but I got a feeling and I wanted to tell you right away."

Jerry sat up in his easy chair and tilted his head slightly and said, "Yeah, what's up?"

"How old would you say your two boys would be?"

Jerry looked at John and said with a sad expression, "Why are you asking me that? You know that shit just about breaks my heart, why do you need to bring it up?"

"Hey," said John, "don't fucking blame me, you sent those fucking crazy bastards to get those papers, and it's not my fault that she was killed. Things got out of hand."

"Yeah, yeah, I know, I'm not blaming anyone. If anything, it was my fault, but I should have gone back. I should have taken care of the boys."

"Sure as shit, if you had gone back there, your ass would have been in a sling. You would have spent the next twenty years in the fucking can, and then your boys would really have been screwed up. At least the whole world thinks that you died a hero." John continued, "I asked you a question, about how old would they be?"

Jerry thought for a moment, turned back toward John and said, "Sean would be thirty-six and Jack thirty-two. Now for Christ's sake, what the hell is this all about?"

John took a dramatic pause, and said, "I'm pretty fucking sure that I just had lunch with your two sons."

Jerry stared at John with disbelief. "You telling me you think that two random guys came to this remote fucking island to take some diving lessons, and now you've come to the goddamn conclusion that they're my boys? What makes you think that?"

"Well, old man," said John. "First, they're from Pennsylvania, and second, they are thirty-six and thirty-two. Jack and Sean are their names. It's them, all right. Your two kids just pulled up and checked in."

"Where are they now?"

"In town. This afternoon we start dive training in the water. Stop by and say hello. They don't know who the hell you are, remember they think you're dead."

"Hold on, shithead, don't you think that it's just a little bit strange that out of the clear blue sky, my two kids just happened to show up? You don't find that just a little fucking strange?"

"What are you getting at?" said John.

"What if they found out something? Maybe my dad left them some of the notebooks. Or they found out about Tony. They could have gone to the VA hospital in Williamsport, and that motherfucker would have told them that we were here."

"No," said John. "Well, Tony may have told them something, I'll give you that, but they didn't say a word about you. I could be wrong, but I am sure that they believe that you were killed in 'Nam. Of course, if that's what they think, then why the hell are they here? Something's weird, just doesn't make any sense. If they think you're dead—" John stopped and said, "You think the little shit told them that I whacked you? You think that they came here to settle the score? I'll be a son of a bitch. Makes sense, if any of your letters survived after all, everything leads to me, yup, that's got to be what it is." John stood and continued. "This is going to be the granddaddy of reunions, and you got a lot of explaining to do."

Jerry said, "Would you please just shut the fuck up and let me think? First of all, we're not even sure they're my boys, and second of all, you aren't doing anything. I'll take care of it. I don't know what the hell I'm going to tell them, but I'm tired of living this fucking lie, it's been too damn long. I need to make things right. If they have found me, both of us, I owe them the truth. I always thought this day would come."

John looked up and said, "That's real fucking noble. I could feel the tears running down my face. You do what you have to do, long as I'm not involved. You hear me loud and clear?"

"Relax," said Jerry. "This has nothing to do with you."

"You need to talk to them and find out exactly what's going on here. If they're here to get their dive certification, fine and dandy, but if they're here to find out what happened to their parents and maybe make things right, then we got ourselves a real bad problem that you're going to have to deal with."

John stood up and walked out. Jerry stood and stared out at the ocean.

Jerry tried to think back. The decision to sign up back in 1969 had changed everything, and so much damage had been done. Was this the moment to make things right? He had wanted more back then, more than what was there, more than a simple life writing for a local newspaper. Sometimes you have to be awfully careful what you wish for, because you might get it, and it doesn't always turn out the way you planned.

Jerry closed his eyes. The last two weeks had been quiet. Most of the medical students had gone home, and there wasn't too much to do for the director of security on Saba in the middle of the summer. Connie would be home soon; he would talk it over with her. As he started to drift off, the memories became vivid, and he found himself back in Vietnam.

It hadn't taken long before Jerry stopped questioning his motives and his methods.

He had been passing information to Tony and John for weeks, and nobody was getting hurt. He was getting thick envelopes of cash, and it all just seemed so easy. And then there was the day everything changed.

Jerry had confirmed that there was a CID agent investigating rumors of theft and trafficking. John and Tony had asked him to keep an eye on the investigation and let them know when the trail was getting hot. Jerry knew he had to tell them the truth. His own position in the Unit was on the line. He met up with Tony one afternoon at the café.

"Listen, Tony, Steve Jacobs has been tracking you guys for a while, and I don't know exactly what he has on you, but he knows your name and John's."

"Should have known it," said Tony with a nasty smile. "That little Jew bastard, we should've known it was him. Anyway, good work. John will be real pleased, and you're getting to understand just how John shows his appreciation, if you know what I mean." Tony stood up, walked around the table, gave Jerry a pat on his back, and walked out of the café.

That same night Steve told Jerry he had a late-night meeting and not to wait up for him. By 3:30 in the morning he still wasn't back. Jerry sat on the edge of his bed and stared at the empty bed across the room. He had a bad feeling about this. He stood up, pulled on his pants and shoes, and started walking through the side streets toward the town. As he got closer to the main street, the lights seemed to be getting brighter; he hadn't remembered the streetlights so bright before. That's good, he thought, streetlights make it a little safer. But it wasn't streetlights that Jerry saw that night, the lights were from MP jeeps. Jerry walked toward the jeeps and saw the MPs standing around something in the street. One of the soldiers stopped Jerry and asked him where he was going at four in the morning. Jerry looked at the young soldier, looked over at the blanket that covered what seemed to be a body, and asked, "What happened?"

"Not sure," said the young MP. "Look likes the poor bastard ran into the wrong guys. They robbed him; then they cut his throat, fucking cold. Poor guy, he probably laid here and bled to death. What a place to die, some dark alley in this godforsaken country. Just not right."

Jerry stared in disbelief, scared to death to ask the only question he must ask. "You got an ID?"

"Nope, looks like they took everything. There was no wallet, no watch, no dog tags, no nothing. Strange, why would they take his tags?"

The soldier turned as an officer walked up to them, and Jerry moved forward to the covered body. His hand shook as he reached for the edge of the blanket. He slowly pulled the cover carefully from the face of the dead man, almost praying he wouldn't see what he expected. Steve seemed almost peaceful as he lay there with his eyes wide open, staring into the darkness. There was a bloody gash that started at one ear and went all the way to the other ear. Jerry knelt in the dirty street beside the dead body of his friend. He understood that this was no random mugging that went bad. He knew that Steve had been murdered, he knew why, he knew who was responsible, and he knew it was him. He had done this.

It was the moment everything turned; the road he had chosen would lead away from the life he had known, the life he had planned. It was a moment when everything John was saying started to make sense. There was no going back. He tried to remember when he had stopped thinking about Lucy and her mother. He tried to remember when he had decided that there was nothing he could do for Chuck and Brian Harris and that it was time for him to move on.

Jerry woke up in the wicker chair on his balcony. He sat for a moment looking out to the ocean beyond the reef. He could see a small boat with four or five scuba divers next to the dive boat, getting their gear ready for an afternoon dive. He peered out and could see two young men, their backs to Jerry. One was bigger, solidly built with dark hair, and the other seemed smaller, tall, but thin, with long hair that hung almost down to his shoulders. Were these his boys? Jerry ran to his desk where he kept the binoculars. He focused, his hands trembled, and he could feel dampness on his forehead, tears in his eyes. He turned away from the dock and took the binoculars away from his eyes, wiping the tears away with his sleeve. He felt light-headed, took a few breaths, then raised the glasses to his eyes again. He could see the thinner of the two men turn. Jerry focused the lenses. He hadn't seen the boy for more than thirty years. He couldn't tell if this was Jack, but maybe it was. This face was drawn, thin, almost gaunt; his hair seemed dull and lifeless. The years had not been kind to this one. He might have been in his mid-thirties, but he looked older, weathered and beat-up. The other brother turned, and Jerry recognized him instantly: it was Sean.

Jerry closed his eyes tightly and remembered walking into his sons' room early on cold, wintry days. "Rise and shine, sleeping beauties, time to get ready for school."

When he opened his eyes, the dive boat was moving out of the inlet. The two boys, their backs to Jerry, were listening and watching John show them how to set up their tanks, and then the boat turned sharp left and moved out of view.

Jerry's mind drifted back to his friend Steve. The betrayal plagued him almost more than the abandonment of his sons. He found himself confessing to his murdered friend. Pleading for forgiveness, but he knew that forgiveness would never come, not for Steve or for Kate or for his father who could have only died from a broken heart. How many lives had he destroyed?

Then the memories took him back to the moment he confronted Tony.

"You lying bastard, you swore to me that nothing was going to happen to Jacobs."

He could see Tony's face; he could hear the words. "Jerry, I swear, we had nothing to do with that. You got to believe me, your friend was just in the wrong place at the wrong time. It's a real bad area, dark streets, happens all the time." It was bullshit, and Jerry knew it, but deep inside, he wanted to believe them. He wanted to be one of them; he had become one of them.

After the last fateful phone call to Kate, that was another turning point: the moment he said to Tony, "I got a problem. I got to talk to John. I need to get home. I got to take care of some things. It's just for a few days, it's important."

Tony looked up from his beer, and said, "What's so important?"

Jerry sat there, staring at Tony, then down at his beer. He knew that he needed to get this taken care of. He needed to get home, burn the papers, and everything would be fine. He would deal with Kate.

Tony reached over and grabbed Jerry's arm, "What's so important?"

"Nothing, I'll take care of it." But he hadn't. In the end, he had to come clean to John and Tony. John had understood, he really had, and Jerry gave him all the information he needed: directions to the house, specific instructions on when to go, avoiding Kate and the kids, and where to find the paperwork. It should have been so easy. It all went so hideously wrong.

Those memories were hard, exhausting. He sat back on his deck and closed his eyes, dozing off for a bit. When he awoke, he looked at his dive watch; they wouldn't be back from the dive for at least another hour. What was he going to say to the boys?

CHAPTER 29

Saba

Once the boys finished the classroom part of the dive course, it was time to take them out for a short deep water dive. John was still sizing them up. They were definitely Jerry's kids. The only question was, why were they here? He had already caught them lying about their last names. He had gone down to the office where they had to give identification to get their National Park passes. He decided not to call them on it yet, as they obviously hadn't thought this through or they would have come with fake identification. Maybe they knew that John had known their father and they wanted to talk about their old man. Of course, his first natural inclination was always to strike out at even the slightest provocation. These boys were possible enemies who would have to be dealt with, but there was no benefit from striking first without knowing the full extent of what they knew. After all, he didn't become a captain in command of the most lucrative structure in the U.S. military by acting irrationally.

He remembered well when Jerry confessed his true intentions about the letters and journals he had sent home. John had to call upon every ounce of self-control in that moment and stay focused on the big picture. Revenge and retributions would come later, much later. Perhaps this was the time to close that chapter. He had made the right decision at that time, and Jerry had provided invaluable services to the Unit over the years.

Sean and Jack walked up the stairs to Alice's café. "Don't eat too much before the deep dive," said John as he walked over to the counter where his hot cup of coffee was waiting. John picked up the cup and came back to the boys. "Last thing you want to do is take a dump at eighty feet with the currents swirling. Could get a little messy for the folks right behind you." He smiled.

"Makes sense. So, you like it here?" asked Jack.

John took a sip and said, "I like it fine. The people are mostly good, even the tourists are decent, for tourists. Not so many entitled assholes. Mostly folks that have blood running through their veins. They come here, and this is no easy trip, to do some serious diving or some serious hiking. Either way, they're here to do something, not just sit on their asses. I like the way this island was made. One big giant mountain, nothing is flat, everything is uphill or downhill." He sat down and continued to talk. "Ten million years ago, in the middle of the Caribbean Ocean just twenty-seven miles southwest of what is now St. Martin, a mighty explosion triggered a seismic volcanic eruption that pushed a land mass a thousand miles in circumference up from the depths of the ocean floor to the surface and surged up over three thousand feet. A crater the size of a thousand football fields formed over the next million years, and over many thousands of years of rain and wind and thrashing waves, the sides began to fall into the sea and all that remains is a pinnacle, just one lone pinnacle, shaped like an upside-down ice cream cone. Someone named it Saba."

Sean looked at John and said, "Did you just make that up? I swear that sounds like a commercial from a tourist board."

John smiled and said, "Yeah, word for word. I memorized it, pretty cool. When you finish up, come down to the shop, we need to get you guys geared up. Thanks for the coffee. What's your shoe size? I'll pull your fins."

John walked out of the café. Sean and Jack followed him down the six steps that led directly into the dive shop.

The interior of the dive shop was like the inside of a cave. It was so narrow that you could stand in the middle of the room, raise your arms out to the side, and nearly touch the walls to the right and left. Two sets of wooden benches were pushed tight to either side of the rock walls. Diving equipment hung on the walls: regulators, masks, and buoyancy compensators were neatly and meticulously inventoried. Fins were stored in boxes numbered by size. The tanks and the weights were always left on the boat. A small table served as a reception desk, cluttered with forms and pencils. A small glass case filled with everything from dive watches to underwater flashlights fit neatly under the desk.

John introduced the boys to Robert Jackson, who served as first mate. He was almost 6'6", and his complexion was darker than most on the island, perhaps from long hours in the sun. His short-cropped hair was as curly as a Brillo Pad with patches of gray dominating the top of his head. He smiled and walked over to Sean, Jack, and John. Robert nodded to John as he pulled up a chair and sat down.

"Need a hand today?" he said, in a deep voice with a rhythm and beat that seemed to be unique to this volcanic island in the middle of the sea. The words sounded like English, but both boys strained to decipher the words.

"Not today, partner, I got this one covered. Just me and the boys, first open water."

Robert stood and offered his hand to John, who grabbed it and pulled hard in a friendly tug of war between the two longtime friends. The sleeve on John's shirt pulled back and there on his right arm was a faded yet clear tattoo: the butterfly, the same one on Tony's arm, fangs and all. If Jack had harbored any doubt that this was the right John, he was sure now. Jack turned slowly toward Sean, his face was ashen, a distant look in his eyes.

"You okay, Jack? You feel up to making the dive?" Sean asked quietly.

"Yeah, I'm fine."

John hadn't heard the exchange; he was pulling down the necessary equipment. He called over to them. "Let's go, guys. Pick up your gear. First dive will be just working on your skills: buddy breathing, clearing your mask, and getting in and out of your buoyancy compensator, which we call the BC, and learning the signs. It'll be a piece of cake for you guys. We won't be too late. Robert will give you a ride up the mountain to the cottages when we are done. You get a good night's sleep tonight, and then tomorrow we'll head out to open sea."

The first dive went well. They did what they were told to do, their bodies flooded with adrenaline. They were almost giddy with the tension. In spite of all that was going on in his head, Sean was enjoying the experience. He was looking forward to the dive the next day, somehow pushing the reality of what they were actually doing there deep into the back of his mind.

When they got back to the dock, Robert helped them unload their gear, and they all walked back up to the shop.

"These guys did a hell of a good job for newbies," John told Robert. "We'll have a great dive tomorrow. Take it easy, boys, see you around 9 a.m."

They shook hands with John and went out to the street. They got into Robert's old and dented station wagon that sat in front of the dive shop. The road up to the Cottage Club was long, narrow, and steep, but not like any steep they had ever seen; this was steep like climbing a wall. The view was unbelievable. Looking up, the top of the mountain was shrouded in the heavy mist of the rainforest, and far below was the blue ocean, water so clear that the reflection of the sun's rays off the surface was bright enough to make you shade your eyes. They climbed and climbed the narrow road. Sean held on tight and found himself holding his breath when he would see a car coming in the other direction. Robert would pull over a bit, hugging the side of the road, coming right up against the brush, with only a few feet to the sheer drop off of the edge. Jack, on the other hand, was as calm as if he were lying on the beach; he looked like he was at peace with himself.

Sean began to say something, but then stopped, turned back to the window, and just held on tight.

It took about fifteen minutes to weave through the steep hills and sharp curves that led to a picturesque hillside with colorful buildings surrounding the water treatment center that provided fresh water for the island.

The Cottage Club was not so much a hotel as it was a grouping of small cabins that sat on the side of the mountain overlooking the Caribbean Ocean. The two boys checked in and were taken to their cabin by a young girl who turned out to be one of the daughters of the owner.

What the room lacked in amenities it surely made up for in a breathtaking view of the ocean below. The room held two beds, a couple of old chairs, a kitchen table, stove, refrigerator, and a small TV against the wall. There was a screen door that led to a small deck, with room for only one chair, overlooking the ocean, maybe a thousand feet below them. It had been a long day for both boys, and Sean threw his bag on one of the beds and sat down. He turned toward his brother, who was staring out the window.

"Jack," said Sean, looking at his back. Jack stood there, unmoving, looking down at the ocean below. Sean stood up and walked to Jack and placed his hand on his brother's shoulder. Jack turned toward him. The confused and flat expression that had dominated his face over the last few days was no longer there. Instead there was a brightness in Jack's eyes, an almost serene expression that replaced his previous sad and sorrowful look.

"Sit down, Sean," said Jack.

They both sat down, and for a moment, Jack said nothing and Sean waited.

Jack said, "I need to tell you some stuff." He hesitated for a moment and then continued, "I know it was a long time ago, but for me, the day that Mom died was like yesterday."

"For Christ's sake, Jack," said Sean in a shaky voice. "You were six years old."

"I saw her die, Sean, and even after she stopped moving and crying, she was still looking at me. After he got off her, she was still staring at me. I just sat there, I couldn't move. Maybe if I had screamed or yelled or something, it would have helped. Could have saved her. Maybe they would have left if they'd realized someone else was in the house. But I couldn't move, not a fucking inch. I know that afterward you guys thought I was spaced out. I guess I was. It was like being in a dark cloud, no sunlight, no blue sky, no laughter, no crying, nothing. I remember a doctor telling me later that your mind has a safety switch. If there is trauma, it can just turn off. That was the only way I could survive."

"Jack," said Sean. "Look, one way or the other, it's all coming to an end. We're here together, and it ends here."

Sean stood and walked over to the little refrigerator and found two cold beers; the hotel staff had stocked it for them. He handed one to his brother. Neither spoke. The sun was getting lower on the horizon, a bright orange-red glow surrounded it. The sky was cloudless with a slight breeze that seemed to cool things down a bit.

Finally, Jack spoke. "Did you notice the tattoo on John's arm? It was kind of faded, but it was there. A butterfly with teeth and fangs, just like Dad talked about. Did you see it?"

"I saw he had a tattoo, couldn't see it that well."

Jack continued, "Tony had the same tattoo, a butterfly with fangs and teeth. I saw it, and Dad talked about Chuck having the same tattoo. I remember seeing it from the top of the stairs that day. I saw his hands around her neck, and I saw that tattoo on his arm, the same tattoo that Tony Ramo has. The doctors told me that someday it would all come back. Something would happen, I would hear something or see something, and all the details would come back."

Jack grabbed his brother's arm with a strength that he hadn't felt in years, and said, "It was him. It was definitely John Murphy that day. That son of a bitch killed our mother. He didn't just give the order like Tony Ramo told us; that was total bullshit. John must have found a way to fly back to the U.S. himself. And you know what,

I'll bet Tony was with him. God is doing his job, he's taking care of Ramo, and we've got to do ours."

"I'm with you all the way, but there is no way in hell we can prove it. The police will never reopen the case even with the stuff we have, and there is no way we could get this bastard back to the States to stand trial. We know what happened now. I don't know what more we can do."

"You got it all wrong, brother. I am taking this guy out, and when that motherfucker is dead, that's when we can let it go and both start living our lives."

"I get it, Jack, but he looks pretty hard to kill. How do we even plan something like that? He is an ex-soldier. And what if we got caught? I mean, don't take this the wrong way, but you haven't exactly been a model citizen, and I don't feel like spending the rest of my life in some fucking prison. So look, let's just think this whole thing out. First we take the diving course and just go with the flow, and we'll figure out how to bury that bastard. Okay?"

Jack said, "Look, man, I'm fucked. What I mean is that I ain't got much longer to live, maybe a few more years, and tell you the truth, I'm tired of being sick. I'm tired of being angry and feeling bad all over. Let me do it. I'll do it, and you go home to your family. I'll stay here, nobody's waiting for me. I'll take my time, hang out, and when the time is right, and his guard is down, I'll do to him just what he did to us. And you know what, Sean, I'll make sure he knows it, that it's going to be slow and painful. Before he's dead, he'll be begging for me to end it, and then I will."

Sean stood up and looked down at his brother. There were tears in his eyes, and he put his hand on Jack's shoulder. "Jack, listen to me, please, you're not alone. This isn't just about you. It's about all of us, you, me, Mom, and Dad. I am not leaving you here, no matter what you say."

CHAPTER 30

Saba

J erry jumped, startled, the bang on the door bringing him back from the daydream.

The door opened and Jerry knew who it was. He pulled himself up from his easy chair and walked to the bathroom. He looked in the mirror. The years and the sun had taken their toll— where did the time go?

He felt old, tired. He put his hands on the sink and closed his eyes. This wasn't supposed to happen, it was supposed to be over, and now his two boys had somehow stumbled back into his life.

"What the fuck you doing in there," shouted John, "taking a bath?"

Jerry turned and walked into the living room, where John was sitting on the couch.

"I sent two guys over to the VA hospital in Williamsport to pay a visit to our old friend," said John. "I said to myself, how in the hell do those two kids end up here, right at our door? No way it's just coincidence, that bastard told those kids everything,"

John hesitated for a moment. "It was my Christian duty, 'Thou shall not let your friends suffer.' They turned up the old morphine drip and Tony is now our dear departed friend."

Jerry, in a fog, looked up at John with a bewildered expression, "Tony's dead?"

"Yup," said John in a matter-of-fact way. "They tell me it was peaceful. He might have been a lying treacherous motherfucker in the end, but all in all he was a good guy, and I swear to god, he was my friend.

"They tried to talk to him first, but couldn't get a word out of him. It would have been helpful if we could have found out what he told the boys. I guess we're just going to have to assume the worst. Your boys are here for a reason. They're not here to learn how to scuba dive, you can bet your ass on that. They're here to revenge your supposed death, or the death of their mother. They think I had something to do with it. You know what happened to Kate was never my fault. It was those crazy bastards that blew the fucking mission to shit. Look, I can't let those two kids destroy everything we built. There are too many good men and women that are depending on us to make the right decisions. When it comes right down to it, Jerry, I'll do what I have to do. I sure wish those boys would have just let old dogs lie."

Jerry sat up straight, then stood up and slowly grabbed John by his shirt collar. "Over my dead body. The killing has stopped. What was the point of killing Tony? What the fuck is wrong with you?"

John spun around, Jerry lost his grip, and in an instant John was behind him with his arm tight around Jerry's neck. Jerry grasped for John's arm, but already the lack of oxygen was having its effect. Jerry's body slumped and fell to the floor.

John knew the sleeper hold would keep him unconscious for enough time. John dragged Jerry's body across the floor, lifted him over his shoulder, and walked slowly down the stairs to the old Ford station wagon. Robert Jackson opened the back door of the wagon and helped John push Jerry in the back.

"He's not dead," said John, "just fast asleep. I was always real good at that shit. Take him to the safe house at the top, and lock him in the money room. I need him out of the way for two days."

"What are you going to do with the two boys?" asked Robert, with a cold expression on his face.

"You know the tug that sunk two years ago, ended up right behind the pinnacles?"

"Yeah, what about it?" said Robert.

"It's perfect. I'll tell them that if they both get their skills down I'll give them a tour of the sunken tug. First, we'll take a good look at the coral, work on some skills, and use up most of their air. Then as a special treat I'll take them into the tug. I'll have them follow me into the captain's cabin. It's pretty dark and gloomy, lots of wires, broken piping, all kinds of shit hanging from the ceiling. I'll lead them to the back of the cabin; there's a little alcove in the corner with a small air pocket. The air's rancid but still breathable. And while they're checking it out, I'll slip behind them and head to the door and lock it behind them. I'll just swim out of the tug, spend another twenty minutes at forty feet looking frantically for them, and by the time I get to the surface and call the Coast Guard, it will all be over. I'll be inconsolable. What a tragedy, two young men in the prime of their youth drowned today in that old sunken tugboat. What a shame."

Robert nodded his head slowly. "It's a good plan, John, might just work. You'll have to be a little lucky, and they'll have to be a little unlucky, but I guess it'll work."

"What about him?" Robert pointed to Jerry and said, "He's not going to believe that line of bullshit for one second, and he ain't going to be too happy when he finds out you drowned his only two sons."

"He'll be upset, sure, but the fact is, he hasn't seen those boys in years. Jerry's a smart guy; he'll figure out soon enough that this was the only way."

"It doesn't matter if it's been years. Fathers avenge their sons and sons avenge their fathers. It's biblical stuff, eye for an eye, that shit never goes away, it's just human nature. So if you ask me, and god knows I like that boy, but if I were you, I would do all three."

John looked up and said, "Don't you know that I know killing Jerry is the smart play? I know that, but he's been my friend for thirty fucking years. Nothing happens to him, you understand? Nothing happens to him."

"Okay, okay," said Robert. "No worries, boss. I'll take him to the safe house; he'll be just fine. But I know Jerry, he ain't gonna let this go. But you're the boss."

The following morning Robert Jackson drove his Ford station wagon up the narrow road that led to the Cottage Club to pick up Jack and Sean.

Sean stood looking out the window that overlooked the ocean below. He was waiting for Jack to come out of the bathroom. They would be picked up soon. He was very uneasy about the lack of a clear plan. He felt a hand on his shoulder and turned.

"Let's talk about this. We got some time before we get picked up."

Jack walked the few steps to the table and sat down slowly. He picked up his coffee and sipped it carefully. "Sean, I've asked you for nothing over the years. If there is anything to forgive, then I swear that I forgive you and Grandma. But just this once, you need to hear me out. Please, let me do this. I don't have much time left."

Jack continued, "I'm not even one hundred percent sure it's him, but I remember that fucking tattoo. Maybe I'm wrong. So look, let me hang out here for a while, let me make sure that John is the guy. If he is, I'll take care of him, but you need to be gone. You can't have anything to do with this. I'll just say that I'm staying for a while and you're heading home to your job and your family. Makes perfect sense, and I'll keep in touch. I swear I won't do anything unless I let you know."

"You can't do it on your own, you're not strong enough."

Jack looked at his brother. "Are you fucking nuts? What do you think, I'm going to challenge him to a fucking duel to the death? Trust me, Sean, I'm not that crazy. I'll find a way. I always do."

The sky was crystal blue with only a few scattered clouds. It seemed a perfect day in paradise, a tranquil ocean with just an occasional white cap skipping over the water and shimmering as the sun rose higher in the eastern sky. It was always a little cooler at 1,500 feet, just below the rainforest that shrouded the top of the mountain. Looking up at the sky, turn your head 360 degrees and all you could see was ocean and sunshine.

It was a short walk up the brick path to the main house where Robert would be waiting for them. The road down to the dive shop and the dock was steep and narrow. Robert had made this trip a thousand times; he could do it drunk or sober, didn't matter. Sean knocked on the window.

"Rise and shine, sleeping beauty," he called into the window that was only partially closed. Robert didn't move at first, but a smile came to his face, and he looked up slowly as he turned his head to the boys and said, "That's what my mom would say. I haven't heard that in a very long time. Let's get going, you've got a big day. You boys ready for your first real dive?"

"Yeah, looking forward to getting in the water. Do you dive?" asked Jack as Robert pulled out of the narrow curve of the Cottage Club and started down the long, narrow, and winding road.

"No, man. Well, sometimes I'll go out if they got a big group. I've got my divemaster card, but only when they need me. I guess I've seen everything there is to see. Besides, if the Lord meant for us to be underwater, he would have given us gills, not lungs. Right?" Robert had a booming laugh, and whether or not you found the story or the joke funny, you couldn't help but laugh when Robert laughed.

Jack, still smiling, turned toward the ocean. He could hear the tires as they rolled over the concrete road inches away from the dirt and gravel shoulder that stood between the car and the cliff edge.

John was waiting for them on the stone wall that surrounded the dive shop. When the station wagon pulled up, he stood slowly and walked into the shop. He was finishing up the paperwork as the two boys walked in.

"Morning," said John, and he picked up the forms, giving them a tap on the counter to straighten them out. "You guys get a good night's sleep? We got a big day. First we work on your skills—mask clearing, buddy breathing, getting your tanks on and off at the surface. And then in the afternoon, if you both check out, which I know you will, we'll do a little excursion dive to the old tug that went down a couple of years ago. She's in shallow water, right out there."

John pointed to two stone pinnacles that seemed to have sprouted from the ocean, like a giant Popsicle with double sticks that was driving straight up from the blue sparkling water into the pristine and bright blue sky.

"It will be fun. Only about eighty-five feet down, and still in great shape, sitting on its side, but we can have a look in. How's that sound?"

"Sounds great," said Jack with a smile on his face.

"Good. Got your gear all laid out in the back. Large BC for you," he said, pointing at Sean. "And the medium for you, you can put on a little weight you know," he said, smiling at Jack and pointing toward the back room, where all the dive equipment was hanging. "The weights will be on the boat. Let's get going, we got a lot of work to do. Want to get you boys underwater."

Sean and Jack threw the dive bags over their shoulders and headed down the dusty dirt road that led to the dive boat. There were two men waiting, the captain and one crew member to help the divers with their set-ups and getting in and out of the water. Both looked like they were from the island. The boys threw their gear to the younger crew member and jumped into the boat. The tanks were lined up along the sides, with flexible cords tied around each tank to keep them from rolling around when the seas got a little rough.

"Jack," said Sean as he gingerly moved to the front of the boat. "You think this is a good idea, that crazy bastard taking us down to some old fucking wreck? Maybe he knows who we are. I mean, if he wanted to drown us, this would be a pretty good time."

Jack looked up at his brother with a quizzical expression and said, "Come on, get your regulator on your tank. Don't forget to check your air pressure. Make sure you have at least 3,000 PSI." Jack smiled and gave his brother a gentle slap on the back and moved toward his tank. They stood side by side on the rocking boat as the captain slowly maneuvered around the buoys that marked the trail out of the harbor into the ocean.

"Everything a-okay?" John stood behind the boys and began to help them set up their tanks. "You've got to be careful, make sure everything is in good working order. After all, we would feel mighty bad if anything happened to you boys, being your first serious dive."

John smiled and checked all their equipment, turned on their air, and watched the PSI gauges each shoot up to just a little over 3,000.

"You guys are all set," said John. "Your first dive is just ten feet, sandy bottom, really good visibility this morning. We'll run through your skills. Depending on how things go, it shouldn't take more than thirty minutes, and we'll surface together. Then we'll hang out on the boat, around thirty minutes of surface time, and then we'll do your first real dive. You boys stick with me. I don't want you chasing some guppy and ending up lost, we clear?"

Sean and Jack each gave John a bit of smile and said, "Yup."

Deep in the rainforest, well off the dirt road, almost 3,000 feet above the village of Johnson Town, and buried beneath more than five feet of dirt and rock, was the safe house. The Unit's safe house on Saba was a secure location that served as a holding spot for drug shipments when U.S. surveillance was detected, and it served the same purpose for men and money heading back to Colombia and Mexico.

Their DEA mole, a former Vietnam veteran and marine, would get a message to the Saba team if a shipment was being tracked. The small and sleek boat, with a false bottom in case they needed to dump the drugs, would detour to Saba until the heat died down.

The walls were solid concrete, as were the floor and the ceiling, with only one reinforced steel door. There were only three people that knew of this place: Robert, Jerry, and John. It took almost a year to build the safe house. The five local men that built it had done a good job, and then all five had tragically died in a single boating accident soon after its completion. There were five large rooms, about 5,000 square feet in all, fully ventilated and stocked with plenty of fresh water and enough canned food to last up to six weeks, depending on the numbers hunkered down. The soft brown carpet and the light green paint on the walls and ceiling gave the underground bunker a comfortable and secure feeling.

It had only been about twelve hours since Robert had taken the unconscious Jerry up to the house. Jerry sat in one of the dozen chairs thinking about the choices that he had made more than thirty years ago. Why couldn't Tony have kept his fucking mouth shut? Maybe it wasn't too late, maybe, but only if he could get out of this fucking coffin.

The sound of the bolt being pulled out of the hinge on the door alerted Jerry to his chance. He didn't move. The metal door opened. "Jerry," whispered Robert. "You awake, man?" Robert moved toward Jerry, whose back was to him, apparently sleeping. Robert kept his hand in his pocket, ready to pull his gun out if Jerry tried to escape.

"You awake, Jerry? You awake?" asked Robert again. "I come to see how you doing, man, don't want no trouble. Just brought you some food and yesterday's paper."

Jerry didn't move a muscle, waiting. He had one chance. Robert turned around toward the table that stood against the wall and put down the bag that held fresh food and a six-pack of local beer.

Jerry flew from the chair, lunging at Robert's back with the frying pan in his hand. Robert turned around as Jerry came at him, and he

403

reached up to block the pan, but Jerry still hit him on the side of the head. The glancing blow knocked Robert into the table, spilling the food and beer on the floor. He grabbed at Jerry, but Jerry moved back and swung the pan at Robert's head, this time knocking him down to the floor. Robert grabbed for Jerry's ankle, and Jerry hesitated momentarily. Robert was his old friend, but he had no choice. His only chance to save his boys was to get out and down to the dock.

He lifted the pan high over his head and brought it crashing down on his friend's head. Robert lay there, moaning on the ground. Jerry quickly found the duct tape that they used to seal the large boxes filled with drugs or money. He tied Robert's hands and legs, five or six turns around his feet and around his neck, pulling his neck back toward the back of his feet. Robert lay on his side, still moaning and trying to move. Jerry kneeled down beside him and looked him in the eyes and said, "I'm going to ask you one time, and only one time, and then I start cutting off fingers, you understand?" Robert nodded his head.

"Where are my boys, and what does John have planned?" Jerry reached for the scissors that they used for cutting into the boxes and brought the points close to Robert's face.

"Okay," said Robert. "John is crazy, Jerry, I didn't want this to happen. I tell the man he's out of his fucking mind, but he doesn't listen to a word."

Jerry moved the opened scissors so that the tip of Robert's nose was between the two blades.

"Come on, man, I'll tell you. Take those blades away from my nose."

Jerry tightened the scissors and blood began to drip down Robert's upper lip. He could taste the saltiness.

"Jerry," pleaded Robert. "Okay, he's taking them diving, to the old tug wreck just behind the pinnacles. He's going to lead them into the captain's cabin and lock them in and wait till they drown. Then he's going to make it seem that they got lost or disoriented and drowned before John could save them."

"When? Goddamnit, when are they going?" screamed Jerry.

"They're doing their skills this morning and right after lunch they're heading out to the wreck. I guess around one o'clock."

Jerry looked at the wall clock; it was a little past 11:30 a.m. He moved to the door then turned back to Robert and said, "I thought you were my friend." He didn't wait for an answer. He was frantic. He had no idea where Robert had parked the car, and he realized the safe house door had locked behind him. Robert had the key, but he was tied up. He wouldn't be able to get out for hours. As for the car, they would never park it near the safe house for fear that they would give away its location, and they never parked in the same place, afraid that someone would notice and follow them to the house.

Jerry started running down the dirt trail that led to the nearest town. He knew these woods well; he had become quite adept at moving quickly and silently up and down the steep mountainside. He felt an energy that he hadn't felt since he was in the army. As he ran, thoughts came flying into his mind. "This time," he said out loud to himself. "This time I'm going to be there for my sons."

He could feel his heart pounding in his chest as he stumbled down the narrow, steep trail. It was around 11:40 when Jerry finally reached Johnson Town; he had to find a way to get down to the dock, still fifteen minutes away. He knew he was cutting it close—he still had to find a boat and get out to the tug location in time. He started running up the street towards the Cottage Club where Sean and Jack were staying.

Jerry crashed through the door into the small reception area and found Tom, the son of one of the brothers that had owned the Cottage. Jerry said, panting, "I need to borrow your car, or I need you to drive me to the dock, right now."

Tom looked up from the magazine that he had been reading and said with a smile, "Relax, sport, I'll take you down, no problem. What's the rush?"

Jerry reached across the desk and grabbed the kid by the shirt and said, "Tom, I don't have time, I need to get to the dock NOW!"

"Okay!" said Tom, hearing the urgency in Jerry's voice, and he leaped over the desk, grabbed the keys that were hanging on a hook, and ran out the door, with Jerry close behind him. They both jumped into the dark green jeep and headed down the mountainside toward the dock.

The August sun was already high in the sky as the captain guided the dive boat toward the towering pinnacles.

"Okay, boys," said John. "We'll run through your skills one more time before heading down to the wreck. You guys did great this morning, just want to make sure you got the skills down pat. So, maybe ten minutes at about ten feet. You do mask clearing, buddy breathing, signs, and just a little navigation. Officially you're not required to have any navigation skills, but it's always a good idea to know where the fuck you are, right? In five minutes we'll get your gear on, and we'll be at the dive site in ten minutes. We'll back-roll off the railing, inflate your BCs, give me an "okay" hand sign, then swim to the back of the boat and hold on to the line. We'll go down together, about ten feet," he repeated. "We'll swim around for a few minutes and then head down to the wreck. We clear?" said John.

Jack looked up and said, "Loud and clear."

The two boys sat close together on the small boat as she gently rocked back and forth in the calm Caribbean waters. The sun felt warm on their shoulders; both leaned their backs against the tanks that were lined up for the next dive. Jack turned to his brother and said, "What are you thinking?"

"I was thinking that it would have been nice if we—I mean, if things would have been different. Never mind, let's just get through the day."

Jack said, "When we get back to the dock, let's invite John up to the cottage, you know, a first dive celebration, get to be real buddies. We'll tell him that you're heading back home, but I've decided to hang around, and maybe he could find a job for me."

Sean stared at his brother and said, "I don't feel good about this. Who knows what he's thinking." Sean grabbed hold of Jack's arm and turned him so they were face to face and said, "We don't know what he's thinking, what he's planning. He's a survivor, Jack. He's not one of your street thugs; he's serious military. John is a killer, he would cut your throat and feed you to the fishes in a heartbeat."

"Nothing is going to happen today, maybe another time, but not today. We're going to make this dive, you're going home, and when the time is right, I'll do what I need to do."

Sean looked at his brother closely; his eyes were sunken and glassy. Jack's skin was pale and seemed to have a grayish tint to it.

Sean began to say something when Jack put his hand up to motion Sean to stop.

John walked back to the stern of the boat and lit a cigarette. Sean watched him as he stood there gazing at the ocean.

"There's no fucking way he would be going through all this bullshit if he had any idea who we were," said Jack.

Sean began putting on his wetsuit, turned toward Jack, and said, "I guess."

John came over and checked out their gear and turned the air valves all the way on and then a slight turn back, checked the PSI gauge again. "Let's get ready," he said.

The boys got into their fins, slipped into their BCs, put their masks on, and pulled themselves up so that they were sitting on the rail next to John. He put out his hand with his thumb pointed up, looked at both boys, smiled, and then turned his hand pointing his thumb downward.

All three grasped their masks with one hand, leaned back, and slipped back into the clear blue waters. The waves were gentle and the boys bobbed in the water, relaxing into the motion. John signaled them to descend, and they all drifted down around ten feet to the sandy bottom. For the next ten minutes, they went through all the required skills to become a certified open water diver. The two boys rested just off the surface of the sandy bottom. They both had equalized their BCs, which left them floating like angels at the surface. After each task was completed, John would give them a thumbs up. After all the tasks were completed, John gave the boys another thumbs up with both hands and nodded his head as a "well done" sign.

John motioned with his hand to tell them to swim around and enjoy the underwater world of Saba. No tough currents here, just a nice leisurely dive for about thirty minutes. John signaled for the boys to check their PSI gauges; Sean signaled back that he had 2,100; Jack signaled that he had 1,600. John signaled to Jack to slow his breathing to conserve air.

Sean thought back to the divers that looked for the remaining boy after Chuck had rescued the father and his other son from the Susquehanna all those years ago, and he had always felt sad that they weren't able to save the other boy. Maybe if he and Chuck would have moved faster, maybe they could have saved them all. Sean smiled. He thought maybe when his two boys got older, they could all go on dive trips and perhaps Jack would join them. *Yeah*, he thought, *that would be great, a real family vacation, better than sitting on the beach all day.* He smiled to himself and a slight trickle of water settled at the bottom of his mask. He pulled his head slightly back and cleared his mask.

John signaled to follow him to the drop-off leading down to the tug that had just two years before been swamped and sunk by a hurricane that had blown through the islands of the Caribbean.

The visibility seemed endless as they kicked their way down right behind John. The boys turned their heads from side to side, taking in the beauty of this underwater theater. John pointed straight ahead; coming toward them was a giant eagle ray. She glided effortlessly through the water as if she didn't have a care in the world, and then she was gone. Sean and Jack noticed that they were working harder just to keep up with John. They noticed that the underwater grasses and even the coral were being pushed or pulled toward them, like an underwater wind that was blowing against them as they moved forward, following closely behind John.

The deep current seemed to come from nowhere; the boys began to kick harder and harder and faster and faster, just to hold onto the distance that they had traveled. They looked up and watched as John used rocks to pull himself forward, like an anchor in the sand. The tug was just ahead; Sean noticed that his air was down to just less than 1,500 PSI. It seemed like just a moment ago he had over 2,100;

struggling against the current had caused his oxygen level to plunge. He signaled to John that he was running low on air, but John signaled "okay" and just kept on moving forward toward the sunken tugboat.

The tug was leaning on its side, and small fish and brightly colored coral had begun to make a home on the boat. The boys reached out for the railing and pulled themselves over the side and gently floated to the deck. John turned and signaled the two boys to follow him as he moved toward an open hatch in the deck. The two boys swam forward as John disappeared through the opening.

Sean swam first into the opening and out of sight of his brother. Jack followed Sean into the hole and into the darkness of the interior of the small boat. They saw John slip through an open metal door and into a large room beyond. John turned as the two boys floated just outside of the doorway. He signaled to them to come in and take a look at the engine room of this ill-fated tugboat.

As the two boys moved forward, John motioned for them to come closer, floating above them, while they took a good look at the rusting controls and the wooden wheel.

Sean reached out to touch the wheel and gave it a turn; he smiled and turned to his brother. And then it seemed like the lights went out. The boys suddenly could barely see their hands before them. Sean moved forward to where he thought the door leading to the deck had been, feeling his way along the engine room wall. He could feel his brother swimming close by, and then he reached what he thought was the door; he moved his hands over the metal, looking for a handle. There it was, and he pulled down, but it didn't move. He pulled down again with all his might, and still nothing happened. He felt Jack moving around, lost in the darkness, and he reached out and grabbed his brother and pulled him toward the handle. Sean took

Jack's hand and put it on the handle so that both boys could pull together to open the door and get to the deck. No more than thirty seconds had passed and then it came to Sean: where's John?

CHAPTER 31

The density of the water plays against the normal forces of strength and will. It slows you down, like you're moving in perpetual slow motion. And then the moment comes when it's all so clear. This was his plan, his plan to murder them both and make it look like a tragic diving accident. Sean saw it perfectly now. He and his brother both pushed and pulled on the handle trying to force the rusted metal door open. But it never gave. And then came the moment when they both realized that it was all for nothing. All there ever was, all there would ever be, was gone in a moment. They were supposed to win, after all the pain, they were supposed to prevail. They were supposed to avenge their parents. Win the victory and claim the spoils. Jack stopped first; he was exhausted, and he had nothing left. Sean pulled with all his remaining strength, but then he gave up too. Sean looked at his gauge now that his eyes had adjusted to the dim light. It was close to the red line. Jack looked at his brother, no longer hopeful. He glanced down at his gauge too; maybe he had only a few more minutes. John had led them here to drown.

As their eyes became more accustomed to the darkness, they could make out the interior of the small room and see each other.

Sean motioned to Jack to look around the room, to see if there was maybe another way out. Sean grabbed for Jack's air gauge and saw that he had only 900 PSI left in his tank; Sean had just over 1,100. Sean motioned his brother to try to stay calm and conserve as much air as possible, but Jack knew he was breathing harder and faster, as the reality was setting in. They had been lured into the tug; John had obviously figured out who they were.

Jack moved slowly through the cabin, his hands reaching out. Wires and cables littered the small room, and then he saw a thin ray of light glitter over his hand. He looked up at a small hole that had been torn in the ceiling when the boat sank, no more than a few inches in diameter. He reached out and held onto one of the pipes along the ceiling to steady himself while he pulled himself close to the hole. He could see a small part of the deck and the railing that surrounded the boat. Holding on the rail was John with a grin on his face under his mask. Jack pulled away from the small opening and closed his eyes in disbelief and shock. He was waiting there, waiting for them to die.

The jeep came to a sharp halt next to the dock.

Jerry jumped out and ran toward the Zodiac that was tied to the piling and threw his gear into the boat. "For Christ's sake, Tom, would you move your ass? I'm not letting this happen, there is no fucking way I'm letting this happen."

On the drive down Jerry had told Tom that John was planning on taking the boys to the old tug wreck and locking them inside to drown. Tom was willing to help do anything to save the boys. Tom got the engine started and hit the throttle; the Zodiac lurched forward, flying over the surface of the water. Only ten minutes from the site, maybe there was enough time, maybe not. Tom turned her sharp to the right and headed for the two pinnacles that marked the location of the sunken boat.

"There she is," cried Jerry, looking at John's dive boat tied to the buoy that marked the dive location of the tug. There was another boat nearby too; this was a popular dive spot.

"Pull her right up here," said Jerry.

Tom cut the engines on the Zodiac and grabbed the line that was attached to the buoy line. Jerry had already slipped the tank in the BC, secured the regulator, then pulled the BC over his shoulders, slipped into his fins, put on the mask, and rolled into the cool blue Caribbean Ocean. Jerry headed straight down, equalizing his ears as he swam down to the wreck that lay on the bottom of the ocean.

Jack watched his brother move around the small cabin looking for a way out, knowing that it was futile. Jack understood that John had planned this well, and that this was going to look like just another accidental drowning of two inexperienced divers who had apparently gone where they weren't supposed to go.

Jack steadied himself as he peered out of the small opening in the deck of the boat. It was a jagged opening with sharp strands of rusty metal pointing downward. The hole was no more than two inches around, just large enough to see out of, but much too small to push his hand through. He tried to bend back the sharp metal that protected the opening, but the rusted, sharp edges didn't move. Jack could see John swimming around the deck, as if he were looking for something, and he maneuvered himself to get a look from a different angle and saw what John was looking at. Swimming down toward the boat was another group of divers; he could make out a handful of divers heading for the tug. Somehow he had to get their attention, but how?

Jack turned his head from side to side looking for his brother in the semi-darkness of the engine room. Sean was still trying in vain to move the door handle. Jack turned his eyes back to the jagged hole. He had less than 200 PSI left, and he realized that there wouldn't be more than five minutes left of his air. He had to do something immediately to attract the other divers.

With his left hand, he held tightly onto the pipe on the ceiling, and moved his right hand up and into the small opening. He could feel the sharp metal against his fingertips. He began to push up even while the razor blade edges of the metal began to dig into the tender skin of his right hand.

Jack figured the divers would see the blood coming from the hole in the deck and surely investigate. They could get him and his brother out in time. This was the only way to get their attention. The salt water stung in his open wounds as he pushed harder and harder. He could see his blood, but with his hand blocking the opening he couldn't see outside the tugboat anymore. The blood from his open wound seemed to be swirling down into the cabin instead of up and out into the open ocean—would they even see it? Jack understood what he needed to do, the only way he could think of to get the divers attention for sure. He turned once again to his brother, just as Sean turned toward him in time to see Jack thrust his hand through the small and jagged hole with all his strength, ripping the flesh of his wrist to shreds. What was left of his hand and wrist, open to the bone, was sticking out of the deck, with blood pouring out and getting picked up by the light current. Jack knew he could be bleeding to death, but he didn't care. He understood that this was the end for him, but not for his brother.

John couldn't believe his eyes as a torn and shredded hand came thrusting through the small and jagged opening in the deck. The blood poured from the open wound and swirled all around the deck. Surely the new divers, who were pulling themselves up and over the railing already, would see the blood and then, of course, Jack's hand.

John still had time if he moved fast, and he pushed himself off the railing and swam toward the hole, his mind working furiously. He would force the hand back down through the opening, purposefully cut his own hand doing it, and make like it was his blood all over the deck.

The divers would surely help him to the surface immediately, with John fighting all the way up—it would keep their attention on him. All he needed was a few minutes; he would kick and thrash so that the other divers would think that he was in trouble. By the time the others figured out what John was trying to do, it would be too late. John could dive down to the tug in a vain attempt to rescue the brothers, but they would already be dead.

John swam toward what was left of Jack's arm. He tried pushing it down into the hole, back into the cabin.

But suddenly, a strong underwater current surged and John's body was propelled forward. He lost the grip he had on the bloody and slippery hand. As the current moved him, John felt something grab the strap that held his BC in place and pull him hard down toward the deck. Jack had felt John's body moving past his hand and had grabbed onto anything he could, and although he didn't know it, his outstretched fingers took hold of John's BC strap. He pulled down with all his might, not knowing what he had hold of, but knowing that this might be their only chance to be rescued.

John's body lay on the deck like it had been nailed there, and the blood from Jack's ravaged hand poured out from under John and seemed to surround him like a blanket. John struggled, but to no avail, and Jack's hand, or what was left of it, held fast to the only hope he had; he wasn't about to let that go.

The stinging pain that surged through Jack's arm seemed to fade, and he felt light-headed. He closed his eyes and prayed for the first time in many years. He felt something grab hold of his shoulder; Jack looked to the side and saw his brother. Sean reached for Jack's gauge and saw that it read empty. Jack smiled as best he could; he felt no pain and was at peace. Jack was running out of air and beginning to lose consciousness, but with whatever strength he had left, he held onto the strap that pulled John down onto the deck as Jack's blood flowed over him.

The new divers had just pulled themselves over the railing and immediately saw what appeared to be a man lying on the deck bleeding profusely. Without a moment of hesitation, they began to move as fast as they could to help the injured diver, obviously in serious trouble.

Blacktip reef sharks are generally not aggressive, but the smell of blood and what appeared to be a fish in distress brought them to the deck of the tug like a lightning bolt. The frenzied attack came out of nowhere and was terrifying. The incoming divers froze in fear and then retreated quickly off the deck and moved back up toward the surface. In just seconds more than twenty sharks attacked John as he lay pinned against the deck. His screams were silenced by the deep water; his face contorted into agonizing pain and suffering as his mask filled with water. He desperately tried to move away from the attacking sharks but the grip on his strap held him firmly against the deck of the tugboat. The reef sharks tore at John's limbs as they went into a feeding frenzy.

The loss of blood and lack of oxygen was causing Jack to hallucinate.

There he was, back at the breakfast table; he brushed his small hand over the smooth surface. Jack's mom sat to his left, his dad to his right, and his brother across the small yellow table. The four of them reached out for each other and held hands; they all smiled and bowed their heads.

Jack's left hand fell from the piping and drifted lifelessly in the semi-darkness of the tugboat cabin. Jack said no goodbyes, no I'm sorry; there was just cold silence in this dark coffin at the bottom of the ocean.

Sean glanced at his air gauge, it read under 100 PSI, and his breathing had become labored. He realized then that Jack wasn't moving anymore. Sean saw Jack's hand and wrist torn to shreds in the jagged opening, and he grabbed his facemask and turned Jack's face toward him. Jack's eyes were closed, like he was sleeping, and Sean understood that his brother was dead. He knew that in just a few moments, he too would be dead. Sean held on to Jack's left hand and closed his eyes; he thought of his family while he waited for his air to completely run out.

Jerry descended toward the sunken tug; the sight on the deck was horrifying. He recognized John's brightly colored wetsuit even though it had been torn to shreds. He could see what the sharks had done; they were satiated now and moving away from the boat. Jerry avoided them, slipped quickly into the interior of the tug, moving toward the cabin. He reached the cabin door; there was a pipe lodged under the handle, and he pulled it away and opened the hatch. The open door brought the light into the dark cabin as he swam in. Cables and wires littered the small room, and he looked around frantically; he knew they were in there somewhere. He moved forward and felt something brush the top of his head. Looking up, he saw the two boys near the cluttered ceiling. One was moving, but the other still.

With what little breath he had left, Sean tried one more time to pull his brother's hand out of the jagged hole. He didn't even realize that suddenly he could see more clearly as light flooded the room. He held onto the same pipe that Jack had held onto to anchor himself, and slowly moved his arms around his dead brother. Jack was gone, and in just a moment his own tank would be empty and then he would die with his brother. *Finally together*, Sean thought, *after all these years.*

Jerry pushed off the floor and grabbed Sean and turned his face toward him and stared at his son. Jerry pulled Sean's mouthpiece out of his mouth and shoved his spare regulator into Sean's mouth.

Jerry held tight to Sean's BC while his son was gasping for air. Jerry floated, hanging onto one of the pipes on the ceiling, looking at his two sons, the sons that he had deserted so many years ago. He could see Jack's face beneath the mask and knew he was gone. One boy dead, one still alive. The choices that he had made had led to this, and all the suffering and pain that he had caused.

Sean was still desperately trying to get Jack's hand and arm out of the hole, and Jerry reached up and tried to push back the metal shreds that clutched and tore into Jack's bare skin. Father and son, they tried, while Jack's dead body floated in the hazy, murky water.

Jerry looked down at his air gauge; the needle was in the red, under 300 PSI. The tank that he grabbed had never been refilled. Jerry knew they needed to get to the surface now. With both men breathing on the same tank, they wouldn't last more than five more minutes.

Jerry turned and grabbed Sean by the straps on his BC; he pointed to the PSI gauge and frantically signaled that they needed to get to the surface. Sean hesitated; he couldn't bear to leave his brother, but he knew that he had to.

Sean continued to hold onto the pipe next to Jack. He tried to let go, but somehow he couldn't. The lack of steady oxygen was clouding his thinking and he couldn't see that clearly. The cabin water had become clouded with Jack's blood. Jerry was desperate, they were running out of time. He reached up and pulled the regulator out of Sean's mouth. Sean frantically reached out for it and let go of the ceiling pipe. Jerry popped Sean's mouthpiece back in and Sean glared at Jerry, but he was thinking more clearly now. He couldn't make out who it was in the murky water. They both swam to the open door and through the small, narrow corridor that led to open water and the deck of the tug.

A few sharks were still milling around as Sean and Jerry came out of the boat and onto the deck.

John's lifeless body had been torn apart, but most of him still lay pinned to the deck, held fast by the clenched fist of the unseen diver whose hand alone had protruded through the jagged hole in the deck. Jerry stared at his old friend, feeling nothing, but then he thought that he hadn't felt very much in the last thirty years. He turned toward Sean and pointed his thumb upward and they both rose to the surface together, Jerry holding tight onto Sean's BC.

When they reached the surface, they swam the short distance to the Zodiac that bobbed up and down in the gentle sea. Jerry pulled himself up and into the boat, released the strap that held the BC, and pulled himself out of his gear before reaching for Sean, who was holding onto the side of the boat, to pull him in. Sean was exhausted and fell to the bottom of the small boat and lay there for a moment saying nothing. Jerry sat on the metal bench, put his hand on Sean's shoulder, and said, "Let me help you out of your gear."

Jerry gently pulled Sean up and helped him out of his BC, and laid his gear on the bottom of the boat.

"Are you all right, Jerry?" The Coast Guard boat had pulled up and tied up to the Zodiac. Three divers were pulling their fins and masks on and ready to plunge into the ocean.

"Yeah, we're okay. John, or what's left of him, is lying on the deck. You've got to go into the cabin, right under where Murphy is lying." Jerry hesitated for a moment and then said, "You'll see what I mean."

Sean stared in shock at the man who saved his life who they just called Jerry. The names: Jerry, John. Sean, still lying on the bottom of the Zodiac, tilted his head out of the resting pool of water that had collected at the bottom of the small boat. He could taste the saltwater. The man who sat near him on the bottom of the boat, his hands stretched out, was holding onto the ropes that circled the Zodiac. He'd seen this man before. Sean pulled himself up while the Zodiac was speeding toward the inlet. He glared at the man across from him. Jerry looked at him and said, "We need to talk. I'll explain everything when we get back to shore."

Sean moved forward. Slowly, he moved his hand toward Jerry as if reaching out. Jerry reached out and held his son's hand.

Sean stared and said, "Who are you?"

Jerry looked back at his son and said, simply and clearly, "I'm your father."

THE END